RUTHLESS ARRANGEMENT

THE DIPLOMAT
BOOK 1

M. S. PARKER

D1714364

BELMONTE PUBLISHING, LLC

CHAPTER ONE

Lea

MOST PEOPLE SEE POWER IN NICO VARELA'S SMILE; I SEE the architect of my father's destruction.

The grainy photograph, blown up on my laptop screen, shows the exact moment he'd completed some deal, his face contorted with a smug, controlled curve of the lips that promises ruin disguised as opportunity.

Rain lashes against the cheap glass of my apartment window, blurring the gritty Chicago skyline. The distorted view mirrors the confusion churning inside me. *This city,* my father used to say, *operates in the shadows. Power isn't loud here, Lea. It's silent. It waits.* He learned that lesson the hard way.

My fingers touch the cool metal of the laptop. Tonight isn't just the eve of my first day at the Chicago Investigative Journal; it is the eve of battle. Packing my bag feels less like preparing for work, more like donning armor. Laptop, my sword. Notepads, my shield. Pens, my daggers. Each item, carefully selected and placed into the worn leather satchel that belonged to my father. A relic from his time at the Journal, before Varela, before the silence.

The Journal. It isn't just a building downtown, a prestigious byline I'd chased through four years of journalism school. It is the arena where my father's reputation was destroyed. He'd gotten too close. Asked the wrong questions about the network of influence Varela commanded. It was a web spun through politics, business, and the city's murky underworld. Then, suddenly, sources dried up, stories were killed, and my father, once a celebrated investigative reporter, found himself sidelined, discredited, broken. He never named Varela outright, not in the aftermath, but the fear in his eyes whenever that name surfaced spoke volumes. *Some men cast long shadows, Lea. Don't get lost in them.*

I slam the laptop shut, the click loud in the small space. My apartment, usually a sanctuary of books and half-finished articles, feels tight, the walls pressing in. The rain intensifies, drumming a relentless rhythm against the fire escape. This isn't just about vindicating my father. It is about finishing what he started. It is about dragging the shadows into the light. Tomorrow, I walk into the place that broke him. *This time, the story won't end with silence.*

THE CHICAGO Investigative Journal newsroom hits me like a fucking freight train. A storm of ringing phones, clattering keyboards, and overlapping conversations fills the vast, open-plan space, housed in what looks like a converted warehouse. Exposed brick walls climb toward high ceilings crisscrossed with industrial ductwork. Cheap fluorescent lights cast a harsh glare on the busy mess below. It smells of old paper, burnt coffee, and something unexplainable, like a hunter's energy that hums beneath the surface noise. Desks are crammed together, islands adrift in a sea of discarded coffee cups, overflowing in-trays, and monitors displaying scrolling news feeds. Photos of past triumphs, exposés that had felled mayors and exposed corruption, line a far wall, a gallery of reporting coups.

"Song! Wells wants you. Now," a harried-looking assignment editor commands, pointing a nicotine-stained finger toward a glass-walled office at the far end without breaking stride.

So much for easing in. I adjust the strap of my father's satchel on my shoulder, take a breath, and navigate the maze of desks, sharply aware of the curious glances flicking my way. My skin prickles. *The new kid. Fresh meat.*

Harrison Wells's office is proof of controlled chaos. Stacks of newspapers tilt precariously, threatening an avalanche onto the floor; manila folders overflow from every surface; the air hangs thick and acrid with the aroma of stale cigar smoke. Wells, a well-set man in his late fifties, himself looks like he slept in his clothes with his rumpled shirt, tie askew, silver hair defying gravity. He sits hunched behind a massive, cluttered desk, peering over reading glasses perched on his nose. His eyes, magnified and piercing, size me up with weary cynicism as I enter.

He doesn't offer a handshake, doesn't waste time on pleasantries. He gestures toward the worn visitor's chair opposite him. "Sit." His voice is gravelly, impatient.

I sit, placing my satchel by my feet.

He grunts, shuffling through a pile of papers before finally extracting a thick, battered manila folder. He tosses it onto the desk. It lands with a thud. The sound seems to suck the air from the room and from my lungs.

"Nico Varela," he rasps, tapping the folder with a blunt finger. "Word is, you know the name."

My insides hammers, a violent, thrilled surge colliding with a wave of pure, raw terror. *Varela. On my first day.* It is what I'd hoped for, prayed for, maneuvered for through application essays and interview answers hinting at my interest in Chicago's power structures. And yet, the reality of it, the sheer nerve of being handed this assignment, now, feels like a trap sprung too soon. A cold dread washes over the initial thrill. *This is too perfect. Why?* I force my expression into neutral territory, a mask of professional interest.

"I know of him," I say, keeping my voice steady. "Everyone in Chicago does. Owner of Club Purgatorio, major political donor, incredibly well-connected."

Wells snorts, a humorless sound. "Don't bullshit me, Song. Your senior project paper was on navigating hidden power structures. You cited three articles your father wrote for this paper before he..." He trails off, waving a dismissive hand. "You didn't just stumble in here wanting to cover city council meetings."

He leans forward, the cynicism in his eyes hardening into something pointed. "Let's get one thing straight. Your Northwestern degree means jack shit here. This," he taps the Varela file again, harder this time, "isn't some academic exercise. This isn't play-acting journalism where you write a scathing piece and get an A. People who poke around Varela have a bad habit of disappearing. Or finding their careers torched."

His gaze holds mine, intense, steady. *He knows.*

"Varela eats people like you for breakfast," he continues, his voice dropping lower, gravel turning to granite. "He's smarter, richer, and more ruthless than anyone you've ever met. He has judges in his pocket, cops on his payroll, and eyes everywhere. You think you're walking into a story? You're walking into a goddamn minefield."

The warnings land like body blows, each one echoing my father's hushed fears. But mixed with the fear is a fierce, stubborn determination. *This is it. The chance.*

"Why me?" I ask bluntly. "My first day. This feels... loaded."

Wells leans back, the springs in his old chair groaning in protest, folding his hands behind his head. "Let's just say, you weren't my choice."

The admission jolts me. "What?"

"Got the call yesterday," he says, his gaze drifting toward the ceiling. "From the top floor. Said you were ambitious, hungry, had the right background. Said to give you Varela." He shrugs, a gesture heavy with unspoken frustration. "Publisher wants you on this, Song. Don't ask me why."

He pushes the folder across the desk. The name NICO VARELA is scrawled in faded black marker. It feels heavier than it looks, pregnant with secrets and danger.

"That's it. Go investigate. Report back to me at least once a week on *all* the events in details. And try not to get yourself killed."

I FIND MY ASSIGNED DESK, a small gray island in the swirling sea of the newsroom. Tucked away near the back, flanked by towering filing cabinets and a pillar plastered with old union notices. Functional, anonymous, perfect for fading into the background. I sink into the standard-issue office chair. The Varela file lands on the desk, its physical weight nothing compared to the burden of its contents and the questions swirling around how it got there.

The Publisher. Why would the Publisher, someone more concerned with ad revenue than deep-dive investigations, hand a rookie the most dangerous target in the city? It makes no sense. Wells's reluctance, his explicit statement I wasn't his choice—the words ring through my mind. *Am I being set up? Thrown to the wolves for some unseen political maneuvering upstairs? Or is it simpler? Did they genuinely believe my academic background made me suited for this, unaware of the personal firestorm Varela's name ignites within me?*

"You look like you went ten rounds with Wells and lost."

I jump, startled. A woman stands beside my desk, holding out a steaming paper cup. She has keen, intelligent eyes that seem to take everything in, short dark hair in a stylish bob, and an air of calm competence striking in the surrounding frenzy.

"Uh, something like that," I manage, accepting the coffee. Its warmth seeps into my stiff hands. The coffee itself tastes burned, institutional. "Thanks. I'm Lea Song."

"Sienna Park," she replies, pulling over an empty chair and sitting, lowering her voice. "And you didn't lose. You just got handed the grenade with the pin already pulled."

I blink, surprised by her directness and apparent knowledge. "You know about Varela?"

Sienna nods, her expression serious. "Wells pulled me aside. Assigned me as your handler, for lack of a better term. Unofficially."

"My handler?" *The term sounds illicit.*

"Look," Sienna leans closer, her voice dropping further, compelling me to lean in. "Wells doesn't trust this. The Publisher giving Varela to a rookie on day one? Especially when the order comes directly from the Publisher, who wouldn't normally hand out the assignments to junior journalists? It stinks. He thinks you're being set up to fail, or worse, being fed to Varela."

Her words solidify my churning suspicions. "So, what's your role in this?"

"To watch your back," Sienna says bluntly. "Help you navigate the inner secrets to investigating high society in this city. I've been here five years, doing photography, but I've covered the crime and politics intersection. I know the players, the landscape. Wells wants me to provide intel, whatever you need. But, and this matters, we keep our arrangement, and the real depth of our work on Varela, completely off the radar. Especially from the top floor."

A handler. A secret ally. Relief wars with suspicion. *Why would this seasoned reporter agree to babysit a newbie on a suicide mission? Is this another layer of the game?*

Sienna seems to read my hesitation. "Look, Lea, I heard about your father. Getting pushed out for doing his job too well. It was bullshit. Maybe Wells feels guilty, maybe he just hates seeing the Publisher play games with reporters' lives. He asked me to help, and I said yes. Varela needs exposing. But you need to survive doing it."

The mention of my father, the quiet understanding, chips away at my reserve. Maybe I am not entirely alone in this.

"Okay," I say, the word feeling small. "Okay. Thank you, Sienna."

"Don't thank me yet," she warns, her gaze sweeping the bustling newsroom. "First rule: assume everyone is watching. Listening. Varela has ears everywhere. City Hall, CPD, probably even in here."

She glances at the Varela file on my table. "In fact, we can't plan a strategy here. Too many eyes." Her gaze flickers around the open-plan chaos, lingering a split second on a figure near the elevators, then snaps back. "Let's grab a proper coffee. There's a place half a block away."

The thought of escaping the overwhelming noise, of processing with someone who understands the stakes, is appealing. "Yes. Please." I gather my things, reaching for the file.

"And Lea?" Sienna's voice is crisp, stopping me. "That file? Never let it out of your sight. Ever. Consider it fused to your hand."

The danger Wells described suddenly feels real. Caution isn't just smart; it is survival. I tighten my grip on the folder, its cardboard edges digging into my fingers.

The elevator ride down feels like descending into a pressure cooker. Sienna, leaning against the cool metal wall, doesn't waste time. "Second rule: trust no one. Cops, sources, colleagues. Verify everything. Twice. Varela's network isn't just wide; it's deep. He builds loyalty through fear and favor."

The doors open onto the skyscraper's lobby with its polished marble, soaring ceilings. The newsroom's frantic energy is replaced by hushed, reverberating calm. It feels like crossing a border, still potentially dangerous, but masked by expensive surfaces.

"He owns pieces of legitimate businesses all over," Sienna continues, voice low but clear, as we walk toward the massive revolving doors. "Restaurants, real estate, distribution. Fronts, mostly."

We approach the imposing glass and steel mouth of the revolving doors. Michigan Avenue vibrates beyond. A river of taxis and pedestrians under a gray sky threatening more rain. "Decent café around the corner," Sienna says, nodding left.

My mind swirls with all the new information and questions: the Publisher's motive, Wells's distrust, Sienna's sudden guardianship, Varela's reach. Distracted, I push into an empty section of the heavy glass door as it begins its slow turn.

And then I freeze.

Coming through the adjacent section, moving with unnerving calm, is Nico Varela himself.

Time stretches. My eyes lock with his through the curved glass. Not movie-star handsome. His hair shaped in a unique style, blond on top, dark on the sides, and pulled back into a tiny man-bun. His face is sharp, angular, his presence predatory. His jaw-dropping fit body, too fit for someone in his forties, radiates power, pulling the air taut. Dressed in an impeccable charcoal suit, he looks less like a businessman, more like a panther poured into expensive fabric.

He doesn't look surprised. *Why would he? He doesn't know me.*

Or does he?

As the door rotates, bringing us parallel, a slow, chilling smile spreads across his face. Not warm. Not friendly. The smile from the photograph. The smile of a man who owns the game. Recognition flickers in his cold, dark eyes. Not of a stranger, but of someone expected.

The glass partition slides away. Face-to-face for a fraction of a second, the lobby's muffled sounds yielding to the city's hum. His voice, low and smooth, cuts through, meant only for me.

"Careful there, Miss Song."

He knows my name. *How?* The question steals the air from my lungs. A dizzying wave washes over me, making the polished lobby tilt.

His intense, assessing gaze flicks down to the manila folder clutched against my chest. The VARELA file. His smile widens, a predatory curve that makes my stomach plummet.

Then the door completes its turn. He is past me, stepping into the lobby, vanishing as I am deposited onto the damp sidewalk.

I stand rooted to the spot, the revolving door whispering shut, Michigan Avenue crashing back in with its horns blaring, people hurrying past. My muscles feel locked, unresponsive. He knew my name. He saw the file.

"Holy shit!" Sienna emerges a moment later, eyes wide, fixed on where Varela had entered. "Lea! Did you see—? That was Varela! How the hell? Did he talk to you? Did he just address you as Miss Song?"

I'm getting dizzy, spiraling. Numbly, instinctively, I reach into my satchel for my phone. *Need normalcy, connection. Calling someone. My mother? No.*

My thumb hovers over the screen. As it flickers to life, a tiny icon looking like a stylized microphone flashes briefly in the top status bar. There for less than a second, almost imperceptible, then gone.

"What was that?" Sienna asks, her reporter's eyes missing nothing. She'd seen it too.

"I...I don't know," I stammer, voice thin. "A glitch?"

Assume everyone is listening. Sienna's warning slams back. *A glitch? Or confirmation? Is my phone compromised already? Is he listening now?*

I look back toward the imposing skyscraper Varela had just entered, its doors now spitting out oblivious workers. The anonymity I'd craved, the chance to investigate from the shadows, had vanished before my first day had barely started. I feel stripped naked, exposed, and hunted.

The game hasn't just begun. I am already marked. And Nico Varela is holding all the pieces.

CHAPTER TWO

Nico

THE BLADE OF LIGHT SLICING THROUGH THE ROOM catches the edge of my whiskey glass, casting amber shadows across the smooth, cool surface of the polished mahogany table. I turn the glass slowly, watching the interplay of darkness and illumination. It fits. This whole damn city, the clusterfuck brewing for this meeting, even the woman still cooling her heels downstairs. Control. It's always about control.

Below me, Purgatorio has come to life. The heavy bass, bleeding through even these soundproofed walls, is a distant heartbeat reminding me of the empire I've built. Up here, in my private conference room, a different kind of music is about to play. The grating noise of rival egos, forced into line by the only authority they both dread. Me.

And then there was her. Lea Song. Emerging from the elevator lobby just as I arrived. Clutching that manila folder, my folder, placed in her hands as I'd orchestrated through the pliable publisher. The look on her face when she recognized me? Priceless. Fear, yes, but something else beneath it. Defiance? Intrigue? That flicker in her dark eyes, a refusal to simply shatter, sparked something within me. A challenge. Mine. Let her wonder how I knew her name. Let her feel my attention land on her, a pressure point she can't ignore, before her first day is even an hour old. Good. The game has already started.

I adjust my diamond filled platinum cufflinks, which was a gift from my uncle Alessandro on my thirtieth birthday. "Power," he had said, "is in the details others miss." The platinum's cool presence on my wrists anchors me, physical proof of the authority I wield. I run my finger along the smooth edge, feeling the engraved 'V' that marks them as mine. Everything in my world is marked as mine, eventually. Even ambitious junior reporters digging into their fathers' ghosts. Especially them.

The double doors open, Marco conducting his customary sweep before admitting the two sources of my current irritation. Animosity radiates between them, a palpable static charging the air. Diaz barely contains his restlessness; Kostya carries his resentment like a cheap cologne. Inconvenient. Two snarling dogs disrupting the equilibrium, expecting me to settle their backyard squabble. Predictable.

"Gentlemen." I don't rise. My stillness anchors the room. "Dispense with the pleasantries."

Marco closes the door, taking his position. The air crackles with their resentment. Diaz drops into a chair like it owes him money. Kostya lowers himself more deliberately, already composing justifications I have no interest in hearing.

Before either can speak, I cut them off. "Your disagreement," I state, the word dripping with disdain, "has become a liability. It affects profits, complicates logistics, and worse, it makes noise." I let that hang in the air. Noise attracts the wrong attention. My attention.

I take a deliberate sip of whiskey; the silence amplifying their failures. Their postures shift as Diaz bristles and Kostya tightens. Good. Let them feel the weight of their incompetence before I provide the solution they don't have the intelligence to devise themselves.

"Fortunately," I continue, my voice smooth, "I have formulated a resolution."

At my nod, Marco places identical folders before them. They open them, scanning the contents. Predictable disbelief flickers across their faces, quickly followed by shock as they realize the depth of information contained within: operational details, vulnerabilities, opportunities they thought secret. My information. It's always startling to them how much I know.

Kostya protests, a flush rising on his neck. "This doesn't account for—"

I arch an eyebrow. The objection dies in his throat. Silence returns, absolute. The speed with which they learn obedience is always informative.

"The terms," I state, making it clear there will be no discussion, "are not suggestions. They are the new reality. A reality caused by your inability to manage your affairs without disturbing the ecosystem." A small smile plays on my lips. "You seem surprised I understand the intricacies of your operations so thoroughly. A lapse in judgment on your part."

I let my gaze drift between them. "My neutrality allows

business to function. When that function is disrupted, my solutions become mandatory."

Diaz, quicker to grasp the inevitable or perhaps just more afraid, reaches for the pen Marco offers. Kostya hesitates for three seconds, his pride warring with the obvious, unspoken threat, before following suit. Pens scratch against paper in the heavy silence.

Marco collects the signed agreements and provides copies. His movements are economical, practiced.

"Your organizations will understand a resolution has been reached." I rise, the signal for dismissal clear. "Ensure it remains resolved."

Diaz mutters a hasty thanks, avoiding my eyes. Kostya offers a stiff nod, pride wounded but survival instincts intact. Marco escorts them out.

When the door closes behind them, I take a moment of stillness, as the quiet hum of control restored settles over me.

Marco returns, locking the door behind him. "They'll hold to it," he says, not a question but an assessment.

"For now." I loosen my tie, the only concession to comfort I permit myself during business hours. "Kostya will test boundaries within a month. Have Emilio keep eyes on the northwest hospital supply chains."

Marco nods, making a note on his phone. Our relationship requires few words; after fifteen years working together, he anticipates my thoughts with unsettling accuracy.

"And the journalist?" he asks, tucking his phone away.

The journalist. Lea Song. The file clutched against her chest like armor. The flash of fear and defiance in her eyes when she recognized me. An unexpected variable, yes, but one proceeding according to plan. "The Publisher delivered.

She has the assignment," I confirm, a smile touching my lips. "Phase one complete. Now we wait." Her reaction in the lobby was intriguing. She didn't crumble. There's fire there, beneath the initial shock. That fire will make her useful. And breaking it will be satisfying.

Marco studies me. "The encounter in the lobby was unplanned. You could have ignored her. Kept her in the dark."

"Where's the fun in that?" I counter. "Let her know I see her. Let her feel the pressure early on. She needs to understand who holds the board." I move to the window, gazing down as the city lights ignite against the twilight sky, scattering like jewels on black velvet. *My* city. *My* board. "She thinks she's hunting a story about her father's ghost. She has no idea she's walking into a cage I built specifically for her."

Marco remains silent, knowing better than to question my methods when it comes to manipulation. He's seen them work too many times.

"Surveillance," I instruct, turning back from the window. "Full coverage. Her apartment, her communications, her movements." I pause, considering the most effective way to undermine her confidence, to understand her vulnerabilities. "Also, search her apartment. Discreetly. I want a full inventory of her life. Find out what drives her besides this obsession with her father." A predatory edge creep into my voice. "And bring me something personal. A journal, maybe. Something that reveals her secrets. I want to know her weaknesses before she even realizes she has them."

Possessing something intimate, something she believes is hidden, is the first step to possessing her.

Marco nods, the professional mask firmly in place,

though I detect a flicker of understanding of the game I'm playing. "And the strategic objective?"

"Remains the same," I confirm. "Her mother. According to our reliable source, Professor Song is the key to intercepting the Korean pipeline before Dante Moretti locks it down. Lea is our way to control the mother. Ambitious, driven, blinded by pride and vengeance. She'll chase the breadcrumbs I lay down, thinking she's uncovering the truth." I glance toward the city again, the skyline spread out below like my personal playground. "She just doesn't realize the truth will lead her to where I need her to be. And that she, herself, is a story I'm writing."

Marco processes this, his loyalty absolute. "How deep do we let her dig before we leverage her?"

"Deep enough for her to believe she's winning," I reply, picturing Lea's defiant eyes. "Deep enough that when I pull the curtain, she won't just be compromised. She'll be broken." A wave of satisfaction settles over me. The game is afoot, and I always win.

CHAPTER THREE

Lea

I drag the red string from Nico Varela's club, Purgatorio, a name dripping with ironic salvation, to the zoning commissioner's name, pinning it to my living room wall. *Click.* Another from the commissioner to three property acquisitions that sailed through approval despite neighborhood protests. The pin sinks into the plasterboard. A third connects those properties to shell companies. *Thwack.*

"Got you," I say to the empty apartment, stepping back to survey my work. Or maybe I'm saying it to the man whose image stares back from a dozen grainy surveillance photos tacked between the documents. My personal devil, enshrined on plasterboard.

My once-normal living room has morphed into what my mother would call a "conspiracy cave," laying Nico Varela's invisible empire bare on my wall. News clippings, property records, corporate filings, and my own frantic notes are all connected by a web of colored strings. Red for confirmed connections. Yellow for suspected. Blue for the agonizing gaps, the questions still unanswered.

There are far too many blue strings. And too many pictures of him. That sharp jawline, those eyes that promise nothing good, a mouth that looks like it could ruin you with a word or a kiss. I trace the outline of his face in one photo, my finger hesitating over his lips before I snatch it back, disgusted with myself. *Focus, Song.* He's the target, the monster who maybe...probably...had your father killed. He's not a fixation. But the lie feels hollow, brittle. He is a fixation. Has been for six long years.

I rub my eyes, which feel like they've been scrubbed with sandpaper. Three days. Since Harrison dropped that file in my lap, I've been lost in this research fugue, surfacing only for bathroom breaks and to accept food deliveries I barely taste. My laptop screen glows accusingly from the coffee table, surrounded by empty coffee cups and half-eaten containers of takeout.

The record of my latest failed attempt to reach him still displays on the screen: *Dear Mr. Varela, I'm reaching out regarding a profile piece for the Chicago Investigative Journal focusing on your business success and community impact.*

Polite. Professional. Utterly ignored, just like the five previous messages I've sent to various official channels since getting the assignment. He's playing with me. He knew my name. He knew I had the file. He's letting me dangle, enjoying my frustration. The bastard.

"Damn it," I mutter, collapsing onto my couch. A caffeine-withdrawal headache hammers behind my eyes, and my spine feels fused into a painful hunch. I need a shower, actual food, and twelve hours of uninterrupted sleep. Maybe an exorcism to get his face out of my head.

What I need more is a breakthrough. Something concrete linking him not just to shady deals, but to the suspicious brake failure that sent my father's car into the river six years ago, just months after the Journal let him go for digging too deep.

Harrison's deadline looms. I'm four days away from having to present my first report, and so far I have jack shit. "Get me something substantial," he'd growled when I checked in yesterday. "Not just public records. I need an angle, Song. Something with teeth."

Something with teeth. I glance back at my wall of connections, my eyes snagging again on a close-up of Varela. Those eyes. Sienna wasn't wrong; they look right through you, even in a photograph. The patterns are there, tantalizingly clear: he's built a legitimate empire that serves as a perfect shield for whatever lies beneath. His public persona as a successful businessman, philanthropist, and neutral mediator is immaculate. No arrests, not even a parking ticket. But the gaps in the public record speak volumes, dark spaces where money and influence flow unseen. Spaces big enough to hide a murder.

My phone buzzes, startling me. It's lying face down on the coffee table, the vibration making it skitter. A text from Sienna: *Checking you're still alive. Blink twice if Varela's goons have you tied up in a basement.*

Despite my exhaustion, a small smile touches my lips. Sienna's humor and grounded cynicism have been the only things keeping me sane since she appeared at my desk that first day, my designated guardian angel in this descent into hell. I text back: *Still breathing. Drowning in research. No goons yet, just Varela's ghost.*

Her response comes immediately: *Give it time. Staying late at the office finishing a piece. I'm swinging by after with reinforcements (Korean food & wine). No arguments.*

I don't have the energy to argue, anyway. I set my phone down and stand, stretching muscles that protest loudly. Suddenly, the walls seem too close, the strings and papers suffocating. The air prickles against my skin like unseen eyes are tracking my movement. I shake my head. Paranoia. Harrison warned me. Sienna warned me. Varela gets under your skin. The memory of that microphone icon flashing on my phone screen surfaces unbidden. Maybe it isn't paranoia.

I walk to the kitchen, fill a glass with water, and drink it down in long gulps. The calendar on my refrigerator is a gift from my mother, featuring serene Korean landscapes. It reminds me I missed our weekly Sunday call. My stomach tightens, the usual knot of guilt. I'll have to call her tonight, make up some excuse about work deadlines. Not entirely untrue.

My mother worries constantly. "You have your father's eyes," she told me once, sadness clouding her own. "Always looking beneath the surface. Be careful what you find, Lea." She supported my choice to follow Dad into journalism, but I know she carries the weight of his death, the unanswered questions, even more heavily than I do. His press credentials hang framed above my desk as part shrine, part reminder, part omen.

I run a hand through my tangled hair, grimacing at its greasy texture. Shower first, then back to work. I need to refine my approach, craft one last attempt to reach Varela before Harrison's deadline forces me to go with the circumstantial threads I have.

Thirty minutes later, freshly showered and marginally more human, I sit cross-legged on my couch, notebook in hand, drafting a new outreach strategy. My damp hair drips onto the paper, smudging my already messy handwriting. Appeal to his ego? Hint at information I don't actually possess? Threaten to publish what I have? How do you bait a predator like Nico Varela, especially when he already knows you're coming?

A sudden, insistent knocking on my door makes me jump, sending my notebook flying.

"Lea! Open up! Food waits for no obsessed reporter!"

Sienna. *I lost track of time again.*

I hurry to the door, unlocking it to find her standing there, loaded down with paper bags emitting delicious smells and wearing a concerned expression that shifts to impressed curiosity as she takes in the state of my apartment.

"Whoa, okay," she says, stepping inside and setting the bags on my kitchen counter. "Intense setup, Song. You weren't kidding about diving deep." She moves further into the room, eyes scanning the walls covered in notes, photos, and strings. Her gaze lands on the dense cluster related to Varela. "Damn, Lea. This is...meticulous. The string theory approach, I like it. You've really mapped this out visually. Impressive organization for just three days."

"It's how I process," I say, feeling a flush of pride mixed with the awareness that it still looks crazy. *It is organized, though.*

"Clearly." Sienna turns to look at me, her expression shifting back toward concern, but now framed differently.

"Okay, impressive dedication, but when did you last see your bed? Like, actually horizontal, eyes closed, REM cycle sleep?"

I wave the question away. "I've napped."

"On the couch, I'm guessing? With your laptop balanced on your stomach?" She unpacks the bag with containers of Korean takeout, a bottle of crisp white wine, and a pint of salted caramel ice cream. "You need actual fuel, not just caffeine and whatever delivery app was closest to your thumb."

The smell of jjajangmyeon makes my stomach growl traitorously. I haven't realized how hungry I am until this moment.

"Fine," I concede, grabbing plates from my kitchen cabinet. "Food break. But then I need to get back to work. I'm close to something, Sienna. I can feel it."

She hands me a container and a fork. "Close to a breakthrough, or close to needing institutionalization?" she teases, but her eyes flick back to the wall, admiration still clear. "Seriously though, the number of photos you have of him is thorough."

"Hilarious." I take a bite and moan at the explosion of flavors. Proper food. Maybe Sienna has a point about fuel. "They're for reference," I mumble around a mouthful.

"Reference for his tailoring, or his criminal empire?" She settles onto my couch, plate balanced on her knees. She gestures with her fork toward the wall. "So, talk me through this masterpiece. What connections are strong enough to justify all this?"

"It's the pattern," I say, joining her, needing her to see it, needing her to understand the logic behind the chaos.

"Varela's public record is immaculate. Too clean. But look at the ripples, zoning variances for his associates sailing through while others get shot down, judges giving suspiciously light sentences to people seen at his club, businesses suddenly folding under pressure only to be snapped up by shell companies that trace back to his investment group." I point toward one cluster. "Like Jim Rawlings, the zoning commissioner? Out of nowhere, he buys a vacation home in the Caymans last year. On a city salary."

Sienna raises her head, her fork pausing halfway to her mouth. "Okay, that's shady. Nice catch connecting that timing."

"Exactly," I say, setting my plate down, encouraged by her validation of the *finding*, not just the method. "It's all circumstantial, whispers and shadows, but the pattern?"

Sienna sets her plate down and stands, moving closer to examine my research, her expression shifting now from impressed by the method to concerned by the *implications*. As she leans in to look at a document, my gaze drifts past her toward the corner reading chair where my father's old brass floor lamp stands. Except, it's not standing right. The shade is askew, the heavy base rotated, maybe fifteen degrees counterclockwise from where I always keep it. It's subtle, but wrong.

"Lea, if even half of this is accurate..." Sienna gestures at the chaotic collage, her earlier admiration now overshadowed by the gravity of the potential connections. "This guy operates in the shadows where people disappear." She turns to face me, her eyes serious. "What are you hoping to get out of this? Beyond a byline?"

I almost don't hear the question. My eyes dart back to the lamp. *Did Sienna bump it when she came in?* "Did you...did you move that lamp?" I ask, nodding toward it, my voice sounding tight.

Sienna glances over, frowning. "The floor lamp? No, why?"

My gaze snaps back to it. Faint scuff marks, almost invisible, mar the hardwood beside the base. Marks that weren't there yesterday. My skin goes clammy, prickling with a sudden, invasive chill. My breath catches. *Someone was here. Touching my things. Standing where I sleep.* The violation feels like ants crawling beneath my skin. I force my hand steady as I reach out, moving the lamp back, arranging the shade just so. "No reason," I say quickly, hating the slight hoarseness I can hear in my voice despite my effort to sound casual. "Must have knocked it. Scattered."

Sienna watches me, her brow furrowed with worry now directed at *me*. Not just the wall. "Okay..."

"Look, the professional answer to your question feels thin, inadequate," I continue, trying to recover, pushing the violation aside for now. I look from Sienna's worried face to the wall, to the photos of Varela, to the faded clipping about my father's "accident." The truth lodges in my throat.

"Sienna," I start, my voice low, "You already know my dad worked for The Journal and was fired." She nods slowly. "They said it was budget cuts, restructuring. Bullshit. He was investigating Varela. Asking questions nobody wanted answered." I take a deep breath. "But my father kept digging, even after they fired him. He wouldn't let it go. Then his car. The brakes failed. They called it an accident."

Sienna's eyes widen, understanding dawning. "Oh, Lea. You think Varela?"

"It doesn't matter what I think," I say, the words tight

with six years of grief and suspicion. "I need to know the truth about what happened to my father. I need to prove it. This profile? It's not just a story. It's the only way I can get close enough to find out."

Sienna studies me for a long moment, the newsroom cynicism momentarily replaced by empathy. "Okay," she says softly. "Okay, I get it now. Why you're this intense. Why you took the assignment knowing the risks." She steps closer, putting a hand on my arm. "But Jesus, Lea, that makes this even more dangerous. If Varela was involved, and he knows who you are..."

"He knows," I confirm grimly. "That encounter in the lobby proved it. He knew my name."

"Which means you need to be smarter, not just harder," Sienna insists. "This isn't just research anymore, it's poking a viper. What happens when understanding puts you directly in his path? You seem fixated." She glances again at my slightly too-quick adjustment of the lamp, the tension I hadn't quite managed to hide. "Maybe you should stay at my place tonight. Take a break from," she waves at the wall, "all this."

"Can't," I say, shaking off the unease, though the feeling of violation lingers. *Nico knows I know he's watching me, or at least suspects. Running won't help.* "Deadline. I need to finish my report and make one last attempt to reach Varela." *I need to regain control of the narrative. Of myself.*

Sienna sighs, recognizing the stubborn set of my jaw. "Fine. But promise me you'll get actual sleep. In your bed. Without your laptop."

"Yes, Mom," I tease, grateful for her concern.

We finish dinner, Sienna filling me in on The Journal gossip I'd missed. The conversation is a welcome respite, but my mind keeps drifting back to the lamp, to feeling being watched.

AFTER SIENNA LEAVES, I return to my laptop. The lamp incident has unsettled me more than I admit, layering a new, intensely personal fear on top of the professional danger and the grief for my father. But I can't afford any distraction. Not now.

I open a new email draft. This is it. The last attempt before Harrison's deadline. Professional enough for a response, intriguing enough to pique his interest, maybe even hint that I know more than I do without revealing my hand.

Mr. Varela, The Chicago Investigative Journal is preparing a comprehensive profile examining how Chicago's business leaders navigate the intersection of commerce, politics, and community impact. Your unique position as both a successful entrepreneur and a respected mediator offers valuable insight into these dynamics. I would appreciate the opportunity to include your perspective in this piece, which will explore how influence operates in our city's power structures. Your comments would provide a necessary counterbalance to the other sources we've consulted. I'm available at your convenience for this conversation. Regards, Lea Song Investigative Reporter Chicago Investigative Journal.

The implicit message: *I'm writing this with or without you, and others are talking.* A considered risk. A direct challenge.

With a deep breath that does little to steady me, I hit send. The email vanishes into the digital ether. Then I close my laptop, suddenly bone-weary. The adrenaline that sustained me for days finally ebbs, leaving behind profound fatigue and a simmering unease that tastes like icy dread.

I glance at the wall one last time before heading to the couch, Varela's eyes seeming to follow me from every photo. Tomorrow, I will compile what I have. If he doesn't respond...

But he will. The certainty is unsettling, chilling. He's been watching. He knows I'm digging. He knew my name. This is all part of his game.

THE SMELL of leftover jjajangmyeon wakes me. I blink, disoriented. My phone shows 11:47 PM. I must have passed out after sending the email. The container sits open on the coffee table, dark sauce clinging to the noodles. Hunger cuts through the grogginess. I grab my chopsticks and lift a heavy clump.

My phone buzzes. Sienna checking in again?

Unknown number.

My breath catches. I set the noodles aside, heart suddenly hammering against my ribs. I open the message.

Ms. Song. Your persistence has been noted. Purgatorio. Tomorrow. 9 PM. Nico.

He responded. Not through official channels. Personally. To my private cell number, which I never shared with The Journal, never put on any application.

How?

The lamp. The microphone icon. Feeling being watched. It wasn't paranoia. He's been in my life, in my apartment.

The violation is staggering, intimate. And terrifyingly thrilling.

This isn't just an interview offer; it's a summons. A display of power. *I see you. I know how to reach you. Come.*

My fingers tremble as they hover over the keyboard. The smart response, the safe response, is to suggest a public place, and demand professional boundaries. Safety. Caution.

What would Dad have done?

He would have walked straight into the fire, notebook in hand.

Before doubt can take root, before the fear can paralyze me, I type my response: *I'll be there.*

The reply is instantaneous, a digital echo of command: *Come alone.*

Two words. A blatant disregard for safety protocols. A test. A dare.

Instead of alarm bells, a perverse thrill shoots through me, sharp and undeniable, raising goosebumps despite the fear coiling in my gut. This is it. The abyss Harrison mentioned. The chance to look into the eyes of the man behind the myth, the man who might hold the answers about my father, the man who's already invaded my life without ever properly meeting me.

I set my phone down, looking back at my wall. Each string, each document, feels like a weapon I'm forging for tomorrow night.

Nico Varela thinks he's summoning me to his domain, establishing dominance. He doesn't realize I've been preparing for this moment for six years, obsessed, consumed.

Tomorrow night, I will meet the devil. And I will be ready.

CHAPTER FOUR

Nico

THE MANILA FOLDER LIES OPEN, ITS CONTENTS SPREAD across my desk like a map of someone else's life. Lea Song stares back at me from half a dozen photographs; candid shots captured over the past week. Here she is at a coffee shop, typing like hell on her laptop, that intense crease between her brows. Crossing the street outside her apartment, head tilted up toward the sky during a rare moment of sunshine, a flicker of vulnerability I long to exploit. Leaving the Journal offices late at night, shoulders squared with determination despite obvious exhaustion.

Twenty-three years old. Five-foot-five. Northwestern University graduate, summa cum laude. Daughter of Professor Eunji Song and the late Gene Robert. She immigrated with her parents from England at twelve, after her mother took the Political Science professorship at Chicago University. Interestingly, her mother and father never married, and she took her mother's last name, Song.

And now, Lea is a pawn in my game. She could end up a potential problem, but I suspect she'll prove to be more of a fascinating acquisition.

I lift one of the surveillance photos, studying her face closer. It holds a blend of Southern European and Korean features with high cheekbones, full lips that look soft, inviting. Dark, intense, and challenging eyes that reveal an intelligence rarely found in someone so young.

I trace her face. *Beautiful.* There's something in her expression, like a fierce, unwavering focus that I've seen before, in boardrooms and back alleys alike. The look of someone who believes they can bend the world to their will through sheer determination. Admirable. Dangerous. And ultimately, something I intend to break. The thought sends a low thrum of excitement through me. Recalling her in the lobby, that flash of fear mixed with defiance when our eyes met through the revolving glass, only sharpens the edge of my interest. She didn't crumble then, either.

"What do you think?" Marco asks from where he stands by the window of my private office above Purgatorio. The club won't open for another three hours, but the space is already humming with preparation. The staff restocking the bar, security checking systems, bartenders prepping their stations.

I set the photo down and lean back in my chair, reaching for the tumbler of whiskey at my elbow. The amber liquid catches the light as I swirl it thoughtfully.

"I think Ms. Song is progressing as expected," I reply, my voice measured. "Though her research is more thorough than I anticipated. She's building connections I didn't think she'd find for weeks."

Marco snorts. "Journalists. They never know when to quit."

"That's what makes them useful," I remind him, taking a sip of the Macallan 25. The peat and honey notes linger on my tongue as I set the glass down precisely where it had been. "When properly directed."

I return my attention to the dossier. Marco has been thorough as always. Academic transcripts, social media profiles (sparse, curated), financial records (student loans, modest savings), family connections. The girl's entire life distilled into paper and pixels, laid bare for my examination.

Her thesis catches my eye: "Power Dynamics in Political Reporting: How Journalists Become Complicit in the Systems They Cover." I pull it from the stack, flipping through the pages with growing interest. Her analysis of how reporters gradually adopt the worldviews of their sources, how access becomes a form of subtle corruption is remarkably insightful for someone so young.

"She's smarter than her file suggested," I murmur, half to myself. "Astute. That could speed up our timeline." Or make her more difficult to control. The challenge is invigorating.

"Smart enough to realize she's being manipulated?" Marco asks, crossing his arms.

I consider the question, turning it over in my mind like a curious artifact. Smart journalists are both useful and dangerous. Their intelligence makes them valuable conduits, but also means they might see through the narratives I construct.

"That's a risk we've already accounted for," I say. "If she connects dots we don't want connected, we have contingencies. But for now, her intelligence serves our purpose. The more convincing her reporting, the more effectively she'll lead us to her mother's operation."

I continue through the dossier, noting her workout routine: yoga three times weekly, supplemented with kick-boxing. *Compelling, a fighter beneath the surface, maybe?* Her browser history: heavily focused on investigative techniques and Chicago crime statistics. *Dedicated.* Each detail adds brushstrokes to the portrait forming in my mind, sharpens the focus of my interest.

"What's the latest on her mother?" I ask, knowing Marco has the most current intelligence.

He moves to the desk, pulling out another folder. "Nothing new. Professor Eunji Song continues her pattern. Weekly meetings with the Korean attaché, followed by encrypted communications we still can't crack. The university schedule provides perfect cover. No one questions why a political science professor would meet with diplomatic staff."

I nod, processing the implications. "And the pharmaceutical angle?"

"Three shipments have arrived at the medical research facility where she consults. All legitimate on paper, but our source confirms the manifests have been doctored. Whatever they're bringing in, it's not standard research materials."

The Chicago Investigative Journal assigning Lea to investigate me wasn't a coincidence. It was my orchestrated first move in a complex game. Her mother's possible connection to the new fentanyl pipeline is the prize, and Lea herself is my unwitting pawn. Or perhaps, not so unwitting soon.

"Have we confirmed she's still unaware of her mother's activities?" I ask.

"She has no clue," Marco replies. "Her research is focused entirely on you, not her mother. She's built that wall in her apartment, connecting you to everything from zoning approvals to judicial appointments. Red strings, yellow strings, blue strings—color-coded like a detective show."

A dark spark ignites at the thought of Marco prowling through her space while she slept, rifling through her private things. That invasion, knowing her secrets. The urge to dominate coils tight within me. "Like I said," I say, letting a hint of grudging admiration color my tone. "She's got skills."

"Dangerous," Marco counters.

"Perhaps." I stand, moving to the window that overlooks the empty club below. The soft glow of ambient lighting reflects off polished surfaces, creating pools of shadow and illumination throughout the space. Purgatorio is my creation, my domain. The visible manifestation of my power in Chicago. Lea Song wants to peer behind that curtain. Most would call her naive or suicidal. I find myself intrigued.

"I've invited her here tonight," I say. "Nine o'clock."

Marco's head turns. "Already? I thought we were keeping our distance for another week."

"Plans change," I reply, turning to face him. "She's progressed faster than expected. It's time to escalate."

Marco reaches into his jacket pocket, pulling out a small, clear evidence bag. Inside is a crumpled, wallet-sized photograph. "Almost forgot. Recovered this during the apartment search. As requested, something personal." He places the bag on my desk.

I pick it up. It's an old photo, faded and worn at the edges. A younger Lea, maybe fourteen, laughing, sandwiched between her parents. Her father, Gene Robert, his face familiar from the old Journal archives, is looking proud. Her mother, Eunji, a younger version of the woman in Marco's intelligence files, her smile is not quite reaching her eyes, even then.

"Lea kept this near her bed," Marco says.

I turn the photo. An inscription on the back, in faded ink: *Lea-bug, some truths hide in dark places. Be brave enough to look, but smart enough to know when to turn back toward the light. Your heart is too good for their games. Always, Dad.*

I feel a cold, possessive satisfaction. Knowing what drives her, what hurts her most deeply—this is power.

"That's...sentimental," Marco observes flatly.

"Useful," I correct, tucking the bagged photo into my desk drawer. A piece of her history, now under my control. I'll study it later, dissect the emotions captured within that faded image. For now, it serves as a reminder of the leverage I hold. "Have Damien prepare an Americano with an extra espresso shot, her exact preference, to be served when she arrives," I instruct Marco. "And make sure Tony and Miguel are working the door."

Marco pauses at the threshold. "The usual initiation?"

"With a twist," I reply, returning to my desk to finish my whiskey. "I want to see what she's made of before I decide how to proceed with the next phase."

Marco nods, already pulling out his phone to relay the instructions. "And if she fails?"

I consider the question, studying Lea's face in the photographs once more. There is something compelling in her determination, that fire in her eyes. A quality that would be wasted if extinguished too soon.

"Then we find a more appropriate use for her talents," I say. "But she won't fail. She can't afford to."

Marco leaves to make the arrangements, and I return to the dossier, spending another hour absorbing every detail of Lea Song's life. By the time I finish, I know her better than most of her friends do, perhaps better than she knows herself. Knowledge is power. I never enter an encounter without securing every advantage.

HOURS LATER, I sit in my usual corner booth at Purgatorio, positioned with clear sightlines to both the entrance and the main floor. The club vibrates around me. A low, driving beat thrums beneath the murmur of conversation. Beautiful people in expensive clothes move through the space like exotic fish in a well-maintained aquarium, while my security personnel circulate, their vigilance masked by tailored suits and easy smiles.

A glass of Macallan 18 rests on the table, untouched. A steaming cup of coffee waits next to my whiskey: an Americano with an extra shot, just like Lea Song likes it. Little details matter. They are the foundation upon which control is built.

The high-definition security feed displayed on the discrete screen embedded in my table shows the street outside. Nine o'clock approaches, and I'm curious whether she'll arrive on time or succumb to the temptation to appear fashionably late; a common mistake among those trying to establish dominance in an unfamiliar situation.

At 8:57, Lea appears on the screen, approaching the club

with purposeful strides. Early as I predicted. Her black trousers hugs her curves, paired with a simple, elegant top under a fitted leather jacket. Professional enough to be taken seriously, stylish enough to blend into the club environment. Her long dark hair falls in loose waves around her shoulders, and her expression holds that steel focus I recognize from the surveillance photos. She has dressed for battle. Good. She'll need that armor.

I turn my attention to a second feed, showing Tony and Miguel at the entrance. They have specific instructions to test her, push her, see if she crumbles under pressure. If she can't handle my bouncers, she certainly can't handle me.

Lea approaches the entrance with her head high, confident without arrogance. As she reaches the door, Tony, who's six-foot-four and built like a brick wall, steps directly into her path.

"Not hot enough," he says, his voice clear through the feed's audio.

I'm glued to the screen. This test reveals character. Most people would flinch at such a direct insult; especially women who cultivate their appearance as carefully as Lea obviously has. The shock, the hurt, the scramble for dignity are the predictable human responses.

Lea stops short, blinking. "Excuse me?"

"You heard me," Tony replies, crossing his thick arms across his chest. "Not up to standards. Nico likes them sexy."

I lean forward, anticipating her response. This is the moment most crumble, where embarrassment seeps in; they shrink away or beg for reconsideration.

Lea does neither. She tilts her head, assessing Tony as if

he is the one being scrutinized. Then, to my genuine surprise, she exhales as if bored and smirks.

"Not sexy enough, you say?" she murmurs, reaching for the zipper of her jacket. With zero hesitation, she pulls it open, revealing smooth skin above the edge of a dark lace bra. The hint of cleavage is defiant, not desperate.

Tony freezes, caught off guard.

"These," she says, tipping her chin up, "are the best tits you'll ever see in your life. Now, are you going to let me in for my meeting with Mr. Varela, or are you going to keep standing there pretending you've seen better while I walk right past you?"

A brief, stunned silence follows, stretching through the club's security room as well, I'm certain. Then, without a word, Tony steps aside, nodding almost imperceptibly. "Damn," he mutters under his breath as she walks past.

A quiet chuckle escapes me. "Compelling."

Marco, who has joined me moments before, whistles. "Are you sure about this? She's got some fire, that one."

I watch in silence from behind the floor-to-ceiling glass, tracking Lea as she cuts through my club. Head high, shoulders back. Not a hint of doubt in her posture. The woman moves with the unshakable confidence of someone who's just won her first battle and knows exactly what she's worth.

Most people are overwhelmed upon entering Purgatorio for the first time. The deliberated opulence, the beautiful people, the subtle signals of power and wealth. All of it designed to disorient and establish hierarchy before a single word is spoken. Lea takes it all in her gaze sweeping the room once before focusing forward again, stride unbroken. She's done her homework and studied the club, I realize. Prepared herself for this moment just as thoroughly as I have prepared for her. The unexpected symmetry pleases me.

I watch as she approaches the VIP section, where another of my security staff waits. This time, there is no challenge, just a respectful nod as he steps aside to allow her through. She's earned that much after her handling of Tony.

My gaze tracks her progress across the VIP area toward my corner booth. No hesitation, no nervous glances. The colored lights of the club play across her features, highlighting the determination in her expression. She is beautiful, yes—but it's her composure that catches and holds my attention. Beauty is common in my world. Unshakable poise under pressure is far rarer.

As she reaches my table, I let her stand there for three seconds before acknowledging her presence. A small power play to establish that she enters my space on my terms. Her expression remains neutral, though I detect a slight tightening around her eyes. She notices the manipulation but chooses not to react to it. Another noteworthy choice.

I gesture to the coffee cup set out for her. "Americano with an extra shot of espresso."

Her lips part before she masks her surprise, composure returning almost instantly.

"Ms. Song," I continue, taking my first good look at her in person, not counting the brief run-in in the revolving doors. The photos didn't capture the fire in her eyes, the subtle curve of her mouth when she's assessing a situation. "I've been expecting you. For quite some time, actually."

She holds my gaze without flinching, an uncommon response. Most people find it difficult to maintain eye contact with me for more than a few seconds; a useful tell when assessing potential threats or weaknesses.

"Mr. Varela," she replies, her voice steady. "Thank you for agreeing to meet with me."

I gesture to the seat across from me, an invitation that is really a command. She takes it smoothly, settling into the cool leather with the careful positioning of someone aware they are being assessed.

"Your coffee," I say, nodding toward the cup. "I believe it's to your preference."

Her eyes flicker to the untouched Americano, then back to me. "That's very specific hospitality."

"I believe in knowing who I'm dealing with," I reply, picking up my whiskey and taking a measured sip. The liquid burns pleasantly down my throat, warming without dulling my senses. "You've been investigating me for days. It seemed only fair that I return the favor."

A slight furrow appears between her brows. Not fear, but recalculation. She hadn't expected me to be so direct about my surveillance. Most people in my position would maintain the polite fiction that we are meeting as equals, almost strangers introducing themselves for the first time. But Lea Song doesn't strike me as someone who appreciates fiction, polite or otherwise.

"Is that how you see this?" she asks, leaning forward. "As a favor?"

I set my glass down. "Let's be clear about what's happening here, Ms. Song. You're a junior reporter who's been assigned a story far above your experience level. You've spent the past few days building an impressive, if somewhat fanciful, wall of connections in your apartment, using public records and second-hand accounts to construct a narrative about me and my business interests."

Her eyes widen, as she realizes Marco was indeed in her apartment. She recovers quickly, though, her expression smoothing into professional neutrality.

"And now," I continue, "you're sitting across from me in my club, drinking coffee prepared to your exact specifications, wondering if you've made a terrible mistake by coming alone."

"Have I?" she asks, her voice remarkably steady despite the implication.

I study her for a moment, noting the slight acceleration in her pulse visible at the base of her throat. Nervous, then, but controlling it admirably.

"That depends entirely on your next move," I reply, allowing a small smile to curve my lips. "Chess or checkers, Ms. Song?"

She blinks, confused by the apparent non sequitur. "I'm sorry?"

"Are you playing chess or checkers?" I clarify, leaning back. "Checkers players see only the move directly in front of them. They react rather than anticipate. Chess players see five, ten moves ahead. They understand that sometimes a sacrifice now leads to victory later."

Understanding dawns in her eyes, followed by a flash of something that might be appreciation. "And which do you think I'm playing?"

"That's what I'm determining," I say.

She considers this, then reaches for the coffee I've provided. A studied risk accepting something prepared at my direction. She takes a small sip, her expression revealing nothing as she recognizes her exact preference.

"You've gone to considerable trouble," she observes, setting the cup down. "Research, surveillance, personalized refreshments. Most people would simply have their secretary decline the interview request."

"I'm not most people," I reply, letting my gaze drift over her, taking in the defiant set of her jaw. "And you're not most reporters, are you, Ms. Song?"

"Evidently not." She reaches into her bag, withdrawing a notebook and pen. *Old-school, not digital. Noteworthy.* "May I?"

I nod, leaning back, curious. Let her think she's driving this. "By all means. Begin your interrogation."

She opens the notebook to a fresh page, handwriting neat, precise. When she looks up, the steel is back in her eyes. The journalist attempting to reclaim control. *Cute.*

"Mr. Varela," she begins, tone crisp, "your background is law, yet you built Purgatorio. Why the shift from courtrooms to this?" She gestures at the opulent club around us.

"The law taught me where the actual rules are written, Ms. Song." I lean forward, lowering my voice. "The ones that aren't debated by men in robes but enforced in shadows. Purgatorio is just a more honest venue for the same games." I observe her. "A game you seem eager to join."

She ignores the bait, pen scratching quickly. "And what games are played here? Beyond selling expensive liquor?"

"Ah, the probing question." A hunter's smile curves my mouth. "What do you think I'm selling, Ms. Song? You've plastered my face all over your apartment wall, built quite the monument. What does your gut tell you? Or perhaps, what do you want me to be selling?"

Color flares on her cheekbones, but her voice remains steady. "Public records show you facilitate meetings between competitors. Meetings after which certain criminal conflicts often resolve."

"Public records are so dry, don't you think?" I pick up my whiskey, swirling the amber liquid. "They capture transactions, not motivations. Not the thrill of brokering peace or ensuring compliance." I take a slow sip, eyes locked on hers. "They don't capture the look in a man's eyes when he realizes his future rests entirely in my hands."

Her pen pauses. I see the flicker of fascination warring with professional duty.

"Is that what you enjoy?" she asks, voice neutral. "Holding futures in your hands?"

"I enjoy order," I correct. "And ensuring those who disrupt it understand the consequences." I lean forward again, dropping my voice further, forcing her to lean in if she wants to hear. "Tell me, Ms. Song, what drives someone like you, who's bright, ambitious, with a Northwestern degree, to dedicate so much energy to understanding my specific brand of order? Career? Justice?" I let my gaze drift lower for a split second before meeting her eyes again. "Or is it something more personal? Revenge, perhaps? For dear old Dad?"

The direct hit lands. I see it in the momentary widening of her eyes, the tightening around her mouth before she clamps down on her reaction. She recovers, but the tell was there.

"The truth," she says, falling back on the journalistic shield. "That's what I'm after."

"Truth?" I scoff, setting my glass down with deliberate care. "A rather naive pursuit, don't you think? Especially in this city. Especially concerning men like me." I tap my finger on the table between us. "You want facts? I own this club. I pay my taxes. I donate to the right charities. There's your truth. Write that article."

A flash of irritation crosses her face, quickly masked. "And the backroom deals? The criminal mediations?" she presses, abandoning subtlety.

I chuckle, a low sound in my throat. "Careful, Ms. Song. Asking questions like that...it didn't end well for certain former journalists who did that, remember?" The cruelty is deliberate, a sharp jab to see how she reacts under direct pressure. Will she fold? Lash out? Or hold her ground?

Her knuckles whiten where she grips her pen, but her voice, when she speaks, is remarkably steady. "My father isn't the subject of this interview."

"Isn't he?" I counter. "He seems to be the ghost haunting every question you ask." I study her, the fire beneath her composure. Fascinating. "You're playing checkers, Ms. Song. Rushing the center with blunt questions. It's bold. Reckless, even. But predictable."

She holds my gaze, refusing to look away, refusing to give me the satisfaction of seeing her rattled. Admirable.

"Perhaps," I continue, changing tactics, leaning back with feigned casualness, "I should offer you a different game."

Wariness replaces the defiance in her eyes. "What kind of game?"

"Chess." I offer a genuine smile this time, enjoying the dance. "What if I offered you something more valuable than quotes for your little article? What if I offered you complete access? A ringside seat to the actual games played in this city."

Her eyes widen, journalistic hunger battling innate caution. "Why would you do that?"

"Because you intrigue me," I admit, the truth serving my purpose better than any lie. "Your obsession. Your nerve. That fire in your eyes when you think you've cornered me." I shrug. "Most reporters are predictable bores. You might be entertaining."

Suspicion clouds her features. "And what's the price for this entertainment?"

"Discretion," I say. "And obedience. Complete obedience." I lean forward again, voice dropping to an intimate whisper that belies the harshness of the words. "When you are with me, you follow my lead. Without question a necessity. My world operates by rules you don't understand yet. Break them, and the consequences..." I let the sentence hang, the threat implicit.

She processes this, the internal conflict visible in the slight furrow of her brow. "So, access for obedience," she clarifies, the word "obedience" pronounced like it's tasting of dirt in her mouth.

"Precisely." I watch her, savoring the tension, the silent battle playing out behind her eyes.

"And if I refuse one of your commands?" she challenges me.

"Then our little arrangement ends." I retrieve my business card, sliding it across the table. My fingers brush against hers; a spark of contact, a reminder of the physical reality beneath the power play. "Instantly. No second chances."

She shivers, a reaction she can't hide, her pupils dilating. Fear? Excitement? Both, I suspect. Perfect.

"Think you can handle it, Ms. Song?" I ask, letting the predatory edge show in my smile. "Or are you afraid?"

"I'm not afraid of you," she says, taking the card, her fingers trembling almost imperceptibly.

Liar. The word stays in my mind. Her body betrays her even if her voice doesn't. Instead of leaning back, claiming victory, I lean forward, closing the distance between us until my shadow falls across her. Her scent of jasmine and something sharp, like ozone before a storm, fills my senses.

"No?" I murmur, letting my gaze drop to her delicate throat, then back to her eyes. "Fear isn't always a weakness, Ms. Song. Sometimes it's just awareness. Acknowledging the predator in the room."

I reach out for her face, moving slowly enough that she could pull back, but she remains frozen, caught between defiance and the instinct to retreat. My fingers brush a stray strand from her cheek, tucking it behind her ear. The contact is brief, almost casual, yet loaded with possessive intent. My knuckles graze the sensitive skin of her neck, lingering for a second too long. *Her pulse thumps against my touch, a frantic bird trapped beneath warm skin.* "You should be afraid," I continue, voice dropping to a near-whisper. "Not of me causing you physical harm, that would be crude. But of what you might discover about yourself when you step behind the curtain. What lines you might decide to cross for your 'truth'."

I watch her, expecting a flinch, a gasp, some outward sign that I've finally breached her composure. Instead, she meets my gaze, her eyes dark pools reflecting the club's dim lights.

Her expression settles into something unreadable, almost challenging.

"The only thing I'm afraid of, Mr. Varela," she says, her voice cool despite my proximity, "is not getting the story."

A slow smile spreads across my face. Lea deflects the personal threat, refocusing on her professional goal. She doesn't crumble; she doubles down. Intriguing indeed.

"Then you have nothing to fear," I concede, finally leaning back, allowing her space to breathe. Let her think she's won this round. The victory is mine regardless. "I'll give you what you crave, Ms. Song. A look behind the curtain. But remember: my world, my rules."

She holds my gaze, the journalist warring with the woman, ambition battling self-preservation. The flicker of fear is still there, deep down, but overshadowed now by resolve.

"One condition," she says, reclaiming ground. "Editorial control."

"Of course," I concede easily. Too easily. Let her cling to that illusion. "I wouldn't dream of interfering with your 'truth'."

Her eyes narrow, sensing the deception but unable to pinpoint it. Not yet.

"Then we have a deal," she says, extending her hand.

I take it, noting the strength beneath the tremor, which has lessened now that she believes she has secured her terms. "Indeed we do, Ms. Song."

As our hands separate, I see the hint of uneasy triumph in her eyes. The thrill of having secured unprecedented access battling with the dawning realization that she's just agreed to terms whose full implications she can't possibly understand.

"When do we start?" she asks, closing her notebook with a decisive snap.

I check my watch, a simple, elegant Patek Philippe that has been one of the many gifts from my uncle Alessandro. "We already have," I inform her. "Your test at the door was the first step."

Her eyes widen. "That was deliberate?"

"Everything is deliberate in my world, Ms. Song," I reply. "The sooner you understand that, the better your chances of navigating it successfully."

She absorbs this, reassessing our interaction with new understanding. "So what's the next step?"

I finish the last of my whiskey, setting the glass down with finality. "Tomorrow. Eight AM. My driver will collect you from your apartment."

"To go where?" she asks, unable to hide her curiosity.

"That's your first lesson in our new arrangement," I say, rising from my seat to signal the end of our conversation. "You don't need to know where. You only need to be ready."

She stands as well, gathering her notebook and pen with movements that betray a hint of nervous energy despite her composed expression.

"Until tomorrow, then," she says, extending her hand once more; an attempt to reclaim some measure of professional equality in our interaction.

I take her hand, but instead of shaking it, I turn it slightly, my thumb brushing across her inner wrist.

"Until tomorrow," I agree, releasing her hand after that brief, deliberate contact. "Sleep well, Ms. Song. You'll need your rest."

The subtle threat, or promise, lingers between us as she

turns to leave, her posture rigid with determination as she navigates back through the club.

I watch her go, noting the way she moves, still confident but with a new awareness, as if she can feel my gaze tracking her progress. At the door, she hesitates for just a moment before stepping out into the night, the brief pause revealing more about her state of mind than she probably intended.

"Thoughts?" Marco asks, appearing silently at my side as he always does when needed.

I consider the question, replaying our interaction, cataloging her responses and reactions, calculating probabilities and potential outcomes.

"She's either going to be very useful," I say finally, "or very dangerous."

"Did you just say that the dangerous ones are often the most useful," Marco observes, his tone neutral but his implication clear.

I nod, my gaze still fixed on the door through which Lea Song has disappeared.

"Have the car ready at seven-thirty tomorrow," I instruct. "And tell Alessandro I'll be bringing a guest to breakfast."

Marco raises an eyebrow. My uncle rarely meets with outsiders, especially not at his estate.

"Are you sure that's wise?" he asks. "This soon?"

"No," I admit. "But it will be illuminating."

As Marco departs to make the arrangements, I remain standing, contemplating the empty space where Lea had been. The coffee cup she'd touched still sits on the table, a faint smudge of lipstick marking the rim. A small, tangible proof of our encounter.

Tomorrow will be the first actual test. Not of her courage

or her intelligence since those she's already demonstrated. But of her adaptability, her willingness to surrender control in service of her larger goal.

Few people understand the fundamental truth that has built my empire. True power comes not from controlling others, but from making them willingly surrender control to you.

By this time tomorrow, Lea Song will begin to learn that lesson, whether she wants to or not.

CHAPTER FIVE

Lea

I JOLT AWAKE GASPING, SHEETS TWISTED AROUND MY legs like restraints. Darkness presses thick against my bedroom windows, the digital clock mocking me with 4:23 AM. Fragments of a dream dissolve like smoke, leaving only the hint of dark eyes watching me, the distant fragment of a voice promising access for obedience. *Nico.* His name is a curse, a prayer, a fixation burned onto my brain.

His presence lingers, a phantom heat clinging to the air in my small apartment, hours after I fled his club. I can almost feel the controlled burn of him, the weight of his assessing gaze that missed nothing, the ghost of his fingers brushing mine when he slid his damned card across the table. I kick off the tangled sheets, needing to move, needing air that doesn't somehow remind me of the smell of expensive cologne and danger from the club. The linoleum floor is cold against my bare feet, a grounding shock. Did I really agree to this? Was I insane? One text message to a number I never gave him, *how the hell did he get it?* One promise of a story I'm suspecting is just bait, and I folded like a cheap suit.

The bathroom light feels harsh, unforgiving. My reflection stares back: wild hair, flushed cheeks. My eyes are too bright, burning with adrenaline that hasn't faded. I look like someone running a fever. Or maybe just someone who made a deal with the devil and is only now realizing the fine print involves third-degree burns and possibly eternal damnation.

"Wake the fuck up, Song," I mutter, splashing cold water on my face, again and again. The icy sting does nothing to wash away the sick feeling coiling in my gut. "It's just a story." But the lie dissolves on my tongue, bitter and false. It stopped being just a story the moment he looked at me through that revolving glass, knowing my name, the moment Harrison dropped that file on the desk, the moment I connected Nico Varela to my father's ruined career, his suspicious death six years ago. *His doing.* Nico Varela. The man I swore I'd expose, the architect of my family's destruction.

The shower steams around me, but the heat doesn't reach the chill deep inside. Every crafted word Nico spoke, every lingering glance that felt like both a threat and a caress, his thumb brushing my pulse point as if measuring my fear, it all replays on a loop. *Obedience.* What kind of journalist makes that deal? A desperate one? A compromised one? What kind of daughter, seeking vengeance for her father, puts herself willingly under the thumb of the man she suspects destroyed him? How could I even think about stepping into his world, breathing his air, after what he might have done? What he's capable of doing to me. Dad would turn in his grave, the weight of his disappointment pressing down on me harder than any physical threat.

But you want this story more than you want to admit. The whisper in my head is insidious, seductive. *You felt that treacherous thrill when his dark eyes locked on yours, didn't you? That sickening jolt of power, even knowing he holds all the cards. A thrill that feels like spitting on your father's memory. You saw a flicker of something in him last night...or maybe you just imagined it because you need to believe he's not a pure monster, even though every instinct screams that he is, that he's capable of anything. Anything. Including murder.*

My mind races, a chaotic collision of scenarios: Nico setting me up, the publisher playing a game I don't understand, my father's spirit whispering warnings I refuse to hear. His driver arrives at eight. Less than three hours to prepare for what? He offered no details, just another display of absolute control. *You don't need to know where. You only need to be ready.* Fuck him. Well, two can play. Or at least, one can try to look like she hasn't completely lost her goddamn mind.

I stand before my closet, surveying the meager options like a soldier assessing hopelessly inadequate armor. This isn't just professional attire anymore. I'm dressing for his world now, stepping onto his stage, playing by his warped rules. A world of shadows, violence, and staggering wealth that makes my student loan debt look like pocket change. Every choice feels loaded. Too formal? Uptight, trying too hard. Too casual? Disrespectful, like I don't grasp the gravity of whatever twisted game he's playing. Too provocative? Hell no, not giving him the satisfaction of thinking that's my angle. Too conservative? He might think I'm scared, and showing fear feels like handing him a weapon I can't afford to lose.

I finally settle on a charcoal gray pencil skirt. It's professional, severe, not inviting. A silk blouse in deep burgundy. A rich color with a hint of luxury I don't possess, but projecting a confidence I don't feel. Low heels, practical enough to run if needed. The thought sends an icy dread through me. God, what am I thinking? This isn't a movie. It's just...Nico Varela. Just the man who might hold the keys to everything, or the architect of my ruin, career, sanity, maybe even my life. Armor. It's definitely armor.

My phone rings on the nightstand, the sudden sound startling me so badly I nearly trip over my own feet. Sienna. My only link to normalcy, to the life I had before this Varela vortex sucked me in. I hesitate, hand hovering over the screen. Talking to her feels like confessing to a priest. But the silence in this apartment is suffocating. I answer, bracing myself.

"Hey," I try for casual, aiming for breezy and missing by a mile. "Up early."

"Never slept," she rasps, sounding genuinely wrecked. "Housing scam piece is kicking my ass. You?"

I take a deep breath; the lie forming even as I hate myself for it. "Just getting ready for the day. Early start."

"Right, I got your text last night. Your 'exclusive access' day." I can practically hear her skepticism through the phone. "Did you survive Purgatorio, otherwise?"

"Barely," I say, aiming for dark humor. "But I got what I needed. For now." I give her the fastest, most sanitized version, that Nico agreed to cooperate, certain conditions apply, journalistic boundaries will be maintained. I omit the chilling intimacy of his voice, the demand for obedience, the way a current jolted through me when his fingers brushed mine.

"Conditions? What conditions?" Sienna demands, sharp

as ever. "Lea, this guy is bad news. Like, 'end up in a body bag' bad news. He admitted to surveilling you! Remember what I told you. He guts people! Fuck Lea!"

"I know who he is," I counter, feeling defensive and childish. "This is the kind of access reporters dream of, Sienna. I can handle him."

"Can you? Or are you just telling yourself that?" Her voice softens. "Your career won't matter if you're dead! Look, I'm worried. Seriously worried. Promise me you'll text me. Hourly, even. Promise me you won't get Stockholm syndrome for Chicago's hottest crime lord."

Heat rushes to my face. "I'm using him for the story," I say firmly, the words feeling thinner, less convincing than I want. "That's it. He's a source. A dangerous one, but a source."

"Mmm-hmm," she hums, radiating disbelief. "Okay, Song. Just be smarter than you were last night, okay? Don't let him get in your head."

Too late for that, I think grimly.

The call ends, leaving her words on my mind. *Be smarter.* I glance at Nico's card on my desk. Simple black stock, silver lettering. No title. Nothing needed. I could back out. Call him. Plead illness, a family emergency. Fabricate something. Reassert professional distance. Harrison would understand, wouldn't he? Or was Harrison just another pawn in Nico's game, following orders from the Publisher Nico controls? The thought makes nausea churn in my gut.

Who can I even trust anymore?

The urge to run, to crawl back into my safe, predictable life, is overwhelming. I'm twenty-three fucking years old. I should be worried about paying off student loans and deadlines, not getting into a car with a man who radiates danger like a faulty power line, a man who might have killed my father.

But the thought of backing out feels hollow. This isn't an ordinary story. He isn't an ordinary subject. And this burning need for answers, for justice for my dad; it outweighs the fear. Almost.

Instead of calling Nico to cancel, I draft a detailed email to myself. Everything that happened last night, every word, every touch, every threat implied and stated. My suspicions about Dad. Nico's known connection to the publisher. Insurance. If something goes wrong, if I disappear, there's a record. The act feels chillingly necessary. A final breadcrumb dropped before stepping willingly into the wolf's den.

"WE'VE ARRIVED, MS. SONG." The driver's voice, filtered through the intercom, is the first sound I hear in what felt like an hour of suffocating silence inside the Bentley.

Before I can even process, before my hand reaches for the door handle, it swings open from the outside. Not the driver this time, but a man in formal attire, face impassive, holding the door as if he has been waiting for this millisecond. The air that rushes in is different here: clean, crisp, like the smell of damp earth and old money.

My legs feel unsteady as my heels hit the gravel drive. The house looms—no, presides—over the landscape. Italian Renaissance, honey-colored stone bleeding power under a gray sky, columns reaching like grasping fingers. A fortress built not just of stone, but of generations of influence I can't begin to comprehend. It seems to watch me, its tall windows like cold, evaluating eyes. My charcoal skirt and silk blouse, chosen as armor, feel paper thin.

"This way, please." The butler, because he has to be a butler, speaks without inflection, already turning, expecting me to follow.

He leads me up marble steps wide enough for an army, through massive double doors that open before us, swallowing me into an entryway designed to diminish. Soaring ceilings drip crystal tears from chandeliers the size of a Mini-Cooper. Dark wood paneling drinks the light, punctuated by museum-quality art. A brutal Caravaggio painting dominates one wall, violence rendered beautiful, visceral. The silence is the most unnerving part, heavy, expectant, sucking the sound from my breathing. This isn't Nico's world of pulsing bass and artful cool; this is a legacy made manifest in silent stone and judging eyes, radiating a power so old it feels suffocating. I feel like an intruder, an impurity marring the perfect surface.

We move down a wide corridor. Portraits line the walls—Varela ancestors, judging me with dark eyes and sharp jawlines that mirror Nico's. Their painted stares feel unnervingly real, following me, assessing my worthiness to breathe their rarefied air.

The butler pauses before ajar double doors crafted from dark, gleaming wood. From within drifts the faint clink of silverware on china, the indistinct murmur of conversation. He pushes the doors open, announcing, "Ms. Song," into the room beyond before stepping aside, leaving me exposed on the threshold.

It isn't a study, but a sun-drenched breakfast saloon. Tall

windows overlook manicured gardens still glistening with morning dew. A long table, laden with silver serving dishes, pastries, fruit, and steaming coffee, dominates the space. At the head of the table sits Alessandro Varela, the silver-haired patriarch I've only glimpsed in photos. Opposite him, nursing a cup of coffee, sits Nico.

He looks different here. Less the predator in his natural habitat, more constrained. He glances up as I enter, but he offers no greeting, his attention returning to his uncle. Alessandro, however, fixes me with those pale blue eyes, like ice chips in a weathered, powerful face, and gestures to an empty chair placed down the table, isolating me.

"Ms. Song," Alessandro says, his voice smooth but carrying an edge of command. "Join us."

I cross the room, feeling like I am walking a tightrope over a pit of snakes. The chair scrapes as I pull it out, the sound grating in the otherwise quiet room. A servant appears, pouring coffee into a delicate china cup before vanishing as silently as he arrived.

"Cream? Sugar?" Alessandro inquires, though his tone suggests my preferences are irrelevant.

"Black, thank you," I murmur, wrapping my hands around the cup's warmth.

Nico still hasn't spoken to me, his focus on a silver pot of jam he is ignoring. His deference to his uncle is a contrast to the absolute authority he wields everywhere else. It is jarring, throwing my perception of him off balance.

"So," Alessandro begins, setting down his own cup with meticulous care. "The journalist. Nico tells me you have ambitious plans for this profile."

"I plan to write an accurate portrait, Mr. Varela," I reply, trying to project confidence I don't feel.

"Accurate," Alessandro muses, taking a slow bite of pastry. He chews thoughtfully before continuing. "Accuracy is subjective, wouldn't you agree? Depends entirely on the angle of observation." His gaze sharpens. "Your father, for example. He sought accuracy. Look where it led him."

My breath hitches. The casual, almost bored way he references my father's fate, his ruined career, the suspicious death six years ago that screamed of foul play, possibly *their* foul play, sends heat surging up my neck, blurring my vision for a second with pure, fiery anger.

"My father was an excellent journalist," I say, my voice tight. "He pursued truths others were afraid to touch."

"Commendable," Alessandro replies, though the word drips with condescension. "And ultimately, futile. Some truths are best left buried, Ms. Song. For everyone's benefit." He takes another sip of coffee. "Like the circumstances of certain traffic accidents."

Ice forms around my heart. He isn't just acknowledging Dad's death; he is dangling the possibility of foul play right in front of me, testing my reaction, enjoying my discomfort. Nico shifts in his seat, a muscle twitching in his jaw, but says nothing.

"Are you suggesting my father's death wasn't an accident?" I ask, keeping my voice level despite the tremor beneath.

Alessandro waves a dismissive hand. "Tragedies happen. Engines fail. Brakes give out." His eyes glitter with cold amusement. "Especially when someone becomes inconvenient."

That does it. The implication, the smug superiority, the casual disregard for the shattered lives, my life, my father's life, snaps something inside me.

"Inconvenient to whom, Mr. Varela?" I lean forward, abandoning caution. "To men like you? Men who build empires on foundations others would rather not examine too closely? Men who silence anyone asking uncomfortable questions, perhaps by arranging 'accidents'?"

The air thickens instantly. The cheerful sunlight streaming through the windows suddenly feels tauntingly insincere. Alessandro's smile vanishes, replaced by a stillness more menacing than any overt anger. Nico goes rigid beside him, his knuckles white where he grips his coffee cup. Shit. Too far.

"I believe," Alessandro says, his voice dropping to a glacial calm, "this breakfast is concluded." He dabs his lips with a linen napkin, then rises from his chair. "Bennett will see you out."

He doesn't look at me again. Doesn't acknowledge my existence. He turns and walks toward a side door, leaving me sitting in stunned silence. Nico remains seated, eyes fixed on the wall behind me. He doesn't look at me either.

The butler, Bennett, reappears as if summoned by an unspoken command. "Ms. Song," he murmurs, his tone unchanged.

Numbly, I rise. The walk back through the opulent corridors feels like a perp walk, the Varela ancestors smirking down from their gilded frames. Failure tastes bitter in my mouth, mingling with the lingering flavor of expensive coffee. I've let my anger, my grief, my suspicion get the better of me. I've fucking blown it. My only chance to get close, to find answers about Dad, sacrificed for a moment of righteous fury.

Bennett escorts me out the massive front doors, the gray light feeling harsh after the mansion's curated dimness. The Bentley waits, engine purring, a black hearse ready to take me back to my hollow life. Access revoked. Mission failed.

I slide into the backseat with a nauseating mix of failure, regret, and impotent rage. I've screwed this up completely. The partition remains down as the car sits motionless. The driver stands outside, impassive, waiting. What now? Humiliation burns my cheeks. Do I actually have to ask him to take me home?

The front passenger door opens without warning. My breath hitches. Nico slides in, turning to face me across the empty space, a mask of cool control firmly back in place. Questions are almost on my lips: *What happened? Did I blow it? Is the deal off?* His presence, the sheer force of his contained energy, chokes the words in my throat.

Before I can force out a single syllable, he breaks the silence. "Be ready at nine tonight." His voice is low, controlled, giving away nothing, yet the words land like heavy stones, definitive and absolute. "I'll have a dress delivered. Wear it."

Shock slams into me, leaving a cold hollowness where my defiance was moments ago. *My skin prickles, a wave of heat washing over me despite the chill.* The whiplash is dizzying, nauseating. After that disaster? After Alessandro's icy dismissal? He's still commanding? Still dictating the terms? *My hand instinctively goes to my throat, where his touch lingered last night.*

He doesn't wait for a response, offers no explanation, no

hint of what transpired after I left. As he exits the car as abruptly as he entered, he closes the door with quiet finality. He ascends the marble steps and, without looking back, he disappears into the fortress that has just chewed me up and spat me out, leaving me reeling in his wake.

The car moves, pulling away from the mansion, gliding back toward the city, the world I'm returning to, almost defeated. I sit stunned, clutching my bag, his last words lingering in the sudden, oppressive silence. *I'll have a dress delivered. Wear it.* He knew. Alessandro dismisses me, and Nico? Nico just sets the next appointment. My defiance meant nothing. My anger changed nothing. I earned only this brutal lesson: I am a pawn, moved at his whim. I am not dismissed. The game isn't over. It is still on, and the rules, his rules, are clearer and colder than ever.

Relief wars violently with confusion, anger, and a strange, unsettling excitement that coils low in my belly. I have faced the power behind the throne, stumbled spectacularly, yet somehow remain in play. Tonight, I will wear the dress he sends. I will go where he directs. Obedience isn't a request; it is the non-negotiable price of admission.

The thought should terrify me. It does. But beneath the fear, igniting slowly in the wreckage of my assumptions, I feel something dangerously, addictively close to excitement.

CHAPTER SIX

Nico

I watch the light catch the split in Jasmine's lip in the dressing room mirror, a crimson slash against her olive skin that makeup can't fully disguise. She winces as she dabs concealer over the purple bruise blooming beneath her right eye, her movements careful and practiced. This isn't her first time covering evidence.

I stand in the doorway, watching her struggle, my irritation building with each passing second. Friday night at Purgatorio means capacity crowds, VIPs with six-figure tabs, and performances that need to be flawless. Jasmine is one of my best dancers, her aerial silk routine the highlight of the midnight show. Now she looks like she's gone three rounds with a heavyweight.

"You can't perform like that," I say, my voice flat.

She flinches at the sound, her eyes meeting mine in the mirror before quickly dropping back to her makeup palette. "I can cover it, Mr. Varela. I've done it before."

Before. The word hangs between us, heavy with implication. I step into the room, letting the door close behind me. The air smells of hairspray, perfume, and the particular scent of fear that I recognize over the years. Not fear of me, not exactly, but the fear of disappointing me. That distinction is a particular form of power, one I've cultivated.

"Stand up."

She obeys instantly, rising from her vanity stool with the fluid grace of a trained dancer. But I don't miss the slight hitch in her movement, the barely perceptible hesitation as she straightens.

"Lift your shirt."

Her eyes widen fractionally before she complies, raising the hem of her cropped rehearsal top to reveal a constellation of bruises across her ribcage; some fresh and angry red, others fading to sickly yellow. The systematic pattern speaks of deliberate cruelty rather than a single loss of control.

Cold fury coils in my chest. Not because I care about Jasmine as a person, though she is valuable talent, but because this represents something I can't tolerate: disorder in my domain.

"Your boyfriend," I say. Not a question.

She nods, eyes downcast. "We had a fight last night. He thinks I'm cheating on him with Lenny, the bartender." A bitter laugh escapes her. "As if I have the energy for that after dancing six hours a night."

I study the bruising, calculating. The midnight show is the crown jewel of Purgatorio's entertainment, meticulously choreographed and timed to the second. Canceling Jasmine's act would disrupt the entire sequence, disappoint the high rollers who come specifically for her performance, and signal weakness. In my world, weakness invites challengers. But having her perform on stage damaged would be worse. It would advertise that I allow such things to happen to those under my protection. That violence against what is mine goes unpunished. The thought crystallizes with perfect clarity. Jasmine isn't just an employee. She's an asset. *My* asset. And someone has damaged my property.

"Who can replace you tonight?" I ask, observing her.

Relief flickers across her face, relief that I'm not firing her, that I'm focusing on the practical problem rather than her personal choices. "Selina could cover the aerial routine. She's been understudying."

I nod once. "Then that's settled. You're off until those ribs heal." I turn toward the door, then pause. "Your boyfriend. What's his name?"

Wariness replaces relief in her expression. "Michael. Michael Reeves." She hesitates, then adds, "He's a musician. Plays guitar at The Blue Note on Thursdays."

"A musician," I repeat, the word tasting like copper in my mouth. "How...creative."

I leave without another word, ignoring her stammered thanks for not firing her. The backstage corridor hums with pre-show activity, such as technicians checking lighting cues, servers stocking the VIP bars, and security personnel getting settled at their posts. My club, my people, my orchestrated system of pleasure and profit. All of it requiring precise control.

The first staff member I see is a young woman sorting through costume pieces on a rolling rack. "Find Marco," I order, not bothering to soften my tone. "Tell him I need him backstage. Now."

She scurries away without question, abandoning her task mid-count. Smart girl. She understands priorities.

I return to the dressing room area, this time stopping at the door to the performers' lounge, where several dancers are stretching before the first show. Conversations die as I enter, bodies straightening instinctively, eyes lowered in deference.

"Selina," I call, locating the willowy blonde among the group.

She steps forward. "Yes, Mr. Varela?"

"You're taking Jasmine's aerial silk routine tonight. And for the foreseeable future."

A flash of ambition brightens her eyes before she composes her features into an expression of concern. "Is Jasmine alright?"

"She will be," I reply, the promise in my tone causing several of the dancers to exchange glances. They know what that means. They all do.

The heavy tread of steps approaches from behind me. Marco, right on time, as always.

"You needed me?" His voice is low, meant only for my ears despite the sudden silence in the room.

I turn, gesturing for him to follow me to a more private corner of the backstage area. The lighting is dimmer here, the sounds of the club a distant bass thrum through the walls. Marco waits, patient as always, his broad shoulders blocking the view from any curious onlookers.

"Jasmine's boyfriend used her as a punching bag," I say without preamble. "A musician named Michael Reeves. Plays at The Blue Note."

Marco nods once, his expression unchanged. In the fifteen years he's worked for me, I've never needed to explain the implications of such information. He understands imme-diately what is required.

"Find him. Bring him here tonight." I check my watch—7:38 PM. "After the first show. I want a private conversation."

"Of course." Marco's tone betrays nothing, but I catch the slight narrowing of his eyes, the only outward sign of the controlled violence that makes him so valuable to me. "Any particular condition you want him in when he arrives?"

I consider this. "Functional. Coherent. Unharmed." A thin smile crosses my lips. "Make him think it's a business meeting."

Marco's answering smile is hard. "Understood."

I leave him to make the arrangements and head toward my private elevator at the end of the main floor, accessible only with a key card and fingerprint scan. As the doors close, sealing me into momentary silence, I allow myself the luxury of focusing on the night's other appointment.

Lea Song. The journalist with the sharp eyes and sharper tongue, who walked into my trap thinking it's her story. The convenient daughter of a woman with ties useful in my larger strategy. She'll be the perfect pawn, if played correctly.

Alessandro's warnings still linger in my mind as the elevator ascends to my office suite. My uncle rarely involves himself in my operational decisions, but Lea has triggered something in him.

"A journalist is never just gathering information, Nicolò," he'd said, using my full name as he always does when delivering what he considers essential wisdom. "They are building weapons. The question is not whether they will use them, but when."

Perhaps. But weapons can be redirected. And Lea Song, for all her education and ambition, is still painfully young. Inexperienced in the game I've been playing since before she entered kindergarten.

The elevator doors open directly into my private office, an intentional blend of luxury and functionality. Floor-to-ceiling windows offer a panoramic view of the Chicago skyline, though privacy glass ensures no one can see in. The furnishings are minimal but expensive: a custom desk of polished black granite, a leather executive chair, and a seating area.

Along one wall stands a bank of monitors displaying security feeds from throughout the club and its perimeter. Another shows real-time data on the night's reservations, VIP arrivals, and bar sales. Everything I need to maintain a perfect awareness of my domain.

I cross to my desk, checking the time: 8:40 PM. Lea will arrive soon, assuming she follows instructions. The dress I've sent would have been delivered to her apartment hours ago. I'd picked a deep red silk that the designer assured will make her skin glow and her dark eyes seem bottomless. Revealing enough to ensure every man in the club will notice her, modest enough that she can tell herself she isn't compromising her journalistic integrity by wearing it.

I picture her now, stepping out of a taxi, shoulders rigid with determination and uncertainty. Perhaps checking her phone one last time before surrendering to the night I have orchestrated. Will she be nervous? Excited? Both, I suspect. The combination looks good on her.

Alessandro is right about one thing: Lea Song represents a risk. But calculated risks are the foundation of empire-building. And I have plans that extend far beyond Purgatorio's profitable nightlife business, plans that reach into the lucrative intersection of legitimate pharmaceuticals and their more profitable street alternatives.

Lea's mother, the esteemed Professor Song with her convenient academic connections to East Asia, rumors are she's the invaluable bridge in that equation. And Lea herself? A delicious distraction, at minimum. A potential asset to get to her mother at best.

My phone buzzes with a text from Marco. *Target acquired. ETA 30 minutes.*

Perfect timing. The first show will end just as our guitarist friend arrives for his command performance. And Lea will be here to witness it all. Her first glimpse behind the curtain she's so eager to pull back.

I move to the wall of monitors, scanning until I find the camera trained on Purgatorio's main entrance. The Friday night crowd is already forming. A line of eager patrons dressed to impress and ready to spend. VIP guests bypass the line, escorted directly inside by hosts who know which clients deserve special attention.

At precisely 9:00 PM, a taxi pulls up to the curb. Lea emerges, as I'd imagined her: back straight, chin lifted in defiance of whatever nerves she might be feeling. The dress hangs perfectly on her slender frame; the color transforming her from the professional journalist who'd confronted me at our first meeting into something altogether more intriguing.

She approaches the entrance, where Tony checks her name against the VIP list before recognizing her with an embarrassed grin. Very unusual for my top bouncer and gatekeeper. *The right dress makes all the difference.* I watch as she's escorted inside, bypassing the envious gazes of those still waiting in line. The camera follows her progress through the main floor, capturing the heads that turn as she passes, the appreciative glances from men and women alike.

A dark possessive thrill courses through me at the sight—*mine*, walking into my domain. She belongs to no one in that room. Only I know why she's here, what she hopes to achieve, and how thoroughly I intend to control the narrative she thinks she's writing.

I switch to another camera as she's led up the private staircase to the VIP level, then to the even more exclusive corridor leading to my personal lounge. Her posture remains rigidly composed, but I don't miss the way her eyes dart around, taking in every detail, memorizing faces, cataloging information for the story she believes she's researching. Let her look. Let her remember. By the time she understands what she's really seeing, it will be too late.

I move away from the monitors and position myself at the small bar in the lounge's corner. The space is designed for intimate meetings with soundproof walls, subtle lighting, comfortable seating facilitated conversation while maintaining appropriate distance. No windows, no obvious cameras, nothing to suggest that every word spoken here is recorded and analyzed.

A soft knock precedes the door opening. One of my security team, Blake, a former military man with impeccable discretion, shows Lea inside before withdrawing, the door closing behind him with a soft click.

She stands just inside the entrance, taking in the room with those quick, assessing eyes. The red dress clings to her curves, the hemline stopping just above her knees. Conservative by club standards but still showing enough leg to draw attention. She's applied makeup with a skilled hand, enough to enhance her natural beauty without appearing overdone.

"Ms. Song," I greet, my voice neutral as I pour two glasses of water. "You're punctual, as always. I appreciate that."

"Mr. Varela." She steps further into the room, her heels sinking into the plush carpet. "Thank you for the dress. It's beautiful. It...it wasn't necessary."

"I disagree." I hand her one of the water glasses, our fingers brushing briefly in the exchange. She doesn't flinch, but I catch the slight increase in her breathing rate at the contact. "Appearance matters in my world. The right look opens doors that would otherwise remain closed."

She takes a small sip of water, using the moment to gather her thoughts. "I brought my notebook," she says, reaching for her small clutch purse. "I thought we could start by discussing—"

I raise a single finger, cutting her off mid-sentence. The immediate way she falls silent sends a wave of satisfaction through me. Already learning.

"This isn't a conventional interview," I remind her, moving to circle behind where she stands. "It's not a negotiation. It's a privilege I can revoke at any time."

I complete my circle, coming to stand behind her. She remains perfectly still, though I can sense the tension radiating from her body; the fight-or-flight response held rigidly in check by her determination to get her story.

"Tonight," I continue, placing a hand on her bare shoulder, "is about establishing parameters."

She stiffens at my touch, her skin warm beneath my palm. I let my hand remain there for three heartbeats, long enough to make my point, before stepping around to face her again.

"Your phone," I say, extending my hand. "Give it to me."

Her eyes widen, her free hand instinctively moving to the small clutch where her phone presumably rests. "My phone? Why?"

"Because I asked for it," I reply. "And because while you're in my world, your communications are my concern."

I watch the internal struggle play across her face. The journalist's instinct to protect her source material, the woman's natural resistance to surrendering her privacy, the pragmatist's calculation of how much she's willing to sacrifice for access.

"I need my phone for work," she says finally. "For notes, for recording—"

"All of which can be accomplished with this." I reach into my jacket pocket and withdraw a sleek smartphone, nearly identical to the model I've seen her using during our previous meeting. "The latest model. All the functionality you need."

She stares at the offered device, suspicion clear in her expression. "And what's been added to it?"

A smile tugs at my lips. She isn't stupid. Good.

"Security measures," I answer truthfully, if incompletely. The phone does indeed have enhanced security, along with custom software that will allow Marco to monitor her communications, track her location, and access her data. "For your protection as much as mine."

She doesn't believe me. That much is clear from the skeptical arch of her eyebrow. But she's calculating again, weighing her options, recognizing the inherent power imbalance in our arrangement.

"My contacts," she says. "My photos."

"Will remain private," I assure her. Another partial truth. I have no interest in her personal relationships or family vacation pictures. Only in who she speaks to about me, and what she says.

She hesitates another moment before opening her clutch and extracting her phone. Her fingers curl around it, a last moment of resistance before she finally extends her hand.

I take her phone, replacing it with the new one. "Your number will be transferred within an hour," I tell her. "Your contacts as well. Consider it a professional courtesy." I hand her original phone to Blake, who has reappeared at the door.

She glances down at the device in her hand, then back up at me, her dark eyes unreadable. "Is this how all your interviews begin? Confiscating personal property?"

"You're not here for an interview," I remind her, watching Blake pocket her phone before retreating again. "You're here to observe. To understand. To witness how my world functions." I gesture toward the seating area. "Please, make yourself comfortable. We have a full schedule tonight."

She moves toward one armchair, perching on its edge rather than settling back, ready for flight, maintaining what little control she can. I give myself a moment to appreciate the picture she makes: the red dress against the black chair, her dark hair framing features that are both delicate and determined.

"So, what's it about?" she asks, her reporter's instinct for direct questions reasserting itself.

"Business," I reply, taking the seat opposite her. "Some pleasure. Lessons in consequences."

Her eyes narrow. "Consequences?"

Before I can elaborate, a sharp knock at the door interrupts us. Marco. Perfect timing, as always.

"Enter," I call, not taking my eyes off Lea.

The door opens to admit Marco, followed by two of my security team escorting a thin man with disheveled hair and the particular mix of fear and defiance common to those who abuse those weaker than themselves. Michael Reeves, Jasmine's musician boyfriend.

He stumbles slightly as Marco propels him forward, his eyes darting frantically around the luxurious space before settling on me. Recognition dawns in his expression. He knows who I am. Good. That will save time.

Lea has gone completely still, her attention riveted on the unfolding scene. I can see the questions forming behind those keen eyes. The journalist in her is already constructing narratives, seeking connections, hungry for understanding.

I rise unhurriedly, buttoning my jacket. "Mr. Reeves," I greet, my voice carrying the same polite indifference I might use with a waiter or valet. "Thank you for joining us this evening."

The man swallows hard, his Adam's apple bobbing in his scrawny neck. "I had little choice," he mutters, shooting a resentful glance at Marco.

"Few of us do in the end," I reply philosophically. "Choices, consequences. Cause, effect. The fundamental mechanics of existence."

I gesture toward the center of the room. "Please, stand where I can see you properly."

Marco gives him a not-so-gentle shove forward. Reeves stumbles again before righting himself, his posture a study in barely contained panic.

"I hear you're a guitarist," I say conversationally, circling him slowly. "A virtuoso, even."

Confusion flickers across his face, momentarily displacing fear. "I...yeah. I play at The Blue Note. Other places too."

"How long have you been playing?"

He blinks rapidly, clearly struggling to follow this unexpected line of questioning. "Since I was a kid. Fifteen years, maybe? I practice six hours a day."

I nod, as if this information is what I've been seeking. "Dedication. Admirable." I stop in front of him. "Left or right-handed?"

The question hangs in the air, its significance dawning on Reeves with terrible clarity. His eyes flick in terror toward Marco, then back to me, then toward the door where the security team stands blocking any escape route.

"Right," he finally admits, his voice a whisper. "I use my left hand to chord the guitar, and the right to strum."

From the corner of my eye, I see Lea shift in her seat, her breath catching as she realizes where this is heading. I turn, meeting her wide-eyed gaze for a brief, charged moment before returning my attention to Reeves.

"Good," I hiss. "Then you only need the left hand to keep your career. I mean, you can always strum with a guitar pick glued to your right hand, right?"

What happens next unfolds with the precision of a well-rehearsed performance. At a nearly imperceptible nod from me, Marco moves forward, gripping Reeves from behind, immobilizing him with practiced efficiency. I step closer, taking the guitarist's right hand in mine, examining it with clinical detachment. Long fingers. Callused tips from finger

77

picking. The hands of someone who has dedicated thousands of hours to mastering an instrument. Hands that have also been used to strike a woman under my protection.

"Your right hand contains twenty-seven bones," I inform him, my tone conversational despite the tension vibrating through the room. "Fourteen phalanges, the bones in your fingers. Five metacarpals in the palm. Eight carpal bones in the wrist." I grasp his index finger, the skin clammy with sweat, and bend it sharply backward. The resistance gives way with a satisfying snap of bone beneath my hands. His scream resonates through the soundproofed room, high and thin with shock more than pain. That will come later.

"That's one," I say calmly.

The middle finger follows, then the ring finger, each break executed with precise, controlled pressure. Reeves is sobbing now, his knees buckling so that only Marco's grip keeps him upright. The sound of his distress fades into background noise, irrelevant to the task at hand.

I pause before breaking the pinky, glancing toward Lea. She sits rigidly upright. Her face is pale, one hand pressed against her mouth as if stifling a wave of nausea. It's her eyes that catch my interest, though. Her eyes are wide, fixed on the scene with a disturbing blend of horror and fascination. Not looking away. Not even trying to. A thrill of satisfaction stirs within me. *She's not averting her gaze. She's absorbing it.*

I return my attention to Reeves, completing the set with his little finger. Four clean breaks, each one deliberate, each one a message written in pain and bone.

"Listen," I tell him, leaning close to ensure my words penetrate the haze of his agony. "If you ever lay a hand on Jasmine, or any of my women again, I will ensure that every bone in your left hand suffers the same fate. And then I'll start on the ones that keep you walking upright. Do you understand?"

He nods frantically, tears and mucus streaming down his face. Pathetic. Men who prey on the vulnerable always are once stripped of their imagined power.

"Good." I step back, straightening my cuffs. "My associate will arrange medical attention for you. The doctors are very discreet. Very skilled, too, though I'm afraid you might have to cancel a couple of gigs at the Blue Note, just like I had to replace Jasmine in my act for the next week or two, thanks to you."

I nod to the security team. "Escort him out via the service entrance. And make sure he understands that tonight's conversation remains private."

They move forward, taking the sobbing man from Marco's grip and half-dragging him toward the door. As they exit, I turn back to Lea, studying her reaction with genuine curiosity. She remains seated; her knuckles are white where she grips the arms of the chair, her eyes fixed on the spot where Reeves had stood.

"Think carefully," I tell her, my voice dangerously soft, "about how much of that you want to put in your article."

She looks up then, her composure fragmenting before forcing itself back together through sheer will. "Was that supposed to scare me?" she asks, her voice steadier than I might have expected.

"No," I reply honestly. "It was supposed to educate you." I move closer, noting how she tenses but doesn't retreat. "You wanted access to my world, Ms. Song. This is it. Not the champagne and VIP tables. Not the music and beautiful people. This." I gesture to the space where Reeves had stood. "Order maintained through consequence. Respect enforced through example."

She swallows hard, her reporter's instinct fighting against what she's just witnessed. "He deserved punishment," she says finally. "What he did to Jasmine was wrong. But this?"

"Was efficient," I finish for her. "He won't touch her again. He won't touch any woman again. One moment of discomfort for preventing future violence." I tilt my head. "Isn't that a fair trade?"

"Discomfort?" She almost laughs, the sound strangled in her throat. "You broke his hand. His career."

"I broke the hand he used to hurt someone under my protection," I correct. "His left hand remains perfectly functional for chording. Perhaps he'll develop a new style. Adversity breeds innovation, after all."

I can see her struggling with the moral calculus, the part of her that recognizes the justice in Reeves facing consequences warring with her socialized understanding of acceptable punishment. The conflict makes her even more fascinating to watch.

"You could have called the police," she suggests, though her tone lacks conviction.

This time I do laugh, the sound genuinely amused. "And what would they have done? Taken a report? Held him overnight? Released him with a warning?" I shake my head. "The system you believe in fails women like Jasmine every day. My system doesn't."

She has no immediate response to that, her eyes dropping to the new phone still clutched in her hand. I watch her processing, recalibrating, adjusting her understanding of exactly what she's walked into when she agreed to my terms.

"Our schedule for the evening continues downstairs," I say after allowing her a moment to collect herself. "There's someone I'd like you to meet; someone who might provide a valuable perspective for your article."

Lea rises, her movements careful, controlled. Whatever she's feeling, she's determined not to show weakness. I admire that, even as I recognize it as the same pride that will eventually bring her fully into my world.

"And if I decide I've seen enough for one night?" she asks, an ultimate test of boundaries.

I smile, not bothering to hide the predatory edge. "Then our arrangement ends. You walk out with a partial story and limited understanding. Enough to write something, perhaps, but not enough to matter." I step closer, close enough to catch her perfume, something subtle and floral that suits her perfectly. "But you won't. Because you need this story more than you're disturbed by my methods. Don't you, Lea?"

Using her first name, deliberate and intimate, lands as intended. A flush creeps up her neck, her pupils dilating despite her efforts to maintain professional distance.

"I need the truth," she counters, lifting her chin. "Whatever it is."

"Then follow me," I say, gesturing toward the door. "And prepare yourself. The night is just beginning."

CHAPTER SEVEN

Lea

THE LEATHER SEATS OF THE BENTLEY ARE BUTTERY SOFT beneath me, unlike the knot tightening in my stomach. My fingers trace the sleek lines of the new phone Nico provided last night, the cool glass doing little to soothe the residual tremor in my hands. The memory plays on a loop, unbidden: Nico, standing over the terrified guitarist, the sickening snap of bone breaking in the plush silence of his private lounge, followed by screams that still claw at the edges of my hearing.

I close my eyes, trying to block it out, but the image burns behind my eyelids. The casual brutality, the chilling efficiency; it was like watching a surgeon perform a delicate procedure, only the instrument was pain and the outcome was measured destruction. A shudder racks my frame. Part fear, part recoil, and part something darker, a morbid fascination that leaves a coppery taste in my mouth. He hadn't even raised his voice. The violence was cold, precise, almost impersonal, yet utterly dominating.

And then, minutes later, we were downstairs, Nico introducing me to State Senator Abernathy and Alderman Ross as if nothing had happened. "Ms. Song is observing my operations for an article," he'd said, his hand on my back, a subtle claim of ownership. Both politicians, men whose faces frequently graced the front page of the Journal, had greeted me with practiced smiles, their eyes holding a flicker of wary curiosity but mostly acceptance. *They* knew my name. They acted like my presence beside Nico was normal, expected even.

His operations. The phrase lingered in my mind. Last night wasn't just about punishing an abusive boyfriend; it was a demonstration. A lesson in consequences, as he'd called it. And the seamless shift from breaking fingers to shaking hands with elected officials? That was the actual show of force. His power wasn't just in violence; it was woven into the very fabric of the city's legitimate structures.

The car glides through Chicago traffic, the city awakening around us with delivery trucks rumbling, commuters rushing, the rhythmic clang of the L train overhead. Inside this luxurious cocoon, the city noise silenced to a distant hum, the world feels unreal. My world, it seems, now consists only of Nico Varela and the increasingly murky depths I'm descending into.

My gaze returns to the phone in my lap. His phone. I know, with absolute certainty, that it's a listening device, a tracker, a digital leash. Every call, every text, every search query logged and likely reported back to him or Marco. The thought makes my skin crawl. Yet tossing it out the window isn't an option. Not if I want this story. And maybe there's a sliver of truth in his claim of protection. Being under his surveillance feels suffocating, but perhaps it also places me within the boundaries of his territory, a space where others might hesitate to tread. Or maybe that's just what I need to tell myself to justify holding onto this electronic Trojan horse.

The car slows, pulling to the curb in front of an elegant, ivy-covered brownstone on a quiet, tree-lined street in Lincoln Park. The driver cuts the engine, the sudden silence amplifying the nervous thrumming in my chest. A moment later, the front door of the house opens, and Nico steps out, looking immaculate in a charcoal gray suit. There's no trace of the menace from last night, only cool, controlled composure.

He doesn't look surprised to see the car waiting. He slides into the seat beside me without a word, just a brief, almost imperceptible nod in my direction. The small space instantly feels charged with his presence. The faint, expensive scent of his cologne fills the air, a disorienting reminder of his proximity.

The driver pulls back into traffic. Silence stretches between us. I stare resolutely out the window, focusing on the blur of buildings passing by, pretending my heart isn't hammering against my ribs. What am I supposed to say? *Beautiful morning after the bone-breaking? How's the "hand cording only" going for the guy you maimed?*

He breaks the silence first, his voice calm, measured. "The restaurant is called Oriole. Two Michelin stars. Their tasting menu is exceptional."

Food. He's talking about food. As if we're just two colleagues heading to a business lunch. The cognitive dissonance is staggering.

"I'm sure it is," I manage, keeping my tone neutral.

He glances at me, a faint flicker of amusement in his dark eyes. "You seem tense, Ms. Song."

You think? "Just processing," I say, opting for vague truth. "Last night was instructive."

"Good," he replies, turning his gaze back to the front. "That was the intention."

The rest of the drive passes in silence. We pull up to a discreet entrance, marked only by a small, tasteful plaque bearing the restaurant's name. A valet rushes forward, opening Nico's door with practiced deference before hurrying around to mine. Inside, the ambiance is hushed and elegant, with crisp white tablecloths, gleaming silverware, minimalist décor that speaks of understated wealth. The few patrons already seated are impeccably dressed, their conversations muted, creating a sophisticated buzz.

The maître d' approaches immediately, his smile professional, but his eyes fixed solely on Nico. "Mr. Varela. Your party is waiting in the private dining room."

Party? I thought this was just lunch. Nico gestures for me to precede him, his hand hovering near my back again, not quite touching but radiating warmth. We follow the maître d' through the main dining area to a secluded room at the back.

The door opens to reveal a long table already occupied by about a dozen people, men and women, mostly middle-aged, dressed in expensive business attire. The air hums with conversation and the clink of glasses, but it all stops the moment Nico enters. Every head turns, every smile freezes, every gaze locks onto him with a mixture of respect and fear. It's like watching a predator enter a clearing.

"Nico, glad you could make it," one man says, rising from

his seat. I know him; a property developer whose face I've seen in the business section.

Nico nods curtly, scanning the table. "Gentlemen. Ladies." His gaze lingers for a second on each person, a silent acknowledgement, a subtle assertion of dominance. He then gestures toward me. "This is Lea Song. She's observing."

A murmur of polite greetings follows. Some offer tight smiles, others brief nods. Their eyes flicker over me, assessing, categorizing. I see recognition in a few faces. It's the same city officials and business figures whose photos often accompany articles about zoning variances, development deals, and political fundraising. Just like last night, they seem to be familiar with my name, though we've never met before. More unsettling still is how they accept my entrance at Nico's side; not with surprise, but casual acknowledgment, as if my presence here is routine. These aren't just anybody; these are the puppet masters of Chicago, the ones who keep the city's gears turning, or more accurately, the ones who collect the toll at every turn.

Nico gestures to an empty chair near the head of the table opposite him. I slide into it, pulling out the small, discreet notepad and pen I'd tucked into my purse. The conversation resumes, but the energy in the room has shifted. It's lighter, more performative, everyone acutely aware of The Diplomat.

Platters of intricate appetizers circulate, delicate bites of seafood, artfully arranged vegetable terrines, foie gras parfait. Waiters move silently, refilling water glasses, offering wine. On the surface, it's a perfectly normal, upscale business lunch. Discussions revolve around upcoming city projects, potential investment opportunities, the feasibility study for a new downtown high-rise.

I take notes diligently, capturing snippets of conversation, observing the dynamics. Who defers to whom? Who interrupts? And who seeks Nico's approval before speaking? The patterns are subtle but clear. Nico rarely speaks, but when he does, the room falls silent. His contributions are brief, insightful, often reframing the issue in a way that subtly steers the consensus toward his preferred outcome. He doesn't command; he guides, manipulates, orchestrates.

The main course arrives. Pan-seared scallops with truffle risotto for me, a perfectly cooked filet mignon for Nico. The conversation shifts to a major infrastructure contract currently under review by the city council. An older gentleman, Thomas Abernathy, not the senator I met last night, but perhaps a relative, his nameplate identifying him as head of a prominent construction firm, is outlining his company's proposal. He seems confident, jovial, occasionally directing remarks toward Nico with an air of camaraderie.

But as he gets into the financial specifics, his voice falters. He fumbles with the figures, corrects himself twice, his face flushing slightly. He takes a large gulp of water, then clears his throat. "Apologies," he says with a forced chuckle, dabbing his forehead with a napkin. "Must be the heat. Or perhaps the excellent wine." He jogs his chair back. "If you'll excuse me for just a moment."

He heads toward the door leading out of the private room, presumably toward the restrooms, as Nico watches him go. The conversation at the table pauses awkwardly for a beat before someone else picks up the thread, steering it toward safer territory.

Nico catches my eye across the table. He gives a small, almost imperceptible shake of his head, a silent instruction for me to stay put. Then, he rises smoothly and follows Abernathy out the same door.

My reporter's instinct screams. Something just happened. That wasn't just a momentary lapse; Abernathy looked genuinely unnerved. Nico's quiet pursuit confirms it. His instruction to stay means he doesn't want me to witness whatever comes next. Which, naturally, means I absolutely have to.

I wait, counting silently to twenty, letting the rhythm of the table conversation re-establish itself. Then, pushing my chair back quietly, I murmur a polite, "Excuse me," to the woman seated beside me and slip out the same door Nico and Abernathy used.

The corridor outside the private dining room is dimly lit, carpeted, silent except for the faint scent of polished wood and expensive perfume. It forks left and right. I pause, listening intently. From the left, I hear the faint sounds of the restaurant. From the right, nothing. I head right, my heels sinking into the plush carpet, muffling my steps.

Rounding a corner marked with a discreet sign for restrooms, I freeze. There he is. Thomas Abernathy, pressed back against the polished mahogany wall, not physically touched but effectively pinned by Nico's proximity. Nico stands a foot away, one hand resting casually against the wall near Abernathy's head, blocking any quick escape. He's speaking in a low, calm voice, too low for me to make out the words, but the effect is undeniable. Abernathy's face is pale, slick with sweat, his eyes wide with a fear that borders on panic. He looks like a man staring down the barrel of a gun, even though no weapon is visible.

It's the same controlled menace I saw last night, stripped of the overt violence but no less potent. This is how he operates when broken fingers aren't necessary: quiet threats, implied consequences, the crushing weight of his power brought to bear in a hushed corridor. My heart hammers against my ribs. I should retreat, pretend I saw nothing. But I can't move. I'm rooted to the spot, disgusted yet mesmerized by the raw, quiet display of intimidation. Part of me screams to run; another, traitorous part leans closer, needing to understand the source of such absolute control.

Then Nico's head turns. His eyes find mine in the dim light. He doesn't look surprised, or angry, or anything other than mildly amused. He doesn't miss a beat.

His voice, still low but now carrying clearly down the short hallway, cuts through the silence. "Ah, Ms. Song. Perfect timing." He gestures toward the terrified man pinned against the wall. "Mr. Abernathy and I were just clarifying some discrepancies in his recent projections. Weren't we, Thomas?"

Abernathy flinches at the use of his first name, nodding mutely.

Nico continues, his tone chillingly conversational. "Ms. Song was just wondering,"—my blood runs cold—"if you intended to fully honor the terms of our previous arrangement. The one regarding subcontractor allocation."

He turns his head, fixing me with that intense, unreadable gaze. He's done it deliberately. By invoking my name, by implying I'm privy to their "arrangement," he's made me complicit. He's woven me into the threat, positioning me as his ally, his enforcer-by-proxy in Abernathy's terrified mind.

Abernathy's panicked gaze flicks toward me, his eyes pleading. *And suddenly I feel dirty.* He sees me not as a neutral observer, but as part of Nico's apparatus. Complicit in his fear. Nico didn't just intimidate him; he used *me* as part of the threat.

"Yes," Abernathy chokes out, his voice hoarse. "Yes, of course. Absolutely. A simple oversight. It will be corrected. Immediately."

"Excellent," Nico says, removing his hand from the wall. He steps back, creating space, the immediate threat receding but the underlying pressure remaining. "I knew we could rely on your good judgment, Thomas." He straightens his tie, a gesture of finality. "Now, perhaps you should take a moment to compose yourself before rejoining our guests."

Abernathy nods again, frantically dabbing at his face with a handkerchief. He doesn't look at me as he scrambles away down the corridor in the opposite direction.

I stand frozen, my mind reeling. He used me. Effortlessly, seamlessly, he drew me into his web, painting me as part of his power structure.

Nico turns fully toward me, a faint, knowing smirk playing on his lips. "You seem so eager to get involved, Ms. Song. I thought I made it clear for you to stay put?"

"I..." My voice fails me for a moment. I swallow, forcing the words out. "I needed the restroom." A weak lie, and we both know it.

"Of course you did," he says, the amusement deepening in his eyes. He steps closer, invading my personal space just enough to make me acutely aware of his physical presence. "Did you find what you were looking for?"

The question hangs between us, laden with double meaning. Did I find the restroom? Did I find the truth I claim to be seeking? Did I find the confirmation of what kind of man he truly is?

"I found..." I trail off, unsure how to answer, unsure what answer he wants, unsure what the truth even is anymore.

He doesn't press. Instead, he gestures back toward the private dining room. "Shall we rejoin the others? The lemon tart here is supposedly transcendent."

He turns and walks back the way we came, expecting me to follow. And I do. What choice do I have? My legs feel unsteady, my mind a chaotic whirl of conflicting emotions. Disgust at his methods, fear of his power, and that deeply unsettling flicker of something else, something coiling hot and low in my gut. A perverse thrill at being pulled into the orbit of such dangerous charisma?

Nico didn't just show me his power; he made me touch it. He implicated me, binding me to him in a way that goes beyond mere observation.

I follow him back into the private dining room, my steps leaden. The earlier sophistication of the place now feels tainted, almost suffocating. The lemon tart tastes like crap, despite its apparent perfection. I mechanically pick at it, nodding vaguely when spoken to, my mind still replaying the scene in the corridor: Abernathy's terror, Nico's casual menace, and my own unwilling role in the drama. He hadn't just let me witness his power; he'd splashed it onto me, marking me.

The lunch eventually concludes. Farewells are

exchanged, polite smiles are plastered on faces that, just moments before in Abernathy's case, had been masks of fear. In the Bentley on the ride back, the silence had stretched taut again, but this time it felt different. Less like unspoken tension, more like a settled, uncomfortable reality.

As the car pulls up near my apartment building, Nico finally turns to me. His expression is unreadable, detached.

"I have matters requiring my sole attention for the next couple of days, Ms. Song," he states, his tone leaving no room for questions. "Sensitive negotiations that wouldn't benefit from observation. Marco will be in touch when your presence is required again."

It wasn't a suggestion or a courtesy; it was a dismissal. A temporary release from the leash. A wave of conflicting emotions wash over me, relief so potent it almost makes my knees buckle, followed by a prickle of unease. Is this protection, or am I simply being sidelined because I've seen too much, pushed him too far by following him?

"Understood," I manage, keeping my voice steady despite the tremor wanting to betray me. Arguing wouldn't help me here. I gather my purse and the cursed phone, my fingers brushing against its smooth surface.

He gives a curt nod, his gaze already distant, likely calculating his next move in the city-wide chess game he's playing. I exit the car, the heavy door clicking shut behind me with an air of finality. The Bentley pulls away smoothly, disappearing around the corner, leaving me standing on the familiar sidewalk, feeling utterly adrift.

CHAPTER EIGHT

Nico

I PACE THE LENGTH OF MY PRIVATE VIP LOUNGE, A caged predator finally unleashed, though no suitable prey is immediately apparent within these four walls. The club is alive beneath me, bass throbbing through the floorboards like a second heartbeat, a familiar rhythm that usually soothes the savage beast. Tonight, it merely amplifies the electric tension humming through me.

The past two days have been a crucible of focused intensity, dedicated solely to executing a delicate directive from my uncle, Alessandro. The old patriarch doesn't make requests lightly, and navigating the intricate power dynamics involved requires absolute discretion, the kind that precludes even the most observant shadow. It is done now, concluded successfully, another knot tied securely in the complex web of influence the Varela family maintains. But settling accounts for Alessandro, while necessary, hasn't sated the restless energy coiling deep within me. Power demands control, and control requires sacrifice, but the residual static of the operation leaves a sharp, primal itch that demands a different kind of release. Whiskey isn't touching it.

Marco enters, silent as ever, offering a brief nod that confirms the final loose ends from Alessandro's business are tied off. He then shifts focus, his expression neutral as he consults his phone. "Ms. Song arrived promptly when summoned, Boss," he reports, his tone flat, betraying nothing. "She's downstairs at the main bar. Observing."

Promptly. Good. She followed orders after her two-day dismissal, returning to the fold the moment the leash was tugged. I like it. That outward compliance is crucial, even if I suspect a storm of conflicting thoughts likely rages beneath her composed surface. Marco continues, "She's already been taking extensive notes on staff interactions with customers. She's thorough."

Thorough. Yes, Lea Song approaches everything with that same intense focus: her research, her questions, the way her dark eyes track movements across a room, cataloging details others would miss. I saw it during the lunch two days prior, even after the clarification with Abernathy. I've watched her mind work, quick and ruthless in its pursuit of truth, a quality I both respect and intend to leverage fully.

And then there's the other quality she possesses, the one that has flickered insistently at the edge of my thoughts even while handling Alessandro's sensitive affairs. The flush that crawls up her neck when our gazes lock for too long. The subtle catch in her breath when I step into her personal space. The defiance in her posture that can't quite disguise her body's unwilling response to my proximity.

She wants me. She hates that she wants me. And that

delicious conflict makes her infinitely more intriguing than the countless women who make their availability painfully obvious.

Taking her now would be simple. A word, a look, a touch, and she would follow me to my private rooms upstairs, her body betraying her principles even as her mind rebels. The animalistic urge to do just that claws at me now, sharper than usual after the constraints of the past two days. But Lea Song is not a fleeting distraction to be consumed and discarded. She's an investment. A strategic piece to be carefully positioned before I make my ultimate move. Patience is required. Discipline.

My body, however, has different requirements tonight. Fortunately, there are other, more immediate options for visceral relief.

I check my watch. "Nine-fifteen," I murmur, mostly to myself. "Time for something more entertaining."

Marco adjusts his stance, his face impassive. He's been with me long enough to understand that my appetites, like my business dealings, follow patterns only I fully comprehend, especially after concluding high pressure family matters.

"Tell Vivian I want to see her," I say, moving to the private bar and pouring myself two fingers of Macallan 25. The amber liquid does little to soothe the underlying thrum. "And have someone bring Ms. Song up here. She might find this educational."

Marco nods once and disappears, silent as always. That silence, that unquestioning loyalty, is why he's survived beside me for over a decade in a world where loyalty is as rare as genuine innocence.

I swirl the amber liquid in my glass, enjoying the heat as it runs down my throat. The whiskey is excellent, deep and complex, satisfying on multiple levels. Like power. Like control. Like, the look in Lea's eyes when I push her just beyond her comfort zone.

Vivian arrives first, elegant in a black dress that accentuates her curves while projecting professional competence. As my events coordinator, she handles the more exclusive entertainments Purgatorio offers to its most elite clientele. Private gambling. Exclusive performers. Discreet encounters that never appear on any official schedule.

"You wanted to see me, Mr. Varela?" Her voice is smooth, confident. Another quality I value in those who serve me; the absence of unnecessary fear. Respect, yes. Caution, always. But never the paralyzing terror that leads to mistakes.

"The Velvet Room," I say, setting down my glass. "Is it available tonight?"

A flash of understanding crosses her features. "Yes, sir. It's been prepared for tomorrow's private event, but we can have it ready within twenty minutes if you'd prefer to use it this evening."

"I would. Arrange for the Martinez duo. The full demonstration, not the abbreviated version." I pause, considering. "And make sure they understand this is an audition for potential future bookings. I expect their best work."

Vivian nods, already tapping on her tablet. "Of course. Will you be bringing guests, or is this a private viewing?"

"One guest." I smile slightly, picturing Lea's reaction to what I've planned. "A potential business partner who needs to understand the full range of Purgatorio's offerings."

Another nod, no questions. That's why Vivian earns

twice what most club managers make. She executes without unnecessary inquiry. "Twenty minutes, then. I'll have someone escort you when everything's ready."

She leaves just as Marco returns with Lea in tow. The contrast between the two women is striking. Vivian's polished, practiced allure against Lea's raw intensity. Both are beautiful, but where Vivian offers clinical charm, Lea radiates an energy that's far more potent, especially now. Seeing her again after two days crystallizes the restlessness I've felt. My focus snaps solely to her. The forced distance hasn't diluted her impact; if anything, it's underscored the unique friction her presence creates in my space.

Lea eyes me warily as she enters, her gaze sweeping the room before settling on me. She's dressed more formally tonight than in our previous encounters. Black trousers that trace the line of her curves just enough to be tantalizing without being obvious, a silky emerald blouse that brings out the hidden flecks of gold in her dark eyes. Her hair is pulled back in a sleek ponytail, emphasizing the elegant line of her neck.

I imagine wrapping that ponytail around my fist, using it to tilt her head back, exposing her throat to my mouth. The image sends a fresh wave of heat through my body, a low thrum that confirms the tension the brief separation did nothing to quell, perhaps even honed it.

"Ms. Song," I greet her, my voice smooth, gesturing to the sofa across from where I stand.

She remains standing, her usual wariness perhaps edged with something else now, a flicker of the same charged awareness I feel after the silence between us. "My observations were rather solitary for the past two days, Mr. Varela," she states, her tone neutral but direct. "You mentioned sensitive negotiations requiring your sole attention. I trust they concluded satisfactorily?"

There it is. The probe cloaked in professional courtesy. She hasn't forgotten being dismissed, and she wants answers.

"Always focused on the business at hand, Ms. Song. Admirable." A faint smile touches my lips as I hold her gaze. "My affairs concluded as planned." I offer nothing more on the subject, deliberately closing that door. "But tonight isn't about past negotiations. It's about future prospects. And your perspective."

Her eyes narrow, assessing my deflection. "My perspective?" she repeats, a note of skepticism entering her voice. "Interesting. I'm beginning to think the actual story happens up here, anyway, not down on the main floor."

I smile, appreciating her refusal to be easily sidetracked. "Perceptive as always. Which is why I've arranged something special for this evening." I move closer, invading her personal space. I relish the subtle signs of her control warring with her reaction to my proximity after the break: not backing away. Lea Song is too proud for retreat, but there's a definite tightening in her shoulders, a quickening of her breath beneath the emerald silk, a defiant lift of her chin that doesn't quite mask the awareness sparking in her eyes. She feels it too, this sudden intensity after the quiet. "Purgatorio caters to a wide range of appetites, Ms. Song. Some are more specialized than others."

Her eyes narrow further, suspicion replacing the fleeting spark of awareness. "Meaning?"

"We're considering adding a new act to our private entertainment roster." I keep my tone level, the detached businessman seeking a consultation. "I'd value your perspective on its market appeal."

She doesn't believe my professional facade for a second; I see it in the skeptical arch of her eyebrow. But I also see the competing flicker in her eyes. The journalist's hunger outweighing caution and curiosity beginning to win. "What kind of act?"

I'm saved from elaborating by one of Vivian's assistants, a young woman in the club's signature black uniform, appearing at the doorway. "Mr. Varela, the Velvet Room is ready."

"Excellent." I extend my hand toward the door, not quite touching Lea, but close enough that she can surely feel the heat radiating from my palm, heat that feels amplified just by having her near again. "Shall we, Ms. Song? I believe you'll find this interesting for your article. A glimpse into the more exclusive side of nightlife entertainment."

She hesitates for only a fraction of a second, her mind clearly racing, suspicion battling her journalistic instinct to leave no stone unturned. The desire for the story, for the truth behind the polished surface, wins out. "Lead the way," she finally says, her voice betraying nothing of the conflict I know she's experiencing.

The Velvet Room is tucked away in a secluded corner of Purgatorio's upper level, accessible only through a discrete corridor monitored by my most trusted security personnel. As its name suggests, the walls are lined with deep red velvet, absorbing sound and creating an atmosphere of hushed intimacy. The lighting is subdued, just enough to see, not enough to feel exposed. The air is thick with the faint scent of expensive perfume and something else, something warmer, almost musky.

At the center of the room is a small stage, elevated only slightly above floor level. Surrounding it are plush armchairs and sofas, providing optimal viewing while maintaining privacy. Tonight, only one seating area is prepared, a sumptuous black couch positioned in front of the stage.

I guide Lea to the couch, gesturing for her to sit. She does so cautiously; her gaze taking in every detail of the room with that sharp journalist's focus. I settle beside her, close enough that I can detect the subtle scent of her perfume, something with notes of jasmine and amber, sensual without being overpowering. It suits her.

"This room hosts our more specialized entertainments," I explain, keeping my tone conversational. "By invitation only, naturally."

"Naturally," she repeats, her voice dry. "And what exactly are we about to see, Mr. Varela?"

I smile, leaning back against the soft leather. "A demonstration of the more refined aspects of dominance and submission. Professionally performed by experts, of course."

Her posture stiffens almost imperceptibly. "BDSM? That's the 'specialized entertainment' you're considering adding to your club's offerings?"

"In select contexts, for discerning clients." I observe her reaction. "You seem surprised. I would have thought a journalist of your caliber would be acquainted with the prevalence of such interests among the powerful."

A flash of irritation crosses her features before she masters it. "I'm familiar with the concept, Mr. Varela. I'm just surprised you'd include this in my 'education'."

"All aspects of power apply to understanding my world, Ms. Song. It's what made me who I am. Power and domination." I signal to the attendant hovering by the door. "Including the most intimate expressions of it."

The room goes darker just as two performers slip onto the stage. They're the Martinez pair, the latest hot shit in the Midwest BDSM scene. These two don't just put on a show, they make rope and leather into pure art. Miguel rocks black pants like they're painted on, his bare chest catching the low light. Elise is decked out in this wicked black harness that wraps around all her best parts, hooked to a collar. Her wrists are already tied up nice and cozy in front of her.

They hit their marks without a word; him standing tall, her on her knees, looking like the perfect sub. The quiet in here is electric.

I sneak a peek at Lea. She's playing it cool, but her quick breaths and white knuckles gripping the couch tell a different story. She's not freaked. It's more like she can't look away even though she thinks she should.

Miguel circles Elise with a predator's grace, his fingers mapping her skin like territory to conquer. The way he touches her isn't cruel; it's pure power play, a dance where she gives up control and he runs the show. He whispers in her ear and she melts into it, offering herself up like a gift.

Next to me, Lea gulps. Hard.

The show kicks into high gear when Miguel guides Elise to this padded bench center stage. He bends her over it, stretches those arms high, and locks her down tight. Her wrists, ankles, the works. She's exposed and defenseless, exactly how they both want it.

I split my focus between the kinky theater and Lea's face.

She's inching forward, mouth open, hypnotized. The reporter in her is taking mental notes, but there's something else there too. I can see it. A little spark she's fighting like hell to hide.

Miguel grabs this suede flogger and teases Elise with it first. The way her back arches. Fuck, it's obscene. Her ass tilted up like an offering as he drags that suede flogger across her skin. Each teasing stroke makes her tremble, her breath hitching in these little gasps that hit me straight to my cock. Then he snaps it, sharp, precise, and her moan cuts through the air, low and needy, her thighs quivering as red blooms across her pale flesh. My cock twitches hard against my trousers, already straining from the sight.

Beside me, Lea's pretending she's above it all, but I see through her. Her chest rises a little faster, her fingers digging into the couch like she's anchoring herself. That flush creeping up her neck. It's not disgust, no matter how much she wants to play the detached journalist. She's hooked, eyes glued to Elise's writhing body as Miguel swaps the flogger for a leather crop. He lands a quick, stinging slap across her ass, and Elise bucks, a cry spilling from her lips that's pure, unadulterated want. Lea's lips part just a fraction, but it's enough. I know that look. She's imagining it, feeling that sting, even if she'd rather die than admit it. That's my in, right there, her dirty little secret she doesn't even know she's showing me.

I catch the floor manager's eye with a tilt of my head, voice low. "Bring Loretta." Lea might hear, might not. It doesn't matter. I want her to see this next part, to feel the weight of my world while she's stuck watching. The stage is heating up. Miguel's got a vibrator in hand now, pressing it against Elise's clit while she's still bound, helpless. Her moans turn desperate, hips grinding against the bench as he works her, that buzz mixing with the wet sound of her arousal. My blood's pounding, every nerve lit up, and I'm half a second from dragging Lea onto my lap and fucking her right here.

Then Loretta slips in, all sleek lines and quiet deference, her black dress outlining a figure built for sin. She doesn't hesitate, just glides to my side, sinking onto the couch beside me. Her thigh rests a breath away from mine, a silent offering of proximity. She knows the drill. Her attention stays forward, fixed on the performance, but her awareness of me, of my mood, is absolute.

Onstage, Miguel's barking a command: "Beg for it," and Elise's voice breaks, "Please, sir, please," as he teases her with the vibrator, pulling it back just when she's about to lose it. My jaw clenches, arousal clawing through me. I shift, making myself more comfortable, adjusting myself.

Lea's eyes flick over. She caught the movement, and I don't look away. I hold Lea's gaze, daring her to react as I rest my hand on Loretta's thigh. Not kneading, not caressing. Just resting there. A statement of ownership. Loretta doesn't flinch, doesn't react at all beyond a slight, almost imperceptible intake of breath. Her stillness only amplifies my control over her.

"You like this, don't you?" I mutter, voice rough, meant entirely for Lea, though my hand remains on Loretta's leg. My thumb makes a slow, deliberate circle against the fabric of her dress. Loretta stays perfectly still, a beautiful, breathing prop in the psychological game I'm playing with the woman on my other side. My focus narrows on Lea, the way her eyes are fixed on my hand resting on another woman. My arousal spikes, sharp and visceral, fueled not by Loretta, but by the possessive display, by the control, by the conflict warring in Lea's dark eyes. I'm picturing Lea under me, naked, pinned, that smart mouth gasping my name while I fuck her raw. She'd fight it at first, all defiance and sharp edges, but she'd break so fucking beautifully, begging me to take her harder, deeper.

Elise's screams onstage bring me back. She's coming undone as Miguel growls something filthy, his hand relentless between her thighs. The sound tips me closer to losing control. My cock throbs painfully, demanding release. Loretta shifts almost imperceptibly beside me, aware of my state, but makes no move, awaiting command. And Lea's right there on the other side, close enough I can smell that jasmine on her skin. I look straight into her wide eyes, imagining destroying her composure piece by piece. She'd hate how much she'd love it, and that's what's got me burning, knowing I'll have her soon, in any way I fucking want.

I'm close, fuck, so close to doing something reckless, when there's a knock, sharp and unwelcome. One of my guys steps in, voice low. "Boss, warehouse confirmation is in. Moretti's crew set the meeting." My chest's heaving, my hand still resting possessively on Loretta's thigh, but I nod, forcing control back into my voice. "Good. We're done here." I remove my hand from Loretta's leg as if dismissing an object, not acknowledging her further. She rises and slips away, disappearing with the same quiet discretion she arrived with. I'm left aching, half-feral with need I can't unleash yet. Business first. Always fucking business.

I stand, straightening my jacket, my body humming with frustrated arousal. The timing is deliberate. Moretti knows what he's doing, sending this message now. The warehouse meeting has been in discussion for days; confirmation could have come at any time. That it arrives when I'm otherwise occupied is no coincidence. A small power play, testing my responsiveness, my priorities.

Lea rises beside me, her composure visibly strained. The flush in her face, the shaky hands as she gathers her notebook, these small tells betray what she's trying so hard to hide. I find satisfaction in knowing she'll lie awake tonight, replaying what she witnessed, what she felt.

"We're leaving," I tell her, not a request. My voice still carries the rough edge of arousal, and I make no effort to soften it. Let her hear what she does to me. Let her wonder what might have happened had we not been interrupted.

Elise and Miguel halt their act, their gazes finding mine, awaiting my signal. A single dip of my chin is their dismissal, their cue to undo the bindings. Loretta's already vanished. That quiet exit is why I keep her around. Maybe I'll summon her later, have her take the edge off. But not tonight. For now, this throb low in my gut is fuel, honing my concentration for what comes next.

Out in the hall, Lea strides a few paces in front, her walk fast, purposeful, like putting space between us can somehow rebuild the composure I shattered. I let her escape for a moment, my own steps unhurried as I track the stiffness in her back, the way she holds herself so tightly wound.

The club's main floor is a blur of light and sound as we pass through. My staff recognize my focused expression and give us a wide berth. No one approaches, no one speaks. The crowd parts instinctively, creating a path toward the private elevator that will take us to the garage level where my car waits.

The elevator doors close, encasing us, as the quiet between us prickles. I put myself across from her, leaning a shoulder against the wall, drinking in her profile while she makes a show of watching the floor numbers drop. The confined car fills with her perfume and the undeniable current of thwarted need.

"You're quiet, Ms. Song," I observe, my tone casual. "No questions? No observations for your article?"

Her eyes flick to mine, then away. "I'm still processing the experience."

"Are you?" I smile. "And what conclusions are you reaching?"

The elevator reaches the garage level, doors sliding open with a soft chime. Lea steps out quickly, too quickly, betraying her eagerness to escape the intimate confines we shared. My driver stands beside the waiting car, opening the rear door as we approach.

Lea slides into the back seat, arranging herself as far from the center as possible. A futile gesture. The interior of the Bentley might be spacious, but no physical distance will erase what passed between us in that room. I settle beside her, close enough that she can feel my body heat but not quite touching. A planned intrusion into her space that mirrors what I'm doing to her mind.

"Warehouse Five," I instruct my driver. "No rush." The privacy partition rises, sealing us into our own world as the car glides out of the garage and into the night.

For several blocks, we ride in silence. I don't fill it, content to let her discomfort build, to let her wrestle with the questions she both wants and fears to ask. Her fingers twist in her lap, a rare display of nervous energy from someone who usually maintains such careful control.

Finally, I decide to probe the wound. "So, Ms. Song," I begin, my voice pitched low, intimate, "did the performance meet your expectations?"

She swallows, a muscle in her jaw tightening. "It was... professionally executed."

"Indeed." I shift, angling my body toward hers. "The Martinez duo are among the best in their field. But I wasn't asking about their technical proficiency."

Her gaze remains fixed on the city lights sliding past the tinted windows. "What were you asking, then?"

"Whether it stirred anything in you." I lean closer, invading more of her space. "Whether you recognized something of yourself in Elise's surrender. Or perhaps in Miguel's control."

Now she looks at me, eyes flashing with defiance. "I was observing, Mr. Varela. That's what journalists do."

"Was that all you were doing?" I reach for her wrist, my fingers encircling it before she can pull away. Beneath my thumb, her pulse is a frantic, betraying rhythm that contradicts her composed expression. *The frantic beat against my skin fuels the ache low in my belly.* "You can claim you were just observing, but your heart was racing as much as mine, piccola. Still is. And this kind of racing beat comes not from fear or repulse, but from excitement."

She tries to jerk her hand away, but I hold firm, not hurting her but making it clear she won't break my grip unless I allow it. "Let go," she says, her voice low but steady.

"In a moment." I stroke my thumb over her wrist, feeling the rush of blood beneath her skin. "First, I want you to admit something to yourself, if not to me. What you saw tonight affected you. Not as a journalist. As a woman."

Anger flashes in her eyes, but there's something else there too, a vulnerability she's desperate to hide. "You're the one who arranged that whole display. Brought in that woman to... to..."

"To what, Lea?" I press, enjoying her discomfort, the way she can't bring herself to name what she witnessed. "Say it."

"To parade her?" she finally spits out, cheeks flushing darker. "To use her like some kind of prop while you watched me watching your disgusting performance? Like I was supposed to be intimidated, or jealous, or whatever sick game you were playing by putting your hands all over her right in front of me?"

I laugh, the sound genuine despite myself. "Is that what you think it was about? Making you jealous?"

"What else would it be about?" she demands.

"Education." I release her wrist, but don't move away. "Everything I show you has a purpose, Lea. Every experience, every introduction, every revelation. I'm teaching you to see beyond the surface, beyond the comfortable fictions most people live within."

She shakes her head, disbelieving. "By demonstrating how you own everyone in the room, touching another woman like she's furniture while staring me down? That's not education, it's a power trip."

"It's power." I state it simply, as the fundamental truth it is. "Power expressed, power exchanged, power recognized. On that stage, between Miguel and Elise. Between Loretta and myself, her submission, my control. And yes, between you and me."

Her breath catches, just slightly, at this last part. "There is no 'between you and me,'" she insists, but the declaration lacks conviction.

"No?" I reach out again, this time taking her chin between my thumb and forefinger, tilting her face toward mine. Her skin is warm, soft beneath my touch. "Then why are you still here, Lea? Why do you keep coming back, knowing who and what I am?"

For a moment, I think she might pull away, break contact, retreat into professional detachment. Instead, she holds my gaze, something shifting in her expression. Not surrender, not yet, but a recognition of truth she can no longer deny to herself.

"Because it's the story," she says finally. "The biggest story of my career. Most people's careers."

"Your career has just begun," I reminded her. "Is that all it is?"

Before she can answer, the car slows, approaching the industrial wasteland where Warehouse Five stands. The site of tonight's meeting with Moretti's crew. Another kind of power play, with stakes far higher than the ones I've been exploring with Lea.

"We're here, sir," my driver announces through the intercom.

I release Lea's chin, but my gaze holds hers for one moment longer. "We'll continue this conversation later," I promise, my voice dropping. "When we're not interrupted."

CHAPTER NINE

Lea

THE BENTLEY SLOWS AS WE APPROACH A SPRAWLING warehouse complex on the edge of Chicago's industrial district. Through tinted windows, I watch rusted chain-link fences give way to crumbling concrete and metal buildings, monuments to a manufacturing era long past. A perfect setting for a meeting that exists between legal lines.

"This won't be social like the restaurant," Nico says beside me, his voice low and even. He hasn't spoken since we left downtown twenty minutes ago, both of us watching the city transform from gleaming skyscrapers to this neglected wasteland of abandoned factories.

I turn to study his profile. In the near darkness, his features appear carved from stone, all sharp angles and controlled stillness. Only his eyes move, scanning the perimeter as we pull up to a nondescript metal building with no signage.

"What should I expect?" I ask, my notebook already in

hand. Only a few days into this arrangement, and I've learned to always be prepared to document whatever unfolds around Nico Varela.

His dark gaze shifts to me, assessing. "A lesson in territorial negotiation."

"That sounds ominous."

"It's practical." He straightens his already immaculate cuffs, a gesture I now recognize as his equivalent of checking a weapon. "Several factions need reminding of boundaries."

The car stops. Through the windshield, I spot three other vehicles parked at irregular angles; a black Escalade, a silver Mercedes, and a blue sedan that in some ways looks more threatening than the luxury cars.

Nico's driver kills the engine but remains seated. Marco emerges from the passenger seat, surveying the area with practiced efficiency before opening Nico's door. I reach for the handle, but Nico's voice stops me.

"You can wait here," he says, not quite looking at me. "This particular meeting might become volatile."

It's the closest thing to concern I've heard from him. The words hang there, unexpected. Is it genuine solicitude for my safety? Or just strategic calculation, removing a potential complication? With Nico, the motives are always layered, likely both.

"I thought the arrangement was full access," I counter, matching his cool tone, pushing back against the flicker of what? Relief? Disappointment? "Volatile sounds like an important part of understanding your world. You can't keep dismissing me."

Amusement flickers across his face. "Your choice, Ms.

Song. But you stay behind me, and when I tell you to move, you move without question."

Before I can respond, he exits the vehicle, leaving me to scramble after him.

Marco falls into step behind Nico, his broad shoulders tense beneath his tailored jacket. I've witnessed enough by now to recognize the subtle bulge of a shoulder holster beneath his suit.

A giant metal door creaks open as we approach. Nico pauses, turning to face me with a warning in his eyes.

"Stay close. No questions during the meeting. Your phone stays in your pocket." His voice drops. "And if anyone approaches you directly, you defer to me. Understood?"

I nod, suppressing the instinctive rebellion his commands trigger. This isn't about journalistic integrity or independence. This is about survival in a world where the wrong word or look can have consequences far beyond professional embarrassment.

Inside, the warehouse is enormous and surprisingly well-maintained compared to its exterior. Bare bulbs hang from high ceilings, casting pools of harsh light over a concrete floor. The air smells of dust and something chemical that burns in my nostrils.

In the center of the space, a makeshift conference area has been arranged. Folding tables pushed together, covered with maps and papers, surrounded by mismatched chairs. Already seated or standing around this improvised meeting point are seven men of varying ages, all radiating the particular alertness of predators in proximity.

Their conversation stops abruptly as Nico enters. Seven

pairs of eyes track his movement, then slide to me with expressions ranging from curiosity to cold calculation.

"Gentlemen," Nico greets them, his voice carrying effortlessly across the concrete expanse. "Thank you for accommodating this meeting on short notice."

He moves toward the head of the table with the calm confidence of someone who knows his position is unquestioned. I follow a half-step behind, acutely aware of the stares fixed on me rather than my notebook.

"Who's the girl?" asks a heavyset man with salt-and-pepper stubble and eyes like gun barrels.

Nico doesn't break stride. "Ms. Song is documenting our negotiation for my records." The explanation is smooth, offering no invitation for further questions. "Let's begin."

I position myself behind Nico's right shoulder, close enough to observe but not so close as to appear as a part of his inner circle. From this vantage point, I can study the assembled men without making direct eye contact.

They represent a visual taxonomy of Chicago's criminal ecosystem: two middle-aged men in expensive but understated suits, representing established operations with legitimate fronts; a younger Latino man with a careful smile and watchful eyes; two Eastern European looking bodybuilder types, probably Russian; a wiry Black man who stands apart from the others; and finally, leaning against a support column rather than taking a seat, a man whose entire being screams danger.

This last one catches my attention most sharply. Thin but corded with muscle, he wears a leather jacket despite the warehouse's stuffy atmosphere. His hair is slicked back, and a scar bisects one eyebrow. While the others regard Nico with cautious respect, this man's expression holds something that makes my skin prickle, contempt barely masked by compliance. No one is noticing me as Nico gets ready to speak, and I snap a couple of pictures from my phone, hidden behind my jacket.

"Let's be clear about why we're here," Nico begins without preamble, placing his palms flat on the table's surface. "The arrangement we established six months ago is being tested. Borders are being crossed. Merchandise is moving through channels outside our agreement."

His words are vague, couched in business terminology, but I understand what's being discussed, drug distribution territories, relating to the fentanyl trade that's been ravaging Chicago's neighborhoods. The "arrangements" he references are the negotiated boundaries between competing criminal organizations.

"The North Side corridor remains neutral ground for transit only," Nico continues, showing an area on the map. "No direct distribution within these boundaries. The West Side divisions remain as established."

The heavyset man clears his throat. "We've had incidents along Pulaski. Three last week."

"Isolated," counters one of the Russians. "Not systematic."

"Three is a pattern," the heavyset man insists, his voice roughening.

I watch fingers tense on tabletops, shoulders square imperceptibly. The air in the warehouse seems to thicken with each exchange, oxygen replaced by the invisible currents of power and threat.

And through it all, Nico remains still, his presence the

gravitational center around which these volatile elements orbit. He doesn't raise his voice or make grand gestures. He simply *is* an immovable object against which these forces test themselves.

"The incidents were addressed," Nico says, ending the budding argument with four quiet words. "Compensation was arranged. The territory boundaries stand."

His index finger traces a line on the map, following a street, whose name I can't quite make out from my position. "What concerns me more is the recent activity here."

The wiry man by the column straightens, his posture shifting from affected boredom to alertness. The movement is subtle, but in this room of predators, it might as well be a shout.

"Something to add, Vincent?" Nico asks without looking up.

So this is Vincent. I recognize the name as one of Dante Moretti's top lieutenants. From the files, I remember him as the twin brother to Matteo Rizzo, Dante Moretti's right-hand man. The Rizzos are Dante's cousins.

"Funny you should mention that area," Vincent says, his voice carrying a nasal quality that somehow makes him more unsettling. "My people have noticed unusual traffic there, too. Care to explain why your boys are running your product through our established routes?"

The accusation hangs in the air like smoke. Several of the men shift uncomfortably, gazes darting between Vincent and Nico.

"Misinformation," Nico replies, unruffled. "My organization maintains neutrality in distribution. As always."

Vincent pushes off from the column, taking a step toward

the table. "Neutrality. Right. That's not what we call it when you broker access for some while blocking others?"

Behind me, I sense rather than see Marco tensing, his weight shifting forward on the balls of his feet. My heart quickens in response. The atmosphere has changed, a subtle recalibration from tense negotiation to something more volatile.

"Your concerns have been noted," Nico says, his tone unchanged but somehow carrying more weight. "If you have specific evidence of interference, I'm happy to review it. Otherwise, we'll move on to the South Shore adjustment."

Vincent's laugh is sharp, cutting. "Evidence? You want evidence? How about the Koreans all of a sudden getting premium access to the university district while our product gets held up at every checkpoint? I'm talking about the university district gateway, not the trade to students."

My breath catches. The Koreans. An oblique reference to the North Korea pharmaceutical connection that's been rumored to supply much of Chicago's high-grade fentanyl. Sienna mentioned it a couple of days ago. Not confirmed by any officials yet, though. But, the university district, the place my mother teaches? *No way that's a gateway.* Selling to students? Maybe. *Probably.*

Nico's expression doesn't change, but something in the surrounding air seems to crystalize, like atmospheric pressure dropping before a storm.

"The distribution arrangements through the university corridor were established last year," Nico says, his eyes never leaving Vincent. "All parties agreed to the terms. If Moretti has concerns about the arrangement, he knows how to reach me."

Vincent takes another step forward, and now I can see what makes him so unnerving; his eyes never quite focus on one spot, darting between points as if calculating angles of attack.

"There is more at stake now. And Moretti thinks maybe you've forgotten who helped establish your position," Vincent says, voice rising. "Maybe you need reminding that neutrality only works when the neutral party stays fucking neutral."

The Latino man clears his throat. "Perhaps we should—"

"Perhaps you should shut your mouth, Ramirez," Vincent snaps. "This isn't about your corner of the world."

Ramirez stiffens, one hand disappearing beneath the table. The Russians exchange a glance. The temperature in the room drops several degrees.

"Vincent," Nico says, his voice so controlled it functions like a blade, "you're addressing my guests in my territory. Weigh your next words carefully."

For the first time, Vincent looks directly at me, his eyes raking over my face with deliberate slowness. "Brought a secretary today, Varela? Or is she something more personal? Somebody you value?"

My stomach tightens, but I keep my expression neutral, meeting his stare without flinching. A single week in Nico's world has taught me that showing fear is like bleeding in shark-infested waters.

"Ms. Song's role is not your concern," Nico says. His tone hasn't changed, but something in the air has; a near-imperceptible shift that raises the hair on my arms.

Vincent smirks, taking another step toward the table. "Moretti thinks maybe your judgment is getting clouded. New faces, new distractions. He doesn't like it." His hand moves toward the inside of his jacket. "Maybe time for new leadership in these discussions."

Everything happens in a blur of coordinated movement. Marco lunges forward as Vincent's hand emerges with something metallic. Before I can process what's happening, Marco has Vincent's arm twisted at an unnatural angle, Vincent's gun clattering to the concrete floor.

Vincent howls, a sound more rage than pain, as Marco drives him face-first onto the table, scattering maps and papers. The other men have either frozen in place or taken strategic steps backward, hands hovering near concealed weapons but not drawing them.

Through it all, Nico hasn't moved. Hasn't even raised his voice. He observes the situation with all the emotional investment of someone watching a mildly interesting chess move.

"Hold him there, Marco," Nico says, his voice carrying in the sudden silence punctuated only by Vincent's labored breathing.

For the first time since entering the warehouse, Nico looks directly at me. Something passes between us, a silent communication that sends a chill through my body. Not a warning, but an invitation. A test.

Then he turns his attention back to Vincent.

"You know what the problem is with identical twins?" Nico asks, as if they're discussing a minor business inconvenience.

Vincent spits blood onto the scattered papers. "Fuck you."

"The problem with identical twins," Nico continues, ignoring the outburst, "is that they're difficult to tell apart."

121

He holds out his hand toward Marco without looking at him. "Your knife."

The room goes quiet. Even Vincent stops struggling against Marco's grip, his body tensing in sudden comprehension.

Marco reaches inside his jacket with his free hand and produces a sleek folding knife, placing it in Nico's palm with practiced efficiency. The soft *snick* of the blade opening seems loud in the silence.

"What the fuck are you talking about?" Vincent's voice has lost its earlier aggression, replaced by something thinned with growing fear.

Nico examines the blade with detached interest. "You think I don't know that you and your brother take turns representing Moretti? Trading places, gathering intelligence, testing for inconsistencies in my responses?" He steps closer, the knife catching the harsh warehouse light. "You're Vincent today. Maybe Matteo tomorrow. It's a clever tactic."

I watch, frozen, as understanding dawns on the faces around the table. Several of the men exchange uneasy glances.

"You're fucking crazy," Vincent snarls, but there's panic leaking through his bravado now.

"Which one are you right now?" Nico asks, not bothering to acknowledge the denial. "Vincent or Matteo? Even your employer sometimes wonders, doesn't he? Why don't I make it easier for him to tell you apart?"

He moves behind Vincent, out of my direct line of sight. I should look away. I know. But I don't.

"Marco," Nico says, "ensure his head remains still."

Marco's grip shifts, one massive hand moving to grasp Vincent's hair, pulling his head back and exposing the side of his face. Vincent thrashes in earnest now, his panic fully formed.

"Jesus Christ, Varela," the heavyset man interjects, "is this necessary?"

Nico doesn't respond to him. Instead, he leans down close to Vincent's ear, his right ear, and says just loud enough for everyone to hear: "Now I'll always know who I'm dealing with."

Nico's hand moves in one swift, deliberate motion, a sickening slice that cuts through the air, followed by Vincent's scream tearing through the warehouse. It's raw, animal, ripped from the very depths of him.

Blood blooms bright against his skin, spattering onto the maps below like abstract art. The coppery tang of it hits the air, sharp and metallic, mingling with the underlying scents of dust and chemicals. My vision tunnels, the sounds of the warehouse momentarily muffled by a roaring in my ears. My stomach clenches, but I don't look away. Can't look away. There's a strange, horrifying disconnection, as if I'm watching a film projected onto the concrete wall; brutal, graphic, yet somehow unreal.

When Nico steps back, he's holding something small and bloody between his thumb and forefinger, the upper half of Vincent's ear. He drops it onto the table in front of the still-screaming man, the wet slap of it against the paper loud in the sudden echo of the scream.

"A small price for deception," Nico says, his voice chillingly calm. He pulls a handkerchief from his pocket and wipes the knife clean before returning it to Marco. His eyes find mine across the table, gauging my reaction with scientific detachment.

My breath is trapped somewhere in my chest. Horror claws at my throat, bile rising. This wasn't just punishment; it was mutilation, a permanent marking delivered with the casual indifference of swatting a fly. Yet, beneath the revulsion, a colder, more analytical part of my brain, a part I barely recognize, registers the terrifying effectiveness of the act. The challenge neutralized instantly. The message sent unequivocally to everyone present. In the brutal logic of this world, it was efficient. The thought is sickening, alien, yet undeniably present. I meet Nico's gaze, my expression neutral despite the roaring in my ears and the war raging inside me, the journalist recoiling, the strategist acknowledging, the woman utterly horrified yet disturbingly captivated.

Something passes between us in that moment, an understanding that transcends the horror of what I've just witnessed. I've seen behind the veil, been admitted to an inner circle that few journalists ever access. And the price of admission is witnessing acts like this, understanding their necessity within this dark ecosystem.

"Now," Nico says, turning back to the stunned room as if nothing unusual has occurred, "when Vittorio arrives for our next meeting, the asymmetry will be informative." He adjusts his cuff, that signature gesture that now reads to me as a punctuation mark at the end of violence. "Marco, please ensure Mr. Rizzo finds his way back to his employer. Perhaps the hospital route."

Vincent is hunched over, one hand clasped to his bleeding ear, the other holding the handkerchief containing his ear tip, shock and hatred warring in his eyes. The ear might be saved if he hurries, but a scar will always remain. As Marco hauls him toward the exit, Nico addresses the remaining men, whose expressions range from grudging respect to poorly concealed horror.

"Gentlemen, shall we continue? I believe we were discussing the South Shore change."

Just like that, the meeting resumes. Another of Nico's men, one who had been positioned by the door so discreetly that I hadn't even registered his presence, moves to clear away the blood-stained maps, replacing them with fresh copies.

I stand still, processing what I've just witnessed. Not just the swift, systematic violence, but its aftermath; how quickly order reasserted itself, how completely Nico's authority absorbed the disruption without being diminished by it.

My heart is erratic, doing crazy somersaults, but not entirely from fear. There's another ingredient mixed in, like a humming awareness that feels uncomfortably close to exhilaration. The man I've been shadowing can inflict permanent damage without hesitation or remorse. He's shown me who he is, with no pretense or apology. And I'm still here, notebook in hand, oddly captivated. *What the fuck?*

When the meeting concludes, the men leave in a orchestrated sequence. Never all at once, never creating the appearance of a gathering when viewed from outside. Nico remains until the last has departed, then turns to me with an expression I can't quite read.

"Questions?" he asks, as if we've just left a corporate board meeting instead of a criminal negotiation that erupted into violence.

A dozen queries crowd my mind, fighting for precedence.

What I manage is: "The Koreans you mentioned, is that connected to the pharmaceutical suppliers Marco briefed you about at the club? The delayed shipment?"

Something flickers in his eyes: surprise, perhaps, that this is my first question rather than something about the violence we just witnessed. Or maybe approval of the connection I've made.

"Perceptive," he acknowledges. "Yes. The legitimate pharmaceutical channel and the distribution network Vincent referenced share certain logistics challenges."

"And the university district—"

"Not here," he interrupts. "The car."

I nod, tucking my notebook away. As we walk toward the exit, I'm struck by how different the warehouse feels now. It's emptier but also charged with residual tension, like the air after lightning strikes.

Marco is waiting by the Bentley, his posture relaxed but his eyes scanning our surroundings. Vincent is nowhere to be seen, though a dark stain on the concrete near where the blue sedan had parked suggests his departure wasn't entirely dignified.

The drive begins in silence. I expect Nico to sit opposite me as usual, maintaining the careful distance he's established in our previous car rides. Instead, he slides into the seat directly beside me, close enough for me to feel his body heat, smell the subtle notes of his cologne. The proximity is deliberate, I'm certain. Another test, another boundary being probed.

"You were taking mental notes," he says after several minutes, his voice low enough that it seems to vibrate in the space between us. "Beyond what you wrote down."

It's not a question, but I still answer. "Yes."

"And what did you observe, beyond the obvious territorial disputes?"

I turn to face him, acutely aware of how little space separates us in the confined interior of the car. "That Vincent wasn't just Moretti's messenger. He was there to provoke a specific reaction from you."

Nico's mouth curves slightly at one corner. Not quite a smile, but an acknowledgment. "Go on."

"The gun was theater," I continue, warming to my analysis. "He knew he wouldn't get a shot off in that room. He wanted to force your hand, make you look either weak if you didn't respond, or brutal if you did."

"And which was I?"

"Neither," I answer honestly. "You let Marco handle the immediate physical threat, but what came after..." I pause, the image of the severed ear piece flashing in my mind. "That was something else entirely. Methodical. Precise."

Something shifts in his expression. A subtle lightening around the eyes, a deepening of that almost-smile. He leans fractionally closer.

"You understand the dynamics of power," he says, his voice resonating against my skin. "That's rare."

The compliment, if that's what it is, sends an unwelcome flush of warmth through me. I'm hyper aware of our isolation in the backseat, the privacy partition raised between us and the driver.

"I've been watching powerful men manipulate situations my entire life," I reply, fighting to keep my voice steady. "My mother's academic world isn't so different from yours, just less honest about its brutality."

His laugh is unexpected, a brief, genuine sound that transforms his face for an instant before the careful control returns.

"Honesty is what separates my world from theirs," he says. "Strip away the pretense of civilization, and all relationships reduce to power; who has it, who wants it, what price they'll pay to get it."

His eyes holds mine, dark and intense in the shadowed interior of the car. "The question for you, Lea, isn't whether you understand power dynamics. It's what you intend to do with that understanding."

The heat of him seems to intensify, though he hasn't moved closer. Or perhaps it's something inside me responding to his proximity, to the undercurrent in his voice that suggests layers of meaning beyond the words themselves.

"I intend to write the truth," I say, the answer sounding hollow.

"The truth," he repeats, skepticism clear. "And what truth did you see today when Vincent pulled his gun? When half his ear came off in my hand? When the meeting continued as if nothing had happened?"

I swallow, searching for the professional detachment that seems increasingly difficult to maintain in Nico's presence.

"I saw that you're capable of clinical violence when it serves a purpose," I begin. "And I saw that your power comes from precision, not just force. They fear you not because you're unpredictable, but because you're deliberate in everything you do."

Something darkens in his eyes. "And did that frighten you, Lea? Seeing what I'm capable of?"

The question hangs between us, loaded with implications. The honest answer terrifies me more than anything I witnessed in the warehouse.

"No," I admit, the word barely audible even in the quiet car. "It didn't frighten me."

His eyes never leave mine as he registers my confession. Time seems to stretch and compress simultaneously in the charged silence that follows.

"That," he finally says, "is what should frighten you."

The car moves through the night without a word between us, streetlights washing over Nico's composed features, illuminating the sharp lines but giving nothing away. The earlier intensity has drained out of me, leaving an exhaustion settled deep in my bones.

As the car glides to a stop in the secure underground garage of a building I don't recognize, another of his anonymous holdings, no doubt, the sharp buzz of my phone slices through the silence. Instinctively, I glance at the screen. The name flashes bright and demanding against the dark interior: Harrison Wells. The preview text beneath it leaves no room for interpretation: *Song. My office. Tomorrow morning. 9 AM sharp. Updates.*

My gut twists. The harsh command crashes in from a world that feels impossibly distant, a blunt recall of duties so ordinary they feel ridiculous next to the bloodshed and power games defining my present.

Beside me, Nico shifts. He hadn't needed to lean over; his gaze sharp enough to have caught the name and the tone even from his seat. I feel his attention lock onto the screen, onto my reaction.

"Your editor is impatient," he observes, his voice neutral, devoid of the intimacy or threat from moments before. The strategist is back, analyzing the new variable. "Understandable. He smells a big story."

I look up, meeting his eyes. "I have to go. Need sleep. I have to check in at The Journal tomorrow morning."

A flicker of amusement crosses his face before vanishing. "Of course you do. We wouldn't want you risking your prestigious career yet." He pauses, letting the implication hang. "Go. Check in tomorrow morning. Give your editor enough verifiable details about our more public meetings to keep him satisfied. Bellamy's, perhaps. Mention the Riverside project." He leans fractionally closer, voice dropping. "Nothing more, Lea. Nothing about tonight. Nothing that compromises our arrangement. Understood?"

The subtle pressure is unmistakable. He's not just allowing me to go; he's dictating the terms of my report, framing my professional duty as another component of his control. Caught between Harrison's demands and Nico's veiled threats, the walls feel like they're closing in tighter than ever.

"Understood," I say, the word foul.

He gives a curt nod, satisfied. The driver opens the door, and the sterile air of the parking garage rushes in. Nico makes no move to follow me out, his eyes already distant, calculating his next move in a game where I am still just a chess piece.

As I step out of the car, the weight of the secrets I now carry feels heavier than ever. Tomorrow, I'll walk into the Journal, back into the life I thought I knew, and deliver a truncated version of the truth dictated by the man I'm supposed to be investigating. Nico was right. *That is what should frighten me.*

CHAPTER TEN

Lea

I surface from sleep like a drowning victim breaking the surface, gasping, the phantom stench of blood and ozone clinging to my senses. My own bed. My own cramped dusty apartment. It feels alien after the brutal concrete reality of last night's warehouse and the cold luxury of Nico's car.

That is what should frighten you. His last words are still fucking resonating in my head. He's right. The violence hasn't shattered me. The casual way he mutilated Vincent Gallos, the clinical detachment; it hasn't sent me screaming into the night. It registers as data, as a demonstration of power I've observed with a disturbing lack of revulsion. That is terrifying. *What's happening to the woman who used to cry over sad movies?*

Sleep has been a joke for three days now. Every time I lay down to close my eyes, I keep seeing the glint of Nico's knife, the spray of blood, the chilling calm with which he resumed the meeting. And then I see his eyes in the car afterward, stripping away my journalistic pretense, seeing the disturbing lack of fear I felt.

My body is one big knot of residual stress, muscles locked from hours spent coiled, waiting for the other shoe to drop, for the violence to turn on me. I push my legs over the side of the mattress. The cheap flooring shocks my bare feet, so unlike the deep pile carpets I imagine line Nico's place. Coffee first. Strong enough to strip paint. Then Harrison's goddamn report. He'd left three increasingly irate voicemails yesterday demanding an update, demanding I show my face at the office.

Nico's instructions, delivered with that chilling blend of permission and threat in the car three nights ago, are seared into my brain: *"Bellamy's. Riverside project. Nothing more, Lea. Nothing about tonight. Understood?"*

Understood. Oh, I understand perfectly. He's dictating my narrative, controlling the flow of information back to my editor, ensuring his sanitized version of events is the only one Harrison receives. And I, caught between the devil and the deep blue sea of unemployment (or worse, Nico's displeasure), have no fucking choice but to comply.

Sitting at my cluttered kitchen table, nursing coffee that tastes like bitter grounds, I stare at my laptop screen. *How do you write about power dynamics when you've just seen a man's ear sliced off as a negotiating tactic? How do you describe "business meetings" that happen surrounded by armed guards in abandoned warehouses?*

You lie. You obfuscate. You polish the turd until it almost gleams.

I type, delete, type again. Sentences feel hollow, sanitized beyond recognition. I write: "Observed Varela mediating complex stakeholder interests regarding the Riverside development." *True, technically. He mediated the fuck out of Vincent Gallos.* I continue: "Noted presence of key financial figures, including Richard Calloway, showing Varela's significant influence in legitimate markets." Also true. Conveniently omitting the other figures present—the ones whose legitimacy was questionable.

It's pathetic. A betrayal of every journalistic principle I hold dear. But the image of Nico's face, expressionless as he wiped the blade clean, remains. *Fear, I am discovering, is a meticulous proofreader.*

BY 7:45, I have a page and a half of the most carefully constructed bullshit I've ever written. I attach it to an email, fingers trembling as I type a brief, professional cover note to Harrison. Hitting send feels like pulling a trigger aimed squarely at my integrity.

Time for a nap.

It feels like I've just closed my eyes when a sharp knock rattles my apartment door.

Not the tentative tap of a delivery person. This is insistent. My chest tightens. *Nico? Moretti?* I look at my alarm clock. 10:30. I slept for almost three hours. I creep toward the door, peering through the peephole.

Sienna. Her face is tight with worry.

Relief washes over me, so potent it leaves my legs trembling. I unlock the door.

"Jesus, Lea, finally!" Sienna pushes past me into the apartment, her gaze sweeping the room before landing on me. "You look like hell. Harrison's been blowing up my phone asking where you are. Said you sent some bullshit report this morning. What's going on? You haven't been in the office for three days, and now I find you looking like this?"

Then her eyes land on the walls. No longer a wall, but all the walls. The conspiracy cave. Her jaw drops.

"Holy mother of God," she breathes, stepping further into the room, eyes wide as she takes in the chaotic web of strings, photos, notes, and clippings dominating the space. Her gaze snags on the cluster of Nico photos. "Okay, wow. Last time I saw this it was bad, but this... this is next level. Look at the sheer number of pictures of him! It's like... like you're trying to crawl inside his head."

"It's organized," I defend, suddenly seeing it through her eyes, the obsessive grid, the slightly too-many pictures of Nico, the sheer manic energy radiating from the plasterboard altar I've built to the man I'm supposed to be destroying.

"Organized insanity!" Sienna turns to face me, grabbing my shoulders. "Lea, talk to me. What happened? What has Varela been showing you? Harrison's worried, I'm worried. This isn't just a story anymore, is it?"

Her genuine concern, the anchor she represents to the normal world I'm rapidly losing sight of, makes the constructed barriers around my secret crumble.

"It's... complicated," I start, then stop. *How do I explain the warehouse? The ear? The way Nico looked at me afterward? The choice he presented?* "He's showing me things, Sienna. How deals get made. How power works in this city. It's...intense."

"Intense?" Sienna's grip tightens. "Lea, I know guys who used to cover the Outfit back in the day. They talk about Varela like he's the devil himself, only smarter and quieter. People who cross him disappear. You saw what happened to your dad! Nico is not just intense, he's fucking insanely intense."

"That's why I have to do this!" The words burst out, raw with grief and a conviction I cling to like a life raft. "For my father. I need to know what happened to him, Sienna. Nico might be the only one who has the answers. This access... it's the only way. Period."

Sienna studies my face, her expression softening with empathy but hardening with resolve. "Okay, I get the dad angle. I do. But this," she gestures around the room, at the walls, at me, "this feels like more than that. This feels like a fucking obsession. He's getting to you, isn't he?" She leans closer. "Lea, be honest with me. Are you sleeping with him?"

"What? No! God, no!" The denial is vehement, immediate. The thought is both horrifying and shamefully, traitorously, not entirely repulsive. Heat floods my cheeks.

Sienna sees the flush, her eyes narrowing further. "Okay. But he wants to. And maybe part of you wants him to, too?" She holds up a hand as I protest. "I'm not judging. The guy radiates dark, dangerous sex appeal. But Lea, that's how guys like him operate. They pull you in, make you feel special, chosen, privy to their secrets... and then, boom! They own you. This 'access' he's giving you? It comes with strings you can't even see yet. You need to walk away. Now. Before it's too late."

Her words resonate with my internal warnings. *She's right. Walk away. Tell Harrison you can't do it.*

"I can't," I murmur, the admission feeling like a betrayal of Sienna, of my father, of myself. "Not yet. I'm close to something." *Or maybe I just can't let go of him.*

Sienna searches my face for a long moment, then sighs, a sound heavy with resignation. "Okay. Okay, I see I can't talk you out of this right now." She releases my shoulders. "But you need to go see Harrison. Face the music about that report. And Lea, promise me you'll keep your head on straight. Don't forget who he is, what he's capable of." She glances at the wall again. "And maybe take down a few of the glamor shots? It's creeping me out."

Despite the tension, a small smile touches my lips. "Okay. Deal."

After Sienna leaves, the apartment feels too quiet, her warnings lingering in the silence. I force myself to get ready, choosing armor once more. A sharp black pantsuit, heels high enough to signal confidence, hair pulled back. *A warrior preparing for battle on two fronts: Harrison's office and whatever Nico has planned next.*

THE WALK to the Journal feels different. The morning hustle of downtown Chicago seems muted, distant. Every passing face feels like a potential threat, every dark sedan could be a possible tail. *Paranoia? Maybe. Or maybe just a necessary adaptation to the world Nico Varela has dragged me into.*

The newsroom crashes over my senses like usual since I started, a wall of sound, fluorescent glare, desperate motion.

The clatter of keyboards seems louder. But moving toward my desk, the chatter doesn't just dip; it flat lines. Eyes follow me, sharp and zeroed in, nothing like the idle speculation my first day just three weeks ago. My skin prickles under the weight of their scrutiny.

They fucking know. They might not know details, but they know I'm involved with Varela. The rumors must be flying; the exclusive access, being seen with him at Bellamy's, maybe even whispers from Purgatorio staff. I'm no longer the rookie. I'm marked. Varela's girl. The label clings like tar.

My small desk in the corner feels less like a refuge and more like an isolation cell.

The shrill ring of my desk phone makes me jump. Harrison's extension. Predictable as sunrise.

"My office. Now." Click.

Here we go. Taking a deep breath, I stand and begin the walk of shame, or maybe the walk of the damned, toward the glass box at the end of the room.

Harrison is pacing when I enter, radiating impatience. He doesn't offer a seat. He just stops, turns, and jabs a finger at the printout of my email lying on top of the usual chaos on his desk.

"Song." His voice is low. "Explain this garbage."

I stand my ground, hands clasped behind my back to hide their tremor. "It's my initial report, Harrison. As discussed. Covering the Bellamy's meeting, the Riverside project financing—"

"Financing?" He snatches the papers, rattling them in my face. "You think I sent you to shadow Nico fucking Varela to get insights on municipal bonds? 'Key stakeholders discussed financing windows'? 'Calloway expressed confidence'? Are you writing for the Journal or Varela's goddamn newsletter?"

"Harrison, I have to build trust—"

"Trust?" He laughs, a harsh, barking sound. "You build trust by bringing me something real! Something with teeth! This reads like you spent an hour at a Chamber of Commerce luncheon, not embedded with the most dangerous man in Chicago!" He throws the papers down, scattering them across the desk. "Where's the grit, Song? Where are the backroom deals? The threats? The names?"

My throat feels dry. Nico's warning, cold and absolute, rings in my ears. *Nothing about tonight.*

"The access I have is unprecedented, but it's fragile," I say, reciting the justification I've rehearsed. "Varela operates on loyalty and absolute discretion. If I report unverified details, if I burn sources this early—"

"Sources?" Harrison leans forward, eyes narrowed. "Are you protecting him?"

The accusation lands like a punch to the gut. *He sees it. He suspects.*

"I'm protecting the story," I counter, forcing conviction into my voice. "Long-term access requires short-term patience. The Bellamy's meeting is significant. Seeing Calloway defer to him, the way the city officials hung on his every word, that shows his reach into legitimate power structures. That's the foundation."

Harrison's eyes bore into mine, his expression giving no quarter. He runs a hand through his messy hair, chewing on the inside of his cheek. The silence stretches, thick with unspoken suspicion.

"Foundation," he spits, clearly unconvinced. He slumps

back into his chair, looking older, wearier. "Alright, Song. Fine. Play it your way. For now." He pins me with a look that promises consequences. "But the leash is short. One more week. Then I want something substantive. Something that makes the front page shake. You understand?"

"Yes, Sir."

"And routinely check-ins," he adds, an edge in his voice. "Email. Phone. Carrier pigeon, I don't fucking care. Every single day. I want to know you're still digging, not just polishing Varela's shoes." He pauses, his eyes softening almost imperceptibly. "And watch your back, kid. No story is worth dying for."

I nod and turn, escaping his office before my composure can crack. Back at my desk, surrounded by the oblivious chaos of the newsroom, I feel alone, trapped between the journalistic ethics I am betraying and the dangerous world I can't seem to escape. The foundation isn't for the story. It is for the tightrope I'm now walking, with hungry predators circling below on both sides. Fuck Harrison's daily check in's. How would I even do that being 24/7 in Nico's world?

LUNCH WITH SIENNA at Briar Café should be my anchor to normalcy after my confrontation with Harrison, but the normalcy feels paper thin. Even the cheerful chatter and clinking silverware can't drown out the background hum of vigilance that has become my new baseline.

"You look like shit," Sienna says the moment I sit down, concern etched on her face.

"You're repeating yourself," I reply, attempting a weak smile. "And Harrison already chewed me out."

"As he should have!" She leans forward. "Lea, after our last talk, I looked into some old cold cases. Your dad's 'accident'... there were whispers back then, things that never made the official reports. Loose ends. Unanswered questions pointing toward..." She hesitates. "toward Varela's circle."

A paralyzing chill grips me. "What kind of whispers?"

"Enough to make me seriously worried about what you're doing." Her gaze is intense. "This isn't just about your dad anymore, is it? You're fucking drawn to him."

Before I can deny it, before I can process the implications of what she's found, movement outside the window catches my eye. Leather jacket. A stark white bandage wrapped around his ear. That bandage. Vincent, Moretti's top lieutenant. Watching us.

His lips curl into that chilling half-smile as our eyes meet through the glass. He gives a subtle nod, not reaching for a phone, but acknowledging he sees me.

"Lea?" Sienna's voice is sharp with alarm, seeing my reaction. "What is it?"

My blood turns to ice. "He knows me, Sienna." The words are barely a breath. "The man from the warehouse. The one Nico..." I trail off, unable to finish the sentence, realizing I never told her any details.

Sienna follows my gaze, her face paling as she sees Vincent now joined by a second man standing just behind him, identical in every way, both now staring into the café. Twins. Cold, hard eyes fixed on us. "Oh my god. Lea, we need to get out of here. Back exit. Now. Don't argue."

The realization hits me again, harder this time: I'm not

just writing about this world anymore. I'm trapped inside its crosshairs.

We move without another thought, abandoning our half-eaten lunch, weaving through tables toward the rear of the café.

Outside, the fall air carries a bite. We turn into the narrow alley beside the building, the shortcut to the parking garage. The smell of damp brick and stale garbage hits me.

"Well, well. Leaving so soon?"

The voice stops us cold. We spin around. Vincent blocks the alley entrance, his twin brother, Matteo, standing shoulder-to-shoulder with him. Two against two. Vincent touches the bandage on his ear almost possessively, his eyes burning into me with raw hatred.

"I told you not to get in too deep," Sienna mutters beside me, her hand reaching for the heavy camera bag slung over her shoulder.

"What do you want, Vincent?" I ask, trying to project a calm I don't feel, using his name deliberately.

"You," he spits, taking a step closer, Matteo mirroring his advance. Vincent gestures toward his bandaged ear. "Because of your precious boyfriend, The Diplomat, I almost lost my fucking ear. Thought you could just walk away unharmed after watching that?" His voice trembles with rage. "Thought you could hide behind Varela forever?"

His twin brother, Matteo remains silent, but his eyes are just as cold, just as dangerous, scanning Sienna before returning his full attention to me, his posture coiled like a snake ready to strike.

Vincent sneers, "Messing with Varela's affairs is bad

enough. Moretti doesn't appreciate it." He glances at Sienna. "And he doesn't like loose ends or witnesses."

His hand darts out faster than I can react, grabbing my wrist. Pain explodes up my arm, sharp and sickening. I cry out, stumbling back against the alley wall.

"Get your hands off her!" Sienna shouts, swinging her heavy camera bag with surprising force. It connects solidly with the side of Vincent's head. He staggers back with a grunt of pain and surprise, releasing my wrist.

Vincent recovers, fury blazing in his eyes. Matteo tenses, stepping forward, knuckles white. This is escalating dangerously fast.

"Run, Lea!" Sienna shoves me toward the parking garage entrance further down the alley. "Go! Get help!"

She turns to face the twins, camera bag held like a shield. She's trying to buy me time, protect me. Guilt and fear war within me. I can't just leave her here with them.

But before I can decide, before Vincent or Matteo can make another move, a sleek black SUV screeches around the corner of the alley, its tires protesting as it slides to a halt, blocking their path. The passenger door flies open.

Marco. His face is grim granite, eyes assessing the scene, Vincent's fury, Matteo's readiness, Sienna's defensive stance, my bruised wrist, with lethal efficiency.

Vincent and Matteo freeze. Recognition flashes in their eyes. They know who Marco is and who he represents.

"Problem?" Marco asks, his voice calm, low, carrying easily down the alley as he walks closer.

Vincent glares, spitting on the grimy pavement near his feet, his hatred for me obvious. He says nothing, but the message is clear.

"Leave," Marco commands, his tone flat, absolute. "Now."

Vincent hesitates, vibrating with contained violence, wanting to finish what he started. Matteo shifts his weight, perhaps conveying caution. They look at Marco radiating deadly competence. After a tense, silent standoff, Vincent gives a sharp, angry jerk of his head. The twins turn and melt back toward the street, disappearing into the lunchtime crowds.

Marco turns his attention to us. His gaze lingers on my throbbing wrist, then shifts to Sienna's pale but defiant face.

"Ms. Song." He nods, his expression unreadable. "The car is waiting."

Sienna looks from Marco to me, her expression torn between relief and deep worry. "Lea?"

"Go home, Sienna," I say, my voice shaking now that the adrenaline is receding. "Please. Go. I'll be okay."

"Will you?" she asks, clearly unconvinced but seeing she has no choice.

"Get in the car, Ms. Song," Marco repeats, his tone leaving no room for argument.

I give Sienna a quick, desperate hug. "I'll call you," I promise, the words feeling like another unavoidable lie in this new reality.

She watches me go, her face etched with worry, as I climb into the waiting SUV. The doors lock with a heavy, definitive thunk. Marco gets behind the wheel, his movements economical and precise.

"Purgatorio?" I ask, my voice a whisper.

He shakes his head, meeting my eyes in the rearview mirror, his expression unreadable. "Penthouse."

My breath catches. *Nico's penthouse. I've only heard rumors about it, a fortress in the sky, impenetrable, accessible only to his innermost circle.*

The drive passes in silence. I cradle my wrist, watching the city blur past. The earlier rehearsal of what I'd say to Nico feels pointless now. Events are moving too fast, pulling me deeper into a current I can't control.

We arrive at a luxury high-rise near the lakefront. Marco leads me through a private underground entrance, past discreet security, and into a dedicated elevator that ascends without stopping. The doors open into a stunning, minimalist space; all glass, steel, and breathtaking views of Lake Michigan stretching to the horizon.

Nico stands by the floor-to-ceiling windows, looking out at the city spread below him like a map. He turns as I enter, his expression opaque.

"Report," he says, his voice quiet but commanding.

I recount the incident, keeping my voice steady despite the tremor beneath the surface. I tell him everything: spotting Vincent outside the cafe, recognizing the bandage from where Nico's knife had marked him, his identical twin brother Matteo joining him, their deliberate confrontation in the alley, Vincent's specific, personal threats driven by revenge for his ear, Sienna's brave intervention with the camera bag, and finally, Marco's timely arrival forcing Moretti's lieutenants to flee. Nico listens without interruption, his eyes locked on my face, his stillness radiating a focused intensity.

When I finish, the silence stretches for a beat before he moves toward me. "Show me your wrist."

I extend my arm with hesitation. He takes it gently, his

thumb brushing over the bruised skin where Vincent grabbed me. His touch is cool, controlled, yet it sends an unwanted vibration through me. A muscle tightens momentarily in his jaw as he studies the marks left by his rival's man.

"Vincent," he says, the single name flat, devoid of inflection, yet somehow more chilling than any outburst. His eyes lifts to mine, dark and unreadable. "So, Dante's top dog thinks he can bite the hand that warned him, bringing his twin along for backup." He releases my wrist but doesn't step back, closing the distance between us. The air crackles with unspoken tension. "Reckless. They crossed a line targeting you. You understand now, don't you?" he says, his voice a low murmur that contrasts with the hardness in his eyes. "There is no observing from the sidelines. You're part of the game whether or not you choose to be. Your association with me makes you a target. And, a pawn."

"So what happens now?" I ask, hating the vulnerability in my voice but needing to know.

"Now," he says, his gaze dropping to my lips before returning to my eyes, "you make a choice." He steps closer still, close enough that I can sense the heat from his body, smell the expensive scent of sandalwood and bergamot that clings to him. "You walk away, disappear back into your safe little world, and hope Moretti and his hounds forget you exist. Or..."

He pauses, letting the silence stretch, letting the weight of the unspoken danger, the actual threat illustrated by Vincent and Matteo's brazen attack, settle between us.

"Or you accept my protection," he continues, his voice dropping to a low, intimate vibration that resonates deep inside me. "Absolute protection. But it comes with condi-

145

tions. My conditions. No more half-measures, Lea. No more pretending you're just a journalist observing my life."

He reaches out, his fingers tracing the line of my jaw, sending electric sparks across my skin despite the fear coiling in my stomach. "If you stay, you're mine. In every way that matters. You answer to me. You obey me. And you trust I will handle threats like the Moretti twins in my way."

His thumb brushes across my lower lip. My breath hitches. This is insane. He's offering safety from men like Vincent and Matteo, but demanding complete possession in return. Every rational thought screams at me to pull away, to run back to Sienna, to the life I understood.

But the memory of the alley, the fear ignited by the targeted violence from Moretti's trusted lieutenants, the certainty that this won't be the last time it holds me frozen.

My phone vibrates in my pocket, a phantom limb reaching from another life. I know without looking its Harrison, probably asking why I haven't checked in, demanding an update for The Journal. I ignore the summons. This is beyond The Journal now, beyond any story I thought I was chasing.

"What are the conditions?" I ask, voice barely a thread of sound, the words feeling like the first step over a cliff edge, like surrender.

Nico's eyes darken, a predatory light entering their depths. His lips curve into that knowing smile that promises danger and intrigue, things I shouldn't want but do.

"Total access to me," he murmurs, leaning closer still, his breath warm against my ear, sending shivers through me. "Requires total submission."

My pulse hammers against my ribs, a frantic bird trapped

against his proximity. *Submission.* The word hangs there, terrifying and thrilling all at once. This isn't about the story anymore. It isn't even just about protection from men like Vincent. This is about him. About the undeniable, consuming pull he exerts. About the boundaries I know, with chilling certainty, I'm about to let him shatter completely.

God help me.

CHAPTER ELEVEN

Nico

POWER ISN'T ABOUT WHAT YOU CAN DO; IT'S ABOUT WHAT others believe you can do.

My uncle Alessandro's words resonate in my mind as I relax in my chair, watching Lea Song shift uncomfortably across from me. The air conditioning hums, a low, constant thrum beneath the silence. She's trying to mask her anxiety with defiance, chin tilted up, shoulders squared, but I can read the truth in every micro expression. The slight tremor in her hands as she tucks a strand behind her ear. The rapid pulse visible at the hollow of her throat. The way her eyes dart toward the door, calculating distance and escape.

It's been forty-eight minutes since Marco brought her to me, her wrist bruised from Moretti's warning. Forty-eight minutes of watching her process the reality of her situation. She's no longer merely an observer, but irrevocably marked as mine. An extension of my operation.

"So these are your terms," she says, breaking the tense

silence that's fallen between us. Her voice carries a forced steadiness that I find strangely admirable. "Complete schedule transparency. On-call status for whatever you decide."

I don't immediately respond. Instead, I rise and circle my desk with measured slowness, savoring how her body tenses with each step I take closer. Fear and anticipation are so often indistinguishable in their physical manifestations. Both make the blood rush, the pupils dilate, the breath quicken.

"Not terms," I correct, stopping beside her. "Necessities. Moretti's men were delivering a message today, Lea. Next time, they'll deliver consequences."

My gaze drift to her injured wrist, which she's cradling in her lap. The bruises are darkening already, purple-blue marks in the distinct pattern of fingerprints. Anger flares in my chest at the sight. Those marks should never have been made by another man's hand.

"You think I can't handle myself? I'm a journalist—danger comes with the territory." Her attempt at bravado would be more convincing if her voice didn't catch on the last word.

"You're not in journalist territory anymore," I say, my tone soft. Gentle, even. It's an intentional contrast to the harshness of my words. "You crossed that border the moment you agreed to shadow me. Today was just your first taste of the consequences."

I watch the reality of this sink in, see the slight widening of her eyes as she grasps the gravity of her position. She's intelligent enough to understand the implications, that she's become a pawn in a game far larger than her investigative piece. What she doesn't comprehend is that she's always been a piece on this board. I've simply moved her from one square to another.

"I could walk away," she says, though we both know it's an empty threat. "Go to the police, tell them everything I've seen."

I smile at that, just enough to let her see my amusement without revealing genuine mirth. "Could you? The police who frequent my club after hours? The ones whose pensions are secretly managed by investment firms I control? Or perhaps you mean the commissioner, who called me when his daughter got caught with enough cocaine to qualify for intent to distribute."

I lean down, placing my hands on the armrests of her chair, caging her in without touching her. Her scent fills my nostrils, something floral underlying the sharp tang of fear. Her pupils dilate further as I invade her space, and I note with satisfaction how she doesn't shrink back, despite her obvious discomfort.

"You're in too deep already, piccola. The only way out is through."

She swallows, her throat working visibly. I can see the war being waged behind those expressive eyes, her journalistic integrity battling with self-preservation, curiosity wrestling with caution. And beneath it all, something else. Something she's trying to hide, even from herself.

Desire.

Not just physical, though that element is undeniably present in the flush creeping up her neck, the slight parting of her lips. No, it's a more complex hunger for knowledge, for access to a world few ever glimpse from the inside. For the power that comes with proximity to men like me.

I straighten, giving her space to breathe again. Return to my desk and sit on its edge, studying her with clinical detachment. Let her feel the weight of my assessment.

"You don't have to decide now," I say, though I already know what her choice will be. "My driver will be at your apartment tomorrow morning at eight. If you're not waiting, I'll take that as your answer."

She's silent for a long moment, her internal struggle is showing across her features with a transparency I find almost intriguing. So young, so unpracticed at concealment. She hasn't yet learned that in my world, revealing one's thoughts is equivalent to baring one's throat to a predator.

"And if I agree?" she asks. "What guarantees do I have that you'll hold up your end? That I'll get my story?"

"You have my word," I reply simply. "Which, in my business, is the only currency that matters."

She gives a short, disbelieving laugh. "The word of a criminal?"

"The word of a businessman," I correct. "One who understands that reputation is everything. Break your word once, and no one will ever trust you again. I've never broken mine."

It's true, though not for the noble reasons she might infer. My adherence to verbal contracts isn't born of moral fortitude, but practical necessity. In a world without legal recourse, where disputes are settled with blood rather than lawsuits, your word must be unimpeachable.

She weighs this, trying to separate truth from manipulation. I allow her consideration, though I've considered the variables. Her assignment. Her ambition. The threat Moretti now poses. The data points all converge on a single inevitable conclusion: she will agree to my terms.

"Fine," she says at last, the word exhaled on a shaky breath that betrays more than she intends. "I'll do it. Daily check-ins. Open schedule. On-call status."

Victory settles in my gut, warm and clean as fine whiskey. Not that I doubted the outcome, but there's always a particular pleasure in watching the moment of capitulation, especially from someone as spirited as Lea Song.

I move toward her again, this time extending my hand to help her rise. A small test. Will she accept this first physical contact, this minor submission to my assistance?

After a brief hesitation, she places her uninjured hand in mine. Her skin is soft, her fingers slender but strong, a writer's hand. I pull her to her feet with controlled gentleness, bringing her close. So close that I can feel the heat from her body.

"There's something," I murmur, letting my gaze drop to her mouth. Her lips part in response, an unconscious reaction that confirms what I've suspected. She's not immune to me, despite her best efforts.

"What?" she asks, voice barely above a whisper.

I lift my free hand and brush my thumb across her bottom lip, a gesture both intimate and assertive. "Lipstick smudge," I explain, though there isn't one. The real purpose is to establish physical dominance, to cross a boundary that sets a precedent for future encroachments.

Her sharp inhale is audible in the quiet office, a small, involuntary sound that sends a beat of satisfaction through me. My touch linger longer than necessary, gauging her response. She doesn't pull away, though I can feel the tension thrumming through her like a plucked string.

"Appearances matter, piccola," I murmur, releasing her hand and stepping back just enough to let her register how easily I've invaded her space, and how intentionally I've now withdrawn from it.

She blinks rapidly, as if emerging from a trance. A flush has spread across her cheeks, and she clears her throat before speaking. "Is that all for now?"

I nod, resuming my seat behind the desk. "Marco will take you home. Rest. Ice that wrist. Tomorrow we continue."

She gathers her bag with movements that betray lingering disorientation, thrown by the sudden shift from tension to dismissal. It's another planned move, keeping her off-balance, unable to anticipate my next action or request.

As she heads for the door, I call after her. "Lea."

She turns, one hand on the doorknob.

"Wear something formal tomorrow evening. We have a charity gala to attend."

Her brow furrows. "I don't have—"

"Something suitable will be delivered in the morning," I interrupt. "Along with a few other necessities."

She opens her mouth as if to protest, then seems to think better of it. With a stiff nod, she exits, the door clicking shut behind her with quiet finality.

I never doubted she would accept my terms. Her type is predictable, driven by ambition, fueled by curiosity, hampered by ethical constraints they believe are immutable until the moment they bend them. What interests me now is plotting the precise sequence of events that will transform her from reluctant ally to willing accomplice.

The seduction, because that's what this is, regardless of whether it culminates in physical consummation, must be methodical. Artfully planned. A series of incremental breaches, each one pushing her further from her moral center until she no longer recognizes the boundaries she's crossed.

My phone vibrates on the desk. Marco's name flashes on the screen.

"Song's security measures are up and running," he reports when I answer. "I've stationed Ricci in the building across from hers. Rivera is doing perimeter checks every thirty minutes."

"The additional surveillance?" I ask, moving to the window that overlooks the Chicago skyline, now bathed in the golden light of the approaching sunset.

"Installed as instructed. Full coverage, all rooms. Audio and visual feeds are live."

"Good." I end the call without further comment and return to my desk, opening my laptop to access the new security feed from Lea's apartment.

The screen flickers to life, revealing multiple grainy views of her modest one-bedroom. The living room, cluttered with books and papers. A small kitchen with its chipped countertops. The bedroom with its unmade bed and overflowing laundry basket. Finally, the bathroom, where the shower curtain hangs askew.

It takes only moments to locate Lea herself, pacing the length of her living room, phone pressed to her ear. I activate the audio feed, adjusting the volume to hear her side of what appears to be an intense conversation.

"—not that simple, Sienna. I can't just walk away now."

A pause as she listens to the response from her friend, the

same woman who intervened during Moretti's warning earlier today. Brave, but ultimately inconsequential.

"I know what I'm doing," Lea continues, though her voice lacks conviction. "This is for my father, you know that."

Another pause. I sense her frustration.

"Of course I'm being careful! But you didn't see what I saw at that warehouse meeting. The connections he has, the power he wields, it goes so much deeper than anyone realizes."

She stops pacing, her expression hardening with determination that's visible even through the somewhat grainy feed.

"I'm not backing out. Not now. I'll check in daily, I promise. But I need to see this through."

The call ends, and she tosses her phone onto the couch with a sigh that seems to deflate her entire body. For several moments, she just stands there, arms wrapped around herself as if for comfort or protection. Then, with sudden violence, she slams her palm against the wall.

"Fuck!" The exclamation is sharp, frustrated. "What am I doing?"

I lean back, watching as she resumes pacing, now muttering to herself, tugging at her hair in agitation. The unguarded display is fascinating, and so different from the composed facade she presents in my presence. This is Lea Song, stripped of performative confidence, wrestling with the consequences of her choices.

I can see her reporter's mind at work, calculating angles, weighing risks against potential rewards, searching for a path that allows her to maintain some illusion of control. It's futile, of course. Control was relinquished the moment she accepted my invitation to Purgatorio that first night.

What captivates me, however, is not her strategic deliberation but the flash of vulnerability that breaks through, like the momentary widening of the eyes, a soft sound of distress quickly suppressed, the nervous habit of biting her lower lip when troubled.

These glimpses of her interior state ignite something in me that surveillance photos and background reports never could. There's an intimacy to witnessing someone's private struggles, their unguarded moments of doubt and fear. An intimacy that feels almost invasive.

I dismiss the thought as soon as it forms. Invasion is precisely the point. Methodical encroachment on every aspect of her life until no barriers remain between us. Between her and my objectives.

On screen, Lea has moved to the bathroom. She turns on the shower, then undresses with mechanical efficiency. I should look away, not out of any misplaced sense of propriety, but because this surveillance has a specific purpose: security monitoring.

Instead, I lean forward, suddenly aware of the painful tightening in my groin, the shallowing of my breath. My body reacts, primal and demanding, to the sight of her naked, vulnerable, unaware. Every instinct screams to unzip and take release now, to claim this moment, this secret knowledge, physically.

My knuckles pop, bone-white against the chair. That little dip just above her hip? Yeah, I'm claiming that territory. This need to unload is a real ball-ache, making my constructed "cool guy observing" act a goddamn workout. Would be easy, though, and feel real good. Prove a point.

Nope. Get a grip, Romeo. Breathe. Uncurl the fucking

knuckles. Not like this. That's just sad, wanking into the void. The real prize isn't some quick solo splashdown. It's the demolition of her world, getting her wired to me, waiting for that beautiful crack when she gives it up, knowing the surveillance state is personal. Making her wait, making me wait. That's part of the goddamn fun. This hard-on gets put on ice, saved for the big bang.

Okay. Look away from the shower show. Click. I switch screens, pulling up a digital dossier labeled "Song, E." Professor Eunji Song's photograph stares back at me. A woman in her fifties with streaks of silver in her dark hair, expression composed and academic. Nothing in her appearance suggests anything beyond an ordinary professor of political science.

But appearances, as I well know, can be deceiving.

The latest intelligence reports reference a covert meeting with a Korean contact suspected of involvement in the fentanyl pipeline flowing into Chicago, a pipeline Dante Moretti has been working to control. The details are sparse, but sufficient to confirm my earlier suspicions: Professor Song's academic interest in criminal power structures is not merely theoretical.

I scroll through additional data: travel records showing multiple trips to Seoul in the past year, cryptic mentions of "logistics" in intercepted communications, untraceable bank transfers routed through a series of shell companies. Each piece of information reinforces what I've long suspected: Eunji Song stands at the crossroads of something massive, something that could reshape the balance of power in Chicago's underworld.

And Lea, unwittingly, could be the perfect leverage.

If I can secure her trust, I'll have a direct line to unravel her mother's operation before Moretti can exploit it. My plan to ensnare Lea isn't mere whim or distraction; it's the key to controlling whatever pipeline is being established.

I shut the laptop, eyes still burning with the dual flames of arousal and ambition. On the closed screen, I can almost see Lea's reflection, no longer the image of her naked in the shower, but as she will be tomorrow: dressed in whatever gown I select, on my arm at the charity gala, a visible declaration of my claim.

The thought satisfies something deep and possessive within me. By the time she realizes how tightly I've woven her fate into mine, there will be no escaping, not from me, nor from the truth about her mother's dangerous associates.

I pour a measure of whiskey, raising the glass in a silent toast to the coming weeks. The game has only just begun.

CHAPTER TWELVE

Lea

THE LIMOUSINE PURRS TO A STOP AT THE FOOT OF THE marble steps. Through tinted windows, I glimpse the flash of cameras, the glide of designer gowns, the sparkle of diamonds catching light. My heart jumps, a frantic bird against my ribs.

"Ready?" Nico asks, his voice smooth and controlled beside me.

Ready for what? I want to ask. *Ready to step into a world where I don't belong? Ready to pretend I'm something I'm not?*

Instead, I smooth nonexistent wrinkles from the red silk gown that arrived at my apartment this morning in a black garment bag. No note, just the dress. A silent command from the man beside me.

"As I'll ever be," I manage, trying to keep the tremor from my voice.

The chauffeur opens the door, and Nico steps out first. I watch his movements, all fluid, confident, the movements of a man who knows his place in the world and claims it without hesitation. He turns, extending his hand to me, and for a moment, I hesitate.

Taking his hand means something. An acceptance, my surrender?

Haven't I already made my choice? The moment I agreed to his terms, his protection? The moment I stepped onto this path?

I place my hand in his. His fingers close around mine, warm and strong, and he helps me from the car with a gentleness that surprises me.

The moment my stiletto-clad feet touch the red carpet, I'm aware of the shift in attention. Heads turn, gazes sweep over us, conversations pause mid-sentence. The air itself seems to change, charged with curiosity and speculation.

"Chin up," Nico murmurs close to my ear, his breath warm against my skin. "You look stunning."

The compliment lands, catching me off guard. I glance down at the gown. The deep red silk feels cool and whisper-soft against my bare shoulders, the neckline dipping low enough to be daring without crossing into vulgar. It's exactly the right shade to complement my golden skin, the perfect cut to accentuate my figure without making me look like arm candy.

I'd expected something more obvious, something that screamed ownership or objectification. Instead, he's chosen a dress that makes me look like the best version of myself. The realization sends a confusing ripple of gratitude through me.

Nico offers his arm, and I take it, feeling the solid warmth of him through the fine fabric of his tuxedo. We ascend the steps together, the solid weight of his arm anchoring me, and with each step, I feel myself transforming from Lea Song, struggling journalist with an overdue electric bill, into someone who belongs in this dazzling world of wealth and power.

"Remember," Nico says as we reach the top of the stairs, "tonight, you're with me. Not as a journalist. Not as an observer."

"As what, then?" I ask, unable to keep the edge from my voice.

His dark eyes meet mine, intense, opaque. "As mine."

The word sends dread through me that I refuse to acknowledge as anything but indignation.

We enter the grand foyer of the Chicago Art Institute, transformed tonight into a wonderland of crystal chandeliers and floral arrangements. The air smells of expensive perfume and lilies. A string quartet plays a classical piece in the corner, the notes floating above the low hum of cultured conversation, reverberating in the cavernous space.

Nico's hand settles at the small of my back, a light pressure that somehow feels like it's burning through the silk of my dress. He guides me through the crowd with the ease of someone navigating familiar territory.

"Mayor Jenkins," Nico says, stopping before a portly man with silver hair and a red face. "A pleasure to see you again."

The mayor turns, his expression shifting from polite boredom to alert interest. "Varela! Didn't expect to see you here tonight."

They shake hands, and I don't miss the way the mayor's eyes flick nervously around, as if checking who might witness this interaction.

"I never miss the Children's Hospital fundraiser," Nico replies. "Allow me to introduce Lea Song."

The mayor's gaze shifts to me, assessing, curious. I extend my hand, summoning every ounce of poise I can muster.

"Ms. Song," he says, taking my hand. "Are you in business with Mr. Varela?"

Before I can answer, Nico's fingers press against my back, a warning, a reminder.

"Ms. Song is a journalist," Nico says, his tone casual but carrying an undercurrent I can't quite interpret. "But she's here with me tonight in a personal capacity."

Personal capacity. The phrase hangs in the air, loaded with implication. The mayor's eyebrows rise, and I see the moment he re-categorizes me in his mind from a potential threat to Nico's...what? Girlfriend? Lover? Possession?

"I see," the mayor says, giving me an entirely different kind of look now. "Well, enjoy the event. The silent auction has some remarkable items this year."

As we move away, Nico's hand slides to my elbow, his fingers brushing against the sensitive skin there, my bruises covered up with make-up. It's such a slight point of contact, but my body reacts as if he's caressed a much more intimate place, heat prickling beneath my skin.

"You need to relax," he murmurs, leading me toward a waiter carrying flutes of champagne. He takes two, handing one to me. "No one here is going to eat you alive."

No one except you, I think, but don't say it aloud. Instead, I take a sip of champagne, letting the bubbles dance on my tongue.

"I'm not exactly in my natural habitat," I admit, scanning

the room filled with Chicago's elite. "The last formal event I attended was my college graduation."

A smile graces his lips. "You're doing fine. Just follow my lead."

And so I do, floating through the crowd on his arm, watching as he navigates the intricate social landscape with masterful precision. He introduces me to judges who greet him with cautious respect, to philanthropists who seem delighted by his presence, even to a minor European royal whose long name I immediately forget.

With each introduction, each conversation, I'm relaxing incrementally. The champagne helps, warming my blood and softening the edges of my anxiety. But it's more than that. There's something almost intoxicating about being here, about being perceived as someone important enough to be on Nico Varela's arm.

A treacherous thought slips into my mind: What if this were real? What if I weren't here as part of some complex game of power and control, but simply as a woman accompanying a man to a gala? What if the heat of his hand at my back, the brush of his fingers against mine when he hands me a fresh glass of champagne, weren't planned moves in his seduction strategy but genuine gestures of affection?

The fantasy burns bright for a moment. Me, belonging in this world of luxury and influence, standing beside Nico not as a pawn but as a partner. It's so vivid, so alluring, that my breath hitches in my throat.

I banish the thought, horrified by my weakness. This is exactly what he wants. For me to lose myself in the illusion, to forget why I'm here, to surrender to the pull of his constructed reality.

"Senator Mitchell is retiring next month," Nico says, leaning close to speak directly into my ear. His breath skims my skin, warm and intimate, and I can't suppress the involuntary tremor that runs through me. "He's spent the last decade on the Judiciary Committee, always voting against increased sentencing for white-collar crimes."

I turn my head, our faces now inches apart. "Convenient for certain businessmen," I murmur back.

His eyes glint with something like approval. "Indeed. He's also blocked every attempt to increase funding for financial crimes investigation units."

"And now he's retiring with a generous pension and a cushy consulting job waiting for him," I say, unable to keep the cynicism from my voice.

Nico's lips curve in a smile that doesn't quite reach his eyes. "Three consultancy positions, actually. All with firms that benefited from his voting record."

The conversation should disgust me. It should reinforce everything I've always believed about the corrupt system that allows men like Nico to operate with impunity. Instead, I feel a twisted thrill at being privy to this inside knowledge, at standing beside the man who understands how the game is truly played.

What's happening to me?

Before I can examine this disturbing response too closely, a snippet of conversation from a nearby group catches my attention.

"—Professor Song's presentation at the security conference next week—"

My head snaps around, searching for the source of the

comment. A small cluster of academic-looking types stands near a display of auction items, deep in conversation.

"—last-minute addition to the program, but her research on East Asia criminal networks is groundbreaking—"

My mother's name sends a jolt through me. She rarely mentions her speaking engagements to me, but a security conference? That's not her usual academic circuit.

"Excuse me," I murmur to Nico, who's now engaged in a conversation with a silver-haired judge. "Powder room."

He gives me a look that suggests he doesn't quite believe me, but nods anyway. "Don't wander far."

The warning in his tone is clear, but I'm too preoccupied with what I've just overheard to care. I make my way toward the edge of the ballroom, slipping through a set of French doors onto a balcony that overlooks the city.

The night air is chilled, a welcome relief after the close quarters inside. Chicago sprawls in front of me, a vast expanse of lights against the darkness. I pull out the phone Nico gave me, the one I'm certain is monitored, and hesitate. Should I call my mother on this device? But what choice do I have? My personal phone is sitting in Nico's office.

To hell with it. I dial the number, my fingers trembling. After four rings, she picks up.

"Mom?"

"Lea?" Her voice sounds tense, guarded. "Is everything alright?"

"I'm fine, Mom," I say, keeping my voice low. "I just...I haven't heard from you in a while."

"Honey, I've been busy with end-of-term papers," she says, the explanation coming a little too rushed. "You know how it is this time of year."

"Right," I say, leaning against the stone balustrade. "I'm at a charity gala at the Art Institute. With Nico Varela."

There's a sharp intake of breath on the other end of the line. Then silence, so prolonged, I check my phone to make sure the call hasn't dropped.

"Mom?"

"Lea," she finally says, her voice now taut with alarm, "what are you doing with that man?"

The intensity of her reaction startles me. "It's for a story I'm working on. He's granted me access to—"

"Listen to me," she interrupts, her voice dropping to an urgent, hushed tone. "His kind sees only assets and liabilities. Nothing more. Stay far away from him."

There's something in her tone that suggests more than general concern.

"Mom, how do you—"

"I have to go," she cuts me off. "There's someone at my office door."

"At nine o'clock at night?" I ask, suspicion flaring. "What kind of academic meeting happens this late?"

"It's a colleague from overseas," she says, the explanation sounding rehearsed. "The time difference makes scheduling difficult. Please, be careful. More careful than you think necessary."

The line goes dead before I can respond, leaving me staring at the phone in frustration and confusion. *What the hell was that about? And what does my mother know about Nico that would prompt such a specific warning?*

I turn back toward the glittering cityscape, my mind racing. My mother has always been secretive about her past in Korea before moving to England where she met my father, but this level of secrecy is new. Between her cryptic warning and the overheard comment about a security conference I knew nothing about, my journalistic instincts scream that there's a story here. One that might somehow intersect with Nico's world.

"Your mother works unusual hours for an academic."

My chest tightens as I spin around to find Nico standing in the doorway, one shoulder propped against the frame. How long has he been there? How much did he hear? The way he watches me, that measured stillness, those dark eyes missing nothing, makes my skin prickle with awareness.

"Jesus," I breathe, pressing a hand to my chest. "You could make some noise when you approach people."

"Nah, that's no fun." His lips curve into that not-quite-smile I'm recognizing. He steps onto the balcony, his tread almost silent despite his Italian shoes. The dim lighting catches the sharp angles of his face, casting shadows that make him look even more dangerous than usual.

"Like I said, your mother works unusual hours for an academic," he comments, voice laced with quiet interest.

My grip tightens on the phone as if I could somehow erase the conversation he clearly overheard. But there's something in his tone that isn't outright suspicion, just curiosity. Like he's filing away another piece of information about me.

"End of term," I say, aiming for casual. "Papers to grade, research deadlines. You know how it is."

"Do I?" He moves closer, and suddenly the spacious balcony feels impossibly small.

"She works too hard," I continue, desperate to sound normal. "Always has."

He stops beside me at the balustrade. We stand close side

by side, looking out at the glittering Chicago skyline. We could be any couple taking a break from the noise and crush of the gala.

Except we're not a couple. And Nico Varela is not just any man.

"You're concerned about her," he observes, his eyes still fixed on the city lights. "That's admirable. Family loyalty is increasingly rare these days."

There's something in his voice when he says "family." A weight, a reverence almost—that catches my attention. I turn to study his profile, struck by how little I know about this man despite the many days I've spent in his orbit.

"Do you have a family?" I ask before I can stop myself. "Besides your uncle, I mean."

His expression doesn't change, but I sense a subtle shift in his posture, a slight tensing of his shoulders. "Family is complicated in my world," he says after a moment. "Blood matters, but loyalty matters more."

It's not really an answer, but it feels like one of the few genuine things he's said to me. I want to press further, to understand more about the man behind the constructed exterior, but the words die in my throat as his hand settles on my bare shoulder.

His touch is light, almost casual, but it shocks me. His fingertips trace the line of my collarbone with deliberate slowness, and heat pools low, spreading outward like fire. My breathing stutters, my body betraying me with a visceral response I can't control.

"Cold?" he asks, though we both know that's not why my skin suddenly feels too tight.

I should step away. I should remind him I'm here as a

journalist, not as whatever this is becoming. I should remember my mother's warning, still in my ears: *His kind only see assets and liabilities. Nothing more.*

Instead, I'm locked in place, my eyes meeting Nico's as his fingers continue their leisurely exploration of my skin. The question I meant to ask about my mother's warning remains trapped in my throat, drowned out by the insistent tempo of my racing heart beat.

"You look beautiful tonight," he says, his voice dropping to a register that seems to vibrate through me. "Red suits you."

"You chose it," I say, hating how breathless I sound.

His smile deepens, satisfaction clear in the curve of his lips. "True. I did. I picked this, because I knew how it would look against your skin."

His fingers drift higher, brushing the sensitive spot just beneath my ear. I can't suppress the small quiver that runs through me, and his eyes darken in response. He's so close now that I can feel the heat from him.

"Why am I here, Nico?" I ask, trying to regain some control over the situation, over myself. "Really. Not the protection excuse. Not the story. Why did you bring me tonight?"

His hand moves to cup my face, thumb brushing across my lower lip in a gesture that's becoming disturbingly routine. "Because I wanted to see you like this," he says. "In my world. Wearing what I chose. On my arm."

The honesty of it, the raw possessiveness, should repel me. Should make me recoil in feminist outrage. Instead, something dark and primal unfurls in my chest, responding to the claim in his words, in his touch.

"I'm not yours," I say, but even to my own ears, it sounds unconvincing.

"Aren't you?" His other hand slides around my waist, drawing me closer until our bodies are almost flush against each other. "For tonight, at least?"

My head tilts back to maintain eye contact, and in that slight movement, I feel a surrender I never expected. I've spent my entire adult life priding myself on my independence, my strength, my unwillingness to be swayed by any man's charm or power. Yet here I am, melting under Nico Varela's touch like I'm made of nothing more substantial than the silk of this dress.

"This is a bad idea," I murmur, even as my hands come to rest on his chest.

"The best ones are," he murmurs, and then his mouth is on mine.

The kiss isn't gentle. It isn't tentative. It's claiming, pure and simple. His lips are firm and insistent, his hand at my waist pulling me hard against him. I should resist. I should push him away. I should remember who he is, what he's done, the blood on his hands.

Instead, I kiss him back with a hunger that shocks me, my fingers curling into the lapels of his jacket. His tongue traces the seam of my lips, demanding entry, and I open to him without hesitation. He tastes of expensive whiskey and barely leashed power, the slight rasp of his stubble against my skin sending sparks across my nerves. I'm drowning in it. I'm drowning in him.

One of his hands slides into my hair, angling my head to deepen the kiss. The other presses against the small of my back, holding me against him so close I can feel every hard plane of his body. A small sound escapes me, half moan, half surrender, and he responds with a growl that vibrates through my bones.

For a moment, the world beyond this balcony ceases to exist. There is only this. His mouth on mine, his hands possessing me, the thundering of my heart against my ribs. Right now, I am not Lea Song, an ambitious journalist. I am not the daughter of Professor Eunji Song. I am simply a woman in the arms of a dangerous man, consumed by a desire I never saw coming.

When he breaks the kiss, we're both breathing hard. His eyes are darker than I've ever seen them, pupils blown wide with desire. His thumb traces my lower lip, now swollen from his kiss.

"Tell me you don't want this," he challenges. "Tell me, and I'll stop."

It would be so easy to lie. To claim this is just part of my investigation, that I'm playing along to gain his trust, to access his world. But the truth burns too hot to deny, even to myself.

"I can't," I admit, the words almost inaudible. "God help me, I can't."

Triumph flashes in his eyes; pure satisfaction mixed with something darker I can't name. His hand tightens in my hair, not painful but assertive, controlling.

"Then stop fighting it," he says, his voice a command wrapped in velvet. "Stop fighting me."

Before I can respond, the sound of the French doors opening startles us both. We step apart, not quickly enough to hide what was happening, but enough to create the illusion of propriety. A waiter stands in the doorway, looking uncomfortable.

"Mr. Varela," he says, his gaze fixed somewhere over our shoulders. "The auction is about to begin. Your table is ready."

Nico nods dismissal, and the waiter retreats. When we're alone again, Nico turns back to me, his composure restored while I'm still struggling to steady my breathing.

"We should rejoin the party," he says. "Let's continue this conversation later."

It's not a suggestion. It's a promise or a threat. Perhaps both.

He offers his arm, every inch the polished gentleman again, as if he hadn't just been devouring my mouth moments ago. As if my lipstick wasn't now smudged across his lips, marking him as clearly as he's marked me.

I take his arm, feeling the solid strength of him beneath my fingers. As we walk back toward the dazzling lights and music of the gala, I can't shake the sensation that I've just crossed a line from which there's no return. That with one kiss, I've sealed some fate I don't fully understand.

But as Nico's hand covers mine, his thumb stroking across my knuckles, a gesture that feels possessive and intimate, *I wonder if perhaps, just this once, my mother might be wrong.*

CHAPTER THIRTEEN

Nico

I WATCH HER ACROSS THE TABLE, MY ATTENTION CAUGHT in the simple pleasure of her enjoyment. Lea twirls linguine around her fork, a small furrow of concentration between her brows. When she takes the bite, her eyes close briefly, a flash of genuine pleasure that's unexpectedly compelling.

The restaurant hums around us. Ristorante Milano is one of Chicago's finest Italian establishments, tucked away on a quiet street where the old money dines discreetly. Piano notes drift through the air, mingling with the gentle clink of silverware against fine china and the indistinct murmur of conversations designed not to carry. I've owned this place for six years now, though that's not common knowledge. The staff knows me as a valued patron, nothing more, which suits my purposes perfectly.

Tonight, however, I'm not calculating profit margins or assessing which tables host potential assets. I'm simply enjoying watching Lea Song eat pasta.

"This is incredible," she says, gesturing with her fork toward her plate of seafood linguine. "How did you know I love seafood?"

I give a small smile. "I pay attention."

What I don't say: I watched the surveillance footage of your grocery trips. I know you lingered in the seafood section each time. I saw the recipe for cioppino you bookmarked on your laptop.

The candlelight flickers across her features, softening the ever-present wariness in her gaze. There's something almost vulnerable about her tonight in the simple black dress she chose. Elegant but not trying too hard, as though she couldn't decide if this was a date or a business meeting.

I resist the impulse, just like I've been resisting a lot of impulses where Lea Song is concerned.

"Wine?" I offer, reaching for the bottle of Montepulciano d'Abruzzo the sommelier selected. It's a good vintage, with notes of dark cherry and spice. It's complex but approachable, like the woman sitting across from me.

She nods, holding out her glass. "Please."

As I pour, I study the graceful line of her neck, the delicate curve of her wrist. There's strength beneath that softness. I've seen it firsthand. Watched her hold her own in situations that would make seasoned players falter. It's part of what makes her so captivating.

"You handled yourself well last week," I say, setting down the bottle. "That ex-cop we had to question? You read his intentions before any of my men did."

I rarely offer praise. It creates expectations, sets precedents I prefer to avoid. But the words feel right in this moment, hanging between us like an offering.

Surprise flickers across her face, a split-second of unguarded reaction before she can mask it. Then, something even more unexpected: a small, genuine smile that reaches her eyes.

"He was fidgeting with his watch," she says with a slight shrug. "Classic tell. My journalism professor called it the 'liar's timepiece' when someone keeps checking the time. It means they're usually planning their escape."

"Most people wouldn't notice."

"I'm not most people," she counters, taking a sip of her wine.

"No," I agree, holding her gaze. "You're not."

A faint blush colors her cheeks, and she looks away, focusing on her plate again. Something shifts in my chest that I acknowledge with clinical detachment. Physical attraction is nothing new. I've wanted her since I first saw her photograph in the dossier Marco prepared. But this quiet moment of connection feels unfamiliar, unexpectedly pleasant.

"Tell me something," she says after a moment, her voice casual but her eyes sharp with curiosity. "How does someone like you end up doing what you do?"

I consider deflecting, as I always do when personal questions arise. Information is currency in my world, and I've built my empire on controlling its flow. But tonight feels different somehow. The dim lighting, the excellent food, the way she's looking at me with something other than fear or calculation. It creates a pocket of suspended reality where the usual rules seem less rigid.

"I was only six years old when my father died," I say, surprising myself with the admission. "Heart attack. Left nothing but debts and a reputation for weakness."

Her eyes widen, clearly not expecting me to answer. "I'm sorry."

I shrug, swirling the wine in my glass. "Don't be. He was a mediocre man who made mediocre choices. My mother had already left years before, couldn't handle the lifestyle. My uncle Alessandro took me in."

"The man I met at the estate?"

"Yes." I take a sip of wine, letting the rich flavor coat my tongue before continuing. "Alessandro was different. Respected. Feared. He saw potential in me that my father never did."

I don't tell her about my unusual "home schooling," after my uncle took me in. The brutal lessons in control, in strategy, in never showing weakness. Negotiation and interrogation techniques. The nights spent memorizing financial records and political connections until my eyes burned. The first time Alessandro put a gun in my hand and told me to choose between my loyalty to a childhood friend who'd betrayed us and my future in the family business. I was fourteen.

Some things don't belong at a dinner table.

"He taught me that power isn't about violence," I continue instead. "It's about positioning. About knowing where to stand when the dominoes fall."

She tilts her head, studying me with that journalist's intensity that both irritates and intrigues me. "And where do you stand now?"

"In the middle," I reply. "Between forces that would tear each other apart if left unchecked. I create balance."

"Through intimidation and blackmail," she points out, though there's less judgment in her tone than I'd expect.

I smile. "Through whatever means necessary. The world

runs on conflict, Lea. I just make sure it's a controlled conflict."

"Like a pressure valve."

"Exactly." I lean forward, surprised and pleased by her understanding. "Someone has to regulate the tension. Otherwise—"

"Explosion," she finishes, mirroring my posture.

For a moment, we're aligned, two minds meeting in unexpected harmony. It's disconcerting.

"What about you?" I ask, steering us toward safer ground. "Always desired to be a journalist?"

She laughs, a soft, genuine sound that catches me off guard. "God, no. I wanted to be a ballerina until I was twelve. Then I realized I had absolutely no talent for it."

I try to picture her in a tutu, all determination and no grace. "Hard truth to face at twelve." I crack a bitter smile.

"Devastating," she agrees with mock seriousness. "I spent a week locked in my room listening to Swan Lake on repeat and declaring my life was over."

"And then?"

"And then my dad gave me my first camera." Her expression softens with the memory. "He said if I couldn't be in the show, I could capture it instead. Tell the story my way."

There's something in her voice when she mentions her father that resonates with some long-buried part of me. I know from her file that Gene Robert died in a car accident when she was sixteen. The official report cited brake failure. The unofficial report, which I accessed through less conventional channels, suggested potential tampering.

I'd never mention this to her. Some truths serve no purpose but pain.

"He sounds like a wise man," I say instead.

"He was." She takes another sip of wine.

For a moment, I imagine a different reality: one where I met Lea Song in some ordinary way. A charity event, perhaps, or a gallery opening. A world where I could pursue her without calculation, without the weight of ulterior motives.

The fantasy is as attractive as it is pointless.

Our waiter appears with dessert, breaking the charged moment. Tiramisu for her, espresso for me. As he sets the plates down, I notice Lea's gaze drifting toward the entrance. A reflexive scan of the room, the journalist's habit of situational awareness.

Without thinking, I reach across the table and cover her hand with mine, drawing her attention back to me. Her skin, warm and soft beneath my palm, the contrast with my callused fingers striking. She doesn't pull away, which I count as a small victory.

"It's delicious," she says after taking a bite of the dessert, though her eyes remain locked with mine.

"Of course." I run my thumb over her knuckles before withdrawing. "I would never bring you somewhere subpar."

A small smile plays at the corners of her mouth. "God forbid the great Nico Varela associate with anything less than excellence."

There's a teasing note in her voice I've never heard before, almost playful. It catches me off guard, this glimpse of the woman she might be outside the pressure cooker of our arrangement. I want more of it.

My phone vibrates against the table, the screen lighting up with Marco's name. I resist the urge to check it, an unusual restraint for me. Usually, business takes precedence over everything. Tonight, however, I'm reluctant to break this fragile peace we've constructed.

Lea arches a brow, her gaze flicking to the phone and back to me. "Trouble?"

I shrug, turning the device face-down. "Business. It can wait."

Even as I say it, a cold certainty settles in my gut. Marco wouldn't contact me during a dinner I'd requested privacy unless something significant was happening. But I let myself have this small moment, this moment of chosen ignorance.

"That's a first," Lea remarks, finishing the last bite of her tiramisu. "The great Nico Varela, ignoring a call."

"Perhaps I find the current company more compelling," I say, watching for her reaction.

She meets my gaze, neither flinching nor preening at the implied compliment. "Or perhaps you're simply biding your time."

"Suspicious by nature, aren't you?"

"Professional hazard," she counters. "Though in your company, it seems more like a survival skill."

I rise from the table, reluctant to end the evening despite the nagging awareness of Marco's message waiting for my attention. The waiter approaches, but I dismiss him with a subtle nod that he understands immediately.

As we walk toward the exit, Lea pauses, looking back at the table. "Wait, we didn't get the check."

I place my hand on the small of her back, guiding her forward. "It's been taken care of."

Her journalist's instinct kicks in. "Taken care of? We didn't even see the bill."

"Let's just say I have an arrangement with the management," I reply, watching her process this information.

"An 'arrangement,'" she repeats, giving me a knowing look. "Let me guess, you either own this place or you have something on the owner."

I permit a small smile. "I appreciate quality, Lea. In all its forms."

"That's not an answer," she challenges, but there's a hint of amusement in her eyes.

"Isn't it?" I counter, holding the door open for her as we head to my car.

Outside, the evening air carries a sharp bite, the promise of fall etched in the crystalline clarity of the night. City lights glitter against the darkness, reflecting off the sleek surfaces of passing cars. The low rumble of traffic provides a constant city soundtrack. Chicago at night has always held a particular beauty for me, an interplay of shadow and illumination, of power and possibility.

Lea draws closer to my side as we step onto the sidewalk, whether seeking warmth or simply responding to the instinctive urge for protection in the darkness, I can't be sure. Either way, I welcome the proximity, as I guide her toward the curb where Dominic waits with the car.

"You're in a hurry all of a sudden," she observes, glancing up at me.

I don't voice my unease. A prickling awareness at the base of my skull that warns of approaching complications. Years of navigating Chicago's underworld have honed my instincts for danger, and right now, they're humming like a live wire.

"It's cold," I say, scanning the street with practiced casualness.

That's when I see it. A black Audi S8 with tinted windows gliding to a stop beside us. My muscles tense in automatic response, hand moving toward the concealed holster beneath my jacket. Then the passenger window lowers, and I relax, though my guard remains firmly in place.

Dante Moretti.

Not an immediate physical threat, then, but more dangerous in the long term. My grip on Lea's arm tightens, a protective reflex I don't disguise. She senses the change in my posture, her own body tensing in response.

"Varela," Moretti greets, his voice carrying the affected smoothness of old money despite his less genteel origins. He steps out of the car with the fluid grace of a predator, his expensive suit doing little to disguise the street fighter's build beneath. At forty-three, he's still in his prime, powerful shoulders, thick black hair with distinguished silver at the temples, and hazel eyes that shift between charm and calculation.

"Moretti," I respond, keeping my tone neutral despite the surge of irritation at this deliberate intrusion. "Bit far from your usual hunting grounds, aren't you?"

His smile doesn't reach his eyes as he runs a thumb across the burn scar on his right hand. "Just enjoying some of the finer establishments the city offers." His eyes slides to Lea, a deliberate assessment that makes my jaw tighten. "And I see you're doing the same. Ms. Song, isn't it? The journalist."

Beside me, Lea stiffens but maintains her composure. "Mr. Moretti," she acknowledges with a slight nod. No surprise, no confusion, she's done her research. *Of course she has.*

"I've been hearing rumors you've expanded your interests," Moretti continues, addressing me while keeping his gaze on Lea. The undertone of threat is unmistakable, but the veneer of civility remains intact; we're both too practiced to break the façade in public.

"I wasn't aware my life was of such interest to you, Dante," I reply. "Should I be flattered by the attention?"

He laughs, the sound sharp and devoid of genuine humor. "Professional curiosity only. You've always been so focused on business. It's refreshing to see you take time for pleasure."

The way he says "pleasure" makes my blood simmer, but I maintain my neutral expression. This is a play of power, a test of boundaries in neutral territory. Any display of emotion would be counted as weakness.

"We all have our diversions," I say with deliberate blandness.

Moretti's attention shifts to Lea now, his expression taking on a thoughtful quality that I like even less than his previous assessment.

"I hear Professor Song's latest lecture is attracting interesting attention," he says. "She has quite the insights on shadow networks, doesn't she?"

The mention of Eunji Song sends a spike of alarm through me. Beside me, Lea tenses, her breathing changing almost imperceptibly. Moretti's knowledge of her mother's work is too specific, too pointed to be random conversation. It's a message, he knows about Eunji's connections, perhaps even more than me.

More concerning, he wants me to know that he knows.

"I'm sure you've got your sources," I reply, voice edged

with steel despite my outward calm. "But her work is of no concern to you."

Moretti's grin curls like a viper preparing to strike. "Academic freedom is something we should all support, don't you think? Though sometimes scholars dig into areas they don't fully understand. Dangerous areas, like shark infested areas."

The threat is obvious, and I feel Lea's pulse jump beneath my fingers where they rest against her wrist. I move her behind me, creating a physical barrier between her and Moretti.

"You two enjoy the evening," Moretti says, lifting a languid hand in farewell. "The night is still young."

I nod to my driver, Dominic, who steps forward to open the car door. Without waiting for Moretti's response, I usher Lea inside, every sense alert for any sudden movement. The door closes with a solid thunk of British engineering, sealing us in the quiet interior of the Bentley.

As we pull away from the curb, I catch Moretti's expression in the side mirror, too pleased, too satisfied. Like a man who's confirmed something important.

"What the hell was that about?" Lea asks once we're moving, her voice steady despite the tension radiating from her. "And why does he know about my mother's work and research?"

I don't answer, my mind racing through implications and contingencies. Moretti's interest in Eunji Song can't be coincidental. If he's investigating her, it means he's aware of the same connections I've been tracking the pipeline between certain academic circles and Asian pharmaceutical suppliers. The question is whether he's simply gathering intelligence or actively moving against her.

Either way, it puts Lea in his crosshairs, both as leverage against me and as a potential path to Eunji.

"Nico?" Lea prompts, interrupting my calculations.

I exhale, hooking an arm around her shoulders in a show of reassurance that serves multiple purposes of comfort, protection, and the simple physical need to keep her close.

"Moretti specializes in pharmaceutical distribution," I explain, choosing my words with care. "Both legitimate and otherwise. Your mother's research touches on East Asia's supply chains. It's possible he sees her work as a threat to his operations."

It's not the whole truth, but it's not a lie either. The best deceptions always contain a solid foundation of reality.

"That doesn't explain why he was waiting outside the restaurant," she points out, her analytical mind cutting straight to the core. "Or how he even knew we would be there."

"He has me under surveillance, just as I have him watched," I say with a shrug. "Its standard procedure."

"There was nothing standard about that encounter," she insists, shifting to face me more directly. The interior lighting catches the determination in her eyes, the set of her jaw. "He mentioned my mother, Nico. Why?"

"He's just messing with you. Trust me." My phone vibrates again. I check the screen to find two messages from Marco, each more urgent than the last. *Shipment intercepted at North Pier. Someone tipped off the Feds. Suppliers demanding immediate report. Mario has spotted Moretti's men at the university. Advise action.*

Cold certainty settles in my gut. These are systematic moves in a game that's accelerating faster than I thought possible. Moretti wasn't just sending a message; he was making dangerous moves with stakes so high, they could start a deadly mob war.

"What is it?" Lea asks, reading the tension in my posture.

I meet her gaze, no longer concerned with maintaining the pleasant fiction of our evening. "I'm dropping you off. Something came up."

"Why? What's happening? You can't drop me off. You promised complete access at all times. Those were the rules." The edge of anger in her voice is clear a day.

I signal to Dominic to change course, then turn back to Lea. "I made the rules, and I can change the rules. Sorry piccola. Decision made."

CHAPTER FOURTEEN

Lea

THE MEMORY OF HIS LIPS LINGERS ON MINE AS I STARE at the barista, who glances up.

"Miss? Your order?"

I blink, realizing I've been standing at the counter, lost in my head again. The line behind me shifts impatiently.

"Sorry. Large Americano, extra shot," I manage, fumbling for my wallet. "And a blueberry scone."

The buzz of Café Lumière envelops me, espresso machines hissing, conversations floating in fragments, laptop keys clicking in rhythmic percussion. It's Friday and downtown Chicago comes alive with weekend anticipation. I chose this spot for its floor-to-ceiling windows and central location, a place where I could pretend to be normal for an hour.

Normal. *I wasn't even sure what that meant anymore.*

My phone vibrates against my hip as I settle into a corner booth. I notice that I have two unread messages from Nico:

You're not in the apartment. Where are you? Followed twenty minutes later by: *Why won't you answer?*

I stuff the device back into my purse with more force than necessary. After last night, after he'd ordered me out of the car like some disobedient child, he has the nerve to demand my whereabouts? So much for the promise that I could shadow him whenever I wanted.

The coffee burns my tongue, but I welcome the pain. It's clarifying, unlike the muddled emotions swirling through me since that dinner with Nico. Since Dante Moretti appeared outside the restaurant with his silky threats about my mother.

My mother. *The worry about her hadn't let me rest.* I called her late last night after tossing and turning for hours, worry gnawing at my insides. She'd answered on the fifth ring, her voice carrying that tone of constructed calm that I've known since childhood.

"Lea, it's past midnight. Is everything alright?"

I'd hesitated. "Mom, I met someone tonight who mentioned your work. Dante Moretti. He seemed interested in your research on shadow networks."

The silence continued so long I had to look at my phone, doubting whether the line was still active. Finally, she spoke.

"Moretti is playing mind games, sweetheart. He wants to rattle you." Her tone was measured, but with an undercurrent I couldn't quite identify. "These men operate by creating uncertainty."

"These men? You know who Dante Moretti is?"

"I'm a political scientist who studies power structures, Lea." She'd sighed, a soft, tired sound. "Of course I know the major players in Chicago's underworld."

"He knew about your lecture. Something about 'attracting interesting attention.' What did he mean by that?"

"Nothing. Academic politics can be vicious, you know this." Another pause. "Be careful with your sources," she'd said, her voice suddenly tight with concern.

"I will," I promised.

The unease remains lodged in my chest like a splinter working its way deeper with each breath after we hung up.

The café door chimes, pulling me from my thoughts. Sienna breezes in, a vision in her red scarf, her photographer's bag slung over one shoulder. Her eyes scan the room until she spots me, and her face lights up with a smile.

I lift my coffee cup in greeting.

"There you are!" She slides into the booth across from me, shrugging off her jacket to reveal a vintage concert tee. "Sorry I'm late. Harrison wanted last-minute changes on the article."

"No worries." I force brightness into my voice. "How's the setup going?"

"Exhausting but exciting." She pauses, studying my face with narrowed eyes. "You look like hell warmed over."

I laugh, though it sounds forced even to my ears. "Thanks. Just what every girl wants to hear."

"I'm serious, Lea." She leans forward, voice dropping. "When did you last sleep? Or is Nico Varela keeping you too busy?"

There's a teasing lilt to her words, but I catch the genuine concern beneath. I fiddle with my napkin, tearing small methodical strips from the edge.

"I've had things on my mind."

"Things?" She arches an eyebrow. "Very specific, journalist."

I shrug, avoiding her gaze. "Work. The story."

"So articulate today." She signals the barista, then turns back to me. "Look, I know this assignment is a big deal, but you seem different."

"Different how?"

"I don't know." She accepts her cappuccino from the server with a quick smile. "Tense. Distracted. Like you're waiting for something bad to happen."

Because I am, I think but don't say.

Instead, I take another sip of my too-bitter coffee and change the subject. "How's Jason at work? Still doing that old school flirting-by-getting-you-coffee thing?"

"Nice deflection," Sienna says her eyes narrowing. "And yes, I may or may not have said yes to go out with him." She taps her nails against the ceramic mug. "But we're not talking about my boring love life. We're talking about whatever has you checking the door every thirty seconds."

I blink, startled. "I'm not—"

"You just did it again." She sets down her cup with a decisive clink. "You're talking like him, you know."

"Like who?"

"Varela." She leans back, crossing her arms. "The way you shrug off questions, how you're watching the exits. Hell, that's new."

My stomach drops. I open my mouth to deny it, but the words die on my tongue because, yes, fuck, she's right. I am scanning for threats, measuring the distance to the door, cataloging faces. *When did I start doing that?*

"I'm just being cautious," I admit.

"Cautious? Lea, have you ever been cautious a day in your life? I heard you once climbed onto the journalism building roof during a lightning storm because, and I quote, 'The shot will be worth it.'"

How did she know that? Then I realized she's a Chicago Journal investigator, like me. We know shit. I smile despite myself. "That was an awesome photo."

"It was insane." She reaches across the table to squeeze my hand. "What's really going on? And don't tell me it's just work. I know you better than that."

For one wild moment, I consider telling her everything, about the warehouses and the broken fingers, about Moretti's veiled threats and the way Nico looks at me when he thinks I don't notice. About how I sometimes catch myself wondering what it would be like to surrender to the electric current that hums between us whenever we're alone.

But I can't drag Sienna any deeper into this mess. I've already put her in danger once, when Moretti's men cornered us in that alley.

"It's complicated," I say.

"Meaning you're sleeping with him," she concludes with the bluntness that's both her best and most infuriating quality.

"I am not sleeping with Nico!" I hiss, leaning forward.

"But you want to."

I feel heat climbing up my neck. "That's so inappropriate."

"That's not a no." She studies me over the rim of her cup. "Look, I'm not judging. The man is walking sex appeal wrapped in designer suits. But he's also fucking dangerous, Lea. Like, genuinely fucking dangerous."

"I know that."

"Do you? Because you've got that look."

"What look?"

"The look of: 'I know this is a terrible idea but I'm going to do it, anyway'."

I wince at the insinuation. "This is totally not that . Entirely different," I insist. "It's professional."

Sienna snorts. "Right."

"I'm being careful," I promise, though the words feel hollow. *How careful can I be when I've already crossed so many lines I once considered uncrossable?*

We finish our coffees, chatting about safer topics, like her upcoming article, the latest fail by some celebrity, the super high rent on Sienna's new apartment. For twenty precious minutes, I almost feel like a normal person.

"I should get going," she says eventually, checking her watch. "Deadlines crisis waits for no woman." She stands, gathering her things. "Same time Tuesday? Or will you be too busy with your 'professional' assignment?"

"I'll be here," I say, hoping it's not a lie.

She hesitates, then leans down to hug me. "If you need to talk, like...really talk, I'm here. No judgment, just listening. Not just work stuff, you know."

"I know." My throat tightens. "Thanks, Sienna."

After she leaves, I order another coffee, not ready to face my empty apartment yet. The caffeine jitters through my system, but I welcome the artificial alertness. Sleep has become a luxury I can't seem to afford, not when every time I close my eyes, I see Nico's face, or worse, feel his hands on me.

I pull out my laptop, determined to make some progress

on my article. The document stares back at me, cursor blinking accusingly at the end of a paragraph about Nico's connections to city officials. I've been careful to encode certain details, using initials instead of names, creating a system only I can decipher. The real names and connections are stored in my head, ready to be inserted once the article is safely filed.

As I type, I feel the weight of someone watching me. The sensation prickles, raising the fine hairs on my arms. Slowly, I glance up.

A man sits by the window, pretending to read a newspaper. His worn shoes are scuffed at the toes. Our eyes meet before he hastily looks away, his discomfort too obvious to be professional surveillance. Something about his posture, the rigid set of his shoulders, the way his fingers clench the paper, sets off warning bells in my head.

I save my document, close my laptop, and gather my things with deliberate calm. Then, instead of heading for the door, I approach his table.

"Are you following me?" I keep my voice quiet but firm, channeling the confidence I've seen Nico use to disarm opponents.

The man flinches, gaze darting around the café as if mapping escape routes. He's younger than I initially thought, maybe early thirties, with nondescript features that would blend into any crowd.

"Not exactly," he mumbles, reaching into his jacket pocket.

My body tenses, preparing to run, but instead of a weapon, he withdraws a folded piece of paper. He thrusts it into my hand, his fingers cold and damp against mine.

"You are in danger," he murmurs. "Your mother is not what she seems."

Before I can respond, he slips past me and out the back door, moving with the efficiency of someone used to quick exits. I stand frozen, the paper clutched in my fist, as his parting words linger in my head.

Heart pounding, I unfold the note. The same warning is scrawled across the page in jagged handwriting. I stare at the words, uncertainty crawling through me like ice water.

Moretti claims one thing about my mother; now this random man offers a warning about her. *What do I believe? The criminal who threatened me, or the stranger who just ran away? Both? Noone?*

A chill traces my neck. I dart outside, scanning the crowded sidewalk, but the man has vanished, swallowed by the sea of pedestrians rushing through their Friday routines.

I pull out my phone and call my mother, pacing in tight circles as I wait for her to answer. The connection clicks after four rings.

"Lea? Is everything all right?" My mother's voice is clear but cautious.

"Mom, where are you right now?" I demand, skipping pleasantries.

"In my office, preparing for a department meeting. Why?"

There's an odd reverberation in the background, like an announcement over a PA system. My journalist's instincts buzz with wrongness.

"What's that noise?"

"Campus construction," she explains in haste. "They're renovating the east wing. Don't worry about it."

It's a lie. I've visited her campus office dozens of times over the years; construction announcements don't carry through the building like that. It sounds more like an airport or train station.

"Mom, are you really at the university?"

"Of course I am." Her tone sharpens with irritation. "Lea, what's going on? Why are you questioning me?"

I hesitate, weighing how much to reveal. "Someone approached me today. They said you might be in danger."

A pause...too long to be natural. "That's ridiculous. You're being paranoid again. I'm perfectly safe."

"Are you sure? Because between this and Moretti's comments last night—"

"Lea, listen to me." Her voice drops, turning urgent. "Stay away from Moretti. And be careful around Varela. Just get what you need for your expose, and then get the hell out. Their world isn't a game, and no story is worth risking your life for."

"But Mom—"

"I have to go. We'll talk later, I promise."

The line goes dead before I can protest. I stare at my phone, frustration and fear tangling in my chest. My mother never used to keep secrets from me. After my father died, it was just the two of us against the world, a team. *When did that change?*

I imagine the worst, my mother being involved in something dangerous, something connected to both Nico and Moretti. But what? Her research is theoretical and academic. She studies power structures and political systems, not—

Unless it's not just research.

The thought hits me like a physical blow. What if my

mother's work is a cover for something else? What if her frequent international conferences aren't what they seem?

Stop it, I tell myself. *You're spiraling. Eunji Song is a respected academic with a thirty-year career. She's not some secret operative.*

But the doubt has taken root, sprouting tendrils of suspicion that wrap around memories I'd never questioned before. The late-night phone calls in Korean, that stopped when I entered the room. The unexpected trips that never quite aligned with published conference schedules. The visitors who came to our house when I was a child—serious-faced men and women who spoke in whispers with my parents.

Drained and distracted, I finally head home, desperate to check my notes for any missed connections. Maybe there's something in Nico's business dealings that intersects with my mother's research. Maybe the key to understanding all of this is buried in the files I've already compiled.

I climb the three flights to my apartment, muscles protesting after too many sleepless nights. The hallway is quiet, most of my neighbors at work or school. I dig for my keys, planning to make a fresh pot of coffee and spread my notes across the living room floor like I used to do in college when tackling a complex story.

The lock turns, and I push the door open, then nearly drop my keys at the sight that greets me.

Nico Varela is perched on my sofa, relaxing like *it's the most* natural thing in the world. He looks up from his phone as I enter, dark eyes opaque.

Anger and adrenaline spike in my veins, washing away my exhaustion. I slam the door behind me, dropping my bag on the floor with a thud.

"What the hell are you doing here?" I demand, voice trembling with a mixture of fear and outrage.

He rises in one fluid motion, tucking his phone into his pocket. "You weren't answering your texts."

"So you picked my lock?" I cross my arms, trying to steady myself. "What are you, a glorified stalker?"

Something flickers across his face, but it's gone so quickly I might have imagined it.

"I was concerned," he says, voice calm. "After Moretti's appearance last night, certain precautions seemed prudent."

"Precautions like breaking into my apartment?"

"I didn't break in. I have a key."

The casual admission steals my breath. "You have a key to my apartment? Since when?"

"Since you became a potential target." He steps closer, and I back up against the door. "Moretti doesn't make idle threats, Lea. His interest in you, and your mother, is cause for serious concern."

The mention of my mother sends a fresh wave of anxiety through me. I think of the stranger's warning, the note a heavy weight in my pocket. *Your mother is in danger. Varela is not what he seems.*

"I can take care of myself," I insist, though the words sound hollow even to my ears.

"Can you?" He gestures around the apartment. "Your locks are substandard. Your windows don't have proper security. You live alone on a floor with minimal foot traffic. If Moretti wanted to get to you, there's very little stopping him."

"And what about you? What's stopping you from—" I cut myself off.

His expression darkens. "From what, Lea? Hurting you?"

199

He steps closer, voice dropping low. "If I wanted to hurt you, I would have done it long before now."

"Then what do you want?"

"I want you to understand the situation you're in." Another step forward. "To recognize that my protection isn't some arbitrary restriction I've placed on you. It's the only thing keeping you from becoming collateral damage in a war you know nothing about."

"A war?" I repeat, latching onto the word. "What war?"

He grunts, a rare gesture of frustration. "Do you have any idea how many actual wars I've prevented in this city? How much bloodshed I've stopped by creating structure where there was chaos?" His voice rises, an unusual crack in his perfect control. "I'm a saint compared to what others do."

The raw conviction in his eyes disarms me. I've never seen him like this before, passionate, almost desperate to be understood. I realize with a jolt that he believes this narrative he's constructed where he's the reluctant hero standing between chaos and order. It's jarring to witness someone so intelligent, completely blind to the destruction that follows in his wake.

"Then tell me about it," I challenge, stepping forward. "Let me write the authentic story. Not just about the negotiations and the deals, but about what drives you. About this 'war' you're fighting."

"It's not that simple."

"Why not? You claim to be the good guy—"

"I never said I was good," he cuts in, voice hard. "Just necessary."

"Fine. Necessary. Then let me understand why." I take another step closer. "Let me in, Nico."

His eyes drops to my mouth, and the air between us changes.

"Who was the man you spoke to at the café?" he asks.

My breath catches. *Of course he knows. Of course he was having me followed.*

"No one," I lie. "Just someone who recognized me from the paper."

His hand shoots out, catching my throat in a gentle but firm grasp. Not squeezing, just holding. Asserting dominance. My muscles lock, a sudden paralysis rooting me to the spot. Fear coils tight in my gut, yet beneath it, heat spreads through my limbs, making my knees threaten to buckle.

"Don't lie to me, Lea," he murmurs, thumb stroking the point beneath my jaw. "It never ends well."

I should push him away. I should be terrified. Instead, I'm transfixed by the intensity in his eyes, the heat radiating from his body so close to mine.

"I'm not—" My protest dies as his grip tightens.

"You are," he insists. "I can feel your pulse racing. You only do that when you're lying or when I'm touching you."

The words hang in the air, charged with implications neither of us has voiced until now. I swallow hard, feeling the movement against his palm.

"Nico—"

Whatever I was going to say is lost as his mouth crashes down on mine. The kiss is ferocious. All teeth and tongue and pent-up hunger. My back hits the door as he presses against me, one hand still at my throat, the other tangling in my hair. I should resist, should remember all the reasons this is a terrible idea.

Instead, I kiss him back with equal fervor, my hands

clutching at his shoulders, his chest, anywhere I can reach. He tastes like coffee and mint and something darker, something uniquely him. The world spins away until there's nothing but this—his mouth on mine, his body pinning me to the door, the low growl in his throat when I bite his lower lip.

Then, abruptly, he tears himself away. We stand there, breathing hard, staring at each other in the sudden, stark silence. His pupils are blown wide, a flush high on his cheekbones. I must look just as wrecked—lips swollen, hair mussed where he grabbed it.

He steps back, smoothing his shirt. If not for the rapid rise and fall of his chest, he might appear unaffected.

"We're going out," he says, voice clipped and final. He crosses to the sofa and picks up a remote, flicking on my TV as if nothing just happened between us. "You have half an hour, Lea. Dress appropriately."

I stand frozen by the door, heart hammering, mouth still tingling from his kiss. He won't look at me again, his attention locked on the news scrolling across the screen. The abrupt shift leaves me reeling, caught between fury at his presumption and lingering desire that makes my body hum like a plucked string.

With a shaky breath, I realize I've got no choice but to comply. Whatever game we're playing, he's determined to control the next move. I straighten my shoulders, forcing steel into my spine.

My half-hour starts now.

CHAPTER FIFTEEN

Nico

THE BASS THRUMS BENEATH MY FINGERTIPS AS I PRESS my palm against the unmarked metal door. I can feel it even before we enter, a heartbeat promising secrets, power, and desires best kept hidden from daylight. Beside me, Lea shifts her weight from one heel to another, uncertainty radiating from her despite the confident tilt of her chin.

I knock three times, pause, then twice more. A pattern as old as the establishment itself.

"Is this really necessary?" Lea murmurs, her breath warm against my ear as she leans closer. "The secret knock thing? Another club? Isn't Purgatorio exclusive enough?"

I smirk, turning toward her. "Purgatorio is where the city sees what I permit it to see, piccola. It's controlled exposure, a velvet glove over an iron fist. Undertow, on the other hand..." I pause, letting the implication hang before continuing, "this is the fist itself." She swallows and I give her a second to compose herself.

"This is where the real mechanisms operate, far from any spotlight. Different levels of business require different levels of discretion. Would you prefer we let in just anyone? This place is where politicians mingle directly with syndicate heads. Not exactly the kind of guest list they want publicized."

"To a journalist like me?" she suggests, the challenge still there.

I shrug with a grin as the door opens. "Precisely."

Her eyes widen, and I savor the brief flash of alarm that crosses her features. *She's still underestimating what she's about to witness. Good. The shock value will make tonight's lesson all the more effective.*

A small viewing panel slides open, revealing a pair of watchful eyes. Recognition flashes, and the door swings inward with a well-oiled silence.

"Mr. Varela," the bouncer murmurs, offering a respectful nod that stops just short of a bow. His gaze slides to Lea, lingering a beat too long for my liking. I feel my jaw tighten, a primal, territorial response I hadn't anticipated. "Please, come in," he adds hastily, unhooking the velvet rope that separates the entryway from the main floor.

My hand is on Lea's back, guiding her forward. The pressure of my palm against the silk of her dress sends a current of awareness up my arm. I've touched countless women with this same practiced gesture, yet something about the heat of her skin through the thin fabric feels different. More conse-quential. *Or maybe I just need to get fucking laid?*

We step from the dimly lit entry corridor into the main space of Undertow, Chicago's most exclusive club that doesn't officially exist. The air feels different here, scrubbed clean of outside signals. Dim neon lights cast everyone in flattering shadows, while low, throbbing music provides both ambiance and convenient cover for conversations not meant for recording devices.

Lea's fingers grip my forearm, her nails pressing through my suit jacket. Not enough to hurt, just enough to anchor herself as she takes in the scene before us.

The club sprawls in elegant decadence. Plush velvet booths line the perimeter, many obscured by sheer curtains that provide privacy. A gleaming onyx bar stretches along one wall, staffed by bartenders whose discretion is worth more than the top-shelf liquor they pour. The central dance floor is thick with bodies moving to a beat that's felt more than heard, while the elevated VIP section offers the perfect vantage point to observe without being observed.

But it's not the opulent surroundings that have Lea clutching my arm, it's the clientele. The faces here weren't just the city's elite mingling with known associates; these were the shadow puppeteers themselves. International players, heads of families usually only whispered about, men and women, whose presence together in any public space, could trigger federal investigations.

"Is that...?" she breathes, nodding toward a booth where Chicago's deputy mayor leans in close to a woman notorious for running the city's most lucrative escort service.

"Yes," I answer, watching understanding dawn in her eyes. "At Purgatorio, he might avoid direct contact with certain associates. Down here, pretenses are dropped. Deals require direct conversation, regardless of titles held in the daylight."

Everywhere we look, the lines between legitimate and

criminal blur to nonexistence: a renowned banker shares cigars with the head of the Ukrainian syndicate; a federal judge laughs at something muttered by a money launderer who handles cash for three different organizations; a celebrated philanthropist discusses "investment opportunities" with one of Moretti's lieutenants.

This is my true domain, not the polished nightclub upstairs where I maintain my public persona, but this underground realm where real power flows like the whiskey in everyone's glasses. *She needed to see this layer. To understand that the deals done over champagne upstairs are merely reflections of the actual power brokered down here in the dark.*

"Tell me," Lea murmurs, leaning closer to be heard over the music. "Why would you show me this? Isn't this the kind of thing that would destroy you if it came out in my article?"

I guide her toward the bar, signaling the bartender with a subtle gesture. Without a word, he slides two crystal tumblers of amber liquid toward us.

"That depends," I reply, lifting my glass in a small toast before taking a sip, "on whether you think exposing this would help or harm Chicago."

Her brow furrows. "What do you mean?"

"Look around, piccola." I gesture with my free hand. "What do you see?"

"Corruption," she says. "Collusion. Crime."

I lean closer, my lips nearly brushing her ear. "I see peace."

She jerks back, skepticism etched across her features. It's this, her stubborn refusal to accept easy narratives, that first drew me to her. That, and the fire in her eyes when she challenges me.

"Peace?" she repeats. "You call this peace?"

"Before I established this place, these same people met in back alleys, in warehouses where bodies could be buried, in locations where violence was the first resort, not the last." I take another sip, letting the whiskey burn a path down my throat. "Here, they sit five feet apart. They drink the same liquor. They remember they're all human beneath their various titles."

Lea's gaze sweeps the room again, this time with more calculation than shock. I can almost see her reassessing, questioning her initial judgment. *Good. That's exactly what I want her to see beyond black and white morality into the complex shades of gray where I operate.*

"And what's your role in all this?" she asks. "What do you get out of it?"

Before I can answer, a waiter materializes at my elbow, leaning in to murmur, "Ms. Vega has arrived. She's asking for you in the VIP section."

I nod my acknowledgment, then turn back to Lea. "Isabel Vega doesn't attend fundraisers or public nightclubs. Our discussion requires a level of discretion even Purgatorio can't guarantee. This neutral, untraceable ground is the only place she'll discuss matters of this sensitivity. You're about to find out what my role is."

We weave through the crowd, my hand never leaving her back. I feel her tense slightly as we approach the roped-off VIP area, where a woman sits alone in a corner booth, swirling an amber drink in a crystal glass.

Isabel Vega, liaison for one of Colombia's most sophisticated cartels, radiates lethal grace in her tailored black pantsuit. Diamond studs wink from her earlobes, the only ornamentation she permits herself, apart from the custom Beretta I know is holstered against her ribs. Her black hair is pulled back in a sleek twist, emphasizing the sharp angles of her face.

She rises as we approach, lips curving into a smile that doesn't quite reach her eyes. "Nico," she purrs, the accent of her native Medellín adding texture to the word. She leans in for the customary cheek-to-cheek greeting.

"Isabel," I respond, matching her formal warmth. "May I introduce Lea Song? She's shadowing me for a journalistic piece."

Isabel's eyebrows rise fractionally. "A journalist? How unexpected." Her gaze slides to Lea, sharpens, and lingers perhaps a beat too long, her assessment shifting from neutral curiosity to something more focused, appreciative. I feel an unwelcome flicker—irritation? No, a disruption. Control slipping. "Especially given our shared aversion to publicity," Isabel finishes, her eyes still holding Lea's.

I feel Lea stiffen almost imperceptibly beside me, preparing for rejection. Instead, she extends her hand with perfect poise.

"Ms. Vega," she says smoothly. "I assure you, my focus is on understanding complex power dynamics, not exposing individuals. Mr. Varela has been quite clear about the boundaries of what I can report."

Isabel's smile warms slightly as she accepts the handshake, her thumb brushing lightly across Lea's knuckles. Another flicker inside me, this one colder. A possessive instinct I refuse to name. "Has he now? How fortunate for all of us." She gestures to the booth. "Please, join me. I'm curious what kind of journalist earns Nico's trust. And catches his eye. They're typically such messy creatures."

We slide into the plush semicircular booth, Isabel deliberately indicating Lea should sit between us. Strategic, yes, but it also places Lea closer to *her*. I signal for fresh drinks, then settle back, draping one arm casually along the back of the seat behind Lea. Not touching, but reinforcing my claim, my presence.

"I was just telling Nico about some potential investment opportunities in the shipping sector," Isabel continues, her attention ostensibly on business, though her gaze keeps drifting back to Lea. "The Panama expansion has created interesting openings."

"Shipping?" Lea inquires, her tone neutral, seemingly oblivious to the undercurrent. "That seems rather conventional for a private meeting in an underground club."

Isabel's laugh is crystal sharp. "Conventional investments rarely require such discreet negotiation, Ms. Song." Her smile, when directed at Lea, is notably brighter. "But perhaps you understand that better than most, given your mother's expertise in international relations."

I feel Lea's body tense beside me, though her expression betrays nothing. Impressive control. I hadn't mentioned Eunji Song to Isabel, which means she's done her homework on Lea. The depth of that research now feels pointed.

"My mother's academic work focuses on theoretical power structures," Lea replies evenly. "I doubt it has much application to shipping investments."

"Theory and practice often intersect in surprising ways," Isabel counters, swirling her drink, her knee subtly brushing Lea's under the table. Accident? Unlikely. Isabel is never careless. "Much like journalism and...what shall we call it? Mediation?"

I intervene before Isabel can push further, steering the conversation back to firmer ground while subtly increasing my proximity to Lea, my shoulder now a breath away from hers. "Isabel has been exploring alternative routes for certain specialty imports," I explain. "The challenge is ensuring these routes remain uncontested."

Understanding flickers in Lea's eyes. "And you provide that assurance," she says.

"For a fee," I confirm.

"What happens if the guarantee fails?" Lea asks, looking directly at Isabel, seemingly unaware of the subtle proprietary game being played around her.

A beat of silence. "Then we would have a very different conversation," Isabel says, her smile never wavering, though her eyes briefly meet mine over Lea's head, a silent challenge. "But Nico's guarantees rarely fail. That's why he commands such respect."

Lea nods. "And these specialty imports," she continues, "they must be quite valuable..."

Isabel's gaze flicks to mine, amusement dancing there. "Your journalist has a talent for understatement, Nico." She turns back to Lea, leaning slightly closer to her. "Let's just say the markup makes the risk worthwhile."

The conversation flows, but I track Isabel's focus. While discussing shipping schedules and port security, her attention is almost entirely on Lea. She listens intently when Lea speaks, her questions occasionally veering toward the personal veiled as professional curiosity. Lea handles it beautifully, deflecting with skill, yet I feel a low growl building in my chest. Not jealousy. It's control. Isabel is attempting to engage *my* asset on her own terms.

Lea's intelligence *is* arousing, her quick grasp of the subtext impressive. But Isabel's appreciative glances, the way her gaze lingers on Lea's mouth when she speaks – it's grating.

"Your distribution network in the university district," Isabel redirects to me, pulling my attention back. "Has it recovered...?"

The question pulls my attention back to business. She's referring to Moretti's recent encroachment on territory I've long kept neutral.

"The situation is being managed," I reply, my tone cooling several degrees. "Temporary fluctuations in market share are to be expected in any enterprise."

Isabel's dark eyes glint. "Of course. I merely wondered if our mutual friend's ambitions might affect our arrangement."

"Dante Moretti's ambitions are precisely that, his alone." I keep my voice level despite the surge of irritation the name provokes. "My guarantees remain solid."

"Good to hear." Isabel sets down her glass with a decisive click. "Then I believe we have an understanding about the first shipment."

I incline my head in agreement, recognizing the natural conclusion of our business. Isabel stands, elegant as a jungle cat. She extends her hand first to me, then turns to Lea, holding her hand perhaps a fraction longer than necessary.

"Ms. Song, it's been truly enlightening," she says, her smile directed solely at Lea now. "Perhaps we can continue this conversation another time? Discuss market dynamics further?"

Lea rises to the occasion. "I always strive for accuracy within the constraints of my agreements," she replies politely, subtly sidestepping the invitation while meeting Isabel's gaze.

Isabel's smile widens. "A diplomatic answer worthy of your companion." She finally turns to me. "She's quick, your journalist. And quite captivating. I see why you keep her close." The possessive pronoun grates. She is *mine* to keep close.

With that parting observation, she glides away. I watch her go, calculating, yes, but also suppressing the urge to physically mark Lea as mine in front of the entire room. This possessiveness is inconvenient, a potential vulnerability. I dismiss it. Control is paramount. Satisfied that the primary business objective was achieved, I return my attention to Lea.

She's staring after Isabel, a complicated mix of emotions playing across her face. Fascination, apprehension, curiosity... and perhaps a touch of flattery she hasn't yet processed.

"You just helped arrange a drug shipment, didn't you?" she asks quietly.

I don't insult her intelligence by denying it. "I facilitated a business transaction between interested parties," I correct. "The specific cargo is not my concern."

"But you know what it is."

"I know many things, piccola. Knowledge is currency in my world."

She turns to face me, challenge sparking in her dark eyes. "And what am I supposed to do with what I've just learned? Write about how Nico Varela brokers cocaine deals in his underground club while politicians drink at the next table?"

"You'll write what serves the greater truth," I reply, placing my hand at the small of her back once more. The contact sends that same current of awareness through me. "Which might not be the same as reporting every detail you witness."

I guide her away from the VIP section, feeling the subtle resistance in her posture. She's conflicted. Torn between her journalist's instinct to expose and her growing understanding of the complex ecosystem she's witnessing.

"Come," I say, changing tactics. "There's more to Undertow than business negotiations."

We move through the crowd until we reach the sunken dance floor. Here, the music is louder, the bass vibrating through the floorboards and up into my bones. Lasers slice through a low haze of smoke, illuminating bodies moving in sinuous rhythm. The energy here is primal and sensual.

Lea hesitates at the edge, her eyes darting across the throng of dancers. The press of bodies, the heavy throb of music, the swirl of perfumes and colognes and sweat, is an assault on the senses designed to lower inhibitions and heighten physical awareness.

I grasp her hand, my fingers encircling her wrist. "Dance with me," I say. Not a request, more a gentle command.

She looks up at me, uncertainty flickering across her features. For a moment, I think she might refuse. Then something shifts in her expression, a decision made, a boundary crossed.

Without waiting for further invitation, I lead her onto the floor. The crowd seems to part instinctively, creating space around us as though sensing the electric charge between us. I position us near the center, where the bass is strongest, and the lights cast alternating shadows and brightness across her face.

I settle one hand on her waist, drawing her close until our bodies align. She's rigid at first, her frame tense against mine. I can feel her warring impulses, the desire to maintain distance battling the need to blend in with the surrounding crowd.

"Relax, piccola," I murmur, my lips brushing the shell of her ear. "Let the music guide you."

She exhales, a small shudder running through her as she surrenders. Not completely, but enough that her body loosens against mine. We move together, finding a shared rhythm as the DJ transitions between tracks. Her hips sway, hesitant at first, then with growing confidence as she acclimates to our proximity.

The song shifts to something slower but more sensual; a pulsing electronic beat layered with breathy vocals in a language I don't recognize. The tempo invites closer contact, more intimate movement. I slide my thigh between her legs, a deliberate escalation that draws a sharp inhale from her.

Her eyes fly up to meet mine, surprise and something darker swimming in their depths. I hold her gaze as I guide her hips with my hands, forcing her to move against me in a way that mimics more primal rhythms. Her body responds even as uncertainty clouds her features. *Such a beautiful contradiction.*

"Your mind may resist," I say, splaying my fingers across her lower back and drawing her closer until I can feel every curve pressed against me. "But this doesn't lie."

A telling tremor runs through her, and I watch her pupils dilate in the flickering lights. Her lips part, breath coming faster, as our bodies move in synchronized motion. The heat between us builds with each beat of the music, with each slide of fabric against fabric.

For a moment, I imagine taking this further. Backing her against one of the shadowed walls, sliding my hand beneath the hem of her dress, discovering if she's as affected by our dance as the flush on her chest suggests. The image is so vivid it sends desire straight through me, and I tighten my grip on her waist to steady myself as much as her.

Lost in this fantasy, I almost miss the figure watching us from the edge of the dance floor. My gaze flicks over Lea's shoulder, and recognition is instant. He's tall, angular, wearing a dark, well-cut suit, with the deliberate stillness of someone accustomed to observing undetected. It's the same man from the surveillance photos with Professor Song. Marco hasn't been able to identify him despite exhaustive research.

The stranger lifts his glass in a subtle salute, his eyes never leaving mine. The gesture carries unmistakable meaning: acknowledgment between players in the same game. Then he melts back into the crowd, disappearing as smoothly as he appeared.

I stiffen, protectiveness surging through me with unexpected intensity. *This man's presence here, tonight, cannot be coincidence. Either he's following Lea, or he's following me. Neither option sits well. And his connection to Eunji Song complicates matters further.*

Lea senses the change in me. "What is it?" she asks, trying to turn to see what caught my attention.

I tighten my hold, preventing her from looking. "Nothing," I lie. "Just someone I'd rather avoid discussing business with tonight."

She doesn't believe me. I can see it in the slight narrowing of her eyes, but she doesn't press further. Instead, she notices how tightly I'm now holding her, how possessively my body curves around hers. A question forms in her expression, but the music swells before she can voice it.

"Come with me," I say, not waiting for her response as I lead her from the dance floor toward a narrow corridor flanking its edge.

The passage is dimly lit and lined with alcoves, each separated from the main hallway by heavy curtains that provide varying degrees of privacy for couples or small groups seeking escape from the club's energy. I guide her toward one at the far end. It's not completely secluded, but discreet enough for what I have in mind.

She follows, unsteady from our dance, or perhaps from the tension still crackling between us. When we stand amidst the subdued lighting and plush cushions of the alcove, she looks up at me with questioning silence.

Heart still pounding from our dance and the unwelcome observer, I crowd her against the velvet-padded wall. The thick curtain conceals us from passing glances, creating a pocket of relative privacy amid the club's controlled chaos. My gaze sweeps over her, taking in the flush that extends from her cheeks down her neck, the way her dress clings to her skin where a light sheen of perspiration makes the silk adhere to her curves.

I lean in, allowing my lips to hover just above her throat. I can feel her pulse hammering beneath the delicate skin, smell the intoxicating blend of her perfume and natural scent. When I make contact, the lightest brush of my mouth, she gasps, her hands flying up to grip the lapels of my jacket.

I trail kisses along the column of her throat, each one a deliberate tease. Her grip on my jacket tightens, her body arching toward mine despite her obvious effort to maintain control. I revel in it, this delicious contradiction of resistance and surrender, the way she fights her own desire even as it overwhelms her.

My hands slide to her hips, fingers digging into the soft flesh with enough pressure to leave marks, a primal part of me wants to brand her, to ensure that long after tonight, she'll carry physical reminders of this moment. I nip at the juncture where her neck meets her shoulder, drawing another sharp inhale from her.

I'm about to deepen the kiss, to taste more of her skin, when voices pass nearby, a reminder that we are, in fact, in a public space, surrounded by people who would pay close attention to any hint of weakness or distraction on my part.

I pull away, noting the flicker of disappointment and confusion that crosses Lea's face. I smooth my expression, affecting a coolness I don't feel as I step back.

"Don't forget your purpose," I admonish, though whether I'm reminding her or myself is unclear. "You came for a story, not this."

The words come out harsher than intended, half-sneer, half-warning, a desperate attempt to regain control over both her reactions and my own spiraling hunger. Something flashes in her eyes, hurt, perhaps, or anger at being reminded of the transactional nature of our arrangement.

I lead her out of the alcove, straightening my jacket with practiced nonchalance. As we emerge back into the main corridor, I cast one last glance at her parted lips, the lingering flush on her cheeks, the slight tremble in her hands as she smooths her dress.

The evidence of her desire only confirms what I already know: she's close to craving this world, and me, more than she dares admit. It should bring me satisfaction, a sense of victory in my careful seduction.

Instead, as we make our way back toward the club's main floor, I'm unsettled by the intensity of my response to her. This is to be a detached game, another move in the complex strategy surrounding Eunji Song and Moretti's ambitions.

Is it become something more?

The question lingers, unanswered, as we step back into the pulsing heart of Undertow, where secrets and desires swirl like smoke beneath the surface of Chicago's power structure and where, I'm realizing, I might be in danger of losing control of the very game I've mastered for so long.

CHAPTER SIXTEEN

Lea

I WAKE WITH A SCREAM LODGED IN MY THROAT, MY BODY jackknifing upright as if pulled by invisible strings. My chest constricts, sweat plastering my thin tank top to my skin. The darkness of my bedroom feels oppressive, closing in around me as I gasp for air.

Mom.

The dream clings to me, my mother running through unfamiliar alleys, her face twisted in terror as someone pursued her. The details are already dissolving, but the raw fear remains, an ache spreading through my chest as if it's my own lungs burning from the chase.

I press trembling fingers to my lips, trying to steady my breathing. *It was just a dream. Just a nightmare.* But deep in my gut, a cold certainty tells me it's more than that. The panic feels too authentic, too visceral to be merely a product of my subconscious.

My fingers fumble for the lamp switch, bathing the room

in a soft glow that does little to dispel the shadows lurking in the corners. The clock reads 3:17 AM. Too early to call anyone, too late to fall back asleep. I swing my legs over the edge of the bed, the floor cool beneath my bare feet.

The buzzing of my phone startles me and I nearly knock it off the nightstand. The screen illuminates with a name that sends a different kind of shiver through me.

Nico.

My finger hovers over the screen. *It can't be coincidence that he's calling at the exact moment I've jolted awake from a nightmare.* Has he somehow sensed my distress? Or is it something more sinister? A camera hidden in my bedroom, watching my every move?

The thought makes my stomach clench, but I answer anyway, some part of me craving the steady anchor of his voice despite everything.

"Bad dream?" His voice slides through the speaker, low and intimate, as if he's lying right beside me instead of wherever he is at this ungodly hour.

A chill traces. "How did you know that?"

"Your breathing." He sounds almost amused. "It's erratic. Panicked. And it's the middle of the night. What else would have you so worked up?"

I glance around my bedroom, eyes darting to every corner, every shadow that might conceal a lens. "Are you watching me?" The question comes out more vulnerable than accusatory.

"Not at the moment, no." His answer leaves room for interpretation, and I'm not sure if that's worse. "Do you want to talk about it?"

I should hang up. I should be outraged at the invasion of

privacy, at the cavalier way he admits to surveillance without actually confirming it. Instead, I'm sinking back against my pillows, my free hand clutching the comforter to my chest.

"I dreamed about my mother," I confess, surprising myself. "She was running from something, someone. She was terrified."

Silence stretches between us for a moment. When he speaks again, the usual hard edge is gone from his voice. "Dreams often manifest our deepest fears, not reality."

"This felt different." I close my eyes, trying to recapture the fading images. "It felt real."

"I had nightmares as a child," Nico says. "About drowning. My uncle would find me thrashing in my bed and tell me that fear was just the mind's way of preparing for threats that might never materialize."

The admission catches me off guard. A glimpse of vulnerability from a man who has built his entire existence around projecting strength and control. I try to picture him as a boy, frightened and small, before the world, and his uncle, shaped him into the dangerous force he is now.

"Did they ever stop? The nightmares?"

"Eventually." There's a hint of something darker in his tone. "Once I learned to control my environment, to eliminate threats before they could touch me."

The implication behind his words sends another wave of cold through me, but there's also something comforting in his brutal honesty. No platitudes, no empty reassurances, just the cold reality of how he's chosen to face his demons.

"Your mother is a capable woman, Lea," he continues, steering the conversation back. "More capable than perhaps you realize."

My eyes snap open. "What's that supposed to mean?"

"That she's navigated complex situations for years. Academia can be its own kind of battleground."

There's something he's not saying, something he's withholding, and it makes my heart quicken again. But before I can press him, he shifts tactics.

"Focus on your breathing. In through your nose for four seconds, hold it for another four, then breathe out through your mouth for six seconds. Repeat. Slow and steady."

I want to resist, to demand answers about what he knows about my mother, but my body betrays me; I follow his instructions, my breathing syncing with the calm, measured cadence of his voice as he continues to murmur directions.

"Better?" he asks after a minute.

"Yes," I admit. My heart rate has slowed to a more normal rhythm, the panic receding like a tide pulling back from shore.

"Good. Now lie back and close your eyes."

I comply without thinking, settling deeper into my pillows. "Are you always this bossy at three in the morning?"

A low chuckle rumbles through the line. "I'm always this bossy, period. You're just more inclined to listen when you're vulnerable."

The observation stings because it's true. In my current state, half-awake, rattled by nightmares, alone in the dark, I'm finding a strange comfort in his authoritative tone, in having someone else take control, even if just for a few minutes.

"Tell me about your first memory," he blurts.

"What?"

"Your earliest memory. I want to know what shaped Lea Song from the beginning."

I hesitate, but the request seems harmless enough, and the distraction is welcome. "We were in London. I was maybe three or four. My mother was teaching me to write my name in Korean. I remember the smell of ink and the way she guided my hand across the paper, her fingers warm around mine."

As I speak, the tension continues to drain from my body. I tell him about the pride I felt when I finally got it right, the way my mother's face lit up with a smile reserved just for me. It's a simple memory, but tender, a glimpse of a time before life grew complicated, before I began questioning the woman who raised me.

"She's always been your safe harbor," Nico observes.

"Yes." My voice catches. "Which is why this dream has me so rattled. I've never seen her afraid like that, not even in my imagination."

"Dreams reflect our own fears more often than reality," he repeats, but there's less conviction this time, as if he too is considering darker possibilities.

We lapse into silence, but it's comfortable. I can hear his steady breathing, the occasional soft rustle as he shifts position wherever he is. It's strange to feel this connected to someone through just a phone line, especially someone who represents everything I should be fighting against.

"You should try to sleep now," he says finally. "You have a long day tomorrow."

"I do?" *This is news to me.*

"We're attending a dinner. Senator Wright's fundraiser. I'll send a car for you at seven."

The abrupt shift back to business catches me off guard. "Don't I get a say in this?"

"You agreed to follow my lead, remember? Besides, the senator sits on the committee that oversees pharmaceutical regulations. His guests might provide valuable context for your article."

He's dangling access again, using my journalistic ambition as bait. The worst part is, it works. My mind begins cataloging the potential connections, the doors that might open at an event like this.

"Fine," I concede, too tired to argue. "But I choose what I wear this time."

"As long as it's appropriate for the setting." His tone, smooth but absolute, makes it clear he'll have the final say, regardless.

I should push back, set firmer boundaries, but exhaustion is pulling me under again, my eyelids growing heavy. "Goodnight, Nico."

"Sleep well, piccola." His voice has that softer quality again, the one that makes my chest tighten with emotions I can't, or won't, name. "No more nightmares tonight."

It sounds almost like a promise, a command to my subconscious. And strangely, as I drift back toward sleep with the phone still pressed to my ear, I believe him.

MORNING LIGHT FILTERS through my blinds, painting stripes across my rumpled sheets. I blink groggily, disoriented until last night's conversation comes flooding back. The phone lies beside my pillow, battery drained from the hourslong call. *I must have fallen asleep with Nico still on the line.*

The lack of disturbance unnerves me.

I drag myself to the shower, letting hot water sluice away the remnants of my nightmares. But no amount of scrubbing can wash away the heavy weight that has taken up residence in my stomach. My mother's terrified face keeps flashing behind my eyelids, along with Nico's cryptic comments about her capabilities.

Forty minutes later, I'm dressed in jeans and a simple blouse, my damp hair pulled back in a loose ponytail. The clock reads just past nine, still early enough to catch my mother at her university office hours if I hurry.

THE CAMPUS IS BUZZING with midweek energy when I arrive. Students hurry between buildings clutching over-sized coffees, professors huddle in small clusters engaged in animated discussions, and tour groups wind their way across the manicured lawns. The Political Science building rises at the far end of the quad, its limestone facade weathered with age and academic prestige.

I take the stairs two at a time, anticipation building with each step. My mother's office is on the third floor, tucked away in the corner of the east wing. I've visited countless times over the years, finding comfort in its familiar smell of old books and the jasmine tea she always keeps stocked.

But today, something feels off the moment I round the corner. Her door stands half-open, which is unusual. She's meticulous about privacy, always closing it fully during meetings and when she's away. Through the gap, I can see the lights are on, but there's no sound of movement or conversation from within.

"Mom?" I call out, pushing the door wider.

The office is empty. Not just of my mother, but of the usual tidiness that defines her workspace. Papers are scattered across the desk, a mug of tea sits half-drunk and long cold, and a drawer hangs open with documents threatening to spill out. It looks as if she left in a hurry, with no time to straighten up.

A chill runs through me, reminiscent of my nightmare. Eunji Song is many things, but disorganized has never been one of them.

"Oh! You're Professor Song's daughter, right?"

I startle at the voice, turning to find a harried-looking young man juggling an armful of papers and a tablet. I recognize him as my mother's teaching assistant, though I can't recall his name.

"Yes, I'm Lea. Is my mother around?"

"No, she left yesterday for a research trip." He shifts the papers, nearly dropping them before regaining his balance. "Rather suddenly, actually. Asked me to cover her under-graduate lectures for the week."

My insides twist. "Did she say where she was going?"

"She didn't specify." He shrugs, looking puzzled. "Just said it was an important opportunity that couldn't wait. No details on location or duration."

That doesn't sound like my mother at all. She plans everything meticulously, especially academic travel. And she always, always tells me first.

"That's odd," I manage, trying to keep my voice casual. "She usually gives more notice."

"Yeah, threw the entire department for a loop. Dean was

pretty upset about it." He gestures toward the office. "I was just coming to grab her lecture notes for tomorrow's class."

I step aside to let him enter, my mind racing. *A sudden, unplanned trip. No communication. An uncharacteristically messy office. None of it makes sense.*

While the TA rummages through a stack of folders on the desk, I edge closer to the open drawer. Through the gap, I can see the corner of a red folder marked with symbols, geometric shapes arranged in a pattern that looks almost like an insignia or logo.

Adrenaline surge as I lean against the desk, allowing my hand to drift toward the drawer. *If I could just get a better look.*

"Here we go!" The TA's triumphant voice makes me jump. He waves a folder labeled "International Security Frameworks: Undergrad." "Found what I needed."

I straighten quickly, my chance lost. "Great. Listen, if you hear from her, could you ask her to call me? It's important."

"Sure thing." He tucks the folder under his arm, then seems to remember his manners. "Oh, I should lock up when we leave. Professor's orders."

"Of course." I grab a textbook from the desk, making a show of leafing through it. "Just give me a minute to check something for my research."

He nods, stepping back into the hallway to reorganize his armful of papers. The moment he's out of sight, I lunge for the drawer, sliding it open further. The red folder sits beneath a stack of academic journals. The paper feels thick and glossy under my fingertips. I lift it, flipping it open to reveal a single sheet of paper covered in what looks like a shipping manifest, columns of numbers and cryptic abbreviations that mean nothing to me.

But what catches my eye is the header: a stylized logo with Korean characters I can't quite make out, alongside the English letters "NK Pharma Consolidated."

A polite cough from the doorway sends me scrambling to shove the folder back and close the drawer. The TA stands there, keys jingling impatiently in his hand.

"Sorry," I say, forcing a casual smile as I hold up the textbook. "Just checking a reference."

He nods, though his expression suggests he's not convinced. "I really need to lock up now. Department policy."

I have no choice but to leave, my mind buzzing with questions. What could my mother be researching that involves pharma companies? And why the secrecy?

Outside, I stand on the steps of the building, trying to make sense of it all. I pull out my phone to call her again, but the call goes straight to voicemail. The dread in my stomach has grown into a solid mass.

What have you gotten yourself into, Mom?

THE SENATOR'S mansion sprawls across a meticulously landscaped acre on Chicago's North Shore, its limestone facade glowing warmly in the evening light. A line of luxury vehicles winds up the circular driveway, disgorging passengers in formal attire who ascend the broad steps with practiced elegance.

I tug at the hem of my midnight blue cocktail dress, self-conscious about my choice. It's the most expensive piece in my wardrobe, a gift from my mother, but among these people, it looks like off-the-rack mediocrity.

"Stop fidgeting," Nico murmurs. "You look beautiful."

He's resplendent in a tailored tuxedo that emphasizes his broad shoulders and lean waist. The fabric is so fine it seems to absorb light rather than reflect it, giving him an almost predatory sleekness.

"I feel out of place," I admit as we hand our invitation to a white-gloved attendant.

"You're not." His voice is firm, brooking no argument. "You belong wherever I bring you, Lea. Remember that."

The possessive edge to his words should offend me. Instead, they send a treacherous warmth spreading through my chest. I've spent the day distracted by worry about my mother, by the mysterious folder and her sudden disappearance. But now, with Nico standing as my silent anchor, I feel grounded in a way I can't quite explain.

We step into a grand foyer where crystal chandeliers cast prismatic light across marble floors. The air is heavy with expensive perfume, cigar smoke, and the particular scent of old money, a blend of entitlement and aged whiskey that clings to those born into privilege.

"Senator," Nico greets our host with a firm handshake. "Thank you for the invitation."

Senator Wright is a silver-haired man with a politician's perfect smile and eyes that calculate your value with every glance. "Nico! Delighted you could make it." He looks at me, assessment giving way to curiosity. "And this lovely young woman is?"

"Lea Song," I answer before Nico can, extending my hand. "Journalist with the Chicago Investigative Journal."

If my profession surprises him, he hides it well. "A journalist! How refreshing to have someone from the fourth estate who isn't shouting questions at me outside a committee hearing." He chuckles, but there's a new wariness in his eyes as he looks between Nico and me.

"Ms. Song is working on a piece about business leadership in Chicago," Nico explains. "I'm one of her subjects."

The senator's eyebrows lift, but he doesn't pursue it. "Well, please enjoy yourselves. Dinner will be served in half an hour. Until then, the bar is open, and the company is, I hope, stimulating."

He moves on to greet other guests, and Nico steers me deeper into the gathering. The dining room opens before us: a lavish spectacle of crisp white tablecloths, gleaming silverware, and floral arrangements. Around the edges of the room, clusters of Chicago's elite engage in the careful dance of networking, their laughter a little too loud, their smiles a little too fixed.

"Try not to look so overwhelmed," Nico says, his lips brushing my ear. "These people can smell fear."

I shoot him a glare. "I'm not afraid. I'm observing."

A hint of a smile tugs at his mouth. "Then observe while looking like you belong. Tonight, you're not an outsider looking in, you're with me, which puts you at the center."

Before I can argue, he's threading his arm through mine, guiding me toward a group. Without missing a beat, Nico introduces me to each one, a federal judge, a shipping magnate, the CEO of a pharmaceutical conglomerate, as if

I'm an integral part of his world rather than a temporary attachment.

What's most unsettling is how seamlessly he moves between personas. With the judge, he's deferential but knowledgeable about recent rulings. With the shipping magnate, he's all business acumen and industry insights. With the CEO, he shifts to casual bonhomie, asking about the man's recent fishing trip to Alaska.

Each conversation reveals a different facet of Nico Varela, yet none seems to capture his true essence. I'm watching him more than participating, fascinated by this chameleon-like ability to be whatever the situation demands.

"Lea Song?" A voice interrupts my observations. "I thought that was you."

I turn to find Professor James Wong, a colleague of my mother's from the Political Science department. His silver-rimmed glasses catch the light as he offers a polite smile.

"Professor Wong," I greet him, pleased to see a familiar face. "I didn't expect to see you here."

"Academic consultants occasionally get invited to the halls of power," he says with a self-deprecating shrug. "Though I suspect it's more for the university's endowment potential than my insights on East Asia politics."

I laugh, relaxing for the first time since entering the mansion. "How is the department? I stopped by my mother's office today, but she wasn't there."

Something flickers across his face, concern, perhaps, or caution. "Yes, her sudden trip caught us all off guard. Very unusual for Eunji to leave without proper arrangements."

"Did she mention anything to you before she left? Any hint about where she was going?"

Professor Wong's gaze darts past me, and I realize Nico has stepped away to speak with the senator. We're unobserved in the crowded room.

Leaning in, Wong lowers his voice. "Your mother's recent work is more extensive than she lets on. She's tapping doors few would dare to open." His eyes hold a warning. "Be careful about the questions you ask, Lea. And perhaps more careful about the company you keep."

My blood runs cold. "What do you mean? What doors?"

Before he can answer, a presence materializes at my side. Nico, radiating that quiet power that seems to bend the air around him. "Professor," he says cordially, though his eyes are cold. "I don't believe we've been introduced."

Wong straightens, offering a tight smile. "James Wong, Political Science. I was just catching up with my colleague's daughter."

"How fortunate for us to have such distinguished academic representation tonight." Nico's tone is pleasant, but the message is clear: this conversation is over.

"Indeed." Wong nods, already backing away. "If you'll excuse me, I should pay my respects to the senator before dinner. Lea, always good to see you."

As he disappears into the crowd, I turn on Nico. "That was rude."

"That was necessary," he counters, sliding his hand into mine and interlacing our fingers. The possessive gesture is both a comfort and a constraint. "Come, they're seating for dinner."

I want to pull away, to chase after Wong and demand answers about my mother's mysterious "doors," but Nico's grip is firm as he leads me toward a table near the center of the room. The placement is deliberate, I realize, close enough to the senator to signal favor, but with clear sightlines to every entrance and exit. *Always the strategist, even at a social dinner.*

We're seated with the pharmaceutical CEO and his wife, a federal prosecutor and her husband, and a state representative whose name I recognize from campaign signs. The conversation flows around me, healthcare policy, regulatory challenges, the upcoming election cycle, but my mind keeps circling back to Wong's cryptic warning.

Under the table, Nico's hand finds mine again, his thumb tracing small circles on my palm. It's a simple gesture, but it sends a warm ripple through me, anchoring me to the present moment. Despite the opulence surrounding us, despite the power players and their purposeful conversation, that single point of contact feels like the most real thing in the room.

I lean into it, allowing myself to be steadied by his touch.

"You've been quiet," he murmurs as dessert is served, a delicate chocolate confection that looks to die for.

"I'm taking it all in," I reply, which isn't entirely a lie. "This is quite a different world from the newsroom."

"Is it so difficult to imagine yourself belonging here?" His eyes hold mine, searching for something I'm not sure I want him to find.

"Yes," I answer. "I'm an observer, not a participant. That's what journalists do."

His lips curve into a smile that doesn't reach his eyes. "And yet, here you are, taking part. Wearing the dress, playing the role, enjoying the benefits of access."

The observation stings because it's accurate. I am playing a role, walking a dangerous line between observer and accomplice. And the most unsettling part is how natural it's beginning to feel.

"It's for the story," I insist, as much to convince myself as him.

"Is it?" His voice drops lower, intimate in a way that makes my blood rush. "Then tell me, piccola, why have your notes become so selective lately? What happened to the ruthless reporter who was going to expose all my secrets?"

My cheeks burn with the realization that he's been reading my notes, another violation of privacy that I should be outraged about. Instead, I'm more disturbed by the truth of his observation. My documentation has become selective, omitting details that might paint him in a damning light: the way he strong-armed that city contractor, his subtle threats to the judge who seemed reluctant to grant a specific motion, the network of informants that keeps him three steps ahead of his rivals.

When did I start protecting him?

"I'm still gathering information," I say. "Building a complete picture."

"Of course." His smile tells me he sees right through the excuse. "And when this picture is complete, what then? Will you write about the monsters or the men? The systems or the individuals caught within them?"

It's a question I've been avoiding, one that grows more complicated with each day I spend in his world. The black-and-white morality I arrived with has dissolved into countless shades of gray, and I'm no longer certain where to draw the line, or if lines even matter in a world where everyone seems to have their own version of right and wrong.

"I don't know," I admit, the honesty surprising us both.

His hand tightens around mine, a gentle pressure that feels like approval. "That's the first true thing you've said all night."

The moment is broken by the tinkling of a spoon against crystal, signaling the senator's closing remarks. As attention shifts to our host, I'm left with the uncomfortable awareness that I've crossed some invisible threshold. My journalistic objectivity is compromised, my moral compass spinning without a clear north.

And the most terrifying part? I'm not sure I want to find my way back.

———

MY APARTMENT FEELS SMALLER than usual when I return, the walls closing in with the weight of unanswered questions. I kick off my heels, wincing as my feet throb from hours of standing on marble floors and pretending to belong among the wealthy and powerful.

The dress joins a growing pile of laundry in the corner, another aspect of my life that's fallen into disarray since Nico Varela entered it. I slip into an oversized t-shirt and pajama shorts, then pad to my desk where my laptop waits, screen dark and accusing.

With a sigh, I open it, pulling up the document that has become both my salvation and my damnation:

Varela Investigation—CONFIDENTIAL

The file has grown to over thirty pages of notes, observations, recorded conversations, those I could sneak without detection, and cross-referenced connections between Nico's various associates.

I scroll through it, eyes catching on phrases that leap from the screen:

Primary source confirms Varela's involvement in mediating territory dispute between Ukranian and Polish factions.

City contract awarded to GreenSpace Development, suspected Varela shell company, despite three lower bids.

Judge Hernandez's son's DUI charges mysteriously disappeared following a private meeting with Varela.

But what strikes me most are the omissions, the details I've chosen not to record. I've left out how Nico intervened when one of his club employees was being stalked by an ex, ensuring the man was arrested on outstanding warrants before he could cause harm. I've omitted the way he funds a shelter for trafficked women, requiring absolute anonymity for his donations.

I've said nothing about the genuine concern in his voice when he called me during my nightmare, or how it anchored me when panic threatened to pull me under.

These are the complexities that don't fit into the narrative of "criminal empire builder" I set out to expose. They're the inconvenient truths that challenge my preconceptions and blur the lines I thought were so clearly drawn.

With growing unease, I realize I'm censoring myself, protecting Nico from the very exposure I promised to deliver. The journalist I was when this assignment began would be appalled at my selective reporting, my willingness to look away from certain truths while highlighting others.

I close the laptop without adding a single word about tonight's dinner, about Professor Wong's warning, or about the pharmaceutical connection I discovered in my mother's office. These threads are beginning to weave together into a pattern I'm afraid to see clearly, one that might implicate not just Nico, but my own mother in something darker than I'm prepared to face.

The question that gnaws at me now isn't just about Nico's world and how deeply I've sunk into it. It's about whether I'll be able to extricate myself at all when the time comes. And more disturbing still: whether I'll want to.

Because the truth, the one I can barely admit even to myself as I curl up on my couch, phone clutched in my hand as if expecting another late-night call, is that I'm starting to crave the complexity of his world. The power, the danger, the inexplicable safety I feel when his hand finds mine under a table full of criminals and politicians.

What kind of person does that make me?

The question hangs in the darkness of my apartment, unanswered, as I drift into a fitful sleep haunted by dreams of my mother running through endless corridors, a red folder clutched to her chest, never quite escaping the shadows that pursue her, or the ones that have taken root in my heart.

CHAPTER SEVENTEEN

Nico

THE SECURITY FEEDS STREAM ACROSS SIX DIFFERENT monitors, each displaying a different angle of Purgatorio's main floor. I relax in my chair, fingers steepled as I track the movements of a particular guest, a city councilman with gambling debts who's been making noise about increased police presence in my territory. His nervous glances toward the VIP area tell me he received my message. *Good. One less problem to manage.*

My office is silent except for the soft hum of electronics and the occasional ice cube settling in my whiskey. This is where I'm most comfortable, surrounded by information, watching the pieces move across my board, orchestrating from a distance. The dim lighting casts everything in shadow, the way I prefer it. Darkness has always been where I excel.

A sharp knock interrupts my thoughts.

"Come in," I say, not taking my eyes off the monitors.

Marco enters and closes the door behind him, waiting for

permission to approach. I appreciate this discipline, the understanding that every interaction follows a protocol.

I wave him forward.

"They've marked her apartment," Marco says, sliding several surveillance photos across my desk.

I pick them up, my face betraying nothing as I examine the images. One of the twins photographing entry points to Lea's building. Mapping security cameras. Timing the doorman's breaks. Methodical. Professional. Exactly what I'd expect from Moretti's men.

My jaw tightens. Not from concern for Lea's safety, but from the cold fury at Moretti's audacity.

"He's targeting my assets now," I state, my voice calm despite the rage building underneath.

Marco nods, understanding the distinction. *This isn't about me going soft on Lea. She's a chess piece in my larger strategy to control the drug trade flowing through Chicago. Lea Song is valuable precisely because of her connection to her mother and the university pharmaceutical pipeline I've been tracking for months. Moretti daring to touch what's mine is unacceptable.*

I rise, buttoning my suit jacket.

"Have the car ready. And initiate Protocol 4 for the safe house on Michigan Avenue."

"Already on it," Marco replies, falling into step behind me as I stride toward the door.

"And Marco," I pause, hand on the doorknob, "double the surveillance on Professor Song's associates and communications. I want to know the moment she makes contact from her 'research' trip. If Moretti is making a move on the daughter, he might try to reach the mother as well."

I don't wait for his acknowledgement. It's unnecessary. In fifteen years, Marco has never failed to execute my orders as intended.

The Chicago Investigative Journal occupies the third floor of a converted warehouse in the West Loop. The space is industrial, exposed brick, steel beams, concrete floors, as if the architectural rawness might somehow translate to journalistic integrity. I find the aesthetic pretentious, much like the profession itself.

Heads turn as I cross the open newsroom, conversations faltering mid-sentence. My reputation precedes me, as always. I've cultivated this effect over the years, the blend of respect and fear that compels people to seek my notice while dreading it.

I spot Lea at her desk in the corner, hunched over her keyboard, oblivious to my arrival. Her hair falls forward, obscuring her face as her fingers fly across the keys. I stand beside her, not announcing my presence, simply waiting to be acknowledged.

One by one, her colleagues notice me looming over her workspace. Their stares eventually alert her to my presence. She looks up, surprise flashing across her features before she masks it with practiced indifference.

"Nico," she says, as if my appearance in her workplace is perfectly normal. "I wasn't expecting you."

I don't waste time with pleasantries. "We need to go. Now."

She frowns, glancing at her screen. "I'm in the middle of something. Can it wait twenty minutes?"

"No." The single word carries enough weight to silence whatever argument she was preparing. Something in my expression must communicate the urgency, because she saves her work and closes her laptop without further protest.

As she gathers her things, I scan the room. At least three people are already on their phones, no doubt sharing the news that Nico Varela collected the junior reporter who's been shadowing him. By tomorrow, the rumors will have evolved into something far more salacious. *Good. Let them talk. Public perception is another tool in my arsenal.*

In the elevator, I position myself close to her, using proximity as both intimidation and protection. She presses herself against the wall, creating distance. I can smell her perfume. It's becoming recognizable to me now, this scent that means Lea.

"Moretti's men are planning to take you," I explain as we descend. "That would be inconvenient for my plans."

Her eyes widen. "Take me? You mean kidnap me?"

"Yes." I see no reason to sugarcoat the reality. "They've been surveilling your apartment building for the past thirty-six hours. Establishing patterns. Identifying vulnerabilities."

She swallows hard, absorbing this. "And you know this because?"

"Because I have people watching your building too." *I don't mention that my surveillance predates Moretti's by several months. Some details are best kept private.*

The elevator doors open, and I guide her through the lobby, my hand touching her back. She doesn't pull away, which tells me the threat of Moretti has already accomplished what weeks of careful manipulation couldn't: made her acknowledge her dependence on my protection.

My driver has the car waiting, engine running. I usher Lea into the backseat before sliding in beside her. The vehicle pulls away from the curb, following the evasive route I've established for high-security transports.

"Where are we going?" she asks, clutching her bag to her chest like a shield.

I don't answer, instead watching the city blur past the tinted windows. We take three unnecessary turns, double back twice, and drive through a parking garage before emerging onto Lake Shore Drive heading north. Standard protocol to ensure we're not followed.

I observe Lea's reflection in the window glass. Her composure is admirable, hands steady, breathing controlled, eyes alert. But there are tells for those who know how to look: the slight tension around her mouth, or the almost imperceptible bounce of her right knee. *She's frightened but refuses to show it. This combination of vulnerability and strength continues to intrigue me, though I'm careful not to let the interest become a liability.*

After twenty minutes of silence, the car pulls up to a sleek high-rise overlooking the lake. The doorman is one of my people, though he's on the building's official payroll. He give me a subtle nod as we enter the marble lobby. In the private elevator, I press my thumb to the biometric scanner and enter a six-digit code.

"Where are we?" Lea asks as the doors slide open to reveal a private foyer.

"Somewhere Moretti can't reach you," I answer, unlocking the apartment door.

I walk in first, performing a habitual scan of the space even though I know it's secure. The apartment is immaculately designed, floor-to-ceiling windows showcasing Chicago's skyline, Italian leather furniture in shades of gray and black, minimalist art on the walls. The air is still, cool, carrying the faint, sterile scent of professional cleaning. Nothing personal, nothing that could reveal anything about me or my tastes. It's designed to be impressive without being informative.

Lea steps inside, taking in the luxurious surroundings. "This is yours?"

"In a manner of speaking." I remove my suit jacket, draping it over the back of a chair. "The bedroom's through there." I gesture down a hallway to the right.

"Bedroom?" she echoes, her expression sharpening. "Singular?"

A slight, predatory smile curve my lips. "This is a safe house meant for one occupant. You're here on my sufferance."

The implication hangs in the air. *She owes me for this protection, and payment will be expected. Whether that debt will be collected in information, cooperation, or something more physical remains deliberately ambiguous.*

She swallows, chin lifting in that defiant gesture I've come to recognize. "So what happens now?"

"Now," I say, rolling up my sleeves, "we wait for Moretti's next move."

I've established additional surveillance displays in the living room, creating a command center that gives me visual access to the building's exterior, elevator bank, stairwells, and lobby. A separate feed shows Lea's apartment building, where two of Moretti's men remain stationed in a black SUV across the street.

Lea watches me work from her perch on the edge of the sofa, arms crossed defensively. She's been quiet, processing the rapid shift in circumstances. I prefer her this way, observing rather than questioning, though I know it won't last.

"Moretti's targeting you to get to me," I explain, voice detached as I adjust a camera angle. "You're seen as my property now."

She bristles at the word "property," as I knew she would. "I'm not anyone's property."

"Perception matters more than reality in these situations." I don't bother looking up from the monitor. "You've been seen with me at multiple locations. You've been granted access to conversations and meetings no outsider would normally witness. As far as Moretti is concerned, that makes you either very valuable to me or a significant vulnerability." I turn to face her. "Possibly both."

Her eyes narrow, processing the implications. "So I'm what...bait? Leverage?"

"You're a journalist who made a deal for exclusive access," I remind her. "That access comes with certain complications."

I continue setting up the security system, outlining the situation with deliberate thoroughness. "The building has armed security. The elevator requires biometric access for this floor. The windows are bulletproof." I notice her glancing toward the door. "You could leave if you wanted. I'm not your jailer. But Moretti's men are watching your building already."

The message is obvious: her choices are my protection or Moretti's brutality.

She stands, pacing the length of the window wall, arms

still wrapped around herself. "How long do I need to stay here?"

"Until I've addressed the situation with Moretti." I don't offer a timeline because I have no intention of providing one. Uncertainty is a powerful tool for maintaining control.

"And what exactly does 'addressing the situation' entail?" She turns to face me, backlit by the city lights behind her.

I manage a cold smile. "Nothing that would interest a legitimate journalist."

She holds my gaze for a moment before looking away first, a small victory that satisfies something primal in me. *She's learning the hierarchy, whether she realizes it or not.*

"I need my laptop," she says. "And clothes. Toiletries."

I nod toward a closet by the entryway. "Marco will retrieve your essentials from your apartment tonight. In the meantime, there are basic supplies in there."

She raises an eyebrow. "You keep women's toiletries in your safe house?"

"I keep necessities in all my properties," I correct her. "Preparation is the cornerstone of effective contingency planning."

AS EVENING SETTLES, the tension between us shifts into something more complex. Sharing space creates an artificial intimacy, a forced familiarity that serves my purposes perfectly. Moretti's move against Lea confirms the situation is escalating, and Marco's preliminary reports suggest the threat might extend to me. Until we have a clearer picture of Moretti's intentions and capabilities, lying low in this secure location is the only prudent course of action, despite the inconvenience. This forced proximity, however inconvenient for business, has its advantages when it comes to Lea.

I order dinner from an exclusive restaurant that rarely delivers or allow takeout, another display of my influence that doesn't go unnoticed by Lea.

Throughout the meal, I study her with predatory interest, cataloging her unconscious habits: the way she touches her collarbone when uncomfortable, how her eyes scan for exits, the slight furrow that appears between her brows when she's thinking deeply. Each observation is filed away for future use, potential pressure points to exploit when necessary.

"Why this place?" she asks after the dishes have been cleared away.

I consider my answer, deciding to offer a crafted truth. "Because nobody knows about it. Except Marco, of course." I watch her process this information, the subtle widening of her eyes showing she understands the significance.

"Is protecting me supposed to tell me I'm special?" Her tone is sarcastic, defensive.

I shrug, deliberately casual. "Maybe just that you're useful. For now."

The ambiguity is intentional, keep her off-balance, uncertain of her status, eager to prove her value. It's a tactic I've employed countless times in negotiations, creating an atmosphere where the other party seeks approval they can never fully attain.

Night falls, and with it comes a different tension. I sit on the sofa, reviewing security feeds on my tablet. The apartment is quiet except for the sound of running water from the bathroom where Lea has retreated to shower.

I scroll through Marco's latest updates. Moretti's men have expanded their surveillance to include the newspaper offices. They're looking for her, which confirms my suspicion that this is a targeted operation rather than opportunistic intimidation. Moretti is playing a longer game, one that likely involves Professor Song and whatever arrangement she's making with the Koreans.

The bathroom door opens, and Lea emerges wearing only my white dress shirt, water darkening patches of the thin fabric where it clings to her still-damp skin. Her legs are bare, hair wet and slicked back from her face. The sight hits me with unexpected force, desire surging hot and immediate.

I set the tablet aside, giving myself time to assess the strategic value of this moment. This attraction is a tool, nothing more. A means to deepen her attachment, to create another layer of control.

"I didn't have anything else to wear until Marco gets here with my stuff," she explains, tugging self-consciously at the shirt's hem.

I rise from the sofa and approach with measured steps, like a predator stalking prey. Her eyes widen, but she stands her ground, chin lifting in that characteristic defiance that has become strangely appealing.

"We need to discuss what happens next," I say, my voice lower than intended.

I reach out, checking the bruise on her arm from Vincent. My touch lingers longer than necessary, tracing the discolored skin. Her arm is warm beneath my fingers.

My hand to slide up her arm to her neck, thumb tracing her jawline with deliberate slowness. Her breath hitches, pupils dilating as she looks up at me.

"Tell me to stop," I challenge, giving her a choice even as my other hand settles on her waist, drawing her closer.

She doesn't pull away as expected. Instead, she leans into my touch, a response that sends a jolt of triumph through me. *Not affection, I don't deal with such weaknesses, but satisfaction at her surrender. This is what I've been cultivating since our first meeting: the gradual erosion of her resistance, the slow-building dependency that will make her an effective tool in my larger strategy.*

I kiss her, claiming rather than connecting. My hands slide beneath the shirt to find warm skin, fingers tracing the curve of her waist, the jut of her hip bones. Her response is immediate and gratifying, fingers clutching my shirt, body arching into mine.

I back her against the wall, lifting her. Her legs wrap around my waist as the kiss deepens, becoming more desperate, more consuming. I'm still calculating every move, gauging her responses for future leverage, even as my body responds with genuine desire. *She's a means to an end, but a pleasurable one.*

My phone vibrates in my pocket with Marco's urgent code, three short beats, pause, two long. Years of discipline make me check it, though I don't disengage from Lea. Her soft moan as I shift against her nearly derails my focus, but the screen shows a code for critical intelligence: 8-5-3.

My mind shifts from conquest to strategy in an instant. This code indicates intelligence that could alter operational parameters, not something Marco would interrupt for unless absolutely necessary.

"I have to take this," I say, voice rough but mind already refocusing on business.

I set Lea down with visible reluctance. Her eyes are dazed, lips swollen from my kisses, the shirt rucked up to reveal the lace edge of her underwear. The image burns into my memory, fuel for later, but for now, discipline reasserts itself.

I move to the windows, putting distance between us as I return Marco's call. My expression hardens into the stony mask of The Diplomat, previous desire compartmentalized. This separation of function is second nature to me, the ability to switch between roles without emotional bleed-through is what makes me effective.

"What do you have?" I answer.

Marco's voice is crisp, professional. "Found the professor. Surveillance picked her up in DC, meeting with some Koreans. But there's more. Dante Moretti's lieutenant was in the background, monitoring the meeting."

My grip on the phone tightens. "Send me the photos."

"Already did. Check your secure server."

I end the call and access the encrypted files. The images are clear despite the low light, Professor Eunji Song in animated conversation with a man I've identified as connected to the Korean embassy. And there, obscured by a pillar but unmistakable, is Matteo Rizzo, Vincent's brother.

This confirms my suspicion that Eunji Song is coordinating something between Korean interests and Moretti's organization, a distribution channel for the fentanyl derivatives that have been flooding Chicago's streets. But something doesn't add up. Why would the South Korean government get involved with drug distribution?

I examine the attaché's face closely His credentials check out. He's registered with the South Korean embassy, but there's something in the body language between him and Professor Song that suggests a deeper connection. A shared purpose beyond diplomatic pleasantries.

The implications enhance Lea's value as leverage exponentially. She's not just bait for Moretti, but the key to controlling whatever pipeline her mother is establishing and uncovering what appears to be an international conspiracy. If Moretti could indeed secure the Korean connection before me, the balance of power in Chicago will shift dramatically.

I add a note to have Marco dig deeper into Professor Song's background. Perhaps there are inconsistencies we've overlooked. Something that would explain why a respected academic would risk everything to coordinate with known criminals.

"Keep this contained," I instruct Marco in a follow-up text. "No one else sees these."

I lock the phone and turn back to find Lea watching me from across the room, arms wrapped around herself again, uncertainty clear in her posture. She's waiting for me to explain, to continue what we started, but the moment has passed. The strategic landscape has shifted, requiring recalibration.

"Business," I say, offering no further explanation.

I move past her to the bathroom, closing the door behind me. My mind is clear, calculating the new variables.

I splash cold water on my face, cooling the heat that still lingers from Lea's touch. Earlier desire is now secondary to strategic objectives. Moretti's knowledge of the Professor's involvement changes everything. Using Lea to get to her mother remains the plan for me, but with higher stakes now that I know Moretti has the same objective. Except, Moretti's version is cruel. If Moretti captures Lea, he will cut her up bit by bit, and return her in pieces to Professor Song until she complies with his commands.

Is Lea aware of her mother's connections? Possible, but unlikely given her genuine confusion about Moretti's interest in her. She's either an exceptional actress or genuinely ignorant of her mother's extracurricular activities.

I dry my face, decision made: accelerate the timeline, deepen her emotional dependence, then leverage that attachment to access her mother's operation. The seduction is no longer merely convenient, it's necessary intelligence gathering.

When I emerge from the bathroom, the apartment is quiet. I find Lea already asleep in the queen bed. *I know I could flip her like a switch. The kisses we've shared so far prove it. Her body responds to mine instinctively, a chemical reaction she can't seem to control despite her intellectual resistance. There will be plenty of time for full-scale seduction, for dismantling every one of her defenses, for finding all of Lea's breaking points and exploiting them for my purposes.*

My cock hardens at the thought of all the ways I will control her, binding her resistance until only need remains, obscuring those defiant eyes until she sees only me, guiding her until she inevitably begs for my touch. The fantasy is vivid and arousing, but with stoic willpower, I shift my thoughts to tomorrow's business matters.

I remove my shirt and trousers, leaving only my boxer briefs, and slide into bed beside her. She stirs, but it doesn't wake, her breathing remaining deep and even. I lie on my back, staring at the ceiling, mind cycling through contingencies and scenarios.

Moretti's move against Lea. Professor Song's meeting with the Koreans. The potential pipeline for pharmaceutical-grade fentanyl. The leverage points these connections create.

Each piece fits into the larger puzzle of control I'm assembling. And at the center of it all is the woman sleeping beside me, blissfully unaware that her journalistic ambition has placed her at the nexus of a power struggle that extends far beyond Chicago's criminal underworld.

I turn my head to study her profile in the dim light filtering through the windows. She looks even younger in sleep, vulnerable in a way she never allows when conscious. It's a reminder that for all her sharp intelligence and stubborn courage, she's still just a pawn in this game, a valuable one but a pawn, nonetheless.

My phone vibrates once with a final update from Marco for the night: *"All secure. Moretti's men still at primary location. No movement at secondary sites."*

I set the device on the nightstand and close my eyes, allowing my body to rest while my mind continues processing. Tomorrow will bring new challenges, new opportunities to advance my position. And Lea Song will be right where I want her, isolated, dependent, and increasingly entangled in my web.

CHAPTER EIGHTEEN

Lea

I JOLT AWAKE. FOR A DISORIENTING MOMENT, I CAN'T place where I am, the bed is too large, the sheets too soft, the silence too complete. Then memories flood back in a rush: Nico's men at my office, the warning about Moretti, being whisked away to this luxury safe house.

And last night. *God, last night.*

My hand moves to the empty space beside me. The sheets are cool to the touch. He's been gone for a while. I close my eyes, remembering the heat of Nico's mouth against mine, his hands sliding beneath the borrowed shirt, lifting me against the wall with effortless strength. The way my body betrayed me, arching into his touch despite every rational thought screaming to maintain distance.

The journalist in me, the one with ethics and professional boundaries, is horrified. The woman in me, however, is something else entirely.

The rich aroma of coffee pulls me from my rumination. I

slide from bed, tugging the white dress shirt down over my thighs. My reflection in the full-length mirror stops me short. Tousled hair, bare legs, face flushed red. I barely recognize myself.

What are you doing, Lea?

I should be maintaining professional distance. This man breaks people's fingers over business disputes. He systematically terrorizes rivals. He's the subject of my story, not some romantic prospect. Yet here I am, wearing his shirt, sleeping in his bed, letting him press me against walls with my full participation.

The bathroom provides temporary sanctuary. I splash cold water on my face, attempting to wash away the lingering heat of last night's encounter. The woman in the mirror stares back accusingly.

After using the fancy toothbrush provided, I steel myself and follow the coffee scent to the kitchen.

Nico stands by the expansive windows, already impeccably dressed in a charcoal suit. His attention is fixed on a document in one hand, coffee in the other. The morning light casts his profile in sharp relief, all angles and controlled power. He doesn't look up, though I know he's registered my presence.

I hover in the doorway, suddenly hyper aware of my bare legs and disheveled appearance. His shirt barely reaches mid-thigh, leaving me feeling more exposed than if I were actually naked. The vulnerability grates against my nerves.

When he glances up, his eyes linger on my legs before meeting my gaze. Satisfaction flickers across his expression, before it's masked by casual politeness.

"Sleep well?" he asks, as if we hadn't been moments away from fucking against the living room wall last night.

I cross my arms over my chest, hating the heat that rises to my cheeks. "Fine." I move toward the coffee maker, focusing on the simple task to avoid his penetrating stare. "Any news about Moretti's men?"

"They're still watching your apartment." He sets his document down, giving me his full attention. "Marco brought your things earlier. There's a bag over there with clothes and toiletries."

"Thanks," I mutter, pouring coffee into a sleek white mug. The surreal normalcy of the action feels absurd given our circumstances.

He moves closer, invading my personal space with that deliberate confidence that sets my nerves on edge. "We'll need to stay here another day, at least until I've addressed the Moretti situation."

I take a step back, coffee clutched between my hands like a shield. "And what does 'addressing the situation' involve? More broken fingers? Ear slicing?"

His smile doesn't reach his eyes. "Nothing that would make it into your article."

The reminder of my professional purpose lands straight. I'm here for a story. Yet last night, I'd forgotten that completely when his hands were on me.

"Speaking of which," I say, forcing my voice to remain steady, "I should work on my notes. Is my laptop in that bag too?"

He nods. "Everything you requested. I'll be on calls most of the morning." He steps closer, fingers brushing a strand from my face with deliberate gentleness. "Try not to miss me too much."

Before I can formulate a cutting response, his phone rings. He answers without breaking eye contact, his voice shifting into that cool, authoritative tone reserved for business. I use the opportunity to grab the bag, and escape back to the bedroom, coffee sloshing close to the rim of my mug.

An hour later, I'm showered and dressed in my own clothes: jeans and a simple black blouse Marco retrieved from my apartment. The normalcy of my attire provides a thin veneer of control I need.

I set up my laptop at the dining table, opening the document that contains my evolving article on Nico Varela. The cursor blinks against the white background, waiting for words I can't seem to form.

The facts are all there: his systematic control over Chicago's criminal landscape, his connections to legitimate businesses, the way he brokers peace between rival factions. I have more firsthand material than any journalist has ever gathered on him.

Yet my fingers hover, paralyzed above the keyboard.

If I write about the warehouse meeting where he sliced off a man's ear, I will expose his methods. If I detail the way politicians and business leaders flock to his club seeking favors, I implicate dozens of powerful people. If I describe his surveillance network, I compromise operations that while morally questionable, actually prevent bloodshed.

And if I'm honest about how deeply I've become involved, I destroy my credibility.

I close my eyes, massaging my temples. *When did this*

become so complicated? When did I start weighing Nico's safety against journalistic integrity?

The answer comes unbidden: *When you let him touch you. When you kissed him back. When you started noticing the real man beneath the monster.*

"Fuck," I mutter, opening my eyes to the damning blank page. This is exactly what they warn about in Journalism Ethics 101, getting too close to your subject, losing objectivity, compromising your reporting.

I force myself to type, documenting the meeting at Purgatorio where Nico broke the guitarist's fingers. The words come mechanically, devoid of the emotional weight of witnessing such casual violence. I describe the facts but omit my reaction at how I'd been both horrified and fascinated by the methodical way he'd administered punishment.

The resulting paragraph reads like a police report, not the vivid, insightful journalism I pride myself on.

I highlight and delete it all with a frustrated jab at the keyboard.

Through the glass doors to the balcony, I can see Nico pacing as he gestures during a phone call. His back is to me, giving me a rare moment where he isn't watching, analyzing, calculating.

My gaze drifts to his open laptop on the coffee table.

The journalist in me stirs, awakening from the stupor of confused attraction. *Information is what I came for. Information is power. And I've been handed an opportunity to gather it without Nico's careful curation.*

I glance at the balcony again. Nico remains engaged in his call, seemingly aggravated in a rare display of frustration.

Before I can second-guess myself, I move to the coffee table and angle the screen so I can see it clearly while monitoring the balcony door.

His computer desktop is organized, folders labeled by date and subject matter. One catches my eye: "Song, L."

My stomach plummets. A folder with my name.

I click it open, dreading what I'll find while unable to resist the pull of truth.

The folder expands to reveal dozens of files, surveillance photos, documents, and emails. With trembling fingers, I open the first image file.

It's a photo of my apartment. From inside my bedroom. Taken while I was sleeping.

Nausea churns as I click through more files. Photos of me in the shower. At my desk. On my couch reading. Moments I thought were private, exposed to Nico's cold scrutiny. Even videos. My vision blurs; the room seems to tilt.

But it's worse than simple surveillance. There are psychological assessments, detailed reports analyzing my personality, identifying vulnerabilities, predicting my reactions to various scenarios. Notes on my relationship with my mother, my new friendship with Sienna, even my coffee preferences and sleep patterns.

The violation is so profound I feel physically ill.

I force myself to keep going, opening an email folder. What I find there shatters what little composure I have left.

Emails between Nico and the publisher of Chicago Investigating Journal. Discussing my assignment. Planning it. The "higher up" order to select me for the Varela exposé wasn't an editorial interest in my amazing fresh talent. It was

Nico pulling strings, manipulating my career for his purposes.

Everything, my big break, my proud calls to my mother, my confidence in my professional abilities, all of it was his elaborate construct. A puppet master pulling strings while I danced, thinking it was my talent moving me forward.

I scroll frantically, finding another folder labeled "Song, E." My mother. But when I click it, a password prompt appears. Whatever information he has on her is encrypted, protected.

The glass door slides open.

With lightning reflexes, I close the folders and return to my phone on the dining table, pretending to check messages. My blood rushes in my ears, so loudly I'm certain he can hear it.

Nico steps inside, tucking his phone into his pocket. "Problems with the article?" he asks, nodding toward my abandoned laptop.

I force a casual shrug, amazed my voice doesn't shake. "Just organizing my thoughts." I gesture at my phone. "Checking in with Sienna. She worries."

He studies me with that penetrating gaze that always makes me feel transparent. *Does he know? Can he tell I've seen behind the curtain?*

"You seem tense," he observes, moving closer.

Because I just discovered you've been manipulating every aspect of these last four weeks of my life, and who knows how much before that, you calculating bastard.

But I don't say that. The journalist in me, the one who's spent years learning how to get people to reveal themselves, recognizes this as a turning point. Confrontation would only confirm I snooped and lose my advantage. If I'm going to uncover what's happening with my mother, why Nico targeted me, I need a fresh approach.

A plan forms, crystallizing with each breath. *If Nico manipulates through seduction and false vulnerability, I'll use the same tactics against him, especially now I have a good idea of what turns him on. He kept those shower pictures for a reason.*

I force my shoulders to relax. "Just cabin fever, I guess." I offer a small smile. "I'm going to shower. Clear my head."

He nods, seemingly satisfied with my explanation, and returns to his laptop. My stomach turns as I walk to the bathroom, hoping he can't read the fury and betrayal in the set of my shoulders, the tension in my jaw.

It's time to turn his own weapons against him.

When I emerge forty minutes later, I'm transformed. I've taken extra time with my appearance, my hair blown out to soft waves, minimal makeup that still enhances my features. But the actual change is beneath the surface. I've locked away the hurt and betrayal, compartmentalizing them to access the cold calculation necessary for what comes next.

I've also shaved every inch of my body in the shower, a detail that won't be lost on Nico when the time comes.

I find him in the living room, watching a news report about a warehouse fire on the south side. His expression gives nothing away, but the tension in his shoulders tells me it's connected to his business.

"Everything okay?" I ask, injecting just enough concern in my voice to seem invested without being nosy.

He glances up, eyes tracking my approach. "Just a minor setback with a competitor."

I settle on the couch near him, not touching, but close enough to suggest growing comfort with his proximity. "Moretti?"

A flicker of surprise crosses his features; he didn't expect me to connect those dots so easily. "Yes. Nothing to worry about."

"When do you think I can go back to my apartment?" I ask, making my tone cautious rather than demanding.

"We'll need to remain here another night," he says, watching me for a reaction. "Moretti's men are still monitoring your building."

Before I knew him, I would have argued, asserted my independence, demanded more information. Instead, I nod.

"I suppose there are worse places to be trapped," I say with a small smile that suggests growing comfort with our situation.

The flicker in his eyes is subtle but unmistakable, surprise followed by recalculation. He expected resistance.

"You're taking this well," he observes, testing my new demeanor.

I shrug, maintaining eye contact. "You were right about the danger. I've seen enough to know when to listen to experts." I use "we" instead of "I" when I add, "Besides, we have everything we need here."

His expression shifts as he processes this apparent surrender. I've studied human behavior enough to recognize when someone is reassessing their approach, adjusting to unexpected data.

We spend the afternoon in a strange dance of proximity

and distance. I work on my laptop, careful to write only innocuous notes about club operations that won't reveal everything I've learned. Nico moves between calls and his own work, occasionally checking security feeds or sending cryptic texts.

I catch him watching me several times, that calculating look in his eyes. *Good. Let him wonder what's changed. Let him think his seduction is working.*

By evening, we've settled into an uneasy domesticity. I help set the table while Nico heats the prepared meals Marco delivered, pasta with a rich tomato sauce for me, something with fish for him. The normalcy of the scene is surreal given what I now know.

Halfway through dinner, Nico excuses himself to use the bathroom. As he stands, I notice his phone remains on the table beside his half-empty wine glass.

The moment he's out of sight, I grab his phone just as screen illuminates with an incoming message. My journalist's instinct kicks in before I can stop myself, eyes darting to the preview displayed on his lock screen:

Moretti making move tonight. Three targets identified. Varela property on Michigan Ave. Shipment at docks. Professor surveillance is in progress.

I stare at the message, heart racing. *Professor surveillance is in progress. Is he talking about my mother? No, it can't be.*

I try to open the phone, but it requires facial recognition to unlock. The preview is all I can see, and it's enough to send a wave of dread through me.

The mention raises genuine alarm. *If my mother is in some kind of danger, and Nico knows where my mother is, I should immediately agree to do whatever he wants; whatever game we're playing, my mother's safety isn't part of it. But what if it's not about that? I would give up all my cards at once.*

But before I can decide what to do, Nico returns, noticing his illuminated phone. His expression darkens as he reads the message in full. "We have a situation," he says, already typing rapidly on his phone. "Moretti's making multiple moves tonight."

I school my features to show surprise and concern rather than confirmation. "Moves? What kind of moves?"

"Attempting to breach several properties," he says vaguely, editing the information for my consumption. "Nothing for you to worry about."

I watch as he retrieves his laptop, issuing instructions to what must be his security team. I note which properties he prioritizes, how he distributes his forces, the cool efficiency with which he responds to threats.

What he doesn't mention is my mother. He's keeping that information from me.

For hours, Nico manages the developing situation, occasionally stepping onto the balcony for private calls. I maintain my role as the concerned but trusting companion, offering coffee and asking just enough questions to seem invested without being intrusive.

All the while, I'm cataloging information, noting whom he calls, what locations are mentioned, the hierarchy of his organization revealed through crisis.

The clock ticks past midnight, and the safe-house kitchen feels like a pressure cooker, the air thick with the aftermath of Nico's ruthless efficiency. He's just neutralized a threat, some of Moretti's men, I presume. His commands barked over the phone with a chilling calm that made my skin prickle.

Now, his posture eases, the lethal edge softening as he accepts the whiskey I offer. His fingers brush mine, deliberate, and I catch the flicker of amusement in his dark eyes. He's The Diplomat, always calculating, always in control.

"The immediate threat is contained," he says, voice smooth as the liquor he sips. "We'll move to my penthouse tomorrow. It's more secure now that Moretti knows this location."

I nod, letting my fingers linger against his as I take my glass, the touch an artful move to draw him in. "You were right," I say, infusing my tone with admiration, just enough to stroke his ego. "About the danger. About needing protection."

His eyes narrow, a predator sizing up prey. He sees the shift in me, this new compliant, yielding version of Lea Song, and he's dissecting it, searching for cracks. I step closer, invading his space the way he's done to me countless times, my chest brushing his. "I'm not good at trusting people," I admit, the truth a weapon in my arsenal my father taught me. "But you've been right about everything so far."

Before he can respond, I strike. My lips crash against his, the kiss bold, feigned to disarm. For a split second, he freezes, caught off guard, but then his hand snakes to the nape of my neck, fingers twisting in my hair with a grip that's anything but gentle. He kisses me back, hard and possessive, claiming my mouth like it's his birthright.

"Interesting timing," he murmurs against my lips, his voice a low, dangerous purr. A faint smile curves his mouth, dark with amusement. "After watching me crush a threat, you decide to spread your legs. What does that say about you, Lea?"

His words hit like a slap, sharp and cutting, exposing the raw truth I'm trying to hide. A mix of fear and heat is pooling low in my belly. He's always analyzing, always one step ahead, peeling back my motives like layers of skin. I lean into the role, letting him think he's got me pegged.

"Maybe I'm just tired of fighting the inevitable," I say, my voice husky. It's a lie wrapped in truth, and I pray he buys it.

His eyes bore into mine, piercing, and for a terrifying moment, I think he sees through me; through the journalist, the spy, the woman playing a dangerous game. Then his mouth descends again, punishing, his tongue forcing mine into submission. He backs me against the kitchen counter, the edge biting into my hips. One hand grips my ass, squeezing hard enough to bruise, while the other tugs my hair, tilting my head to expose my throat.

"The inevitability of this was written the moment you walked into my club," he growls, his lips grazing my pulse point. "Pretending you're just a journalist? That was cute, piccola. But we both know you've been wet for me since I broke that guitarist's fingers."

His teeth scrape the sensitive skin where my neck meets my shoulder, and I gasp, the sound authentic as desire floods my core. This wasn't supposed to feel like this; so raw, so consuming. I'm supposed to be in control, manipulating him, but my body betrays me, aching for his touch.

"I'm still a journalist," I manage, clinging to my cover even as his hand slips under my blouse, palming my breast through my bra with a roughness that makes me arch.

He laughs, the sound dark and mocking, vibrating against

my skin. "Sure you are. And I'm still The Diplomat. But right now, you're not chasing a story. You're begging for my cock."

The crude words should disgust me, but they ignite something primal soaking my panties. He's right, and I hate him for it. His fingers unbutton my blouse with agonizing slowness, each movement a display of absolute control. He's not rushed, not desperate; a predator savoring his prey. The black lace of my bra is exposed, and his eyes rake over me, proprietary, hungry.

"Tell me what you're thinking," he commands, his voice low, dangerous, as he traces the edge of my bra, his thumb brushing my nipple through the lace.

"I'm thinking you talk too fucking much," I snap, reaching for his belt in a bid to seize control, to shift the power back to me.

His hand catches my wrist like a steel trap, squeezing until I wince. "Patience, Lea," he says, his tone a silken threat. "You don't get to call the shots." He pins me against the refrigerator, the cold metal shocking against my back. My wrists are trapped above my head in one of his hands, his grip unyielding. "Tonight, you learn who owns you."

His free hand traces my collarbone, down the valley between my breasts, to the waistband of my jeans. "I've pictured this," he murmurs, his voice rough with desire. "Stripping you bare, fucking you until you scream my name. You thought you could play me, didn't you? With those coy looks, that tight little skirt in my club?"

He unbuttons my jeans, the zipper's slow descent a torture. "You got so wet watching me break that bastard's hand," he continues, his voice dripping with dark satisfaction.

"Your pulse was racing, your thighs clenched. Don't lie to me, Lea. Your body tells me everything."

I try to move, to grind against him, but he holds me still, his strength overwhelming. "You're getting off on this," I accuse, trying to sound defiant, but my voice trembles with need.

"Damn right," he says, his smile wolfish. "And so are you." His hand slips inside my jeans, finding the soaked fabric of my panties. "Fuck, you're drenched. What would your readers say, knowing their fearless journalist is dripping for the monster she's supposed to expose?"

His fingers push the fabric aside, sliding through my slickness, teasing my entrance without entering. I bite my lip, stifling a moan, but a whimper escapes. "Look at you," he murmurs, his voice a dark caress. "So fucking desperate. Beg for it, Lea. Beg me to fuck you."

I shake my head, clinging to some shred of pride, but he circles my clit with maddening precision, and my resolve crumbles. "Please," I whisper, hating myself.

"Louder," he demands, his fingers stilling.

"Please, Nico," I gasp. "Take me to the bedroom and fuck me."

He doesn't smile, doesn't gloat. He just yanks my jeans and panties down in one brutal motion, leaving me exposed. He lifts me onto the counter, the granite cold against my bare ass, and spreads my thighs wide. "Not the bedroom. Right here," he says, his voice rough. "Where you can't hide from me."

He drops to his knees, his breath hot against my core. "You prepared for me," he notes, his palm gliding over my shaved skin. "Thought you could seduce me, control me.

Cute." His eyes meet mine, dark with promise. "Let's see how you taste when you're lying to me."

His mouth closes over my clit, sucking hard, and I cry out, my hands gripping the counter's edge. His tongue is relentless, flicking, circling, while two fingers thrust inside me, curling to hit that spot that makes my vision blur. The dual assault is devastating, his dominance absolute. "Fuck, you're sweet," he growls against me. "So fucking wet for me."

I'm supposed to be playing him, but my body surrenders, my hips grinding against his face. My hands pull him closer, and he groans, the vibration pushing me closer to the edge. "That's it," he says, his voice muffled. "Ride my tongue, piccola. Show me how bad you need it."

The orgasm hits like a tidal wave, my body convulsing as I scream his name. He doesn't stop, licking me through every shudder until I'm whimpering, oversensitive. When he stands, his lips glisten with my arousal, and he doesn't wipe it away, letting me see my surrender.

"Now," he says, his voice thick with controlled hunger, "we go to the bedroom."

He lifts me, my legs wrapping around his waist as he carries me. The hard length of his cock presses against me through his pants. In the bedroom, he drops me onto the bed, and I watch, breathless, as he strips. His body is a map of violence—scars crisscrossing his chest, muscles honed by brutality. Tattoos everywhere. His cock springs free, thick and intimidating, and I swallow hard.

"Like what you see?" he asks, stroking himself, with his eyes locked on mine.

"Yes," I admit, as I fight the urge to lick the drop of pre-cum that slides down the tip of his thick cock.

He climbs onto the bed, pinning me beneath him. His cock nudges my entrance, but he doesn't enter, teasing me with shallow thrusts. "Tell me why you're here," he says, his voice a low growl. "In my bed, in my fucking life."

It's a trap, but I'm too far gone to care. I touch his face, feigning vulnerability. "To understand you," I say. "For the story, at first. Now... I don't know."

He searches my eyes, and for a moment, I think he'll call me out. Then he thrusts into me, one brutal stroke that fills me completely, and I cry out, the stretch exquisite. "Fuck," he groans, his control fraying. "So fucking tight."

He doesn't give me time to adjust, pulling out and slamming back in, each thrust harder, deeper. The bed shakes, the headboard slamming against the wall. "You think you're smart," he growls, his hands gripping my hips, bruising. "Playing me like I'm some mark. But this—" He thrusts so deep I see stars. "This is what you get for crossing me."

My nails rake his back, drawing blood, and he hisses, his pace turning feral. "Fuck, yes," he says, his voice raw. "Mark me, Lea. Show me you feel it."

I wrap my legs around him, pulling him deeper, my body chasing the pleasure despite my mind's protests. "You're mine," he snarls, his hand wrapping around my throat, squeezing just enough to make my blood rush. "Say it."

"Yours," I gasp, the word torn from me as another orgasm builds.

"Damn right," he growls, his thrusts relentless. "This pussy, this body... it's mine."

He shifts, hitting that spot inside me, and I shatter, my scream echoing as my walls clench around him. He follows, his rhythm faltering as he spills inside me, his groan primal, possessive. We collapse, sweat-slick and panting, his weight pinning me to the mattress.

He rolls off, pulling me against him, his arm a possessive band around my waist. "Sleep," he murmurs, his lips brushing my temple. "You'll need it."

He thinks he's won. He thinks I've surrendered, fallen for his manipulations, become another asset in his collection.

Little does he know, I've just executed the opening move in my counter-strategy. Using the very desire he thought would be my weakness as my strongest weapon against him.

CHAPTER NINETEEN

Nico

I WAKE TO THE WEIGHT OF LEA'S HEAD ON MY CHEST, her breath warm against my skin. The specific quality of the early morning light slanting through the blinds paints stripes across her naked back. She sleeps the way innocents do, deeply though I know better than most how deceptive appearances can be.

Last night replays in my mind: her planned surrender, the way she started our encounter after watching me handle Moretti's threats. *Too convenient. Too perfectly timed.*

Marco's voice is still in my head from our last private conversation on the balcony. *"She's playing you,"* he'd warned, eyes narrowed with concern. *"The timing is suspicious. First, she's snooping through your laptop, then she can't wait to fuck you? Come on, boss."*

I'd dismissed him with a wave, though not because I disagreed. *Of course she's playing me. I've encountered enough strategic seductions to recognize one.* What Marco doesn't understand is that manipulation can cut both ways, with each player believing they hold the strings.

Lea stirs against me, her leg shifting across mine. Even in sleep, she's positioned herself strategically, one arm draped across my torso, pinning me while appearing affectionate. I smile at the subtle maneuver. *She's better at this game than I gave her credit for.*

I run my fingers along her spine, counting the vertebrae like rosary beads. She arches into the touch without waking, a purely physical response and therefore genuine. *These unguarded moments are precious, the only times I see past her performance to the woman beneath.*

Her eyelids flutter, consciousness returning. I feel the exact moment awareness hits her, the slight tensing of muscles, the shift in breathing. She makes a deliberate show of stretching languorously, as if untroubled by waking in my arms after all we've done. As if this is where she wants to be.

"Morning," she murmurs, voice husky with sleep. The sound stirs something in me, something I quickly suppress.

"Sleep well?" I ask, keeping my tone casual despite the possessive heat that flares at the sight of the marks I've left on her neck, her collarbone, the soft curve of her breast.

She nods, sitting up to survey the room. The sheet falls to her waist, leaving her breasts exposed. The morning light loves her skin, turning it golden against the white cotton. My shirt from yesterday lies crumpled at the foot of the bed where I tossed it before taking her the second time last night.

"May I?" she asks, reaching for it.

I nod, watching as she slips it on. There's something satisfying about seeing her in my clothing, a primitive marking of territory that appeals to the part of me that operates on instinct rather than calculation.

She rises, the shirt falling to mid-thigh, revealing long legs still bearing faint red marks from my grip. She doesn't bother buttoning it, leaving the top three undone to reveal the curve of her breasts and the constellation of marks I've left there. The sight makes my cock stir despite the thoroughness of last night's activities.

"Coffee?" she asks, padding toward the kitchen with a deliberate sway to her hips.

"Please," I respond, making no move to leave the bed just yet. The view is too enticing.

I listen to her move around the kitchen, the sound of water filling the carafe, the quiet hiss as the machine brews. Ordinary sounds made extraordinary by their domesticity. By the illusion of normalcy, they create.

When she returns with two steaming mugs, I've propped myself against the headboard, sheet pooled at my waist. Her eyes linger on my bare chest, tracking the scars that map my history. Some from childhood, some from business gone wrong, all part of the record that made me who I am.

"Cream, no sugar," she says, handing me the mug. That she remembers how I take my coffee shouldn't please me as much as it does.

"Thank you." I accept the offering, allowing our fingers to brush in the exchange. She doesn't pull away from the contact, another deliberate move in our ongoing chess match.

She perches on the edge of the bed, legs tucked beneath her, studying me over the rim of her mug. "What's the plan for today? Still heading to your penthouse?"

I sip my coffee, appreciating the rich bitterness. "After

breakfast. I have some business to attend to this afternoon, a meeting with international contacts that can't be rescheduled."

Her expression brightens with feigned interest. "Will I be joining you at the meeting?"

And there it is, the journalist beneath the lover, always hunting for access, for information, for the story. I hide my amusement behind another sip of coffee.

"Not this time," I reply, watching disappointment flicker across her features before she masks it. "These particular associates are traditional in their views. A woman's presence would complicate matters."

She nods, accepting the explanation without protest, another sign of her new strategy. *The old Lea would have argued, pushed for inclusion, demanded equal access.* This new, compliant version sets my teeth on edge even as it captivates me.

"I understand," she says, setting her mug on the night-stand. "I should get dressed then."

She makes no move to retrieve her clothes, instead sliding the shirt from her shoulders with deliberate slowness. The fabric whispers against her skin as it falls, pooling around her knees on the bed. She's naked now, her skin flawless in the morning light, her nipples hard, her pussy bare and glisten-ing. She watches me, daring me to react.

My cock twitches, already hard, but beneath the desire, anger simmers. She thinks she's playing me, this 23-year-old journalist with her clever eyes and traitor's heart. She thinks she can manipulate *me*, The Diplomat, the man who breaks empires. Last night was a taste, but today, I'm going to punish her until she can't walk for days.

I set my coffee aside, my eyes never leaving her. "You think you can tease me, piccola?" I growl, my voice low, dangerous. "Think you can flash that pretty body and I'll forget you're a manipulating journalist who thinks she's clever?"

Her eyes widen, maybe a flicker of fear, but she covers it with a sultry smile. "I'm just getting ready, Nico. Don't you want me to?"

The teasing innocent tone is decent acting, but not fooling me. She's still trying to play me. I'm on her in a second, as I yank her head back. She gasps, but her pupils dilate, betraying her arousal. "On your knees. Now."

She hesitates, just enough to test me, and I tighten my grip, forcing her off the bed and onto the floor. She lands on her knees, looking up at me with a mix of defiance and heat. "You're such a bastard," she mutters, but her hands are already reaching for my belt.

"Keep talking," I say, my voice cold. "It'll only make this rougher." I unbuckle my pants, freeing my cock, already rock-hard and leaking. Her eyes widen at the size, and I smirk. "Open that smart mouth, Lea. Let's see how well you take your punishment."

She leans forward, her tongue darting out to lick the tip, and I groan, the sensation shooting through me. But I'm not here for gentle. I grab her head with both hands, holding her still, and thrust into her mouth, hard and deep. She gags, her throat constricting around me, but she doesn't pull back. Fuck, she takes it like a champ, her eyes watering as I fuck her face, each thrust punishing, relentless.

"That's it," I growl, my voice rough with pleasure.

"Choke on my cock, you little liar. You thought you could play me? This is what you get."

She moans around me, the vibration sending a jolt through my balls, and I feel her hands grip my thighs, steadying herself as I push deeper. Her gags are loud, wet, and fucking perfect, her throat tight and hot. Tears stream down her cheeks, but she's not fighting me. She's taking it, her tongue swirling even as she struggles to breathe. "Fuck, you're good at this," I say, my voice thick. "Look at you, gagging on my dick like you were born for it."

She tries to pull back, gasping for air, and says, "You're such a fucking prick." Her voice is hoarse, defiant, and it only fuels my anger.

"Wrong answer," I snarl, shoving back into her mouth, deeper this time, holding her there until she's choking, her hands slapping my thighs. "Talk back again, and I'll fuck your throat until you pass out." I pull out just before I come, my cock slick with her spit, and she coughs, panting, her lips swollen and red. She's a mess, and it's fucking beautiful.

"Get up," I order, yanking her to her feet by her hair. She stumbles, but I don't give her time to recover. I spin her around, bending her over the bed, her ass in the air, her pussy glistening. "You don't get to come until I say so," I say, my hand cracking against her ass, hard enough to leave a red print. She cries out, but her hips push back, begging for more.

"You're an asshole," she gasps, her voice trembling with a mix of pain and need.

I spank her again, harder, and she moans, the sound raw and desperate. "Keep talking, piccola," I say, my voice a dark promise. "Every word makes me want to fuck you even harder." I pull her head back, arching her spine. "You're mine, Lea. Your body, your lies, your fucking soul. I own you."

I line up my cock, teasing her entrance, and she whimpers, trying to push back. I hold her still, my grip bruising. "Beg for it," I demand. "Tell me how bad you want my cock."

"Fuck you," she spits, but her voice cracks, her body trembling.

I laugh, and thrust into her, hard and deep, filling her in one brutal stroke. She screams, her walls clenching around my cock. "That's it," I growl, pulling out and slamming back in, setting a punishing rhythm. "Take it, you little slut. Take every fucking inch."

Her moans are loud, uncontrolled, the bed creaking under us as I fuck her from behind, my hand still fisted in her hair, pulling hard enough to make her gasp. "You like this, don't you?" I say, my voice rough. "Getting fucked like a whore by the man you're trying to destroy. Your pussy's so wet, it's dripping down your thighs."

"Shut up," she gasps, but her hips meet every thrust, her body betraying her.

I spank her ass again, the sound loud in the room, and she cries out, her walls fluttering around me. "Don't fucking tell me to shut up," I snarl, forcing her to arch further. "You're gonna take this cock and love every second of it."

I'm close, my balls tightening, but I want her to come with me, to feel her shatter around me. I lean forward, spitting on her exposed asshole, the act filthy and possessive. She gasps, shocked, and I jab a finger deep inside her ass, no warning, no gentleness. She moans, loud and raw, her body tensing, then relaxing as pleasure overtakes her.

"Fuck, Nico!" she cries, her voice a mix of surprise and ecstasy. "Oh God—"

"That's right," I growl, pumping my finger in time with my thrusts, my cock driving into her pussy, my finger stretching her ass. "Come for me, Lea. Come all over my cock while I fuck your tight little holes."

She's trembling, her moans turning to sobs as the pleasure builds, and I feel her walls clench, her body seizing as she comes, her scream ripping through the room. Her pussy milks my cock, and it's too much. I follow her over the edge, my release hitting like a freight train, spilling deep inside her with a guttural groan.

We collapse onto the bed, both panting, sweat-slick and spent. I pull out, watching my cum drip from her, marking her as mine. She's trembling, her face flushed, her body marked with my handprints, my bites. I pull her close against me, my arm around her waist, and she curls into me, her breath ragged.

"You think you can play me," I murmur against her ear, my voice low, dangerous. "But you're mine, Lea. Every lie, every scheme, every fucking inch of you. Try to run, and I'll drag you back."

She leaves for the bathroom and as I stare at the ceiling, my mind's already shifting to the war ahead. Lea's dangerous, a fucking liability, but she's my liability.

———

AN HOUR LATER, she emerges from the bathroom wrapped in a towel. I'm already dressed in the suit Marco brought from my penthouse, charcoal gray with subtle pinstripes, a burgundy tie that matches the sheets she writhed against earlier.

Lea heads for the bedroom to get dressed, and once she's out of sight, I position my laptop at a specific angle, one that ensures she'll be able to see the screen if she glances over when she returns. Then I open an email thread I've prepared in advance.

From: Dr. Reginald Hammon To: Nico Varela Subject: Academic Conference Sponsorship Request Mr. Varela, Following our discussion at last month's charity gala, I'm writing to formally request your consideration for sponsorship of our upcoming International Economic Systems Conference. As mentioned, we've secured several distinguished speakers, including Professor Eunji Song, whose work on shadow economies has generated significant interest among policy makers. Professor Song's lecture series, "Invisible Networks: How Unofficial Systems Sustain Global Commerce," will be the centerpiece of our program. Given your foundation's interest in international business relations, I believe this would align with your philanthropic goals. Please let me know if you require any additional information. Regards, Dr. Reginald Hammon, Chair of Economics Department Chicago University.

I hear the bedroom door open and continue scrolling through emails as if absorbed in my morning correspondence. From the corner of my eye, I catch Lea's entrance, now dressed in fitted jeans and a simple blue blouse that brings out the warmth in her skin. She moves with a careful stiffness she attempts to disguise, favoring one side, a detail I file away with grim satisfaction. The morning *lesson* left its mark.

She moves to the kitchen to refill her coffee, but her path

takes her behind me. I feel the moment her eyes catch on the screen, the subtle pause in her movement, the hitch in her breath. She thinks I don't notice, but I register every nuance.

"More coffee?" she offers, her voice steady, though perhaps a fraction huskier than usual. A deliberate performance of normalcy.

"Please," I respond, clicking to another email as if unaware of her interest.

She returns with my refilled mug, setting it beside my laptop with perhaps more care than necessary, avoiding any sudden movements. She moves to the other side of the table, settling into her chair with a subtle adjustment I interpret as easing sore muscles.

"This conference sounds interesting," she says, careful to keep her tone casual. "My mother mentioned something about a lecture series, but I didn't realize it was such a big event."

I glance up, regarding her with mild interest. Her eyes meet mine, a challenge beneath the pleasant inquiry. She's putting on a brave face, pretending last night didn't rattle her, didn't break something inside her even as her body surrendered. "Your mother is quite respected in academic circles. Her work on shadow economies is groundbreaking." I pause, watching her eyes. "Have you read any of her research?"

She shakes her head, a flicker of genuine emotion, regret, perhaps, crossing her features. "Not as much as I should have. We don't talk about her work often."

"Interesting," I murmur, filing away the nugget of genuine information. "Most daughters would be proud of such academic achievements."

Something darkens in her expression, a touch of real hurt breaking through the performance. "I am proud of her. We just have different interests."

I nod, allowing the subject to drop though I've confirmed what I suspected: there's distance between Lea and her mother, an emotional gap I might exploit. Knowledge is currency in my world, and I've just acquired another valuable coin.

"We should leave within the hour," I say, changing the subject. "Marco will meet us at the penthouse with updates on Moretti's movements."

She nods, sipping her coffee. Her grip on the mug is tight, knuckles white. She's processing, analyzing, likely trying to reconcile the tenderness I showed her later with the brutality that preceded it. Good. Let her be confused. Let her remain off balance. "I'll be ready."

THE DRIVE to my penthouse passes in comfortable silence. Lea gazes out the window, lost in thought, while I review security updates on my phone. Marco's team has neutralized Moretti's immediate threats, but the underlying tension remains. This is merely a lull in the conflict, not its resolution.

When we arrive at my building, the doorman greets us with deferential politeness, holding the private elevator open. I touch her lightly on the elbow guiding her inside as we enter. She leans into the touch, playing her role perfectly.

The penthouse doors slide open to reveal Marco waiting

in the foyer, tablet in hand. His eyes flick briefly to Lea before settling on me, his expression professional but questioning.

"Everything's secure," he reports. "The incidents at the warehouse and shipping yard have been contained. Moretti's men have retreated for now."

I nod, removing my jacket and handing it to him. "And our other matter?"

Marco's eyes shift toward Lea again. "Under observation as discussed."

Lea pretends not to notice this cryptic exchange, moving further into the penthouse to admire the panoramic view of the city through floor-to-ceiling windows. The morning light streams across the minimalist furnishings, highlighting the curated art collection and the strategic spareness of personal touches. This space, like everything I own, is designed to reveal nothing while impressing everything.

"Make yourself comfortable," I tell her. "I need to speak with Marco privately."

She nods, settling onto one of the sofas with ease. "Take your time."

I lead Marco to my study, closing the door behind us. The room is soundproofed, one of many precautions built into this fortress disguised as a luxury residence.

"Report," I say, moving to the desk where a stack of folders awaits my attention.

Marco hands me his tablet, displaying surveillance photos taken over the past twenty-four hours. "Professor Song was spotted in Washington DC yesterday afternoon, entering the Korean Consulate. She stayed for two hours before leaving in a diplomatic vehicle. This wasn't a casual visit."

I scroll through the images, noting the professor's subtle signs of tension, the tight set of her shoulders, the wary glances toward surrounding buildings. "She knows she's being watched."

"Yes," Marco agrees. "And there's more. Our sources at the university say she's requested an indefinite leave of absence, effective immediately. The conference mentioned in that email you planted? It's been moved up by three weeks and moved to Seoul."

This is unexpected, a rapid acceleration of whatever game Eunji Song is playing. "Moretti's people?"

"Still monitoring her office and residence, but she hasn't returned to either location since yesterday morning."

I lean back in my chair, considering the implications. Eunji Song is making moves that suggest imminent danger or opportunity, perhaps both. And Lea, whether or not she knows it, has just become exponentially more valuable to both myself and Moretti.

"Increase surveillance on all Korean diplomatic channels," I instruct. "And prepare the jet. If Professor Song is heading to Seoul, we may need to follow."

Marco nods, making notes on his tablet. "And the journalist? She's compromised your laptop. How much do you think she knows?"

I smile, remembering the crafted way Lea initiated our encounter last night. "Enough to think she's gaining the upper hand. Not enough to realize she's where I want her."

Marco's expression remains skeptical. "She's smart. And motivated. Whatever game you're playing with her—"

"Is necessary," I interrupt, voice hardening. "Her connection to Professor Song is our best leverage in understanding what's happening with the Korean pipeline. If Moretti secures exclusive access to that supply chain, we can use the welfare of the professor's daughter to have it go our way instead."

I don't need to finish the thought. Marco understands the stakes as well as I do. A single person's life is no match against controlling the Korean fentanyl pipeline to the Midwest market. The economic implications are staggering, and the potential for massive bloodshed if negotiations fail even more so.

"Just be careful," Marco says, his concern genuine beneath the professional demeanor. "Women like her, smart, driven, with something to prove, they're dangerous in ways guns aren't."

I laugh, the sound sharp in the quiet room. "I've been handling dangerous women since before Ms. Song graduated high school. Trust me, I know what I'm doing."

Marco doesn't look convinced, but he knows better than to press the issue. "Your international contacts confirmed for three o'clock at the Blackstone Club. Security protocols are in place."

"Good," I nod. "Keep Lea under surveillance while I'm gone. Discreetly."

"Always," Marco assures me, heading for the door. He pauses, hand on the knob. "One more thing, Alessandro called. He wants updates on the Song situation. Says you're getting too personally involved."

A flicker of irritation courses through me at my uncle's presumption. "Tell him I'll call him tomorrow. After I've gathered more intelligence."

Marco nods and exits, leaving me alone with my

thoughts. Alessandro isn't wrong to be concerned. However, emotional entanglement is a risk in our business. But what he fails to understand is that one can simulate intimacy without succumbing to it. I've spent a lifetime perfecting that skill.

When I rejoin Lea in the living room, she's standing by the windows, silhouetted against the city skyline. The position is vulnerable, back turned, attention elsewhere, a silent signal that she trusts me. *Another artful move in our ongoing game.*

"Everything alright?" she asks, turning as I approach.

"Just business," I reply, moving to stand beside her. The view from here encompasses much of what I control; properties, businesses, territories. "Moretti's retreated for now, but it won't last. Men like him only understand escalation."

She nods, eyes tracking moving boats on the lake below. "What does he want? Territory? Money?"

"Power," I answer. "Like everyone in this city."

"Including you?" she asks, turning to face me.

I smile, trailing a finger along her jawline. "I already have power. What I want is command."

Her pupils dilate at the touch, a physiological response she can't fake. "And what's the difference?"

"Power is the ability to influence outcomes," I explain, voice dropping lower as I step closer. "Command is ensuring those outcomes unfold as you've designed them to. Power can be shared. Command is absolute."

Her breath quickens, whether from my proximity or my words, I can't be sure. The line between her performance and genuine response has blurred, making this interaction all the more intriguing.

"And which am I?" she asks boldly. "An outcome to influence or a design to control?"

Her eyes gleam with that infuriating cockiness, like she thinks she's got me wrapped around her finger. After last night and this morning, she's still playing her game, thinking she can outsmart me, The Diplomat, with her journalist's tricks and that wicked smile. She's about to learn what happens when you taunt a man who breaks men for breakfast.

I laugh, amused by her directness. "That, piccola, depends entirely on your next move."

"You're looking tense, Nico," she purrs, leaning back against the floor-to-ceiling window. "What's wrong? Not used to a woman who can keep up with you?" Her tone is all challenge, her lips curling like she's won something.

My jaw clenches, anger and desire twisting into a dangerous knot. "You think you're in control, piccola?" I say, my voice low, a warning she doesn't heed. "You think you can prance around, tease me, and I'll just roll over?"

She shrugs, her smile smug. "Maybe I just know what you want. And I'm good at giving it." She runs a hand down her chest, popping a button on her blouse, exposing the black lace of her bra. "Admit it, Nico. You're obsessed."

The audacity of her words snaps my restraint. My hand runs up her neck, fisting in her hair, yanking her head back. She gasps, her bravado faltering, but her eyes still spark with defiance. "You're gonna regret that mouth," I growl, my lips brushing her ear. "I'm gonna fuck that cockiness right out of you, Lea. You'll be begging by the time I'm done."

She tries to laugh, but it's shaky. "Big talk for a man who—"

288

I cut her off, slamming my mouth against hers, the kiss brutal, all teeth and dominance. She fights back, her tongue battling mine, her hands clawing at my suit jacket, but I'm in charge. I spin her around, pinning her against the window, her cheek pressed to the cool glass. The city stretches out below, oblivious to the war we're waging. My hands grip her hips, grinding my hard cock against her ass through her jeans, letting her feel what's coming.

"You think you're so clever," I snarl, my voice rough. "Playing me like I'm some mark. Let's see how cocky you are when I'm done with you." I grab the waistband of her jeans, ripping the button open and yanking them down her thighs with a force that makes her yelp. The denim pools at her ankles, and I tear it off, leaving her in her blouse and black lace panties, her legs trembling.

"Spread your legs," I order, kicking her feet apart until she's spread-eagle against the window, her hands braced on the glass. She's exposed and vulnerable, the Chicago skyline framing her like a fucking masterpiece. I step back, admiring the view: her ass round and perfect, her pussy barely covered by the lace, already wet for me. But she's not getting pleasure yet. Not until she's paid for her arrogance.

I reach into the desk drawer, pulling out a pair of scissors, the metal glinting in the light. Her eyes widen, but she doesn't move. "What are you—" she starts, but I silence her with a look.

"Shut up," I say, my voice cold. "You don't get to talk unless I say so." I kneel behind her, sliding the scissors under the edge of her panties. The cold metal brushes her skin, and she shivers, her breath hitching. With one swift cut, I slice through the lace, then the other side, letting the ruined fabric fall to the floor. She's bare now, her pussy glistening, her asshole winking at me, and fuck, I'm so hard it hurts.

"Such a pretty little liar," I murmur, standing and running a hand over her ass, squeezing hard enough to make her gasp. "But you're gonna learn your place." I unbuckle my belt, the leather sliding through the loops with a slow, deliberate hiss. Her eyes follow the movement, and I see the mix of fear and anticipation in her gaze. Good.

I fold the belt in half, gripping it tightly. "Three lashes," I say, my voice a dark promise. "Take them without a word, and I'll reward you. Scream, beg, or cry, and you get nothing but my handprint on your ass. Understand?"

She nods, her jaw tight, her eyes blazing with that stubborn defiance. "I can take it," she says, her voice steady despite the tremor in her legs.

"We'll see," I growl, stepping back. I raise the belt and bring it down, the leather cracking against her ass with a sharp snap. Redness blooms instantly, and she bites her lip, her body tensing, but she doesn't make a sound. Fuck, she's tougher than I thought. "One," I say, my voice rough with approval.

The second lash lands harder, the sound echoing in the room, and her fingers curl against the glass, her knuckles white. Her ass is red now, the red stark against her skin, but she stays silent, her breathing ragged. "Two," I count, my cock throbbing at her resilience.

The third is the hardest, aimed at the sensitive spot where her ass meets her thighs, and she jolts, a muffled whimper escaping before she clamps her lips shut. I pause, watching her tremble, but she doesn't break. "Three," I say, tossing the belt aside. "Good girl. You earned your reward."

I'm on her in an instant, my hands gripping her hips, my cock freed from my trousers and pressing against her dripping pussy. "You're so fucking wet," I growl, teasing her entrance with the tip. "You loved that, didn't you? Getting punished like the slut you are."

"Fuck you," she gasps, her voice hoarse, but there's no real venom in it, only need.

I laugh, dark and cruel, as I thrust into her hard, filling her in one brutal stroke. Lea screams, her walls clenching so tight, it's almost painful. The window rattles as I pin her against it, her breasts pressed to the glass, her legs spread wide. "That's it," I snarl, pulling out before slamming back in, as I set a punishing rhythm. "Take my cock, Lea. Take it like the little whore who thought she could outsmart me."

Her moans are loud, desperate, her hands scrabbling against the glass for purchase. The city sprawls below, oblivious, while I fuck her senseless, each thrust driving her higher. "Look at Chicago," I growl. "All those people, no idea their precious journalist is getting fucked like a slut five hundred feet above them."

She tries to talk back, her voice shaky. "You're not as smart as you think, Nico—fuck!" Her words cut off as I thrust harder, angling to hit that spot inside her that makes her see stars.

"Keep talking," I say, my hand cracking against her already-red ass. "It just makes me want to fuck you harder." I grip her hips, bruising, and pound into her, the sound of skin slapping skin filling the room. Her pussy is soaked, dripping down her thighs, and I can feel her building, her walls fluttering around me.

"You're mine," I growl, my lips against her ear. "This pussy, this ass, this fucking city...it's all mine. Say it."

"Yours," she moans, her voice breaking as she surrenders, her body trembling. "I'm yours, Nico."

"Damn right," I say, my hand sliding between her legs to circle her clit, fast and rough. "Come for me, piccola. Come all over my cock while Chicago watches."

She shatters, her scream echoing as her pussy clamps down, milking me. The intensity pushes me over the edge, and I come with a roar, spilling deep inside her, marking her as mine. We stay locked together, panting, the window cool against her skin, her body trembling in my arms.

When I pull out, she's unsteady, her legs shaking, and I catch her before she collapses. Her ass is red, welted from the belt, her pussy glistening with our combined release. She's a mess, and it's fucking beautiful. But I'm not done with her yet, not until I've shown her every facet of my control, even the gentle side she doesn't expect.

"Come on," I murmur, lifting her into my arms. She's too spent to protest, her head resting against my chest as I carry her to the penthouse's luxurious bathroom. The room is a sanctuary of marble and gold, the bathtub big enough for two. I set her on the counter, her wince as her sore ass meets the cold surface making me smirk.

I fill the tub, adding oils that fill the air with lavender and eucalyptus. She watches me, her eyes wary but soft, like she's trying to reconcile the man who just whipped her with the one preparing a bath. I strip off my suit, letting her see the scars, the muscles, the cock that's still half-hard for her. Then I lift her again, settling us both in the warm water, her back against my chest.

"Relax," I say, my voice softer now, but still commanding. I take a soft cloth, dipping it in the water and gently cleaning her, starting with her arms, her neck, then moving to her breasts. She sighs, leaning into me, and I feel her tension melt. "You took your punishment like a fucking queen," I murmur, my lips brushing her temple. "But you're still mine, Lea. Don't forget it."

I move the cloth between her legs, careful with her sensitive pussy, and she moans, her head falling back against my shoulder. My other hand massages her ass, soothing the welts, and she hisses, then relaxes, the pain blending with pleasure. "You're sore," I say, not an apology, just a fact. "But you loved it."

She doesn't deny it, her silence an admission. I wash her hair, my fingers working through the strands, and she's pliant, trusting in a way that makes my chest tighten. This is the real danger, not her lies, but the way she makes me feel something beyond control.

When she's clean, I lift her out, wrapping her in a heated towel and carrying her back to the bedroom. I lay her on the bed, applying a soothing cream to her welts, my touch gentle but firm. She watches me, her eyes searching, and I know she's still playing her game, still plotting. But for now, she's mine, marked and claimed, and I'll be damned if I let her forget it.

"Sleep," I say, pulling her against me. "Take a nap. We'll go to dinner later."

As she drifts off, her breathing evening out, I stare at the city beyond the window. Lea's dangerous, a wildcard in my controlled world. But I'm The Diplomat, and I don't lose. Not to her, not to anyone. She'll learn her place, even if I have to fuck it into her, one punishment at a time.

———

NEXT DAY, I work from my home office while Lea explores the penthouse, gathering impressions for her article but undoubtedly searching for insights into my operation. I allow it, having already ensured that anything sensitive remains locked away.

When I emerge to prepare for my meeting, she's curled on the sofa with her laptop, typing rapidly. She glances up as I adjust my cufflinks, a new suit for the afternoon's business, this one midnight blue with a subtle sheen.

"You look dangerous," she observes, setting her computer aside.

"That's the point," I reply, checking my reflection in the hallway mirror. "These particular associates respect power above all else. Appearance matters."

She approaches, stopping just behind me. Our eyes meet in the mirror's reflection. "When will you be back?"

"Late," I answer, turning to face her. "Don't wait up."

Something flickers in her expression, disappointment, perhaps, that she won't be accompanying me to gather more intelligence. "I'll be here."

I lean in, brushing my lips against hers in a kiss that's gentle, at odds with the intensity of our earlier encounters. "Good."

The elevator arrives with a soft chime. Before stepping inside, I glance back at her, standing in the foyer with an expression I can't quite decipher. For a moment, brief but disconcerting, I'm genuinely curious about what she's thinking behind that constructed exterior.

I dismiss the thought as the doors close between us. Curiosity about her motivations is useful only where it serves my purposes. Anything beyond that is a distraction I cannot afford.

THE MEETING at the Blackstone Club proceeds as expected, six hours of careful negotiation with Korean business interests whose legitimate enterprises serve as perfect covers for more lucrative endeavors. We discuss shipping routes, import regulations, and the delicate balance of international relations without ever mentioning what will actually flow through these established channels.

Throughout the discussions, I drop casual references to the academic conference, to Professor Song's research on shadow economies. The Korean businessmen exchange glances but reveal nothing beyond polite acknowledgment of her scholarly reputation. They're too disciplined to be baited so easily.

By the time we conclude, it's past midnight. The agreements reached are superficially about textile imports and technology exports. The subtext, the actual business, remains unspoken but mutually understood.

I return to the penthouse exhausted but satisfied. The groundwork has been laid for intercepting whatever operation Professor Song is facilitating between Korean interests and Moretti's organization. Now I need only to leverage Lea's connection to her mother to gain the last pieces of the puzzle.

The penthouse is quiet when I enter, lights dimmed to a soft glow. I find Lea in the bedroom, propped against pillows with a book in her lap. She's wearing one of my dress shirts again, this one crisp white against her golden skin. The sight stirs something possessive in me despite my fatigue.

"Successful meeting?" she asks, setting the book aside.

"Productive," I answer, removing my tie and jacket. "The Koreans are cautious but amenable to my terms."

Her eyes track my movements as I unbutton my shirt, revealing the scars and muscle beneath. "Business or pleasure?"

I smile at her attempt to extract information. "Business is pleasure when done correctly."

I disappear into the bathroom, emerging minutes later in silk pajama pants, chest bare. She's still awake, watching me with those calculating eyes that miss nothing. I slide into bed beside her, propping myself against the headboard.

"Come here," I say, not quite a command but close enough.

She hesitates for just a fraction of a second, before moving into my arms. I position her against my chest, one hand stroking her hair. The intimacy of the gesture is intentional, designed to foster trust, to lower defenses.

"Tell me about your mother," I say, feeling her stiffen against me. "You said you don't discuss her work. Why is that?"

She's quiet for a moment, weighing how much truth to reveal. "She's always been private about her research. Even when I was young, there were topics she wouldn't discuss, papers I wasn't allowed to read."

This rings true, the first genuine information she's offered without calculation. I press, "That must have been difficult, being kept at arm's length from something so important to her."

Another pause, longer this time. "I used to think she didn't trust me enough to share it. Now I wonder if she was trying to protect me from something."

"From what?" I ask, voice gentle, encouraging confidence.

She shakes her head, cheek rubbing against my chest. "I don't know. But lately—" She stops herself, reconsidering what she was about to reveal.

I let the silence stretch, knowing sometimes the most effective interrogation technique is patience. Eventually, she continues.

"Lately she's been even more secretive. Canceling our regular dinners, taking mysterious trips. When I ask, she deflects or changes the subject."

I hum thoughtfully, continuing to stroke her. "Parents often believe they're protecting their children by keeping secrets. Usually, they're just creating distance."

She shifts to look up at me, surprise clear in her expression. "That's remarkably insightful."

I smile, allowing a measured glimpse of vulnerability. "My uncle was the same way. Everything was 'need to know,' growing up."

This is true, though I rarely share it, a selected personal detail designed to foster false intimacy. The strategy works; I feel her softening against me, curiosity piqued by this rare crack in my armor.

"What happened to your father? You said he died of a heart attack?" she asks.

"That not true. He was murdered by a business associate he thought was a friend," I answer. "A situation that might have been avoided if he'd trusted my uncle enough to share his concerns."

Her expression shifts to genuine sympathy, another crack in her performance. "I'm sorry."

I shrug. "It was over thirty-five years ago. But it taught me the value of information, and the danger of keeping it from those who might help you."

The parallel to her situation with Eunji is deliberate, and I see the moment she makes the connection. Her brow furrows, thoughts turning inward. *I've planted the seed, the suggestion that her mother's secrecy might place them both in danger, that sharing information with me could be the safer choice.*

"Enough talk of family secrets," I murmur, tilting her chin up with one finger. "I can think of better uses for this time."

I kiss her then, slowly and deliberately, a careful seduction rather than earlier conquering. The softness of my approach is its own strategy, a honey trap rather than a steel cage.

She responds, melting against me in a way that seems practiced. Her hands slide up my chest as she straddles my lap with artful grace. I let her have this illusion of control, watching with hidden amusement as she believes she's seducing me.

"You're full of surprises, Varela," she breathes against my mouth. "I didn't take you for this gentle."

I smile against her lips. "There are many sides to me you haven't seen yet, piccola."

My hands settle on her hips, guiding her movements as she rocks against me. The friction is maddening even through the barriers of fabric, my silk pants, her damp underwear. I could take her now, hard and fast as I did earlier, but tonight's strategy requires a different approach. *Tonight, I want her to believe she's breaking down my defenses, gaining ground in this silent war between us.*

I lift the shirt from her body, revealing inch by inch of golden skin still marked from our previous encounters. She's beautiful in the dim light, all smooth curves and quiet strength. My hands trace the line of her collarbone, down to cup her breasts, thumbs circling nipples that harden under my touch.

She arches into the contact, a soft sound escaping her lips that seems unguarded. I file it away, another tell, another weakness to exploit. *She likes this gentler touch, this illusion of mutual pleasure rather than dominance.*

I flip our positions, pressing her into the mattress, my weight suspended above her. Her eyes widen before her expression shifts back to feigned desire. I lower my head, trailing kisses down her neck, her chest, taking a nipple into my mouth and sucking gently. Her back arches off the bed.

"Nico," she breathes.

I continue my descent, mapping her body with lips and tongue, noting each reaction, each involuntary shiver. This isn't merely pleasure, it's reconnaissance, learning what makes her respond authentically versus what's part of her performance. By the time I reach the waistband of her underwear, her breathing has quickened, her thighs trembling with anticipation.

I glance up, meeting her gaze as I hook my fingers into the

lace, slowly dragging it down her legs. "I've been thinking about tasting you all day," I murmur, the admission measured to seem like vulnerability while maintaining control.

Her eyes darken, pupils dilating with genuine desire. "Then start tasting."

I settle between her thighs, hands spreading her legs wider. She's already wet, arousal glistening on pink flesh. The sight stokes a primal satisfaction. Whatever game she's playing, this physical response can't be faked. I trace her entrance with my tongue, a slow, deliberate tease that makes her hips buck.

"Please," she murmurs, one hand fisting in the sheets.

I oblige, circling her clit with the tip of my tongue before sucking. Her reaction is immediate, a sharp gasp, thighs tensing around my head. I establish a rhythm, alternating between broad strokes and focused attention, reading her body's responses like a map to her surrender.

When I slide two fingers inside her, curving upward to find the spot that makes her vision blur, she cries out, a sound that seems torn from her, unplanned and uncontrolled. I work her, relentlessly, driving her toward the edge while watching for those moments of genuine response amidst the performance.

Her orgasm builds, flushed chest, quickened breath, the flutter of inner muscles around my fingers. When she breaks, it's with a cry that sounds almost surprised, as if the intensity caught her off guard. Her body arches, thighs clamping around my head as waves of pleasure course through her.

I continue my attention through the aftershocks, only relenting when she tugs at my hair, over-sensitized and breathless. I rise to my knees, looking down at her sprawled across the sheets, skin flushed, expression dazed. *This is power, seeing her undone, vulnerable in ways she can't fake.*

"Come here," she says, reaching for me, voice still unsteady.

I move over her, positioning myself between her thighs. The head of my cock nudges against her entrance, still sensitive from her orgasm. I push forward, inch by deliberate inch, watching her face for each reaction. Her eyes flutter closed, lips parting on a silent gasp as I fill her completely.

"Open your eyes," I command. "I want to see you."

She complies, meeting my gaze as I begin to move inside her. The rhythm is measured, controlled, each thrust designed to build pleasure rather than overwhelm. Her hands trace the scars on my back, fingertips exploring the map of old wounds with a gentleness that feels almost like genuine curiosity.

"You feel so good," she murmurs, lifting her hips to meet each thrust. "So deep."

I adjust the angle, hitting the spot that makes her breath catch. "Is this what you wanted, piccola? To have me inside you again?"

She nods, biting her lower lip in a way that seems contrived to appear vulnerable. "Yes. I've been thinking about it all day."

I smile, seeing through the performance while appreciating its execution. "Such a hungry little thing. So eager to be filled."

Her eyes narrow at the shift in my tone, a flicker of wariness beneath the desire. I maintain the gentle rhythm, though, lulling her back into complacency.

"Tell me what you want," I urge, voice honeyed with false surrender. "How do you want to be fucked?"

She hesitates, perhaps sensing the trap but unable to identify it. "Like this," she says. "Slow. Deep."

I oblige, maintaining the measured pace while escalating the depth of each thrust. Her breathing quickens, inner muscles tightening around me as another climax builds. I feel my release approaching but hold it at bay as control is the objective here, not pleasure.

"You're getting close again," I observe, watching the flush spread across her chest. "So responsive."

She nods, beyond words now as sensation overwhelms performance. Her nails dig into my shoulders, leaving crescent marks that sting pleasantly.

"Tell me you want me," I demand, voice low and commanding. "Say it."

"I want you," she breathes, eyes glazed with pleasure. "God, Nico, I want you."

"Again," I insist, driving deeper. "Louder."

"I want you!" she cries, the declaration appearing to surprise her with its vehemence.

"What else?" I press, maintaining the relentless rhythm. "Tell me what else you want."

She shakes her head, clearly struggling to form coherent thoughts as pleasure builds. "I—I don't—"

"You want information," I supply, voice hardening. "Access. The story. Isn't that right, piccola?"

Her eyes widen, clarity breaking through the haze of arousal. "That's not—"

I cut her off with a particularly deep thrust that makes her gasp. "Don't lie. Not here. Not like this." I wrap one hand around her throat, applying just enough pressure to make her skin flush beneath my palm. "You think you can fuck your way into my confidence? That I don't see what you're doing?"

Fear flashes in her eyes, subsumed by a darker heat as my grip tightens. Her inner walls clench around me, betraying her arousal at this display of dominance. "You're just as calculating," she manages, voice strained beneath my hand. "Using me to get to my mother."

The accusation, so accurate it can only be confirmation she's seen more of my files than I intended, should anger me. Instead, it triggers something darker, more primal. The pretense of a gentle lover falls away like a discarded mask.

"Smart girl," I praise, increasing the pressure on her throat while my other hand pins her wrists above her head. "But not smart enough."

I withdraw almost completely before slamming back into her, setting a brutal pace that makes her cry out. The gentleness of before is gone, replaced by raw possession, each thrust a claiming. My hand releases her throat to grab her hip, fingers digging into soft flesh hard enough to bruise.

"This is what you want, isn't it?" I growl, feeling her respond to the rougher treatment with undeniable enthusiasm. "To be taken. Controlled. Owned."

She shakes her head in denial even as her body betrays her, inner walls fluttering around my cock, thighs trembling with impending release. "No—"

"Yes," I counter, leaning down to bite the junction of her neck and shoulder, marking her. "Your body can't lie, Lea. Not to me."

The words seem to break something in her. She arches beneath me, walls clenching as orgasm crashes through her with unexpected force. The sight of her coming undone, eyes wide with shock at her own response, pushes me over the edge. I follow her into release, emptying myself inside her with a low groan.

For several moments, we remain locked together, both panting. I see calculation returning to her eyes as the haze of pleasure recedes, the journalist reasserting control over the woman. Still buried inside her, I brush a strand of hair from her face with unexpected gentleness.

"We understand each other now, I think," I murmur, watching her process the implications of what just happened, how her body responded to dominance despite her mind's resistance.

She swallows hard, voice hoarse when she finally speaks. "That wasn't—I didn't."

I smile, pressing a kiss to her forehead with false tenderness. "Yes, you did. And we both know it."

I withdraw from her body, rolling to lie beside her on the mattress. She remains still for a moment before turning away, curling on her side with her back to me. The position speaks volumes, an attempt to process, to rebuild defenses, to regain control of her narrative.

I watch the subtle tension in her shoulders, the careful regulation of her breathing. She believes she's concealing her thoughts, unaware that her very posture reveals everything, how she's positioned herself to see my nightstand, my phone, the door to the bathroom where my laptop sits charging.

She's still playing the game, still gathering intelligence, still believing she can maintain the upper hand. I smile in the darkness, admiring her persistence even as I counter it. *She doesn't realize that every move she makes only confirms what*

I already know: she's in far deeper than she planned, responding to me in ways she never anticipated.

The mattress shifts as she slips away, her movement quiet toward the bathroom like a cat trying to be sneaky. I roll over with an amused smirk, pulling the sheets up to my chest. *She'll be sore tomorrow, but if she thinks she's hurting now, the surprise awaiting her is far bigger.*

CHAPTER TWENTY

Lea

I step under the scalding spray, a hiss escaping between clenched teeth as water hits sensitive skin. Every movement is a reminder. Muscles I didn't know I had protest, small pains blossoming in unexpected places. I brace myself against the shower wall, unsure if my legs will hold me.

This wasn't just rough sex like these last few days. Today was something else entirely, a demonstration of power that went beyond physical domination. The calculating coldness in his eyes when he flipped me over, the precise way he applied pressure, knowing how much would hurt without leaving lasting damage. *This wasn't passion; it was methodical.*

I reach for the soap, lathering it between trembling hands. As I wash, I catalog every mark, every ache, not just as evidence of what happened, but as data points in understanding Nico Varela. The man I thought I was manipulating revealed something primal tonight, something beyond the controlled exterior he typically presents.

Even now, the journalist in me takes notes.

My throat feels raw from his squeeze and sounds I don't remember making. I close my eyes under the spray, trying to process all the sensations still going through my body. Behind the soreness and discomfort lurks something more complicated, a response I'm reluctant to acknowledge.

There had been moments, brief, disorienting flashes, when pain transformed into something else. When his controlled brutality had triggered responses in me, I never knew existed. When I'd found myself pressing toward rather than away from his punishing grip.

That realization is more unsettling than any physical discomfort.

I press my forehead against the cool tile, letting water run down my back. "You can handle this," I mutter to myself. "You've been through worse."

Have I, though? The question floats unbidden.

I shut off the water with more force than necessary, wrapping myself in one of his soft towels. *Who am I? The ambitious journalist? The scheming seductress? The willing participant in whatever just happened on that bed?*

All of them, I decide. *And yet, somehow, none of them.*

Back in the bedroom, Nico sleeps soundly, his face relaxed in a way it never is while conscious. I study him from the doorway, this man who just dismantled me piece by piece. In sleep, he looks almost vulnerable, a dangerous illusion.

I know what I have to do. Retreat isn't an option, not with Moretti's threats hanging over my head, not with my mother's safety at stake, not with the story of a lifetime still unfolding. I've ventured too far into the labyrinth to turn back now.

No, I need to be smarter. More strategic. The game has escalated, and so must my approach.

I move to the dresser, retrieving a t-shirt. The soft cotton slides over my marked body, falling to mid-thigh. I could sleep on the couch, part of me wants to, but that would be a tactical error. Instead, I slip back into bed, careful not to touch him.

The mattress dips as I settle in, and I stiffen as Nico stirs beside me. His eyes remain closed, but his voice, thick with sleep, fills the darkness.

"Your lip is split."

I touch the tender spot where he bit down too hard earlier. "It's fine."

"No, it's not." His eyes open now, focusing on me with surprising clarity for someone just waking. "You'll need to conceal it tomorrow."

"Tomorrow?" I keep my voice neutral, though my heart-beat quickens.

He shifts onto his side, studying me in the dim light filtering through the curtains. "We have an event. Private gathering at the club. International interests. High-profile."

My mind races. *An event means witnesses, visibility, information.* "What kind of event?"

"The kind where appearances matter." His fingers reach out, brushing my swollen lip with unexpected gentleness. "This won't do."

I resist the urge to flinch away, forcing myself to remain still under his touch. "I'll handle it."

"See that you do." His hand moves from my lip to my

hair, stroking it with deceptive tenderness. "You'll need to look the part."

"The part of what, exactly?" I dare to ask.

His smile in the darkness makes my stomach clench. "My companion. My chosen partner. The woman with exclusive access to my world."

The word 'exclusive' hangs between us. It's what I wanted, access no other journalist has obtained. But the price keeps rising.

"I'll have something appropriate delivered for you to wear," he continues, his hand now trailing down my neck to my shoulder, tracing the outline of bruises he left there. "Something that covers these. For now."

The implication being that next time, perhaps, he won't be so considerate.

"What am I walking into, Nico?" I ask, steadier than I feel. "Who will be there?"

His fingers pause their exploration. "People who can open doors. Or close them permanently." He leans closer, his breath warm against my ear. "People who know things."

Ice floods my veins. "What are you talking about?"

But he's already pulling away, settling back onto his pillow. "Get some sleep, Lea. Tomorrow will require your full attention."

I lie rigid beside him, mind spinning. *Is it a threat? A lure? More manipulation?*

I slide further under the covers, wincing as the movement awakens fresh aches. Nico's breathing has already deepened again, but I don't trust his apparent return to sleep. He's shown me plenty times that nothing about him is as it seems.

I SIP MY CHAMPAGNE, letting the bubbles dance across my tongue as I observe the room through lowered lashes. The five-star hotel's private event space vibrates with quiet power; an exclusive gathering of international figures whose wealth and influence cast long shadows across both legitimate and shadowed realms. The lighting is dim, casting everyone in the most flattering glow while concealing the subtle tells that might reveal too much.

My midnight blue dress whispers against my skin as I shift my weight, the fabric chosen by Nico, modest enough to be taken seriously, revealing enough to mark me as his. The bruises from last night's "lesson" remain concealed beneath the high neckline, my split lip artfully camouflaged with makeup.

I catch fragments of conversation around me: shipping routes discussed in the same breath as stock portfolios, political shifts mentioned alongside supply chains. Every sentence seems to carry double meaning, and I'm recording it all in my mental notebook.

"Impressed?" Nico materializes beside me, one arm sliding possessively around my waist. His touch ignites a conflicting storm of responses, desire and wariness, comfort and alarm.

"It's quite the gathering," I reply, careful to keep my voice neutral while leaning into his touch, a purposeful response that affirms his ownership for any watching eyes. "The mayor's chief of staff speaking so openly with that shipping magnate from Singapore is particularly interesting."

Nico's lips quirk upward, approval glinting in his dark eyes. "You notice the right details. Good."

The praise shouldn't warm me, but it does, a pavlovian response I'm struggling to control. *Four weeks ago, I was an ambitious new journalist chasing a career-making story. Now I'm playing girlfriend to Chicago's most dangerous power broker while trying to unravel his connection to my increasingly mysterious mother.*

And my body still aches from how thoroughly he claimed me last night.

"The Korean delegation arrives in twenty minutes," Nico murmurs against my ear, his breath warm on my skin. "Stay close when they do."

I nod, taking another sip of champagne. "Should I prepare to be invisible or engaging?"

His fingers trace small circles at the small of my back. "Observe first. Take part if invited. These men respect intelligence but resent presumption, especially from women. Balance the line carefully."

"I always do," I remind him, meeting his eyes.

Something flashes in his eyes, pride mixed with caution. He's still recalibrating after last night, when I proved I could match his brutal honesty with my own. When I acknowledged that we're both using each other while refusing to back down.

My phone buzzes in my clutch, three short beats that signal a message from Sienna, my only remaining tether to the normal world. *I'll check it later, when Nico is occupied. For now, I need to focus on navigating this landscape of predators in bespoke suits.*

"Varela." A silver-haired man approaches, hand

extended. "A pleasure to see you outside of negotiation rooms."

Nico's posture shifts subtly, straightening, hardening, though his smile remains perfectly calibrated. "Senator Harrington. I didn't expect you until later."

I recognize the name. Senate Intelligence Committee, three terms, rumored to be eyeing a presidential run. *What's he doing at a gathering of international business interests with known criminal connections?* The journalist in me practically salivates at the potential story.

"Plans change," Harrington replies with practiced affability before turning to me. "And who is your charming companion?"

Nico's hand tightens at my waist. "Ms. Lea Song. A journalist working on a profile piece." The way he phrases it, not quite a lie, not fully the truth, reminds me how skilled he is at operating in gray areas.

I extend my hand, channeling the poise my mother drilled into me since childhood. "Senator. Your work on the Pacific Rim Security Act was quite illuminating."

Surprise flickers across the senator's features before settling into appreciation. "You follow international policy?"

"Among other things," I reply, keeping my tone light. "The implications for trade agreements with Korea were particularly interesting, especially regarding pharmaceutical exports."

It's a deliberate probe, watching for reactions. Nico's fingers press warning into my side, but I maintain my pleasant smile. The senator's eyes narrow before he chuckles.

"Ms. Song, you're better informed than most policy advisors on my staff." He turns to Nico. "Careful with this one,

Varela. Beauty and brains. That is a dangerous combination."

"I'm well aware," Nico responds, voice carrying an edge only I can detect.

The senator excuses himself to greet another guest, and Nico steers me toward a quieter corner of the room. His grip is firm but not painful, a controlled display of displeasure.

"That was bold," he murmurs, voice low enough that only I can hear. "Mentioning Korean pharmaceuticals to a man whose committee oversees international drug enforcement."

I meet his gaze. "I'm doing what you brought me here to do, observing while gathering information. Unless you'd prefer I stand silently and look pretty?"

A muscle in his jaw ticks, the only sign that I've struck a nerve. "There's a difference between intelligence and reck-lessness, piccola." The endearment sounds like a warning. "The senator has significant interests in maintaining certain trade relationships. Probing them directly is unwise."

"Then perhaps you should be more specific about which questions I'm allowed to ask," I counter, keeping my voice sweet while my eyes challenge him.

Before he can respond, a ripple of subtle movement sweeps through the room. Conversation volumes lower as all eyes shift toward the entrance. The Korean delegation has arrived.

The group is smaller than I expected, three men and one woman, all impeccably dressed. The woman's gaze is sharp, assessing. They move with practiced coordination, the oldest man ahead as their apparent leader.

"Mr. Park," Nico greets the leader, stepping forward with calibrated deference. "Welcome to Chicago."

The older man inclines his head. "Mr. Varela. Your hospitality is appreciated." His English is perfect.

"May I introduce Ms. Lea Song," Nico continues, drawing me forward.

I bow slightly, enough to show cultural awareness. "안녕하세요," I greet them in Korean. "It's an honor to meet you."

Mr. Park's eyebrows rise, reassessing me. "You speak Korean, Ms. Song?"

"Poorly," I admit with a self-deprecating smile. "My mother insisted on teaching me, but I fear I've neglected practice."

"Your mother is Korean?" asks the woman in the delegation, her gaze suddenly more intense.

"Yes," I reply, watching for their reactions. "Eunji Song. She's a professor at Chicago University."

A look passes between the delegates so quickly I almost miss it, confirming my suspicion that my mother's academic work intersects with their interests.

"Professor Song is highly regarded," Mr. Park says. "Her work on shadow economies provides valuable insights."

Nico touches me, a silent signal to tread carefully. I heed the warning, steering the conversation to safer topics. The exchange continues for several minutes, a masterclass in saying nothing while appearing engaged.Nico guides the conversation toward their real purpose.

"Perhaps we should discuss the proposal in more private settings," he suggests, gesturing toward a door I hadn't noticed before.

Mr. Park nods, but his gaze lingers on me. "Will Ms. Song be joining us?"

The question surprises me. Nico recovers instantly. "That would be unusual for these discussions."

"But perhaps valuable," counters the Korean woman, studying me. "A fresh perspective."

"While Ms. Song's insights are always appreciated," Nico replies, "these particular matters require absolute discretion among primary parties. I'm sure you understand."

Mr. Park smiles, accepting the polite refusal. "Of course. Business requires certain protocols."

Nico nods to me. "Enjoy the party, Lea. I won't be long."

I watch them disappear through the private door, my mind buzzing. They know my mother. They were interested enough in me to research me. What exactly are they discussing in there? The implication of "specialty pharmaceuticals" and "shadow economies" hangs heavy in the air.

I mingle for a while, gathering snippets of conversation, observing the power dynamics, but my thoughts keep returning to the Koreans and my mother. What is she involved in?

Sometime later, the delegation emerges from the private room. As they pass me on their way out, the Korean woman pauses.

"Your mother speaks of you often," she says, her voice pitched for my ears alone. "She would be proud of your poise today."

Before I can respond, she glides away, leaving me frozen with shock and confusion. My mother speaks of me to these people? Enough for it to be "often"? The implications make my head spin.

Nico is pulled into conversation with another group. I

touch his arm. "I need a moment," I murmur, nodding toward the ladies' room.

He studies me before nodding. "Don't be long."

I weave through the crowd, maintaining a composed exterior while my thoughts churn like a storm-tossed sea. The women's restroom is luxurious. To my relief, it's empty.

I lean against the counter, releasing a shaky breath as I mutter to myself, gripping the cool marble. "You need clarity, not panic."

What I need most is to contact my mother, to demand answers about her connection to these people. But that will have to wait. For now, I need to process what I've learned and maintain my composure long enough to get through the evening.

I head to one of the stalls, needing a moment of complete privacy to collect myself. The door clicks shut behind me, and I lean against it, closing my eyes. My chest feels tight, each beat a reminder of how far I've strayed from the relative safety of normal journalism into a realm where information isn't just power, it's life and death.

My mother knows these people. They know her, not just as an academic but as someone involved in their operations. And they know about me. The realization sends a fresh wave of dizziness through me.

I take several deep breaths, forcing my racing thoughts into order. Whatever she's involved in, I need to approach it methodically. Gather information, connect dots, identify leverage points. The investigative process is familiar territory, even if the stakes have escalated beyond anything I anticipated.

After using the facilities, I linger a moment longer,

mentally preparing to return to my role as Nico's attentive companion. When I emerge from the stall, the sight that greets me stops my breath mid-beat.

Dante Moretti leans against the counter, arms crossed over his chest. The air seems to crackle around him, heavy with something dangerous.

In the men's bathroom, this would be strange enough. In the women's restroom, it's beyond alarming. It's threatening. I freeze, adrenaline flooding my system as instinct screams danger.

"Ms. Song," he greets me, voice casual as though we're meeting at a coffee shop. "Don't look so frightened. If I wanted to hurt you, you wouldn't see me coming."

The statement does nothing to calm my racing heart. I straighten, forcing steel into my backbone as I step toward the sink furthest from him. "Mr. Moretti. This is unexpected."

"Is it?" He watches me through the mirror as I wash my hands with deliberate care, pretending a composure I don't feel. "I think we both know this conversation was inevitable."

I meet his gaze in the reflection, refusing to show weakness. "I wasn't aware we needed to have a conversation."

He smiles, a predator's expression that never reaches his eyes. "Varela's latest playtoy should know what game she's playing in."

"I'm not his toy," I counter, reaching for a towel to dry my hands. The slight tremor in my fingers betrays me.

"No?" Moretti pushes away from the counter, taking a step closer. "Then what are you? His confidante? His partner? His weakness?"

The last word hangs between us, loaded with implication. I turn to face him, refusing to be cornered against the sinks.

"What do you want, Mr. Moretti?"

He studies me with unsettling intensity, head tilted as though examining a curious specimen. "To offer a warning, out of professional courtesy."

"Professional courtesy," I repeat, skepticism clear in my tone. "Why would you extend me any courtesy, professional or otherwise?"

"Not to you," he clarifies, his smile widening. "To your mother."

The mention of my mother sends ice through my veins. I struggle to maintain my expression, but something must show in my eyes because Moretti nods, satisfied by my reaction.

"Ah. So he hasn't told you everything. Interesting." He takes another step closer, invading my space with deliberate intimidation. "Nico Varela is going down, Ms. Song. I've made certain of it. The only question that remains is whether you'll go down with him."

I swallow hard, mind racing to process the implications. "Why would you care?"

"I don't, particularly," he admits with casual cruelty. "But your mother is a valuable associate. It would be inconvenient if her daughter became collateral damage in Varela's inevitable fall."

My breath catches. "What kind of business could my mother possibly have with someone like you?"

Moretti's expression shifts to something like amusement. "Someone like me? You're sleeping with Nico Varela. The moral high ground isn't exactly yours to claim."

The barb hits its mark, but I push past it. "You didn't answer my question."

"No," he agrees, checking his watch with exaggerated casualness. "I didn't."

I take a risk, stepping closer rather than retreating. "My mother is an academic. A professor of political science. Whatever you think she's involved in—"

"Is what Varela is trying to control," Moretti interrupts, all pretense of amusement vanishing. "Ask yourself, Ms. Song, why is a man like Nico Varela suddenly interested in a junior journalist? Why is he keeping you so close? What does he hope to gain that's worth the risk you represent?"

The questions strike too close to my own doubts, my own suspicions about Nico's motivations for bringing me into his world. I struggle to maintain my composure.

"You should return to the party," Moretti continues, straightening his already-perfect tie. "Your keeper will be looking for you. But remember my warning, Varela's interest in you has nothing to do with your charm or your body. It's about what you represent, what you can lead him to."

"And what's that?" I demand, voice steadier than I feel.

His smile returns, sharp as a blade. "The same thing I already have, your mother's cooperation in matters far beyond your understanding." He moves toward the door, pausing with his hand on the handle. "Choose carefully which puppet master pulls your strings, Ms. Song. Only one of us will still be standing when this is over."

With that parting shot, he slips out, leaving me alone with my racing thoughts and pounding blood.

I grip the counter, force myself to breathe, to think through the implications of what just happened.

Moretti knows my mother. Is doing business with her. And believes Nico is using me to access whatever she's involved in.

The pieces don't quite fit, my mother, the dedicated academic, involved with not one but two of Chicago's most powerful criminal figures? It seems impossible, yet the evidence keeps mounting. First the Korean delegation's familiarity with her work, now Moretti's explicit confirmation of their "association."

I splash cold water on my wrists, a trick my mother taught me years ago to calm a racing pulse. My mother. The woman who raised me alone after my father's death, who pushed me to excel, who always kept certain parts of her life compartmentalized. Who's been increasingly distant and secretive in recent months.

Who might be at the center of whatever power struggle is playing out between Nico and Moretti.

I need to find her, to demand answers. But first, I need to get through this evening without revealing to Nico that Moretti approached me. *Something tells me that information is valuable currency I should hold on to until I understand more.*

After reapplying my lipstick and pinching color back into my cheeks, I exit the bathroom, scanning the room with newfound awareness. The gathering no longer appears elegant and exclusive, it's a battlefield where invisible currents of power and information flow beneath polite conversation and crystal champagne flutes.

I spot Nico, his tall figure commanding attention even in a room full of powerful people. He's engaged in conversation with a Japanese businessman, but his eyes find me the moment I emerge, tracking my movement across the room. *I wonder if he can read the confrontation on my face, if my mask of composure has slipped enough to reveal the turmoil beneath.*

As I approach, Nico extends his hand, drawing me to his side with practiced ease. His fingers interlock with mine, warm and steady.

"Everything alright?" he asks, voice pitched for my ears alone.

I smile, the expression not quite reaching my eyes. "Of course. Just needed a moment to freshen up."

His gaze lingers, searching my face for something, lies, perhaps, or signs of distress. I meet it steadily, revealing nothing. After a beat, he turns back to the Japanese businessman, reintegrating me into the conversation.

"Mr. Tanaka was just discussing the challenges of navigating regulatory differences between markets," Nico explains, his thumb tracing small circles against my palm, a gesture that appears affectionate but feels possessive, evaluative.

I slip back into my role with practiced ease, making appropriate comments, asking intelligent questions, playing the part of the captivating companion. But beneath the performance, my mind races with new questions and suspicions.

What does my mother know about all this? How deeply is she involved? And most pressingly, is Nico's interest in me just a means to access her?

CHAPTER TWENTY-ONE

Nico

I FEEL IT BEFORE ANYTHING HAPPENS, THAT ELECTRIC charge in the air that precedes catastrophe. Some men call it intuition. I call it survival instinct, honed through years of navigating Chicago's underworld. Tonight, that instinct screams danger.

The security feeds stream across multiple screens in my office, the low electronic hum a familiar counterpoint to the taste of the Macallan on my tongue. I watch my client's latest shipment arriving at the warehouse. Everything appears normal, the men efficient, the transfer smooth. Yet something feels wrong. I can't place it, but the sensation prickles at the back of my neck, a phantom warning I've learned never to ignore.

"Third checkpoint confirmed delivery," Marco says, standing by the window overlooking the main floor of Purgatorio. The club is busy below us, unaware of the tension building in this room. "All inventory accounted for."

I nod, eyes still tracking movement on the screens. "And our lookouts?"

Marco shifts his weight, a subtle tell I recognize. He's concerned. "Garza and Rivera haven't checked in for the last hour."

My fingers still on the keyboard. *Garza never misses check-in. Even when the feds were crawling all over his neighborhood last month, he found a way to signal all-clear.*

"Both of them? Same location?"

"Different posts. East and south approaches." Marco's voice remains professional, but I catch the underlying worry. He's been with me long enough to read the same warning signs.

I lean back, considering. *Two lookouts going dark simultaneously isn't coincidence. It's coordination.*

"Call them again," I instruct, already rising from my desk. "Then initiate shutdown. I want the club cleared in twenty minutes. Staff too. Keep only security team Alpha."

Marco nods once, already dialing. I watch as his expression hardens when the call goes straight to voicemail. He switches to the other number with the same result.

"Something's coming," I murmur, more to myself than to Marco. I cross to the hidden panel behind my bookshelf, entering the code that reveals a compact arsenal. My Sig Sauer P226 slides into my hand with its usual weight. I check the magazine, the action smooth and practiced.

"Boss, tonight's revenue—" Marco begins.

"Leave it. If my instinct is wrong, we lose one night's profit. If I'm right..." I slide the gun into my shoulder holster, adjusting my jacket to conceal it.

Marco doesn't argue. In fifteen years at my side, he's seen

my instincts proven right too many times. "What about the journalist?"

I pause. Lea. Currently downstairs interviewing my staff for her article. She's a planned risk that now threatens to become a liability.

"Find her. Bring her up here. We leave in ten minutes."

As Marco exits, I turn to the security system controls, initiating lockdown protocols. Bulletproof shutters descend over external windows. Access points reduce to minimum essential entries. The system is designed to transform Purgatorio from nightclub to fortress in under two minutes.

I pull out my phone, scrolling to Alessandro's contact. My finger hovers over the call button, then withdraws. *No need to alarm him yet. If this is Moretti making a move, I want confirmation before I involve my uncle.*

Instead, I dial our backup team stationed three blocks over.

"Status check," I say when the line connects.

"All quiet, boss," comes the response. "Traffic normal. No unusual activity."

"Move to position Bravo. Be ready to extract on my signal."

"Copy that. ETA eight minutes."

I end the call, my mind already mapping contingencies. If this is Moretti, he'll have planned thoroughly. The man is many things, volatile, ambitious, brutal, but never sloppy. If he's coming for me, he'll have multiple angles covered.

The door opens, and Marco returns with Lea. Her expression shifts from mild annoyance to alert concern as she reads the tension in the room.

"What's happening?" she asks, dark eyes scanning the security monitors, the visible weapon at my side.

"Possible security situation," I answer, vague. Despite our arrangement, there are limits to what she needs to know. "We're leaving. Now."

To her credit, she doesn't waste time with unnecessary questions. She gathers her materials, notebook, recorder, phone, and slips them into her bag with efficient movements. I've noticed this about her: beneath the journalistic persistence and sharp intelligence, there's a pragmatic survivor.

"Marco, take point. Standard extraction path C." I turn to Lea. "Stay between us. Move when we move. Stop when we stop. Understand?"

She nods once, eyes steady on mine. No fear yet, just focused attention and the slight flush of adrenaline across her cheekbones.

I check the monitor one final time. The club has emptied considerably in the past few minutes, my security team ushering patrons toward the exits with minimum fuss. Most will assume it's a routine closure, perhaps for a private event. By tomorrow, they'll hear about a gas leak or electrical issue that required evacuation.

If tomorrow comes.

The thought flits through my mind unbidden. I dismiss it. Doubt is a luxury I cannot afford.

"Let's move," I say, gesturing toward the private exit behind my office. This route will bypass the main floor, leading to the service area where a vehicle should be waiting.

Marco leads the way, his movements controlled yet alert. Lea follows, her steps measured and quiet. I bring up the rear, scanning constantly, the weight of my weapon a reassuring presence against my ribs.

We descend the narrow stairwell in silence. The music from the club grows fainter, replaced by the dull hum of industrial air handling systems. The service corridor stretches before us, dimly lit and utilitarian with concrete floors, exposed pipes overhead, steel doors at regular intervals.

We're halfway to the exit when I hear it, the subtle click of a side door being tested. Marco freezes, hand raised to halt our progress. Lea stops, her body tensing as she registers the change in atmosphere.

Three seconds of absolute stillness. Four. Five.

The door at the end of the corridor bursts open.

Everything happens at once.

The gunshot cracks through the confined space, deafening in its intensity. Glass shatters as a bullet strikes an overhead light fixture. Marco reacts with practiced efficiency, shoving Lea behind a concrete support pillar, drawing his weapon in the same fluid motion.

I'm already moving, dropping into a crouch as I draw my Sig. Four men in tactical gear pour through the doorway, professional killers, not street thugs. No masks, no hesitation. They're here to eliminate, not intimidate.

The first attacker advances, weapon raised. I center my sight picture and squeeze the trigger twice in rapid succession. Center mass. The impact drives him backward, weapon discharging harmlessly into the ceiling as he falls.

Marco engages the second, the exchange of gunfire creating a disorienting barrage of sound in the enclosed space, the sharp scent of cordite stinging my nostrils. The emergency lighting kicks in automatically as more fixtures shatter, bathing everything in pulsing red. Blood appears black in this light, shadows writhing like living things against the concrete walls.

I adjust position, seeking better cover as the third attacker moves laterally, attempting to flank us. My mind operates on two tracks simultaneously: the immediate tactical situation and the broader strategic implications. *Why tonight? What intelligence did Moretti receive that prompted this timing?*

The questions evaporate as a second team breaches from the opposite direction. We're caught in a classic pincer movement, escape routes closing rapidly.

"Panic room!" Marco shouts over the gunfire, already maneuvering toward the concealed entrance twenty meters away.

I assess instantly. We're cut off. The distance is too great, the cover too sparse. We'd be exposed for a critical five seconds. Unacceptable risk.

"Negative!" I call back, gesturing toward a service alcove to our right. "Alternative route!"

Marco nods, understanding. We've rehearsed contingencies for years, mapped every potential escape path. He provides covering fire as I grip Lea's arm, pulling her toward the alcove.

She moves with surprising coordination, staying low as instructed. No screaming, no freezing in panic. Her adaptability continues to impress, even in this chaos.

We're three meters from cover when it happens. A bullet clips my side, tearing through my jacket and shirt to score a burning path across my ribs. White-hot pain flares, but adrenaline keeps it manageable. *I've experienced worse. This is superficial, painful but not debilitating.*

We reach the alcove, temporary shelter from the immediate gunfire. I check my wound. It's bleeding steadily but not arterial. Manageable. Lea's eyes widen at the sight of blood darkening my shirt, but she says nothing, maintaining the composed silence.

Marco provides suppressing fire from his position, buying us precious seconds. I'm calculating our next move when catastrophe strikes.

Marco takes a hit to his right leg. The impact spins him, driving him to one knee. Even from this distance, I can see it's bad, femoral involvement likely from the volume of blood already darkening his pants.

Despite the injury, he maintains fire discipline, continuing to engage the approaching attackers. But his mobility is compromised. He can't make it to our position.

Time slows as I watch one of Moretti's men advance on Marco's position, weapon raised for a kill shot. It's one of the fucking twins. Matteo. I try to establish a firing line, but the angle is wrong, the distance too great for a reliable headshot around Lea's position.

Marco knows. I see it in his eyes as he glances my way, not pleading for help, but offering absolution for what we both know is about to happen. Then he turns back to face his executioner, defiance written in every line of his body.

"Tell Moretti he still shoots like a bitch," he spits, blood on his teeth, chin raised in one final act of loyalty.

The gunshot reverberates through the corridor like a thunderclap. Marco's body jerks once, then slumps forward, motionless on the concrete floor.

Something breaks inside me.

The cold, strategic calculation that has defined my

survival for decades shatters, replaced by a white-hot rage that consumes rational thought. Marco isn't just my right hand, he's the brother I chose, the one person who has stood beside me through every trial, the only man I trust completely.

Was. Was the only man.

I move before conscious decision forms, advancing on Matteo with single-minded purpose. As I move past another attacker, a blade slashes across my shoulder. I register the burning pain distantly, irrelevantly. My world has narrowed to a single objective: Matteo, the man who executed Marco will die by my hand.

Three shots in rapid succession. Center mass, center mass, throat. Matteo crumples, weapon clattering to the ground. The visceral satisfaction is immediate but hollow as Marco remains motionless on the floor, blood pooling beneath him.

I don't see his brother coming from my blind side until it's almost too late. A crushing impact between my shoulder blades drives me to my knees. Something cracks, ribs giving way under the force. My weapon skitters across the concrete floor, beyond reach.

Copper floods my mouth. *Internal damage, possibly lung involvement.* The tactical part of my brain catalogs injuries automatically, even as I try to regain my feet.

Too slow. Vincent looms above me, tactical knife raised for a killing stroke. In that crystalline moment of clarity, I recognize my failure. *After decades of perfect strategy, I'm going to die because I let emotion cloud judgment. Marco would be disappointed.*

Vincent laughs hysterically. "Look who's got the knife

now, motherfucker!" The blade descends in what feels like slow motion.

Then impossibly, Lea emerges from cover, my fallen weapon gripped in both hands. Her stance is all wrong, clearly unpracticed, but her determination is absolute. The first shot catches Vincent in the shoulder, spinning him away from me. The second finds his throat with devastating accuracy.

The sound he makes as he falls is grotesque, wet, gurgling and final. He collapses in stages, first to his knees, then forward onto the concrete. Arterial blood pulses in diminishing spurts from the ruined neck.

Lea stands frozen, the gun still extended, eyes wide with shock. The weapon trembles in her grip as the reality of what she's done registers on her face.

I struggle to my feet, pain now screaming through every nerve ending. The adrenaline buffer is fading, allowing full awareness of my injuries to surface. "Lea," I gasp, but she doesn't respond, transfixed by the dying man at her feet.

Distant sounds of movement snap me back to tactical awareness. We're not clear yet. More of Moretti's men are approaching, drawn by the gunfire.

I grasp Lea's arm firmly, the contact breaking her paralysis. "We need to move. Now."

Her eyes finally focus on me, pupils dilated with shock and residual adrenaline. I pry my weapon from her unresisting fingers, checking the magazine. Three rounds remaining. Not ideal, but workable.

Moving hurts. Each breath sends shards of pain through my chest. Definitely broken ribs. Blood soaks my shirt on two sides now, the shoulder wound deeper than I initially assessed. But Marco's body lies just meters away. Surrender isn't an option.

"This way," I direct, leading Lea toward a service passage concealed behind what appears to be a maintenance panel. Few know of these hidden routes, a security feature I insisted on when renovating the building. Now, that paranoia might save our lives.

The narrow passage is designed for maintenance access, barely wide enough for two people. The air here is stale, thick with the smell of dust and machinery oil. I navigate by memory and touch, each step a negotiation with increasing pain. Twice I'm forced to stop, leaning against the wall as vision blurs and darkness threatens at the edges of consciousness.

Lea supports me without being asked, her slim shoulder braced under my arm, taking weight I can no longer fully bear. The shock of her first kill seems contained by the immediate need for survival. *That breakdown will come later, if we survive long enough to allow it.*

After what feels like an eternity of painful progress, we reach the concealed safe room. I press my palm against a seemingly solid wall section, revealing a biometric scanner hidden within the paneling. A soft click, and a door swings inward to reveal a small space equipped with surveillance monitors, weapons, medical supplies, and basic provisions. The air inside is cool, sterile, smelling faintly of antiseptic.

My legs finally surrender as we cross the threshold. I collapse into a chair, each breath a stabbing reminder of damaged ribs and continuing blood loss.

"Lock the door," I instruct, voice rough with pain. "The code is 3-9-8-4."

Lea's fingers tremble as she automatically enters the sequence. She turns back, her face ashen. Abstract patterns of blood, not her own, stain her clothes.

"Marco's dead," she states flatly, as if saying it aloud might make it less real.

I nod once, sharply. The grief is a separate wound, deeper than the physical ones bleeding through my clothing. Marco has been my constant for fifteen years, the one person who knew every aspect of my operation, who could anticipate my needs before I voiced them. His loss is more than personal; it's a strategic catastrophe.

But grief is a luxury I cannot afford right now. Survival first. Then vengeance.

"Check the monitors," I direct. "Are they still in the building?"

Lea moves to the surveillance station, fingers leaving smudges of blood on the controls as she cycles through camera feeds. "I see three men searching the main floor," she reports with surprising steadiness. "Two more at the exits."

Five hostiles remaining. Against one wounded defender and a civilian who's never held a weapon until tonight. The tactical situation is untenable.

I assess our options. I'm losing blood from two wounds. My broken ribs compromise mobility and combat effectiveness. The safe room is secure but ultimately a dead end as we can't remain here indefinitely.

For perhaps the first time in my adult life, I face a scenario without a clear strategic advantage.

"My phone," I say, the decision forming as I speak. "Call Alessandro."

Lea retrieves the phone from my jacket pocket, now

sticky with dried blood. She navigates to contacts with remarkable composure, considering the circumstances. The call connects as she turns on the speaker.

"Nephew?" Alessandro's voice, precise and cultured as always.

"It's Lea Song," she answers, her voice steady despite everything she's witnessed tonight. "Nico's hurt. Marco's dead. Moretti's men hit the club."

A beat of silence follows as Alessandro processes the catastrophic implications of those three short sentences. "How bad?" he finally asks, voice shifting to the cold efficiency I recognize.

Lea looks at me, assessing visible injuries. "Bullet graze on his side, deep cut on his shoulder, maybe broken ribs. He's losing blood."

"Can he move?" Alessandro directs the question to her.

I take the phone from her hand, unwilling to be discussed as if absent. "I can move," I assert, though the claim feels increasingly tenuous as shock and blood loss take their toll.

Alessandro doesn't waste time questioning my assessment. "I'm sending a team. Five minutes. Get to the east service entrance if you can. If not, stay put and they'll extract you."

Five minutes. The timeframe is both reassuringly brief and dauntingly distant. We need to move now, while Moretti's men are still searching other areas of the building. The entrance is two hundred meters from our current position, a distance that would normally be trivial but now looms as a significant challenge.

I force myself to stand, using the back of the chair for

support as the room tilts alarmingly. Pain radiates from my ribs in waves that threaten to buckle my knees.

"I need your help," I admit to Lea. The admission costs nearly as much as the physical agony. Vulnerability has never come easily.

She steps forward without hesitation, sliding her arm around my waist, positioning herself to take my weight while avoiding the worst of my injuries. Her strength surprises me and not just her physical strength, but the steadiness of purpose after everything she's witnessed tonight.

We move together toward the exit, each step a negotiation between necessity and physical limitation. I focus on controlling my breathing, minimizing the stabbing pain from my ribs while maintaining consciousness. One step. Another. The door. The corridor beyond.

Our progress is painfully slow. Every few meters, I'm forced to pause, leaning against the wall as dizziness threatens to overwhelm me. Lea remains steadfast, her body pressed against mine in necessary support, her expression grimly determined.

We pass the main corridor where the initial confrontation occurred. Marco's body lies facedown on the concrete, surrounded by a pool of blood. I force myself to look, to bear witness to the consequence of my miscalculation, to burn this image into memory as fuel for what must follow.

Moretti has always been ambitious, ruthless in pursuit of territory and power. But this act...executing Marco, and attempting to eliminate me in my own club, crosses a threshold from which there is no return. The debt incurred tonight will be paid in full, with compound interest. Moretti has signed his own death warrant; he simply doesn't know it yet.

We continue our painful progress toward the east service entrance. Twice we freeze at sounds of movement nearby, pressing into shadows until the threat passes. Lea adapts to these necessities without instruction, her body language mirroring mine with surprising intuition.

Finally, the service entrance comes into view, a utilitarian steel door illuminated by a single emergency light. I check my watch. Four minutes and thirty seconds since Alessandro's call. His team should be approaching now.

As if summoned by the thought, the door opens. Four figures enter in tactical formation. It's Alessandro's personal security detail, professionals with military backgrounds and absolute loyalty. Their weapons sweep the corridor efficiently, identifying us without needing verbal confirmation.

The team leader, Danny, former special forces, approaches with contained urgency. "Secure for transport," he says, gesturing to his men. Two of them move to flank us, providing support while the others maintain perimeter security.

"Marco," I manage, gesturing back toward the corridor. "Retrieve him."

Danny nods once. "Secondary team is already tasked. Clean extraction, full protocol."

The assurance steadies something in me. Marco will receive appropriate handling. His body retrieved, and evidence eliminated. Small comfort, but necessary.

They guide us toward an armored SUV waiting just outside, engine running, windows tinted to opacity. The transition from the building to the vehicle passes in a blur of coordinated movement and professional efficiency. Lea remains at my side throughout, her presence a constant in the shifting chaos.

As we pull away from Purgatorio, I turn to watch through the rear window. The building recedes. My club, the center of my operations, the physical manifestation of everything I've built over the past decade. Now compromised. Violated. Stained with Marco's blood.

In the SUV's climate-controlled interior, the immediate danger receding, adrenaline begins its inevitable decline. Pain floods my awareness with renewed intensity. Each breath brings a stabbing reminder of broken ribs. Blood continues seeping through makeshift bandages applied by Danny's team.

Lea sits beside me, her hands still stained with dried blood, mine and the man she killed to save me. The initial shock has faded from her expression, replaced by something harder, more resolute. She's crossed a line tonight that cannot be uncrossed, transitioned from observer to participant in the violence that defines my world.

"He died because of me," I say hoarsely. Not to Lea specifically, not to anyone in the vehicle. Simply a truth that demands acknowledgment, a failure I must own before I can address it.

Lea's hand finds mine in the dim interior of the SUV, her fingers intertwining with mine in a gesture that should feel intrusive but somehow doesn't. "He died protecting what matters to you," she corrects, her voice soft but firm. "And so would you."

I turn to look at her fully, really see her for perhaps the first time. This woman who just killed to preserve my life.

Who's witnessed me at my most vulnerable: wounded, failing, losing. Who should be running from me and my world as fast as possible, yet instead sits here, holding my hand, covered in blood that isn't hers.

"Why'd you do it?" The question emerges unbidden, raw with genuine confusion. "Why save me?"

Lea meets my gaze, and for once there is no calculation in her eyes, no performance, no strategic positioning. Just raw, unfiltered honesty.

"I don't know," she murmurs. "I just knew I couldn't watch you die."

The confession hangs between us as the SUV speeds toward Alessandro's estate. My vision narrows, darkness creeping in at the periphery as blood loss and pain take their inevitable toll. The last image I register is Lea's face above mine as consciousness slips away, determined and afraid, yet somehow still here despite everything she now knows about the reality of my world. *And the last thought that follows me into darkness is unexpected, almost foreign in its simplicity: I don't want her to leave.*

CHAPTER TWENTY-TWO

Lea

Blood never comes out from under your fingernails completely. I've been scrubbing for ten minutes straight, the water running from pink to clear and back again as I find new crimson crescents to clean.

I killed a man tonight.

The thought surfaces for the hundredth time as I scrub harder, my skin turning raw under the scalding water. It should feel monumental, earth-shattering. Instead, there's a disturbing practicality to my movements. Soap. Scrub. Rinse. Repeat.

Alessandro's estate bathroom is all marble and gold fixtures, obscenely luxurious compared to the violence that brought us here. The mirror shows a stranger. My hair is wild, specks of dried blood on my neck that I missed, eyes too wide and bright. I barely recognize myself.

A sharp knock breaks my trance.

"Ms. Song?" A clipped, professional voice. "The doctor requires your assistance."

I shut off the water, watching the final swirl of diluted red disappear down the drain. My hands are shaking again as I dry them. I've been cycling between mechanical efficiency and trembling shock since we arrived twenty minutes ago.

When I open the door, a severe-looking woman in a pressed uniform gestures for me to follow. "Quickly, please."

We hurry down the hallway to a bedroom that's been transformed into a makeshift medical station. Nico lies on the bed, pale and still. His shirt has been cut away, revealing the full extent of his injuries. He has a ragged graze along his side where the bullet passed, a deep laceration across his shoulder, and bruising already darkening across his ribs. A gray-haired man in a sweater vest works efficiently, cleaning the wounds.

"Ah, good. Hold this," he says without looking up, extending a bloodied gauze pad in my direction.

I take it automatically, my brain disconnecting from the horror of the situation and focusing on the immediate task. The doctor, I assume he's a doctor, though no one has actually said so, doesn't bother with introductions or explanations. He simply points to where he needs pressure applied, hands me instruments, while giving me clipped instructions.

"Keep that steady. More pressure there. Hand me the suture kit."

Nico's eyes are closed, his face unnaturally slack. They've given him something for the pain. Without his usual intensity, he looks different. Younger, almost vulnerable. It's jarring to see him this way after witnessing his ruthless efficiency in the club. After watching him put three bullets into a man without hesitation.

After seeing him nearly die lost in rage over Marco.

The memory makes me shudder. Marco's body jerking as the bullet struck, the pool of blood spreading beneath him on the concrete floor. The look in Nico's eyes when he realized his friend was gone. That animal fury that sent him charging forward, abandoning all his careful control.

And then...

I close my eyes, but it only makes the images sharper. Vincent standing over Nico, knife raised. My hands finding Nico's fallen gun. The unfamiliar weight of it. The recoil shocking up my arms as I fired, the acrid smell of gunpowder sharp in the air. The horrible, wet sound of the second bullet striking Vincent's throat. The gurgle as he fell.

"Pressure, Ms. Song." The doctor's voice snaps me back. "I need steady hands if you're assisting."

I refocus, pressing gauze against the wound as he begins stitching. My hands are steady now, surprisingly so. Some part of me has shifted into crisis mode, compartmentalizing the horror to deal with later.

"The bullet graze is superficial," the doctor explains as he works. "The shoulder laceration is deeper but missed anything vital. Ribs are bruised, possibly cracked. We'll need X-rays to confirm."

His movements are precise and practiced. This isn't his first gunshot wound. *I wonder how many times he's patched up Nico or others in Alessandro's organization. How many bullets and knife wounds he's sewn closed without ever filing reports or asking questions.*

"You did well," he says quietly, eyes on his sutures. "Most people freeze in situations like that. Fight, flight, or freeze. Freeze is most common."

It takes me a moment to realize he's talking to me, about what happened at the club. About me killing someone.

"How do you..." I start.

"Alessandro's men briefed me on the extraction. You saved his life." He glances up. "That's not something Alessandro will forget."

I don't know what to say to that. *I don't want Alessandro's gratitude or his memory. I don't want any of this to have happened. I want to be back in my apartment with my article half-written, my biggest worry being whether Harrison will approve my draft.*

But that world doesn't exist anymore. It disappeared the moment I pulled the trigger. Actually, the moment I agreed to shadow Nico.

"Will he be okay?" I ask instead.

"He'll live. Infection is the primary concern now." The doctor finishes the last suture and begins applying antiseptic. "He'll need monitoring through the night. Fever is likely given the circumstances."

When he's done with the bandaging, he leaves detailed instructions about when to change dressings, what signs of infection to watch for, how often to check his temperature. He hands me a small case of medical supplies and medications.

"You're leaving?" The panic in my voice surprises me.

"I have other patients who need attention, Ms. Song. Mr. Varela is stable." His voice softens at my obvious distress.

"The staff will check in regularly, but it's best to limit who has access to him right now. Alessandro's orders."

And just like that, I've become Nico Varela's nursemaid. The absurdity of the situation would be laughable if I weren't so exhausted and traumatized. *Four weeks ago, I was pursuing him for an interview. Now I'm changing his bandages after killing a man to save him.*

The doctor leaves, and silence fills the vast bedroom. I sink into a chair beside the bed, suddenly overwhelmed by everything that's happened. My muscles ache from tension and exertion. My head pounds. I haven't eaten since before we went to the club, and that feels like a lifetime ago.

I look at Nico's sleeping form. He seems almost human like this, no calculating gaze, no controlled movements. Just a man, wounded and vulnerable. His breathing is even but shallow, careful even in unconsciousness to avoid straining his injured ribs.

Without thinking, I reach out and brush a strand of hair from his forehead. The gesture is so intimate it startles me. I jerk my hand back as if burned.

What the hell am I doing?

This man has manipulated me from the beginning. He's been surveilling me, used me, drawn me into a world of violence and moral compromise. I should hate him for that. I should use this opportunity to gather information for my article, to finally gain the upper hand in our ongoing power struggle.

Instead, I watch the rise and fall of his chest, reassuring myself that he's still breathing.

I killed a man tonight.

The thought keeps returning, relentless as a tide. Each time it feels less shocking, which terrifies me more than the act itself. *Is this how it happens? How someone like me becomes someone like them? One compromise, one act of violence at a time, until the extraordinary becomes mundane?*

I press my hands against my eyes, trying to block out the thoughts, the images. I need to focus on something immediate and concrete. Nico needs monitoring. I'll check his temperature, change his bandages as instructed, watch for infection. One step at a time.

When I lower my hands, Nico's eyes are open, watching me.

"You're still here," he says, voice rough with pain and medication.

"Where else would I be?"

He doesn't answer, just holds my gaze before his eyes drift closed again. I'm not sure if it's a genuine question or if he's too drugged to maintain a conversation. Either way, it hangs in the air between us.

Where else would I be? Running as far from this world as possible, if I had any sense of self-preservation. Going to the police, if I believed in their ability to protect me from Moretti. Writing my article, if I were still the journalist I thought I was.

Instead, I'm here, watching over the man whose world has consumed mine. The man for whom I crossed a line I can never uncross.

I settle in deeper, preparing for a long night. Outside the window, rain falls, soft and steady against the glass, washing away another day I never could have imagined.

I jerk awake to the sound of muttering. The room is

dark except for a small lamp in the corner, casting long shadows across the walls. For a moment, I'm disoriented, unsure where I am or why my neck aches from sleeping upright.

Then I see Nico.

He's moving restlessly in the bed, sheets tangled around his waist. Even in the dim light, I can see the sheen of sweat on his skin. His head turns back and forth on the pillow, lips moving in words too low to catch.

Fever. The doctor warned this might happen.

I hasten to his side, laying my palm against his forehead. His skin burns under my touch. Too hot. Much too hot.

"Shit," I mutter, fumbling for the thermometer in the medical kit. I press it against his temple, waiting for the digital readout: 102.8. Not life-threatening yet, but definitely cause for concern.

I hesitate, uncertain whether to call for help or try to manage this myself. The doctor left antipyretics, but Nico's too restless to take pills. Cold compresses then, to bring the fever down.

I hurry to the adjoining bathroom, soaking washcloths in cold water and wringing them out. When I return, Nico's mumbling has grown more agitated.

"Marco," he says as I approach, the name like a knife twist in my chest. "Left flank. Check the left."

He's reliving the attack, I realize. *Trying to warn Marco even now.*

I place a cold cloth on his forehead, another on the back of his neck. "Shh," I soothe. "It's okay."

His eyes open but don't focus, glazed with fever and memory. "They took the shipment," he mutters. "Have to secure the north side. The families will..." He trails off, gaze drifting past me to some point only he can see.

I replace the cloths, which have already warmed against his overheated skin. "You're safe," I tell him, though I have no idea if that's true. *Moretti's men could be surrounding the estate for all I know.* "Try to rest."

"Can't rest," he argues, voice clearer though his eyes remain unfocused. "Too many depending on me. The city needs..." He struggles to sit up, wincing as the movement pulls at his stitches.

I press him gently back. "The city will be there tomorrow. Right now, you need to heal."

He subsides, but his expression remains troubled. "You don't understand," he insists. "If I don't maintain balance, others will fill the void. Moretti doesn't care who gets caught in the crossfire. The streets will run red."

I freeze adjusting his bandages. *Is this fever talk, or is he revealing something genuine?* The idea that Nico sees himself as some kind of necessary evil, a control valve on Chicago's violence, is not new, but still seems like self-serving justification. And yet there's something in his intensity that gives me pause.

"Balance," I repeat cautiously. "Between the crime families?"

He nods, eyes drifting closed again. "Someone has to maintain order. Better me than the alternatives."

I continue cooling his burning skin, replacing cloths as they warm. His breathing gradually steadies as the fever medications I've administered sets in. The restless movement calms.

But his words linger in my mind. *Is it possible there's*

more to Nico's role as "The Diplomat" than simple self-interest? The idea that he sees himself as a guardian of sorts who prevents worse violence by controlling and channeling it? The idea is both absurd and strangely compelling.

As the fever spikes higher, his mumbling becomes more disjointed. Fragments of conversation with invisible others. Names, I don't recognize. And then, unexpectedly, a child's voice, plaintive and frightened.

"Papa, wake up. There's blood. Papa, please wake up."

A chill runs through me despite the heat radiating from his body. This isn't the calculating crime lord speaking. This is a memory, a child finding something terrible.

"They won't let me see," he continues in that younger voice. "Uncle Alessandro says I can't go in there. Why won't they let me see Papa?"

I swallow hard, continuing to bathe his face and neck with cool water. *I shouldn't be hearing this. It feels like a violation somehow, accessing memories he would never willingly share.*

The fever continues to rise despite my efforts. His restlessness increases, movements growing more agitated until he nearly tears his stitches. I need to cool him more effectively.

I glance at the bathroom door, considering my options. A cool bath would help, but I can't possibly move him in this state. Which leaves...

"Dammit," I mutter, making my decision.

I pull back the sheets and begin to remove his remaining clothing. It's a clinical process, or it should be. But as I expose more of his body, it becomes anything but clinical.

His chest and arms are sculpted muscle, testament to a physical discipline I hadn't fully appreciated when he was clothed. But it's the scars that capture my attention. A roadmap of violence and survival. A puckered bullet wound on his abdomen. A long, jagged line across his left pectoral. Smaller marks scattered across his skin like constellations.

Each one represents a moment where he nearly died. Each one a testament to the violence of his world.

By the time I've stripped him down to his boxer briefs, my hands are trembling. I focus on my task, running cool, damp cloths over his chest, arms, and legs. His skin is furnace-hot beneath my touch, but gradually, the relentless heat recedes.

Throughout the process, his mumbling continues, fragments of memory and current fears blending together. Marco's name appears repeatedly. References to Moretti, to balances of power, to protection and territory.

And once, startlingly clear: "Lea." Just my name, but spoken with such complex emotion that my hands still.

After what feels like hours, the fever breaks. His restlessness subsides, his breathing deepens, and his skin cools to a more normal temperature.

Exhausted, I sink back into the seat. The clock on the wall shows 4:17 AM. Dawn isn't far off.

I study Nico's face in repose, trying to reconcile the different versions of him I've witnessed. The calculating manipulator who orchestrated my assignment from the beginning. The ruthless enforcer who broke a man's fingers without hesitation. The grieving friend who lost control at Marco's death. The feverish man who spoke of protecting the city. The child who found his father's blood.

Which is the real Nico Varela? Perhaps all of them. Perhaps none.

And where does that leave me, the woman who killed to save him?

I close my eyes, overwhelmed by exhaustion. *Just a moment's rest,* I tell myself. *Just until morning comes.*

———

I BLINK, disoriented, my neck stiff from sleeping in the chair. The events of the night rush back, the fever, the cooling cloths, Nico's delirious confessions.

I straighten, checking the bed. It's empty, sheets thrown back.

Panic flares until I hear water running in the bathroom. A moment later, the door opens and Nico appears, wearing only pajama pants riding low on his hips, fresh bandages stark white against his skin. He moves slowly, mindful of his injuries, but the improvement from last night is remarkable.

"You should be resting," I say, rising.

"I've rested enough." His voice is stronger, his gaze clear and focused. The vulnerable man from last night is gone, replaced by the controlled, calculating Nico I've come to know. But now that I've seen beneath the mask, I can't unsee it.

"How are you feeling?" I ask. The answer is clear in his posture, in the return of his intensity.

"I've had worse." He crosses to a wardrobe and selects a shirt, moving with deliberate care as he slides it on, not bothering with the buttons.

"You had a fever last night," I tell him. "You were... talking."

His hands pause in the act of pouring water from a carafe on the nightstand. "What did I say?"

"Different things. Some of it made little sense." I hesitate, uncertain how much to reveal. "You mentioned Marco a lot. And something about protecting the city."

He turns to face me, expression opaque. "And that surprised you."

It's not a question, but I answer anyway. "It contradicts the narrative that you're only in this for personal gain."

The faintest of a smile touches his lips. "Perhaps that's the narrative you constructed, not the reality."

Before I can respond, there's a knock at the door. Nico calls for them to enter, and Alessandro steps into the room, impeccably dressed despite the early hour. He carries a silver tray with coffee service, the domestic gesture incongruous with his aura of controlled power.

"Nephew," he greets Nico, eyes assessing his condition with clinical detachment. "You look better than expected."

"I had good care," Nico replies, with a nod in my direction that feels like more than simple acknowledgment.

Alessandro turns to me, his expression warming. "Ms. Song. I thought you might appreciate coffee after your long night." He sets the tray on a side table. "Black, if I recall correctly."

That he knows how I take my coffee is unsettling.

"Thank you," I manage, accepting the cup he offers. The coffee is perfect, of course, strong and rich, how I prefer it.

"I'd like to speak with Ms. Song," Alessandro says to Nico. "If you're stable enough to be left alone for a few minutes."

Nico's expression tightens almost imperceptibly. "I'm fine. Take all the time you need."

I follow Alessandro from the room with a feeling of foreboding. What could he want to discuss with me alone? Has he somehow learned that I've been playing his nephew, using seduction as a strategy just as Nico has been using me?

We walk in silence through the grand hallway of the estate. Alessandro leads me to a sun-drenched conservatory filled with exotic plants. The air is warm, humid, smelling of damp earth and sweet blossoms. The glass walls offer a panoramic view of manicured gardens extending to a distant tree line. It's beautiful, peaceful, a stark contrast to the violence that brought us here.

"Please, sit," he gestures to a comfortable chair. "I imagine you're exhausted."

I sink into the seat, cradling my coffee cup like a shield. "It was a long night."

"You saved his life," Alessandro states, taking the chair opposite mine. "That creates a certain bond between people. A debt."

"I didn't do it for a debt," I say.

His smile is knowing, even indulgent. "No, I don't imagine you did. Which makes it all the more significant." He studies me for a long moment. "Our first meeting...perhaps I underestimated the mettle beneath the journalistic curiosity." "You're not what I expected, Ms. Song."

"What did you expect?"

"Someone more malleable. Someone who would be overwhelmed by Nico's world, either running from it in terror or succumbing to its allure." He sips his coffee. "Instead, you maintain a curious balance, neither fully rejecting nor entirely embracing what you've witnessed. It's unusual."

I'm not sure if it's a compliment or an accusation. "I'm here to document, not judge."

"Are you?" His tone suggests he knows better. "Is that why you picked up a gun last night? For documentation?"

The coffee suddenly tastes bitter on my tongue. "I acted on instinct."

"Yes. That's my point." Alessandro leans forward. "When instinct overrides calculation, we reveal our true selves. And your instinct was to protect him, even at the cost of taking a life."

I have no answer for that. The truth of his observation settles uncomfortably in my chest. My actions last night weren't those of a detached journalist or even a manipulative strategist. They were raw, unfiltered impulses that revealed feelings I've been trying to deny.

Alessandro seems to take my silence as confirmation. "Nico had a difficult childhood," he says, changing direction. "His parents were killed when he was seven. A business disagreement that turned violent."

The image of the feverish Nico calling for his father flashes in my mind. "He found them," I say softly, the pieces connecting.

Alessandro's eyebrows lift in surprise. "Yes. How did you know?"

"He was delirious last night. He remembered being kept from seeing his father."

"I tried to protect him from the worst of it," Alessandro says, voice distant with memory. "But he heard the gunshots. Saw the blood before I could get him away from the scene." He sighs heavily. "No child should witness such things."

"So you raised him," I prompt, curious despite myself about the forces that shaped Nico into the man he became.

"I did what was necessary. Taught him to protect himself in a world that had already shown its cruelty." Alessandro's gaze sharpens. "The first lesson was control of himself, then of others. The second was strategy. Never act from emotion. Never reveal weakness."

"You taught him to manipulate," I translate.

"I taught him to survive," he corrects. "And he has done more than survive. He has thrived in a world that would have destroyed a lesser man." There's unmistakable pride in Alessandro's voice. "But he has paid a price for that success."

"Marco," I say quietly.

Alessandro nods. "Marco was the closest thing to a friend Nico allowed himself. His death. It will change him."

"He was different last night," I admit. "When the fever broke through his control."

"Vulnerability is not a state Nico permits himself," Alessandro agrees. "Which makes what I observed between you even more remarkable."

I tense. "What do you mean?"

"I've never seen him react to anyone the way he reacts to you. How he trusts you." Alessandro's gaze is penetrating, as if he can see through my constructed masks to the confusion beneath. "And I've never seen him more dangerous than when he thought you were threatened."

The statement lands hard. Trust. The word feels like mockery when I know our entire relationship has been built on mutual deception. I've been playing him just as he's been playing me and using seduction as strategy, intimacy as a weapon.

"You're wrong," I say, voice steadier than I feel. "Nico doesn't trust me. He's been manipulating me from the beginning."

Alessandro's smile is knowing. "The two aren't mutually exclusive, Ms. Song. Nico can manipulate you while also trusting you. Human emotions are rarely tidy or consistent." He rises. "Think about what I've said. And consider your own motives with equal honesty."

He leaves me sitting in the sunlight, surrounded by exotic flowers and troubling thoughts. The coffee has grown cold in my cup, forgotten during our conversation.

I'VE NEVER SEEN *him trust anyone the way he trusts you.*

The words resonate in my mind, colliding with the knowledge of our mutual deception. How can there be trust between people who are lying to each other? Who are using each other for their own ends?

And yet, I killed for him. Not for my story. Not for strategic advantage. But because, in that crucial moment, the thought of losing him was unbearable.

What does that say about me?

When I return to the bedroom, Nico is seated by the window, a laptop balanced carefully to avoid his injured side. He looks up as I enter, his expression guarded.

"What did my uncle want?"

"To talk about you, mostly." I cross to the bed and begin straightening the tangled sheets, needing something to do with my hands. "About your childhood. How he raised you after your parents died."

Nico's fingers still on the keyboard. "He's not usually so forthcoming with family history."

"Maybe he thought I should understand the man whose life I saved." I turn to face him. "Or maybe he was testing me, seeing how I'd react to a curated version of your past."

"And how did you react?"

"With more questions than answers." I move closer to him, noticing the stiffness in his posture, the careful way he holds himself to minimize pain. "You should be in bed."

"I have matters that can't wait." His tone is dismissive, but when he shifts position, a flash of pain crosses his features before he can mask it.

"At least let me help you to the bathroom," I insist, seeing how he's avoiding movement. "You need to clean up properly, change those bandages."

He starts to refuse, then seems to reconsider. "Fine."

I offer my arm for support as he rises. He accepts the help with visible reluctance, but once standing, his arm slides around my shoulders, leaning more heavily than I think he intended. We move slowly toward the bathroom, his body warm against mine.

Inside, I help him remove the shirt, then step back as he braces himself against the sink, staring at his reflection in the mirror. The bandage on his shoulder is spotted with seepage, the bruising on his ribs darkened to deep purple overnight.

"Let me," I say, reaching for the medical supplies. He watches in silence as I peel away the old bandage and clean the sutured wound. My fingers slide over his skin, clinical in their purpose but intimate in their care.

"You've done this before," he observes.

"My roommate in college was in nursing school. She practiced on me." I apply fresh antiseptic, noting how he doesn't flinch despite the sting it must cause. "And I've patched up my minor injuries over the years. Hazards of being a curious kid."

A ghost of a smile touches his lips. "You? Curious? No way..."

"You can keep joking all you want, but hold still." I secure the new bandage and step back to examine my work. "There. Better."

He turns to the sink, wetting a washcloth to clean his face. I hand him a toothbrush already prepared with paste, our fingers brushing in the exchange. These small, domestic acts feel strangely more intimate than our sexual encounters. There's no performance here, no strategic seduction. Just basic human care.

When he finishes, I help him back to the bedroom. He sits on the edge of the bed, clearly tiring but unwilling to admit it.

"You should rest," I tell him.

"So should you." He studies my face. "You were up all night with me."

"I'm fine."

"No, you're not." His voice softens. "None of this is fine, Lea. What happened at the club? What you did..."

The gentleness in his tone threatens to undo me. I've been holding myself together through shock, through necessity, through sheer force of will. But his simple acknowledgment of the trauma cracks something in my maintained composure.

"I killed someone," I say, the words finally spoken aloud between us. "I picked up your gun, and I shot a man in the throat and watched him die."

Nico reaches for my hand, his grip warm and steady. "You saved my life."

"That doesn't make it okay!" The emotion bursts out of me, uncontrollable. "None of this is okay! Marco is dead. I killed someone. I'm hiding in a mansion with a man who's been manipulating me from the moment we met. Everything about this is wrong!"

"Is it?" he asks quietly. "You found evidence on my laptop, didn't you? About the surveillance. About arranging your assignment."

I freeze, caught off-guard by his directness. "How did you—"

"You're not the only one who can observe patterns, Lea. Your behavior changed. You became more strategic in your approach. More calculated in your responses." His eyes hold mine, unflinching. "You started playing the game on my level."

I should deny it, maintain the pretense, but I'm too exhausted for more lies. "Yes. I found the surveillance photos. The emails to my publisher. All of it."

He nods slowly, no surprise in his expression. "And you decided to turn it to your advantage. To seduce information from me while letting me believe I was the one in control."

"Just like you've been doing to me from the beginning," I counter, defiance rising through the fatigue.

"Yes." The simple admission surprises me. "We've both been performing. Both been calculating each move, each response." His hand still holds mine, thumb brushing mine in a gesture that feels genuine despite our conversation. "And yet here we are."

"What does that mean?"

"It means when it mattered, when there was a knife at my throat, you didn't calculate. You acted." His gaze is intent, searching. "Just as I would have done for you."

The statement hangs between us, weighted with implications neither of us seems ready to fully examine.

I pull my hand from his, needing distance to think clearly. "So what now? We just acknowledge we've been manipulating each other and move on? Continue the game with new awareness?"

"Or we stop playing," he suggests quietly. "Put down the masks, the strategies. See what's left when the performance ends."

The offer is tempting. Dangerously so. But I've been deceived too many times to trust easily, even now. "How do I know this isn't just another manipulation? A more sophisticated level of the game?"

"You don't," he admits. "Just as I don't know if your vulnerability right now is genuine or crafted to lower my defenses." He sighs, the sound heavy with exhaustion and something that might be regret. "That's the price we pay for starting as we did."

I turn away, moving to the window to gather my thoughts. Outside, the estate grounds stretch in manicured perfection, a deceptive tranquility. Everything in Nico's world is controlled, arranged for maximum effect, including me, from the beginning.

But last night wasn't controlled. The fever, the vulnerability, the memories that slipped through his defenses, those were real. Just as my instinct to save him was real, cutting through all the layers of deception between us.

"I can't do this anymore," I say, turning back to him. "The constant calculation, the strategic moves and countermoves. I'm exhausted."

"Then don't." He watches me, something almost hopeful in his expression. "Be honest instead. Tell me one true thing, Lea. Something you haven't planned or constructed."

The request is simple but terrifying. *One true thing*. After all the layers of deception between us, can I even distinguish truth from performance anymore?

But as I look at him, all wounded and vulnerable despite his attempts to hide it, waiting for my response with uncharacteristic patience, the truth rises unbidden.

"I'm afraid," I admit, voice low. "Not of you, or Moretti, or even what I did last night. I'm afraid of how much I care. How easily I crossed a line I always thought was absolute. How much I'm changing, becoming someone I don't recognize." I take a shuddering breath. "I'm afraid because when I had to choose between my principles and your life, it wasn't even a choice."

The confession hangs in the air between us, raw and unfiltered. Nico's expression shifts, softens in a way I've never seen before. He rises from the bed, moving to stand facing me despite the pain it must cause.

"Your turn," I whisper. "One true thing."

His hand lifts to my face, fingers gentle against my cheek. "When I was on that floor, bleeding out while Vincent stood over me, my thought wasn't of revenge, or regret, or even Marco." His voice drops lower, intimate in its honesty. "It was of you. Of all the moments between us I would never see."

The confession shatters my last defenses. I move into him carefully, mindful of his injuries, my forehead resting against his chest. His arms encircle me, holding me as if I'm something precious rather than a pawn in his game.

"What are we doing, Nico?" I murmur against his skin.

"I don't know," he admits, the uncertainty so unlike his usual measured confidence. "But I don't want to stop."

I lift my face to his, and the kiss that follows is unlike any we've shared before. No power play, no artful seduction. Just the simple, devastating truth of connection.

He winces as my hand brushes his injured side, and I pull back. "You need to rest."

"Stay with me," he says, the request unguarded in a way I've never heard from him.

I help him back to the bed, arranging pillows to support his injured side. When he's settled, I hesitate only briefly before climbing in beside him, careful not to jar his wounds. His arm curls around me, drawing me against his uninjured side.

The intimacy of the moment, this quiet, unguarded closeness, feels more significant than any of our previous encounters. There's no audience here, no strategic advantage to be gained. Just two people finding comfort in each other after surviving something terrible together.

As his breathing steadies into sleep, I remain awake. The man beside me is still Nico Varela, manipulator, criminal, dangerous in ways I'm only beginning to understand. But he's also the man who held me with unexpected tenderness, who admitted fear and vulnerability when he could have maintained his mask.

The truth settles over me like a physical weight: I'm no longer pretending. The feelings that have been growing since that first meeting at Purgatorio. All of it, the fascination, the desire, the deepening emotional connection are real, despite all the reasons they shouldn't be.

And that makes me more vulnerable than any surveillance or manipulation ever could. Because now, when Nico Varela inevitably returns to being the calculating strategist I know him to be, it won't be a performance that's shattered.

It will be my heart.

CHAPTER TWENTY-THREE

Nico

Blood feels different on your hands when it belongs to someone you care about. An unfamiliar thought, unwelcome. I've had blood on my hands before, figuratively, literally; the distinction blurred years ago. But watching Lea's peaceful breathing beside me, the memory of my blood coating her fingers as she pressed compresses against my wounds is sharp, insistent. The sight of her, determined amidst the chaos, working to keep me alive...it complicates things.

The pale light of early morning filters through the curtains, catching the curve of her cheekbone, softening the sharp intelligence that usually guards her features. The urge to touch her in this unguarded state, is surprisingly strong. I resist, not wanting to break the spell.

My body aches, a constant reminder of vulnerability. The wounds are manageable, physical pain a familiar companion. But the *other* exposure from last night unnerves me more: the fever that cracked open defenses, revealing fragments I keep locked away. What did I say in that delirium? What weakness did she witness?

I've taken countless women to my bed. None have seen me stripped bare like Lea did. Not just physically, but the shards of memory, the grief over Marco I haven't allowed myself to process, the raw uncertainty that follows losing the one man I trusted implicitly. And then there was the shift afterward, when the fever broke, when we acknowledged the game we were both playing and somehow chose... something else.

I trace the line of her jaw with my eyes, remembering the taste of her lips, the feel of her yielding against me. That wasn't strategy, not entirely. Not on my part. An emotional impulse overriding decades of calculation. The thought should terrify me. It does.

"You're staring," she murmurs, voice husky with sleep, eyes still closed.

"Force of habit," I reply, keeping my tone light. "I observe."

Her eyes open then, dark and knowing, a faint smile touching her lips. "And what have you observed about me this morning?"

That you're a dangerous complication. That you make me question everything.

"That you snore," I say instead.

She makes an indignant sound, fully awake now. "I do not."

"Lightly." I trace a finger along her collarbone, feeling the slight tremor beneath her skin, watching the way her breath catches. "Almost imperceptibly."

She swats my hand away, but the smile lingers. This easy intimacy, the shared space, the quiet rhythm of waking together is unfamiliar territory, destabilizing in its simple normality.

A sharp knock interrupts the moment. Lea tenses, pulling the sheet higher. The pattern is Alessandro's.

"Alessandro," I say, resigned.

He enters, his gaze taking in the scene with neutral assessment. "Moretti's men are still probing the perimeter," he states. "Testing defenses. We should discuss our response."

I glance at Lea. She's already reaching for clothes, wrapping the sheet around herself as she stands. "I'll give you two a moment," she says, her composure remarkable. She disappears into the bathroom.

Alessandro watches her go. "Less adversarial than I expected," he remarks.

I swing my legs over the side of the bed, ignoring the sharp protest from my ribs. "Moretti is the priority," I say, reaching for my shirt, wincing.

He studies me. "She's quite remarkable, your journalist."

"She's not mine," I reply.

His smile is knowing. "Keep telling yourself that." He departs, leaving the words hanging in the air.

When Lea emerges from the bathroom, dressed in fresh clothes, I'm struggling with the buttons of my shirt, my injured shoulder protesting. Without a word, she crosses to me, her fingers moving efficiently. The simple intimacy, Lea standing between my knees, tending to me, stirs something deeper than desire, a startling flicker of need.

"Thank you," I say when she finishes.

She steps back, perceptive eyes searching mine. "What did Alessandro say?"

"His men are probing the perimeter." I stand carefully, moving to the window. "We need to determine our next move."

"Our?" she asks, the word significant.

I turn. "Yes, *our*. Unless you'd prefer to be excluded?"

A slow, genuine smile transforms her face. "No, I wouldn't prefer that."

"Good." We make our way through the hallways, my pace slow. Lea matches her stride to mine without comment, observing everything.

"You grew up here?" she asks as we pass a portrait.

"After my parents died, yes," I admit. "Alessandro raised me. He believed comfort bred complacency. This was a place for learning strategy."

"Seeing people as pieces to be moved," she mumbles.

"Yes." I meet her gaze. "Including you, initially."

She doesn't flinch. "And now?"

Before I can answer, we reach the study where Alessandro waits with his team. The briefing is concise: Moretti is assessing, not attacking immediately. I keep the details minimal for Lea, but her presence beside me feels... necessary. She's become a stabilizing force, sharp mind cutting through assumptions. This dependence disturbs me. Weakness. Yet I bring her deeper in.

As afternoon turns to evening, I suggest a walk on the grounds, needing movement, needing distance from the weight of command. We move along a gravel path toward the lake. The setting sun casts long shadows. Lea walks beside me, close, respectful of my injuries.

"Why did you really bring me into the briefing?" she asks when we're alone. "Not because I 'earned it'."

A smile tugs at my mouth. "Perceptive."

"What's the truth, Nico?"

What is the truth? About us? "I wanted to see what you'd do," I admit. "Whether you'd use the information, or..."

"Or treat it as confidential because it came from you," she finishes. "A test."

"Yes."

She considers this. "Did I pass?"

"Which matters more to you now?" I ask, sitting on the bench by the lake.

She sits beside me. "A few weeks ago, my article. Now..." She looks across the water. "I'm not sure who I am anymore, Nico."

As darkness falls, the temperature drops. Without thinking, I slip my arm around her shoulders, drawing her against my uninjured side. She comes willingly, fitting against me.

"We should head back," I say, reluctant to end this.

She nods but turns her face up to mine. Her eyes are dark pools in the fading light. I lower my mouth to hers, the kiss gentle at first, then deepening. By the time we break apart, we're both breathing harder.

"Yes," she says, rising and offering me her hand. "We should head back."

The walk is charged with anticipation. Despite the pain, my body responds, and as we step into the room, the door clicking shut with a finality that seals us away from the world, the air between us crackles. Lamps cast a warm, amber glow, painting Lea's skin in hues of gold. Her eyes, dark and fathomless, lock onto mine, and I feel the pull. Raw and undeniable. My injuries ache, a dull reminder of the fight, but they're nothing compared to the fire igniting in my veins. She hesitates, her gaze flickering to the bandages beneath my shirt, concern etched into her delicate features.

"Lea," I say, my voice low, a command wrapped in velvet. "Stop worrying about me."

Her lips part, a protest forming, but I close the distance in two strides, my hands framing her face. The kiss is immediate, hungry, my tongue claiming hers with a possessiveness that makes her gasp into my mouth. Her fingers clutch my shirt, and I feel the tremor in her touch, the desire warring with restraint. I pull back just enough to meet her eyes, my thumb tracing the curve of her lower lip.

"You think I'm fragile?" I murmur, a dark chuckle rumbling in my chest. "Sweetheart, I'll fuck you so good you'll forget your own name. Injuries be damned."

Her breath hitches, pupils dilating, and I know I've got her. My hands move to her blouse, fingers deftly undoing the buttons, each one a slow, deliberate tease. The fabric parts, revealing the swell of her breasts, the lace of her bra barely containing her. I slide the blouse off her shoulders, letting it pool on the floor, and step back, taking my time to, once again, drink her in. She's a vision: curves and shadows, her skin glowing under the lamplight.

"Fucking perfect," I growl, my voice thick with want. "I can't stop looking at you, Lea. Made for me. Every inch of you."

A delicious flush spreads across her chest, but she doesn't look away. Good. I want her to see the hunger in my eyes, to feel the weight of my desire. I reach for her skirt, unzipping it with a slow, deliberate pull, letting it fall to join her blouse.

Her panties are next, and I hook my fingers under the lace, dragging them down her thighs. She steps out of them, and I take another moment to admire her, standing bare in front of me.

"On the bed," I order, my tone leaving no room for argument. "Now."

She obeys, moving with a grace that makes my cock throb. She lies back, her hair fanning out on the pillow, and I shed my shirt, ignoring the sharp twinge in my side. The pain is irrelevant. All that matters is her: spread out, waiting, her eyes tracking my every move. I climb onto the bed, settling between her thighs, my hands gripping her hips as I lower my mouth to her skin.

"Nico," she whispers, her voice trembling with need.

"Oh, baby," I purr, my lips brushing the sensitive skin of her inner thigh. "You have no idea what I'm gonna do to you. I'm gonna taste every fucking inch of you until you're screaming my name."

I start slow, my tongue tracing patterns along her thigh, teasing closer to her core. She squirms, her hips lifting, and I pin her down with a firm hand, my fingers digging into her flesh. "Stay still," I command, my voice a low growl. "You move when I tell you to move."

She whimpers, and the sound goes straight to my dick. I part her with my fingers, exposing her to my gaze, and fuck, she's glistening, already so wet for me. "Look at this pretty pussy," I say, my voice dripping with reverence. "So fucking wet, just for me. You want my tongue, don't you, piccola?"

"Yes," she breathes, her voice a whisper. "Please, Nico."

I don't make her wait. My mouth descends, and I lick her slow and deep, savoring the taste of her, the way she

arches under me. Her hands fist the sheets, and I grin
against her, my tongue circling her clit with relentless precision. "That's it," I murmur, the vibrations of my voice
making her gasp. "Let me hear you, Lea. Tell me how good it
feels."

"So good," she moans, her head thrashing. "Nico, please.
Don't stop."

"Stop?" I laugh, dark and wicked. "Baby, I'm just getting
started."

I slide a finger inside her, curling it just right, and her cry
is music to my ears. I add another, stretching her, pumping in
time with the flicks of my tongue. She's tight, so fucking tight,
and the thought of being inside her again has me grinding
against the bed, desperate for friction. But this is about her.
Her pleasure, her surrender. I work her relentlessly, my
mouth and fingers driving her higher, until her thighs tremble
and her moans turn to sobs.

"Nico—oh God, I'm gonna—"

"Come for me," I growl, sucking her clit hard. "Come all
over my tongue, piccola. Let me taste it."

She shatters, her body convulsing as she screams my
name, her release flooding my senses. I don't stop, lapping at
her until she's writhing, oversensitive, begging for mercy.
Only then do I pull back, licking my lips as I crawl up her
body, my hands skimming her curves.

"Fuck, you're beautiful when you come," I say, my voice
rough. "But we're not done. Not even close."

I shed my pants, freeing my cock. I stroke myself once,
twice, letting her see how hard she makes me. "You want this,
Lea?" I ask, my tone taunting. "You want me to fuck you
deep, make you mine again?"

"Yes," she says, her voice desperate. "Please, Nico. I need you."

I position myself at her entrance, teasing her with the tip, and she arches, trying to pull me in. I grip her hips, holding her still. "Patience, baby," I murmur. "I'm gonna give you what you need, but you take it my way."

I push in slowly, inch by torturous inch, and fuck, she's heaven. Hot, tight, gripping me like a vice. Her moan is low and guttural, matching mine as I bottom out, buried to the hilt. For a moment, I hold still, letting her adjust, letting the connection sink in. It's more than physical. It's deeper, rawer, like she's peeling back every layer of me.

"Look at me," I command, my voice softer now but no less intense. Her eyes meet mine, dark with desire, and I start to move, slow at first, each thrust deliberate. "You feel that?" I say, my voice a low rasp. "That's me claiming you, Lea. Every fucking inch of you belongs to me."

She nods, her hands clutching my shoulders, nails digging in. I pick up the pace, driving into her harder, deeper, the bed creaking under us. "Tell me," I demand, my lips brushing her ear. "Tell me who this pussy belongs to."

"You," she gasps, her voice breaking. "It's yours, Nico."

"Damn right," I growl, slamming into her, my control fraying. "You're mine, Lea. My woman, my everything. Tonight, you'll be fucked so good you'll never forget it."

The words pour out, filthy and reverent, as I lose myself in her. Her legs wrap around me, pulling me closer, and I angle my hips, hitting that spot that makes her cry out. "That's it," I murmur, my lips grazing her throat. "Take it, baby. Take every fucking inch."

She's close again, her walls fluttering around me, and I'm

right there with her, the pressure building. "Come with me," I say, my voice raw. "I wanna feel you come when I fill you up."

Her eyes lock onto mine, and the trust there, the raw, unguarded vulnerability, undoes me. We move together, frantic now, chasing the edge. She comes first, her scream muffled against my shoulder, and the feel of her pulsing around me sends me over. I bury myself deep, my release hitting like a freight train, her name a ragged prayer on my lips.

For a moment, we're suspended, bodies locked, hearts pounding. I collapse beside her, pulling her into my arms, her head resting on my chest. Her breathing slows, and I stroke her, contentment settling over me like a rare, fragile thing. I truly care about her.

But as she drifts toward sleep, the weight of what comes next creeps in. Love is a luxury I cannot afford, not when the stakes are this high. The warmth I felt earlier recedes, replaced by the familiar detachment that has served me so well for so long.

I disentangle myself from Lea's sleeping form, sliding out of bed without waking her. I dress quietly in the darkness, movements precise despite my injuries. Looking back at her one last time, I feel the weight of what might have been.

Then I turn away, heading to Alessandro's office to plan our next move. The Diplomat is back in control, even as part of me mourns.

I close the door behind me, leaving her to sleep in peaceful ignorance of the storm that's coming.

CHAPTER TWENTY-FOUR

Lea

COLD SHEETS. THAT'S WHAT WAKES ME. NOT A SOUND, not a nightmare, but the absence of warmth where Nico's body should be. I blink in the darkness, disoriented, my hand patting the empty space beside me. The indentation of his head on the pillow remains, but the sheets have long since cooled. He's been gone awhile.

I squint at the ornate clock on the bedside table: 3:17 AM. My throat feels dry, cottony. I tell myself that's why I'm getting up, for water, but even in my half-awake state, I recognize the lie. *I'm looking for him.*

Sliding out from beneath the silken sheets, I wince as my bare feet touch the cold hardwood floor. Alessandro's estate is all old-world luxury, but apparently heated floors didn't make the cut in whatever century this place was built. I grab Nico's discarded shirt from the floor and pull it on. It smells like him, that indefinable scent that's just him. My chest tightens at the comforting smell, at how quickly it's become a comfort to me.

The hallway outside our bedroom is dimly lit by small wall sconces that cast more shadows than light. During daylight hours, Alessandro's mansion hums with quiet efficiency, staff moving purposefully, security personnel checking in, phones ringing in distant offices. Now, it's unnervingly silent, as if the building itself is holding its breath.

My tread seems obscenely loud against the polished floor as I make my way toward the grand staircase. The massive oil paintings of Varela ancestors watch me pass, their eyes following my movements with aristocratic disapproval. *You don't belong here,* they seem to say. *You're just passing through.*

Maybe they're right.

I pause at the top of the stairs, listening. The house remains stubbornly silent, but there's a tension in the air that I can't quite place, like the pressure drop before a storm. My journalistic instinct, the same one that's led me into countless dangerous situations in pursuit of a story, prickles at the base of my neck.

Something's happening. Something important.

I descend the stairs, careful to avoid the third step from the bottom that I've learned creaks loudly. The main floor is darker than upstairs, the elaborate chandelier in the foyer extinguished, leaving only the ambient glow from outside security lights filtering through the windows.

I'm halfway to the kitchen when I notice it. There's a thin sliver of light beneath a door down the hallway. Nico's office. The one place in Alessandro's mansion that is exclusively his territory, where even the house staff enter only by invitation.

Water forgotten, I change direction, drawn to that ribbon of light like a moth to flame. It's likely nothing, Nico suffering from insomnia, catching up on business, making calls to associates in different time zones. There are a dozen innocent explanations.

Then why does my heart suddenly hammer against my ribs?

As I approach the door, I hear the low murmur of voices, Nico's and Alessandro's, their tones hushed but intense. The rich scent of old wood polish hangs heavy in the corridor. I slow my pace, years of investigative instinct taking over. My bare feet make no sound on the thick carpet as I move closer, close enough to see that the door isn't fully closed. A gap of perhaps two inches provides a partial view into the room.

I shouldn't eavesdrop. This is the kind of boundary violation that would reinforce every suspicion Nico has about journalists, about my motives. We've moved beyond that in the past few days, found something real beneath the layers of calculation and performance.

Haven't we?

I lean closer, telling myself I'll just check if he's okay. If it's nothing important, I'll announce myself, make up some excuse about insomnia or thirst. But what I see freezes me in place.

Nico is hunched over his desk, posture rigid with tension, so unlike his usual fluid confidence. Alessandro stands beside him, one hand braced on the desk's edge, the other gesturing emphatically as he speaks. Between them, documents are spread across the polished wood surface, and Nico's laptop casts a blue glow across both their faces.

"—confirmed by three separate sources," Alessandro is saying, his voice sharp with urgency. "The timeline matches."

Nico shakes his head. "It can't be a coincidence. Not with the Moretti connection. Not with the university shipments."

Alessandro's response is too quiet for me to catch, but Nico's reaction is immediate. His head snaps up, eyes hardening.

"She can never know," he says, the words carrying clearly to where I stand frozen. "Not until we're certain."

Ice forms in my veins, an instant, visceral reaction. *She. They're talking about me. Or...*

"Your sentiment is understandable, but misguided," Alessandro replies, voice low but sharp. "The woman killed a man to save your life. She deserves the truth, however painful."

My mind races. *What truth? What are they hiding from me?*

Alessandro reaches into his jacket pocket and extracts something small, a thumb drive. He places it on the desk between them.

"Everything's here," he says. "The border crossing records. The academy photos. The chemical shipment manifests. It's comprehensive, Nico. Irrefutable."

Nico takes the drive, inserts it into his laptop. The blue glow intensifies, illuminating the harsh angles of his face as he scrolls through whatever contents the drive holds. His expression transforms from skepticism to stunned disbelief.

"Jesus Christ," he mutters, the profanity shocking coming from his usually controlled lips. "All these years. Right under everyone's noses."

A cold dread spreads through me. *They're not talking about me.*

Alessandro leans in closer, lowering his voice further. "What about Lea? She'll have to be told—"

"Not yet," Nico cuts him off. "There's still a chance this isn't what it appears to be."

My fingers grip the doorframe, knuckles white with tension. *What isn't what it appears to be?*

Alessandro sighs, the sound heavy with resignation. "Nico, if Professor Song is actually a North Korea operative coordinating a fentanyl pipeline through Moretti's distribution network, we need to—"

A sound escapes me, half gasp, half strangled cry, before I can stop it. The words slam into me like physical blows: *North Korean. Operative. My mother. Fentanyl.*

Both men whip toward the door. Nico's face, when he recognizes me, does something I've never seen before. It crumples, just for an instant, with what looks like genuine regret. Then the mask slides back into place, but it's too late. I've seen beneath it.

I push the door fully open, stepping into the room on legs that threaten to give way beneath me.

"What did you just say about my mother?" My voice sounds foreign, distant, as if someone else is speaking through me.

Nico rises slowly from his chair, hands raised in a gesture that might be meant to calm but feels patronizing. "Lea—"

"Don't." I cut him off, turning instead to Alessandro. "Say it again. What you just said about my mother."

Alessandro's eyes flick to Nico, seeking permission, I

realize with a flare of anger. *As if I'm some delicate flower who needs protection from the truth. As if I haven't spent the last six years digging for buried facts that powerful men would prefer to keep hidden.*

Nico gives an almost imperceptible nod, and something in his expression shifts. The diplomat retreating, the strategist emerging.

Alessandro straightens, assuming the formal bearing that seems to come naturally to him. "Your mother, Professor Eunji Song, emigrated to the United Kingdom about twenty-five years ago, and then together with you and your father, moved to the United States under false pretenses. Your mother..." he hesitates, but only briefly, "is not South Korean. The evidence suggests she is a deep-undercover North Korea operative, using her academic credentials to facilitate a major drug trade operation to help finance military expenses for the regime."

The words hang in the air between us, monstrous and incomprehensible. I want to laugh, to dismiss this as an absurd conspiracy theory, but the gravity in Alessandro's tone, the documents spread across the desk, the way Nico won't quite meet my eyes. The room seems to shrink, the air thinning until I can barely draw a breath.

"SHOW ME!" I demand, the words tearing from my throat.

Nico hesitates only a moment before turning his laptop toward me. The screen is split into two images side by side. On the left is a young woman in a crisp North Korea military uniform, her posture rigid, her expression severe but unmistakable; my mother's eyes, my mother's mouth, my mother's distinctive cheekbones. On the right is the graduation photo

I've seen a hundred times on her office wall. Eunji Song accepting her doctorate from Seoul National University, beaming with pride.

"That's..." I start, but can't finish. Because it is her. Unmistakably her, in both images.

My fingers move to the trackpad, scrolling through the open files with a detached, mechanical precision that belies the earthquake happening inside me. Shipping manifests for pharmaceutical components moving through shell companies with innocuous names. Bank transfers through offshore accounts, the money trail obscured by layer upon layer of corporate facades. Surveillance photos, recent ones, of my mother meeting with a man I recognize as one of Moretti's lieutenants, the same one who confronted me at the gala.

Each new piece of evidence is another blow, dismantling the foundation of everything I've ever known. A lifetime of memories reconfiguring themselves in sickening new patterns.

The bedtime stories she told me about escaping from an oppressive regime—true, but not the one I'd been led to believe. The "research trips" that took her away for weeks at a time. The locked filing cabinet in her study that I was never allowed to open. The way she stiffened whenever certain political topics came up, steering conversations in safer directions.

Oh god. My father. Did he know? Was he part of it? Or was their relationship just another cover to hide behind?

I can feel myself swaying, the room tilting around me. A strong hand grips my elbow, steadying me. Nico. I jerk away from his touch as if burned.

"Did you know?" The question scrapes my throat raw. "Is

that why you targeted me? Was I just collateral intelligence to you, so you could get first dibs at the biggest fentanyl distribution deal the world has ever seen?"

Silence stretches between us, heavy with unspoken truths, with all the calculations and manipulations that have defined our relationship from the beginning. Nico's face hardens, the vulnerability of moments ago replaced by something cooler, more controlled.

"That's not how it happened," he says finally.

A bitter laugh escapes me, sharp and ugly. "Bullshit! You're the brilliant manipulator, the master diplomat! You're the one who got me that job straight out of college, got me the dream exclusive just like that, all so you could get close to me and my mother!"

The pieces fit together with terrible clarity. I already knew he facilitated the circumstances so the publisher would assign me, a rookie, to profile Chicago's most powerful criminal mediator, but of course he also made sure I got the job at The Journal in the first place. Heck, he's probably even responsible for my accolades in college. *It was all a setup, a long con with me as the mark.*

But Nico is shaking his head, his expression grim. "You're right that I arranged the expose, but I didn't get you that job, Lea."

"More lies? Really?" I spit the words at him, fury burning away the shock, cauterizing the wound with white-hot rage.

Alessandro shifts uncomfortably behind the desk, exchanging a look with Nico that sends a fresh wave of dread through me. *Something worse is coming. Somehow, impossibly, there's more.*

Nico nods almost imperceptibly. "Show her."

Alessandro hesitates, actual concern flickering across his aristocratic features. "Are you sure? This will—"

"Show her," Nico repeats, his voice leaving no room for argument.

With obvious reluctance, Alessandro reaches for a folder on the desk, extracting a single sheet of paper. He places it with the care one might use handling a live explosive.

It's a handwritten note, the paper high-quality, the ink a distinctive shade of blue that I recognize. My mother has used the same fountain pen with the same indigo ink for as long as I can remember, a gift from my father, she always said.

The note is dated a few weeks before I started at the newspaper. The handwriting is unmistakable, each perfectly formed character a testament to her meticulous nature. The message is brief, devastating in its simplicity:

"Asset now in place at Chicago Investigating Journal, starting 08-22 . Confirmation received."

My legs finally give out. I sink into the chair behind me, the world narrowing to this single sheet of paper, these nine words and one date that demolish everything I thought I knew about my life.

Not Nico, but my mother. She orchestrated my entire career. The university scholarship that seemed like such a blessing. The internships that led me step by step toward investigative journalism. The sudden job offer from Chicago's premier newspaper when dozens of more qualified candidates were passed over.

All of it, every achievement I'd been so proud of, every

obstacle I'd congratulated myself on overcoming—nothing but careful manipulation, pieces being moved into position on a board I couldn't even see.

"No," I breathe, the word a plea rather than a denial. My fingers are numb as I push the paper away. "No, that's not... she wouldn't..."

But she would. She did. The evidence is right in front of me, written in her own hand.

The laptop slides from my knees, clattering onto the desk. I barely register the sound, barely notice as Nico lunges to catch it before it falls to the floor. My mind is elsewhere, racing backward through a lifetime of memories, re-examining every conversation, every choice, every seeming coincidence through this new lens.

My mother's quiet pride when I announced my journalism major. *"You have the mind for it, Lea. You see connections others miss."* Had she been grooming me even then? Steering me toward a profession that would give me access to powerful people, to sensitive information?

Her sudden interest in my exclusive with Nico. *"Be careful, Lea. Men like him see only assets and liabilities."* Not a warning from a concerned mother, but from a rival operator worried about her asset being compromised.

The mysterious man warning me. The texts about Moretti, had those been from her too? Part of some elaborate game between criminal enterprises with me as an unwitting pawn?

I'm on my feet without consciously deciding to stand, backing away from both men, from the evidence, from the truth that's shattering me from the inside out.

"Lea—" Nico reaches for me, his expression softer than I've ever seen it, almost pleading.

I don't want his pity, or his comfort. I don't want anything from him or from my mother or from anyone in this godforsaken world of lies and manipulation.

I turn and run, out of the office, down the hallway, bare feet slapping against the cold floor. I don't know where I'm going, just away, anywhere but here, anywhere but this moment where everything I believed about myself has been revealed as fiction.

Behind me, I hear Nico call my name, his voice sharp with command and something else... concern? Fear? I don't stop to analyze it. I can't bear to look at his face, to see the calculation behind his eyes as he decides how best to handle this new development in his grand strategy.

The front door looms ahead, massive and ornate. I wrench it open, the night air hitting me, cold and damp, carrying the scent of approaching rain. I don't care. I charge down the steps, across the manicured lawn, my feet numb to the rough texture of gravel and then grass.

I keep running until my lungs burn and my legs tremble, until the mansion's lights have receded to distant pinpricks behind me. Only then do I slow, gulping air that tastes of earth and the coming storm.

The reality of my situation penetrates the fog of betrayal and fury. I'm standing at the edge of Alessandro's vast property in the middle of the night, wearing nothing but Nico's shirt, with no phone, no money, no identification. Out there stretches the dark mass of forest that surrounds Alessandro's estate with miles of wilderness between here and the nearest town.

Behind me, the lights of the mansion burn like a false beacon of safety. Inside wait one of the two greatest manipulators in my life: Nico Varela, who seduced my body and perhaps my heart in service to his ambitions, and somewhere out there, my mother, or whoever the hell she is, who engineered my entire existence to serve her own hidden agenda.

A drop of rain strikes my face, then another. The storm is breaking.

I have nowhere to go. No safe harbor in a world that has revealed itself as built entirely on lies. Every instinct screams at me to run, to put as much distance as possible between myself and those who have used me so thoroughly.

But run where? To whom?

Lightning splits the sky, illuminating the forest edge in stark white relief. In that brief flash, I see a path leading into the trees. It's narrow and overgrown, but unmistakably a path. Somewhere to go that isn't back to that house of lies.

Thunder follows, a deep rumble that seems to resonate with the turmoil inside me. The rain intensifies, soaking through the thin fabric of Nico's shirt, plastering it to my skin. I barely feel it. The physical discomfort is nothing compared to the psychological devastation of the past thirty minutes.

I take one step toward the forest path, then another. The darkness seems to vibrate, alive and waiting. *Is this wise? Absolutely not.* The rational part of my brain, the part that isn't howling with betrayal and rage, knows that wandering into unfamiliar wilderness during a thunderstorm is the textbook definition of a terrible decision.

But what's the alternative? Return to Nico's arms, pretend I can trust anything he says? Call my mother and listen to more lies?

Lightning flashes again, closer this time, the accompanying thunder almost immediate. The forest path beckons offering escape, and solitude, a chance to process the implosion of my world without Nico's calculating gaze or Alessandro's cool assessment.

Behind me, I hear a door slam, then a voice calling my name. Nico, coming after me. *Of course he is. I'm a loose end now, a complication in his careful plans. Can't have the journalist daughter of a North Korea operative running around uncontrolled, especially one who's seen the evidence, who could expose everything.*

I take another step forward. The forest looms, dark and forbidding, yet somehow less frightening than what waits behind me. Rain courses down my face, mingling with tears I hadn't realized I was shedding.

"LEA!" Nico's voice is closer now, urgent, almost frantic. So unlike his usual controlled tone.

Just another performance. Another mask. I can't trust anything about him, not his touch, not his words, certainly not the tenderness I thought I'd glimpsed beneath his methodical exterior.

I take a final step forward, crossing the threshold between the manicured lawn and the wild unknown of the forest. The path is barely visible in the darkness, muddy and treacherous beneath my bare feet. Each step takes me farther from light, from comfort, from the people who have shaped my life through deception.

Into the storm. Into the dark. Into a world where everything I thought I knew about myself, about my mother, about Nico was built on lies.

. . .

LIGHTNING FLASHES ONE LAST TIME, illuminating the path ahead. In that brief, brilliant moment, I make my choice.

I step forward into the darkness.

Continues in *Savage Reckoning*, the thrilling conclusion to The Diplomat.

Made in United States
Cleveland, OH
27 May 2025

17276532R00216